Improper English

"Funny, quirky, and enjoyable. Don't miss this one!"
—*USA Today* bestselling author Millie Criswell

"Charming and irresistible. A tale to make you smile and pursue your own dreams."
—*USA Today* bestselling author Patricia Potter

"Alix and Alex steam up the pages . . . funny . . . amusing."
—*Publishers Weekly*

"Katie MacAlister knows how to hook the reader from the very beginning and not let them go until they've turned the last page."
—The Best Reviews

continued . . .

Noble Intentions

"Sexy, sassy fun!" —Bestselling author Karen Hawkins

"If there is such a thing as a Screwball Regency, Katie MacAlister has penned it in this tale of Noble, Gillian, and their oh-so-bumpy path to love. Readers are in for a wonderful ride!" —*The Romance Reader*

"This is without a doubt one of the funniest historicals I've read . . . [an] outstanding book."
—The Best Reviews

"[MacAlister has a] captivating voice and charming story-telling skills [and] impeccable style."
—Inscriptions Magazine

"Delightful and charming! A wonderful romp through Regency England." —Lynsay Sands, bestselling author
of *The Reluctant Reformer*

MEN IN
KILTS

Katie MacAlister

AN ONYX BOOK

ONYX
Published by New American Library, a division of
Penguin Group (USA) Inc., 375 Hudson Street,
New York, New York 10014, USA
Penguin Group (Canada), 10 Alcorn Avenue, Toronto,
Ontario M4V 3B2, Canada (a division of Pearson Penguin Canada Inc.)
Penguin Books Ltd., 80 Strand, London WC2R 0RL, England
Penguin Ireland, 25 St. Stephen's Green, Dublin 2,
Ireland (a division of Penguin Books Ltd.)
Penguin Group (Australia), 250 Camberwell Road, Camberwell, Victoria 3124,
Australia (a division of Pearson Australia Group Pty. Ltd.)
Penguin Books India Pvt. Ltd., 11 Community Centre, Panchsheel Park,
New Delhi - 110 017, India
Penguin Group (NZ), Cnr Airborne and Rosedale Roads, Albany,
Auckland 1310, New Zealand (a division of Pearson New Zealand Ltd.)
Penguin Books (South Africa) (Pty.) Ltd., 24 Sturdee Avenue,
Rosebank, Johannesburg 2196, South Africa

Penguin Books Ltd., Registered Offices:
80 Strand, London WC2R 0RL, England

First published by Onyx, an imprint of New American Library,
a division of Penguin Group (USA) Inc.

First Printing, October 2003
10 9 8 7 6

Copyright © Marthe Arends, 2003
All rights reserved

 REGISTERED TRADEMARK—MARCA REGISTRADA

ACKNOWLEDGMENTS

Many people helped me in my quest to understand sheep farming in the Scottish Highlands, but no one helped me more than Iain MacNichol of Turnalt Farm; I greatly appreciate Iain's patience in answering my hundred and one sheep questions. My appreciation and thanks also go to my agent Michelle Grajkowski (for always believing in me), to my editor, Audrey LaFehr (for making my dream come true), and to my critique partner, Vance Briceland (for laughing at all the funny parts).

Chapter One

The e-mail came while I was trying to figure out how to connect my hair-dryer adapter.

OK, so you've been in England for what . . . seven hours, now? my friend Cait wrote. *Have you met any men yet? How come you haven't written to me? You're a writer, for Pete's sake, so write! Tell me everything! Every single detail!*

I just got here, I wrote back, giving up on the adapter. *I'm tired, the only man I met was a street person who hit me up for a pound by promising to write my name in urine on the sidewalk, and I'll tell you more when I have something to tell.*

Two minutes later there was another e-mail waiting. *Was the street guy cute? Did you watch him write your name? Did he spell it correctly?*

Not cute, I replied. *No, I didn't stay, and boy, will I be glad when you start dating again!*

I turned off my laptop, changed into my party wear, looked longingly at the bed, and with a tired sigh, grabbed my purse and headed down to where the action was.

"Kathie Williams? Here's your bag. There's a cocktail party this evening," the Murder in Manchester registration woman told me as she shoved a book bag in my hands before tossing me a printed program. "You have to buy your own drinks, but everyone will be there. You're an author, correct?"

"Yes," I agreed, still stunned with jet lag. It was a ten-hour flight from Seattle to London, and I had to catch a train to Manchester from Heathrow, leaving me more than a bit comatose after . . . my mind balked at trying to figure out how long I was past due sleep. "Yes. Author. Kathie. Drinks."

"Then you'll want to be at the party. Everyone will be there," she repeated, and leaned sideways to see the person behind me. "Next!"

I clutched my book bag full of books, promotional materials, and conference-related items and shuffled off to find a spot to sit and let the fact that I was in England soak in. I found a deep, comfy chair in a corner of the hotel lobby and parked myself there, intending on browsing through the mystery-conference material to familiarize myself with the events of the weekend. After struggling for half an hour to keep my eyelids propped open, I decided that a few minutes resting my eyes were in order before I had to go dazzle everyone at the cocktail party. Surely, I thought as I snuggled back into the chair, I wouldn't actually sleep. Not in a busy lobby. Not in a strange country. I'd just rest and recharge my batteries for the party.

I woke up to the feeling of someone stuffing a tissue under my cheek.

"Oh, you're awake. I'm sorry if I woke you, but you were sleeping so soundly and that blouse looks as if it's made of silk . . ."

I blinked at the short, elegantly spoken white-haired lady who was bending over me.

"Uh . . ."

She fluttered the tissue at me and stared pointedly at my shoulder. I looked. There was a huge saucer-sized damp mark.

"Oh, great, I drooled on myself!"

"That's why I was trying to tuck this under your chin. I do hate to see such a lovely blouse ruined. The embroidery on it is quite exquisite. You're American?"

I took the proffered tissue and tried to mop up the big drool mark. "How humiliating! I save up for years to come halfway around the world on a dream trip only to slobber on myself in public on my first day here. Yes, I'm American.

Thank you for the tissue, but I think it's too late. I can't go to the cocktail party with a big old slobber mark on my shoulder!"

"No, indeed," the white-haired woman agreed. "Such a shame, too. The detail on the embroidery is lovely. Beaded, as well."

"It was made just for tonight," I mourned with her.

"You'll probably want to hurry if you intend on having time to meet people at the party," she suggested as she started off toward the elevators. "I just came from there and I don't believe it is scheduled to last much longer."

"Hell!" I swore as I glanced down at my watch. I had slept three hours! With my mouth open! Drooling! Where everyone could see me! I slunk out of the lobby and escaped to my room, did a quick change from my lovely beaded, hand-embroidered silk blouse into a plain black one, ignored the wrinkles in my pleated wool skirt, and dashed back downstairs to the party.

"Deep breath," I told myself as I stood in the doorway and assessed the situation. "Probably no one saw you sleeping. Probably no one will recognize you at all. Probably no one will talk to you and you'll spend a long, lonely weekend by yourself, an outcast, a pariah, a public drooler."

I girded my mental loins and stepped into the room, dodging scattered tables and smiling hopefully at the groups of people clutching drinks as they laughed and chatted amiably, all the while searching desperately for other lost souls like myself who didn't know anyone there. I searched in vain, but my family code has always been that appearance is everything, so I slapped a confident *I'm not scared to death of being halfway around the world in a room full of people I don't know and can barely understand, oh, no, I'm not* smile on my face and marched over to the bar to ask for something without alcohol. I'm not at my best when I drink. I flush and get silly and very, very sleepy, which is not at all the sort of impression one wishes to make at a gathering of one's peers.

As I turned away from the bar I noticed a man next to the door leaning up against the wall watching the crowd.

"Aha," I muttered to my tonic and lime, "someone else who doesn't know everyone here. A very large someone, too, with a marvelous white woolly sweater."

A woman nearby glanced over her shoulder at me standing in front of the bar talking to no one.

"I'm writing dialogue," I told her. "Mentally. And . . . er . . . out loud, of course. I'm a writer. We do that."

She pursed her lips in a pained expression of disbelief, and made sure not to make eye contact with me for the rest of the evening. I shrugged and turned back to give the old once-over to the guy standing against the wall.

He really was a sight to make the mouth water—a big, burly sight in a lovely sweater and dark brown corduroy pants, but what intrigued me was the expression he wore: this was plainly a man who was not having fun. He looked bored to tears and kind of lonely standing there holding up the wall all by himself. I decided it was my duty to further Anglo-American relations by helping him, so I wandered over in what I hoped was a nonchalant manner, flashed him an *I'm not flirting with you, just being friendly, all in the furtherance of goodwill between nations, and not at all because you are an extremely dishy man* smile, and parked myself next to him.

We stood that way for about five minutes, just watching the crowd, me sipping on my tonic and lime, he occasionally peering morosely into a pint of beer.

"Tch!" he said finally, making that curious noise of derision that only the Scots seem to make, and drained the last of his beer. "You read mysteries then, do you?" he asked me without turning his head.

I almost melted on the spot. I had lucked out and how! A Scot. A real live, woolly sweater wearing, brogue-thick-enough-you-could-trot-a-horse-on-it Scot. Right next to me! My knees went a bit weak.

I love Scotsmen. I love everything about them—I love the way they talk, I love the way they dress, I love that wonderful little noise they make in the backs of their throats, and I love the way they smell. Yes, it's true, they have a smell all their own, and it's glorious. To me, Scottish men smell like the outdoors, with an overtone of bagpipe and an amusing little hint of something wild and craggy and utterly indefinable.

There I was, halfway around the world, friendless, alone in a room full of people who, judging by the enthusiasm with which they greeted one another, all knew each other on a level approaching that of biblical, and standing next to me was a Scot.

Oh, be still my heart.

"Yes, I do read mysteries," I answered with what I hoped was an insouciant smile, wishing all the while I could just jump him and be through with it. "But I also write."

"Ah, do you now? And what would you be writing?"

The man's voice rumbled, positively rumbled. My knees went even weaker. I clutched the wall in a desperate attempt to keep from slipping to the floor.

"Um." My mind went blank. What was the name of the book? Come to think of it, what was *my* name? "I write mysteries. My last book was *The Death of Artemis.*"

I watched closely to see if he recognized it. He didn't. I sighed. "I take it you read mysteries as well?" I asked politely.

"Aye."

My knees slipped a bit further. He actually said *aye*. How on earth could I resist a man who said *aye* as casually as I would say *potato*? I couldn't. I melted even more. It was a bit confusing, this instantaneous overwhelming attraction, but who was I to question fate? I pushed him to the top of my fantasy-men list, and smiled encouragingly.

"Aye, I read a fair bit."

"Ah." No one ever claimed I was the queen of conversation. "Who do you read?"

That's a legitimate question at a mystery convention. Everyone swaps favorite authors, garners recommendations of new authors to read, and takes notes on whom to avoid. The Scot listed a few familiar names, but most were new to me. I asked him about the ones I didn't know, and he told me what they wrote, who was good, and who was great. Most were Scottish writers, but there were a few Brits in the bunch, and one American (not, I was disappointed to note, me).

"I'm Kathie," I said, holding out my hand, extremely pleased I remembered my own name in the face of such distraction as unbidden, overwhelming lust.

"Iain," he replied, taking my hand in his. His fingers were warm and strong around mine, and I let him hold my hand while I gazed at him with a smile that I hoped indicated polite interest, but feared came out as a smut-riddled leer.

"Iain," I said, trying not to dwell overmuch on the pleasure I was receiving from the feel of my hand in his. "That's a nice name. I take it you're from Scotland?"

"Aye, I've a sheep farm in the Highlands."

"Ah." My wellspring of conversation dried up as I stared at his big hand holding mine. A few scars stood out white against the tanned darkness of his skin, giving his hand character and depth I didn't think possible in a mere extremity. Reluctantly, or so it seemed to my bemused self, he released my hand, leaving me to transfer my stare to his face.

"So," I said, rallying the few wits I had left, "is this your first mystery conference?" I almost cringed at the inanity of my question, but was simply unable to summon anything resembling intelligent speech when he was looking at me with those lovely dark eyes.

"Aye, my sons gave me this." He waved his beer around to encompass the room. "As a birthday present because I read so many mysteries."

Sons. Where there were sons, there were usually mothers.

"How very thoughtful of your sons," I said, glancing covertly at his left hand. There was no ring, but that could mean anything and nothing.

"They're good lads," he agreed, taking a pull on his beer.

"Indeed. And your wife is . . . ?" I peered around as if hoping to discover her, which was, of course, the last thing I truly wanted.

"I've no wife," he said, the lines around his eyes crinkling slightly as he smiled.

I smiled back. "Too subtle?"

"No, I prefer a woman who can say what it is she has on her mind."

I turned my smile into a little resigned moue. "That won't be a problem with me. So, tell me all about Scotland. I've always wanted to go there."

We had a nice conversation, or rather, *he* had a nice conversation; I was alternately palpitating and twitching whenever he spoke. His voice was very deep, rumbling around in the big chest housed in that lovely sweater, finally spilling out with an accent you could almost taste. Despite the fact that my hormones kicked in upon hearing that voice, it was his eyes that were my doom, ensnaring me, trapping me, making me a slave to their mysterious depths. Iain had lovely eyes—lyrical eyes—wise, deep, dark eyes. Warm, sultry brown eyes you wanted to teeter on the brink of, then fall into. Dark, dark eyes with lovely little gold and black flecks. I loved watching his eyes when he spoke, enjoyed how his laugh lines crinkled up whenever he smiled, and spent several minutes imagining all of the ways I'd like to kiss around those eyes—amongst other locations.

I won't say there were little heart-shaped bubbles popping over my head at that point, but it was a close thing.

"How are you enjoying England, then?" he asked.

"Eyes," I breathed, drowning in his.

"Aye, you've a lovely pair."

"Hmm?" I blinked and tried to yank my attention from fantasies that featured the dishy Scot, two feathers, and a small jar of pitted olives.

"Your eyes. They're lovely."

"So are yours," I replied, blushing madly, and quickly steered the conversation away from my unseemly instant physical attraction to him. We chatted for about an hour, Iain talking books, me murmuring agreements, saying whatever it took to keep him talking. I positively wallowed in the glory of his voice rolling around me, deep and dark and full of Scottish mystery. Occasionally he'd throw me completely, his accent just too new to my ears. I'd back him up and have him repeat whatever it was I didn't understand.

"The lads at the Twa Brithers—"

"What?" I interrupted him.

"Twa Brithers."

"Come again?"

"Twa . . . Brithers."

"Let's break that down, shall we? *Twa* as in . . . ?"

"Twa." He held up two fingers.

"Oh, *two.* Silly me!" I gave him a fatuous (and infatu-ated) grin. He smiled back, chuckling his sexy chuckle as he repeated the second word again until it penetrated the thick fog of lust circling my head. "OK, you were down at the Two Brothers . . . is that a pub?"

"Aye," he nodded, and continued to tell me an anecdote about a local author.

I listened to that lovely voice, my entire body humming in response to him, but it wasn't just his accent that sent shivers down my spine, it was the cadence in his voice and the way his body moved when he spoke. He described the opening scene of a book to me, throwing his whole body into the telling. Now, you might think that would be an im-pressive undertaking for a man six feet six inches tall. It was—but at the same time it wasn't. He wasn't clumsy in the least. All that walking around the fields and hefting sheep had obviously given the man muscles. Even at his age—mid forties, I was guessing—he was exceptionally fit. And he moved—well, he *moved*, with an innate sense of grace lacking in most men.

At that point, the lust began to clear and something far more profound settled in. I was in serious trouble, but I didn't know it.

What I *did* know was that my conversation with the deli-cious Scot had to end at some point. The evening would draw to a close, we would part, I would talk to others, and life would go on. Only I didn't want it to end, didn't want to talk to anyone else, and didn't want to move on and forget him. I was in the process of being bemused, and it's just not that easy to pull out of a partial bemusement and switch your attention to someone else. Regardless, I smiled brightly as Iain returned from the bar with another pint for himself and a cup of coffee for me.

"You're sure you'd not like a glass of wine?" he asked as I clutched the coffee to me.

"No, no, coffee is fine, coffee is good. I need the caffeine. I'm a bit jet laggy still."

He nodded and took a sip of his beer, those deep, dark, sexy eyes of his twinkling with a devilish glint that made me want to do wicked, wicked things to him. With my tongue.

"Aye, I saw you earlier. You looked a wee bit fashed then."

"You saw me earlier?" How could I possibly have missed this delicious large hunk of man? It wasn't possible! I shook my head. He nodded back.

" 'Twas in the lobby. You were sleeping."

Oh, no! Not the lobby! Not when I was . . .

"Sleeping very soundly," he added, eyeing my blouse speculatively. Aaaaaack! He had seen! He had seen me drooling all over myself! My unfettered lust for the dishy Scot weakened significantly in the ensuing embarrassment.

As I was mentally cringing and about to explain that I normally don't sleep in public—let alone sleep with my mouth open and vast cascades of saliva flowing free and wild—a thin, balding man with a handlebar mustache stopped next to me.

"Good evening. I was told you're the American author on my panel. I'm Daniel Johannson." He held out his hand, a pleasant smile on his lips. I wanted to smack him. How dare he interrupt my lovely conversation with Iain? Who cared about a stupid panel when there was serious ground to be made up with the dishy Scot?

"Kathie Williams," I dutifully replied, and even more dutifully slapped a smile on my face as I shook his hand. He edged around in front of me, more or less pushing Iain to the side. What a rotter! "This is Iain," I added, and took a step nearer to him.

"Evening." The man greeted Iain with another smile. "I don't recognize you. I take it you're not an author?"

"No, I'm not," Iain said, giving me a long look. "As you've business to talk, I'll be on my way. It was a pleasure to meet you, Kathie."

"Likewise," I said, my heart dropping to my loafers as he glanced quickly around the party, then shrugged slightly and left the room. "Well, hell!"

"Sorry?"

"Nothing," I answered, my eyes on the door in case Iain changed his mind and came back. He didn't though, and I was hard put to maintain polite conversation with Daniel since I resented him heartily for interrupting my little tête-à-tête with a much more interesting man, but I did refrain from snapping his head off much in the manner of a peeved praying mantis, a fact which surely must merit me some sort of cosmic brownie points.

He discussed the upcoming panel, then introduced me to some of the other authors, but despite having come all the way around the world just to meet my British peers, I didn't enjoy myself. The evening had lost its warm glow.

"You're an adult, Kathie," I lectured myself later, when I was in my hotel room finishing the task of unpacking. "You didn't spend all that time and money saving for this trip just to moon over a man you've known for all of an hour. Cease your pouting and get over this infatuation!"

The lecture didn't do me any good; they seldom do. For some reason I was unable to explain even to myself, meeting the Scot had rocked my world back on its heels. I didn't quite understand what had happened, but I knew it was something momentous.

Love at first sight strikes some people like that—daft, that is.

I didn't stop thinking about Iain that night—not when I was talking with other authors at the party, not when I was taking a shower later and wondering if he liked faux-auburn-haired women of medium height and no outstanding physical attributes—nor did I stop thinking about him when I lay in bed and listened to the sounds of the hotel settling into sleep.

I thought about him the next day as I went from panel to panel and listened to mystery authors and fans talk.

I thought about him when I went out to dinner that night with Daniel and his group of cronies, only partially paying attention to the publishing gossip and mystery talk, my mind more consumed with wondering whether I hadn't imagined the whole hormone-stirring episode with a nonexistent Scot.

I thought about him every time I spied a tall, dark-haired man.

It's disgusting, I e-mailed my best friend Cait the second day of the conference. *I feel like a schoolgirl with her first crush. I just can't stop looking for him. I can't stop wishing I could talk with him again. I keep trying to figure out what it is about him, what makes him so intriguing, why he's having this effect on me, but all that sort of analysis does is end up in smutty fantasies. I CAN'T THINK OF ANYTHING ELSE BUT THE DISHY SCOT!*

Cait responded almost immediately with a request for full details, and her approval to go ahead and give in to my lust.

Just exactly how dishy is DISHY? she wrote. *What's he look like? Was he wearing a kilt? What did he have on under his kilt, and don't tell me you didn't look, I would have looked for you. Stop angsting over your lust, it's not like you've gotten any in the last decade. So go ahead! Live a little! If you fancy this guy, jump him! You did bring raincoats with you, didn't you? I TOLD you to bring raincoats!*

Condoms were the least of my worries. I argued with myself a lot that day, repeatedly pointing out to my saner self that I was a mature adult, I had been married before, I had fallen in love and fallen out of love. I had engaged in mild infatuations in the past, and they always ended up the same. I told myself to stop mooning about and get on with my life.

I think I had more conversations with myself that day than I did with anyone else. I didn't enjoy either. I didn't enjoy much of anything, and that made me even angrier.

"Oh, Kathie," one of my newly made acquaintances called after me the next morning as a panel ended and everyone was filing from the room. "We're going out to dinner tonight, and we thought as you were at a loose end you might want to come with us."

"Not unless you've got a Scot named Iain in your

pocket," I mumbled softly, then thanked the woman and declined.

"Honest to Pete, I am the grand champion of idiots!" I chastised myself a few minutes later in the ladies' room where I was trying to make myself look presentable for my upcoming panel, always a challenge when you are battling with waist-length hair that never heeds the desire for it to stay confined. It wasn't my hair that bothered me as I stared at my reflection, it was the sour look of discontent that, try as I might, I just could not erase. "I am *wasting* my precious few days of vacation by walking around all grouchy and unhappy because the object of my temporary and doomed-from-the-start fascination is not to be found. What a boob! What a maroon! What a . . . what a pitiful and hopelessly smitten person I am."

Chastisements seldom do much to buoy the spirit, and this instance was no exception. I swallowed my misery and obediently followed the moderator into the panel room, prepared to discuss, to the best of my abilities, writing a mystery series. My fellow panelists were all well-known, respected members of the profession. They were intelligent and witty and had things of great import to share with the audience.

I, on the other hand, sat at the end of the long speakers' table and said little. I responded to questions when they were asked of me, and *tried* to look intelligent, but I know I failed. I didn't have anything to say. Not anything related to the subject of discussion, not anything the people in the audience wanted to hear. Not anything that would make sense.

Instead, I sat like a lump and never once took my eyes off the man sitting in the back row. Iain had come to my panel. And he smiled.

At me.

Chapter Two

As luck would have it, I had to do a book signing after my panel. We all did, all of the authors who were on the panels. It gave readers the chance to meet the authors, chat with them a bit, and have them sign a book or two.

Imagine my horror when I found I couldn't race from the panel and throw myself upon the sexy Scot lurking at the back of the room.

Imagine my disgust with myself when that's all I could think about on the way to the signing area.

Imagine my delight when the aforementioned Scot showed up at the signing as well.

"Well, I like to live dangerously—Janice doesn't, but I do—so I will take a chance that you are as good as you say you are," a middle-aged stocky woman in a powder blue jersey was saying when he arrived.

She thrust a copy of my book under my nose. I peered around her solid form and smiled at Iain. He smiled back, melting me on the spot. The powder blue body in front of me rocked slightly so as to block my lovely view.

"Oh, yes, of course, thank you," I said to the woman, who, with her twin in a matching jersey, had been my sole visitors to the signing table.

"We're from Devonshire, Janice and I are. Janice works at Oxfam," the bulky woman said chattily. I smiled at Janice. She tittered in response.

"I'm a secretary, but we both read quite a bit. Mysteries, mostly, but Janice likes to read those women's books." She

leaned down to whisper in my ear. I glanced over her back
and raised an eyebrow at Iain. He winked. I puddled. "You
know, those books with sex in them."

Now, *that* had my attention. "Sex?"

Janice's twin nodded. "Romances. Fellatio," she added
helpfully.

My eyes almost popped out of my head. I glanced back
at Iain again. He was looking at his watch.

"I beg your pardon?" I managed to squeak out.

"Felicia." She pointed to the opened page of the book I
was about to sign. "My name is Felicia."

"Oh," I said, relieved that she wasn't either proposition-
ing me or reading what my mind was doing with images of
Iain stretched out stark naked on a white sandy beach. . . .
"Felicia. Of course. What was I thinking? Felicia isn't at all
similar to . . . er, yes, it's a lovely name."

She nodded. Janice bumped her arm and dipped her head
toward me in question. "That's right, Janice thought we
should ask you about our little problem."

I handed her the book and leaned sideways, trying to
cover up my shift in position as a simple desire to lean on
my elbow. I fluttered my lashes at Iain. He grinned and
moved slightly to the side so he could nab a book from the
stack in front of me.

"Problem?" I asked, wishing the two of them would go
pick on someone else, but a sale is a sale, and a reader is a
reader, and it doesn't pay to spurn either. "I will be happy to
help if I can."

"We have an uncle—Uncle Beryl—who went to the
States after the war, and we haven't heard from him since.
Thirty-five years it's been now."

"Mafia," muttered Janice darkly.

"Yes," Felicia agreed, bobbing her head. "It must be. All
those gangsters in the Miami area—well, you just know they
must have had a hand in his disappearance!"

I blinked while they continued on with their conspiracy
theory—which, I gathered from the various accusations
thrown out by the terse-lipped Janice, involved Walt Disney,
a myoptic alligator, and Anita Bryant.

"We're going to go to Florida one day to find out what ever happened to Uncle Beryl," Felicia warned as I handed her the signed book. "Just as soon as Janice has the time off and my fungal condition clears up. Then we'll know what's what."

By the time I ran out of "oh, really" and "you don't say" comments, I was blatantly engaged in visual flirting with Iain, and more than ready to pounce on him when the ladies left me for richer fields. Which they did. *Finally*.

"Hello," I said breathily, craning my head to look up at the vision of Scotliness as he strolled forward.

"Morning," he greeted me, handing me a copy of my book and flashing a smile that, if I hadn't been sitting down, would have knocked me over flat. I craned my head even farther back and smiled in return, noting bemusedly that he had a long nose but it fit his face well. He smiled, I smiled, we smiled. My mind took a little vacation and spent some time wandering around a lovely country in which there was Iain, and there was me, and there was not a whole lot else.

His smile grew a little tight. He waggled the book in front of me. "Are you going to sign the bleedin' thing, then, or just stare at me as if your wits have flown out the window?"

What a sweet talker he was!

"Oh. Sign it?" I stared at the book. Had I seen it before? Was it mine? I checked the author's name. It looked familiar, but I couldn't swear to it being me. I wasn't in a state to swear to anything except to the deep, dark, wonderfully warm nature of Iain's eyes and voice. "Um. Sign."

Iain's smile widened and he leaned down until we were nose to nose. "A bit rattled, are you?"

I breathed in his scent, part spicy aftershave, part Iain. A bit rattled? Oh, god, if he only knew!

"If I'd to speak in front of such a large crowd, I'd be a bit daft as well." He nodded sympathetically. His breath fanned out over my face as he spoke, sending goose bumps of sheer pleasure up and down my arms. I bit back the urge to clutch his head, and swallowed. Hard.

"Sure, I'd be happy to sign it for you. Now, I know your first name is Iain, but I'll need a little more information for

the inscription. Such as your surname." And phone number.
And address. And whether or not you are dating anyone at
the moment, and if you like fast women, especially fast
American women.

"It's MacLaren."

I batted my lashes. "Such a *Scottish* name," I said in a
nauseating simper.

His eyes sparkled at me. "Aye, weel, that's because I'm a
Scot."

"Yes, of course," I replied, then realized I was staring at
him openmouthed in a fair imitation of complete imbecility.
I signed the book for him, only just refraining from including a brazen proposition.

"Your book, sir," I said chirpily, handing it to him as he
straightened back up to his full height. It was difficult to
keep a smile on my face since it was fraying badly about the
edges, but I held it in place and tried not to blatantly ogle
him.

He looked down at me, saying nothing. I stared back at
him, a big old pile of mush, quivering on the inside, the
voices in my head screaming at me to say something, *anything* before he walked away.

"Would you be having plans for your supper tonight?"

Tonight? Dinner? Me and him? As in a *date*? I almost
drooled.

"Not a one," I breathed, hopeful, oh so hopeful. Under
the table, I crossed my fingers. I also crossed my toes. If I
had thought he wouldn't have noticed, I'd have crossed my
eyes as well.

"Would you care, then, to have it with me?"

"Delighted to." That husky voice reeking of sultriness really couldn't have been mine answering, but it must have
been, because the vision before me smiled, and asked me
where I was staying. I told him.

"Do you want to meet me here"—he waved a hand at the
conference room—"or shall I knock you up at the hotel?"

Honest to god, I didn't bat an eyelash.

"Well, there's a panel I want to see on serial killers that

ends at five thirty." We're a romantic bunch, mystery writers. "But what say we try the hotel at sevenish?"

He made a date to meet me in the hotel lobby, and with an impish grin that melted my shoelaces, left.

He's asked me out! I screamed into an e-mail to Cait as soon as I made it back to the hotel and my room. *For dinner! Tonight! What should I wear—sexy or sophisticated?*

An hour later I emerged from a steamy, lavender-scented bathroom to check my e-mail.

Sophisticated, she e-mailed me back. *No, wait, you don't have much time . . . sexy, go with sexy. You got raincoats?*

It's only a first date, I replied before powering off my laptop. *I'm not going to sleep with the man, I just want to flirt a little. Well, OK, a lot. But no sex, you know my rules!*

I decided to go with the sophisticated look after all, and pulled out a long, snug-fitting black velvet dress with a square neck that always made me feel romantic. I was downstairs a few minutes before Iain arrived—he was staying at a different hotel—but I spotted him the moment he set foot in the lobby. He took my breath away—actually took my breath away—when he caught sight of me standing by a group of chairs and smiled as he headed toward me. I clutched at the back of the chair nearest me in an attempt to help stiffen my knees, inadvertently yanking a handful of hair owned by the woman occupying the chair.

"Sorry," I apologized as I unclenched my fingers and patted the dislodged puff of hair back into place. "It's my knees. It's a problem I have around Scotsmen."

She must have been related to the woman who caught me talking to my drink two evenings before, because she gave me the very same fish-eyed stare. I ignored her and turned to greet my dream Scot.

It was a lovely dinner. Iain took me to an Italian restaurant a few blocks from the hotel, and we had—well, we had something. I don't remember what. To be truthful, I couldn't actually swear we ate. I do know I fell head over heels in love with Iain that night, which made it difficult to hear his

conversation, what with all the warning bells and whistles
going off in my head.

I ignored them, however. I figured everyone was entitled
to a Katherine Hepburn *Summertime* type of romance, and if
this was it for me, then, by heavens, I was going to jump into
it with both feet. I was through mooning around and lectur-
ing myself; I was going to have some fun before I had to
head home, and I had hoped Iain was thinking along the
same lines. I wasn't sure he was, but figured it was better to
be safe than sorry, so I blithely went about imagining a
wonderfully steamy affair, and how exactly I was going to
seduce him. I was busily plotting a way to innocently show
up naked at his house in Scotland while he walked me back
to my hotel. As we reached the lobby, I realized what I had
done. I had spent the entire evening on autopilot, laughing
and joking with him, but only halfway paying attention due
to the immediate problem that occupied most of my mind—
seducing him. The following day was the last day of the
conference and I had wasted the whole evening!

"Here we are, then," he said as he held the door to the
lobby open for me.

"Um, yes," I replied, my brain suddenly turned to pudding. "My hotel. Uh-huh."

We entered the lobby with me panicking slightly as I
tried to think of what I should do next. Should I ask him to
the hotel's bar for a nightcap? Should I suggest a walk
around to aid digestion? Should I rip off all my clothing and
throw myself at him? Or should I break out the hair shirt and
spend the rest of the lonely evening yelling at myself for my
stupidity?

Iain paused when we reached the elevators. "You seemed
a mite distracted this evening."

Oh, lord, he'd noticed. Thank god he wasn't a mind
reader. I'd die of embarrassment if he knew I'd spent the entire evening plotting his seduction. I blushed just thinking
about that.

"I'm thinking it could be you're feeling the same thing I
am."

What? I spun around and stared up at him, wondering if

my mind had finally snapped under the strain of all that love and lust and adoration, but I wasn't mistaken—there was a definite something in those lovely warm, brown eyes that wasn't entirely innocent. My blush turned up a notch, spreading down my neck and heading for my chest. I tried to swallow. I couldn't.

"Um . . . well, yes, I think I probably do." It was a miracle I could string the words together, really, since my brain had shut down once it realized what he was hinting at.

Iain smiled and waited. I didn't know he was waiting for me to invite him up to my room. I didn't know that his idea of the gentlemanly code of conduct did not allow for a man to invite himself up to a lady's room when he had a particular goal in mind. All I knew was that I was going to die of humiliation if I had misinterpreted his statement.

"So . . . um." Heat flared in my cheeks as I tried to think of a way to invite him to my room without appearing like a wanton woman. "It's been a lovely evening. Thank you for dinner. I really enjoyed it. It was nice."

Nice? *Nice?* Is that all I could say? I wanted to strangle myself on the spot for spouting such asinine words. I was blowing my big chance with Iain! Where was my creative writer's skill when I needed it? My mind ran around in a frenzied circle, searching desperately for something witty and intelligent to say to him—something that would so bowl him over that he would be helpless against the powerful attraction between us, driven by his desire into scooping me up and carrying me off to bed, where he would spend the entire night making mad, passionate love to me.

" 'Twas my pleasure." He smiled, the look in his eyes doing things to personal parts of me that raised the volume of my blush. Still he waited.

I opened my mouth to say something, but all that came out was a pathetic little squeak. Eventually Iain figured out that I wasn't being coy or unreceptive, just naive, and suggested that we might continue our conversation in private. I nodded and quickly calculated how many days I had known him. *Three.*

"Floor?" He had his hand poised over the elevator buttons.

"Three."

Three days. Not within my official Required Length of Time Acquainted Before Sexual Intimacy rule. Damn.

I had a lovely room, but I have to admit never having noticed until then just how much space was consumed by the bed. It was huge, a veritable behemoth of a bed, filling the entire room, drawing the eye and not allowing you to look anywhere else. I think you could have fried an egg on the blush I was now maintaining at a steady rate.

I invited Iain to sit. He took the chair; I took one look at the bed, cranked the blush up to boiling point, and perched gingerly on the edge. I tried desperately to remember my detailed and well thought out planned seduction, but my mind drew a blank. I stared at my shoes and tried to remember why I wanted so badly to seduce him. I tried to remember my own name.

"Kathie?"

Yes, that was it. *Kathie.* I was Kathie, a basket case of nerves sitting on a bed so big it could qualify for its own time zone, staring at a man who melted my bones with just a glance. *Kathie.* I was Kathie. I clung to that fact with the tenacity of a drowning man to a life preserver.

"*Tch*," Iain said, shaking his head. I noticed he had a few gray hairs mixed in with the dark brown. It looked good on him. "I think perhaps this is a wee bit too soon for you, love, so I'll say good evening." Iain stood up and held a hand out for me.

Oh, yes, a bit too soon. Much sooner than I planned. My seduction scenario involved days of casually meeting and passing by his house, not immediately giving in to the admittedly nigh on overwhelming desire to jump his bones. Too soon. It was much, much too soon.

Until he kissed me good night.

Until he got close enough for me to drown in his wonderful manly scent.

"Oh," I said as his lips brushed lightly across mine. I wobbled under the impact of that touch, and melted effortlessly into him when he wrapped his arms around me, bending his head down to kiss me again. I didn't say anything after that; I was too busy trying to remember everything I had learned regarding the art of tongue-play from Joey Marcuzzi, French-kissing champion of North Seattle Junior High. I'm ashamed to admit I didn't put into practice any of the techniques Joey taught the entire seventh grade female class of 1975 because I was too busy trying to respond to Iain without actually swooning.

"Holy cow," I gasped as soon as he pulled away just enough to allow air to enter our lungs. "That was one hell of a kiss! Do you always kiss like that, or was it a fluke of nature, never to be duplicated?"

Iain smiled in response, his lovely laugh lines crinkling alongside those gorgeous eyes. "It was nice, wasn't it? Would you be liking me to leave now?"

I touched a finger to his delicious lower lip. I thought about my rules regarding men and sex. I thought about the folly of starting something that had no future. I thought about how foolish it was to fall in love with a man I'd known for forty-eight hours.

"No," I whispered, and leaned up to suck his lip into my mouth. "I'd like you to stay."

"Ah, good," he said, sighing as I nipped his lip gently. "I'll stay as long as you'll have me, Kathie."

Famous last words, those. It's just a shame I didn't hear them, occupied as I was with allowing him to inventory my teeth while simultaneously trying to catch my breath. I felt like it had permanently been squeezed out of me, leaving me lightheaded and gasping whenever Iain's mouth left mine— which wasn't often, but I wasn't complaining.

Until I felt cool air on my back and knew he'd pulled down the zipper of my dress.

That's when it hit me, the huge wave of embarrassment. I wanted Iain more than I'd wanted any other man, and I knew that given the proper precautions, there was no reason why we shouldn't go full steam ahead with any and all plans dancing around behind those wickedly devilish peaty brown eyes, but at the same time I could feel another blush starting with the realization of exactly how the evening was going to end, with parts of him visiting parts of me that I'd never even seen.

"Um . . ." I said as he slipped both hands down the curve of my hips, tugging my dress with them. I tingled, positively tingled wherever those long fingers touched me, and they touched me in *a lot* of places.

"Um . . ." I gasped as his mouth found the sweet spot behind my ear and starting doing things there that made other parts of me—secret, dark, hidden parts—stand up and yell their approval.

"Um . . ." I moaned as those fiery fingers divested my upper story of its restraining garment, his hands working some sort of magic on my breasts that suddenly transformed them from rather tiresome bits of flesh hanging off my chest into an extremely wonderful place for him to put his hands.

"Um?" he asked, his breath feathering across my collarbone as he set out along a path burning down toward my breasts. "Ah, love, you're so soft—just like satin, you are, and you taste like wildflowers."

I clutched his shoulders as he kissed and nibbled along the undersides of my breasts, avoiding the two spots I was desperate for him to touch, making my breasts swell and ache for the fire of his mouth to claim them properly.

"Wildflowers?" I asked, arching my back and tugging his head to where I wanted it. His mouth closed over the ache that disguised itself as a nipple and I rose up on my toes in ecstasy. "Wildflowers? I taste like wildflowers? You think I taste like . . . *aaaaiiiiiieeeeee*!"

He lifted his head from my left breast, my bones turning to mush as the fingers of one hand went exploring in my southern hemisphere just as he bent over my right breast. "Aye, wildflowers," he breathed on that nipple before closing his teeth over it so gently it felt like velvet brushing against me.

I wanted to do all sorts of wonderfully naughty things to him while he was tormenting me with his fingers and mouth, but I couldn't get my hands to detach their clutch on his shoulders. Somewhere deep inside me I knew if I did, I would fall and never be caught again.

"Do you . . . oh, mercy! . . . do you eat a lot of wild-flowers?"

I toppled slowly backward onto the edge of the bed as his hands swept downward over my hips, down my legs, pushing my underwear and shoes off. I was half-reclined, propped up on my elbows, my legs dangling over the edge of the bed, utterly, completely, totally stark naked before him.

"Do I eat wildflowers?" He sank to his knees before me, hooking my legs up over his shoulders. The dark, promising look he shot me stripped all coherent thought from what was left of my brain. "Aye, love, I eat wildflowers."

"Um . . . Iain," I said as he leaned his head over me, his fingers stroking a serpentine path up my thigh that made every square inch of me tighten in anticipation. "Um . . . I seem to be completely naked."

"Aye, love, you are," he answered, blowing on those parts of me his dancing fingers had uncovered. I shivered in delight and let my arms give way bonelessly under me until the coolness of the comforter was beneath my back.

"You . . . oh, lord, are you going to . . . you are! . . . merciful heaven, no one's ever done that . . . Iain!"

I tugged on his hair until he looked up.

"Iain, I'm naked!"

He grinned, and any solid particles within me that had hitherto remained whole and unaffected by him gave up the ghost and dissolved into goo. "That you are."

I tugged again as he started to return to his previous actions. "But you're not!"

He grinned again—a wicked, sinful, torrid grin that sizzled straight through me. "Aye. It adds a bit of spice, doesn't it?"

He sank one long finger into my waiting depths and I gave up any thought of protest. I had no choice. I couldn't have formed words then if my life depended on it. Luckily, once Iain had me squirming and writhing beneath his hands and mouth, my body licked with flames of desire so strong I'm surprised the smoke alarm didn't go off, once he had me screaming his name in supplication, then he gave in and peeled off his clothes before joining me on the bed. I wanted to push him over onto his back and do to him all of the things he'd done to me, but I was too weak, still quivering in the aftermath of the pinnacle of my entire sexual experience to that date.

I mentioned that to Iain as he stripped off his clothes.

"Granted my sex life hasn't been extensive by any stretch of the imagination," I said a bit shakily as my gaze devoured those bits of him that were being uncovered. My mouth went dry at the sight of that big chest, all muscle and manly chest hair and two impudent nipples that needed badly to be taught a lesson. "But still, that . . . uh . . . wildflower thing you did was the most amazing experience I've ever had. I just thought you'd like to know that before you—" My eyes drifted downward as he shucked his pants.

"Glorioski!" I breathed, staring. Iain tried to look modest. He failed.

I summoned up enough strength to roll over onto my side as he slid into bed next to me.

"Geez, I hope you brought along a shoehorn," I said, then leaned in for a closer look, trailing one finger along a vein that ran on the underside. "Hooo!"

Iain laughed and pulled me up across that lovely expanse of chest, nipping my lower lip before kissing the astonished look off my face. "Ah, love, we're just getting started. I'm looking forward to broadening your experience."

"Amongst other things," I added, peering over my shoulder at the bit of him that was standing up and waving at me. I waved back. He laughed again and set about introducing me to what bliss felt like.

It was . . . *broadening*.

Chapter Three

The last day of Murder in Manchester dawned to gray, overcast skies, the tired eyes of weary conference-goers, and moments of . . . well . . . embarrassment. The last was pertinent only to me. I'm just not worldly enough to wake up to a new man sharing my bed without bursting into unseemly giggles.

I woke up to find myself draped over Iain. Not just part of him, *all* of him. I was terribly comfortable, but it's a wonder he could breathe. I worried about that for a minute, visions of flashy newspaper headlines dancing around my head—YANK MYSTERY AUTHOR CRUSHES LOVER IN HOTEL LOVE NEST—but his chest rose and fell beneath me in a reassuringly steady rhythm, so I assumed he was hale and hearty. I tried to wiggle off him without waking him up, the giggles building even as I thought about it, but that odd skin-bonding thing had happened at some point, and I couldn't slide off.

You know what I'm talking about—when two layers of flesh meet and one compresses the other. Sweat and moisture and all sorts of other things I don't want to think about build up and work to form a bonding agent that would be guaranteed to keep heat tiles securely on the Space Shuttle. From belly to breast I was glued to Iain, unable to remove myself. I desperately wanted to peel myself off him so I could adopt a sophisticated, woman-about-town pose when he woke. No giggles from me, no siree. I was going to greet the man poised and dignified. Maturity would be my by-word.

I felt someone watching me as I was mentally picturing myself as the personification of elegance, and immediately the blush I had thought long dead fired up and over every square inch of my body, the bonded areas excluded. Iain was awake. I could feel him looking down on the top of my head.

It rose up. I couldn't help it. I tried hard not to give in. I fought it, oh, how I fought it, but as soon as I tipped my head back to look up at him, it burst forth.

"Weel, I'm glad to see you so happy this morning, although I thought you had finished that blush last night."

The giggles changed into full-fledged whoops of laughter. Honestly, how much more ridiculous a situation could a thirty-seven-year-old woman find herself in? Stuck to her bedmate, giggling and blushing like a virgin. So much for poise and sophistication.

"We're stuck," I finally managed to say, wiping back the tears of hilarity. Iain's eyes opened a bit wider.

"See?" I said, and gave an experimental push backward. With a noise reminiscent of hot baloney peeling off Naugahyde, my skin separated from his, and I toppled over backward.

"Aye, I do see," he leered at me. All of me. All of me lying there exposed, wearing nothing but a blush.

I couldn't help it. I giggled at him. Giggled until I realized I was looking at him, and he was smiling at me, and we were both in bed together without a stitch of clothing on. The *Good lord, where do I look now?* problem immediately raised its head.

I looked up. Oh, no, there were his eyes, his lovely peaty brown eyes that were giving me a definitely roguish look. I couldn't possibly meet that look. My eyes dropped lower, down to his . . . *whoa!* Too low, it wouldn't do to look there, peeking aside, although I did make a mental note to the effect that Iain woke up in a very happy state of mind. I pulled my gaze up a notch to his chest. A big, broad, muscular chest covered in soft brown curls; a nice chest, a sexy chest. A chest meant to have fingers run over it, through the hair, circling the adorable little nubs of nipples. My fingers itched to . . . nope! Up went the eyes. Aha, an Adam's apple. That had to be safe, right? Yes. Adam's apple, located below a square chin with stubble from a day's growth of beard. There was red mixed in with those brown whiskers, I noticed, but it was his Adam's apple that intrigued me. I just wanted to nibble it around the edges . . .

"Is it shy you are, or just ogling my manly form? I sincerely hope it's the latter, love."

A little moan slipped past my lips. He could drop me at ten paces with that voice. Maybe if I were to just look at one corner of his eye . . . surely an eye corner couldn't possibly hurt.

"It's . . . ah . . . a little bit of morning jitters, thank you. I'm sure there's some sort of Scottish ritual you do on the morning after you've . . . uh . . . but I'm equally sure it involves tea, and since I loathe tea, I'll just have to wing it."

He chuckled. I discovered that you can't avoid someone's eye when they are chuckling at you, especially when the only alternatives are to stare at that person's earlobes (you'd be surprised at just how sexy an earlobe can be), or out the window at Manchester.

"I'm just a bit . . . shy," I explained.

The corners of his mouth twitched. "Shy? After last night? You're thinking you're shy?"

I thought of one or two of the more creative things we'd done the night before. My blush started its climb up my cheeks again.

"There is a difference," I pointed out with great dignity, "between actions taken in the heat of the moment, and the sight of bared flesh in the cold light of morning. I can't help it. I'm just a little shy about these things come the dawn."

"Shy?" Iain repeated in a half snort, his lips curling into a grin ripe with suggestion. My body responded immediately with suggestions of its own. "So it's shy you were when you yelled your pleasure so loud it woke the people in the next room?"

I glared at him, bared flesh or no bared flesh. "That wasn't me," I argued, thumping him on his chest to emphasize the point. The feel of all that heat beneath my hand distracted me for a moment, urging me to investigate further. I dragged my mind back from the lure of his chest and wondered what it was I had been saying. "That . . . uh . . . that was you making too much noise last night. I don't make noise during . . . you know. I never have."

"Love," Iain's hand closed over mine as it stroked along the curve of his chest. I curled my fingers into the hair beneath them and smiled to myself at the change in his breathing. "Love, I hate to disappoint you, but it was you making the neighbors pound on the wall. You're a moaner, Kathie, not that there's anything wrong with that. I'm of a mind it's a compliment."

I pulled my hand out from underneath his and closed my fingers around one of his nipples. "I am not! I am not a moaner! I might make occasional noises of encouragement but that's it, and if you want to see this nipple again, you'll stop shaking your head and admit that it was you making all the noise." I tightened my hold and was gratified when he conceded the point with another of his sexy chuckles.

"You, sir, need to be punished for such foul slander," I declared, merciless in my victory. I slid down along his chest, enjoying the feeling of his skin burning a path down me as I trapped his thighs between mine.

Iain immediately stopped chuckling. "Oh, aye," he agreed quickly as I leaned down to nibble on his hips. "I do. Punish me, love. Punish me now."

And so it was that I found out he was ticklish in one particular spot. I discovered this when I was zerberting him. A zerbert goes by many names, but in my family, it's the noise made when you place your mouth on a flat, smooth stretch of skin, and blow.

Let's pick our minds up out of the gutters, shall we? I said *flat,* smooth stretch of skin.

So there I was, merrily zerberting away and whammo! I hit the ticklish spot, leaving poor Iain helpless with laughter, about at the end of his tether. I removed myself from the area in question, kissed the two nearby protuberances, and sat back on my heels, sniffling and wiping back the tears of merriment. And I knew, at that moment, if I was not able to spend the rest of my remaining days with Iain, I would go stark, staring mad.

"The conference ends today," I tossed out casually, my future with him uppermost on my mind. "When I set this trip up, my plan was to spend a week in the Lake District, then two weeks in other parts of the country. I'm supposed to leave this evening. "

"Are you, now?" he asked noncommittally as he rubbed at his stubbly jaw.

"Yes."

"Why?"

"I told you last night, it's a research trip," I said, suddenly feeling incredibly naked—more naked than just bare-skin naked, naked in a way that I'd never felt before. I was sure he could see right through to my soul as I sat there wanting him, wanting to be with him, wanting to never be parted from him. I shut out the part of my mind that was screaming warnings at me and laid my hand on his chest, right where his heart was beating strongest. He lifted my hand up to kiss my palm.

"Did you not say you were interested in doing some research in Scotland?"

I nodded. "I did."

"Well then, if you'd not be minding a change in your plans, you'd be welcome to ride up with me in the morning."

"Scotland," I said, a thrill going through me at the thought of it. Iain and Scotland. Scotland and Iain. Iain *in* Scotland. Anyway you said it, it sounded perfect to me. "I've always wanted to see it. I've heard it's lovely."

"Aye, the Highlands are like no other. I live near the Spey Valley—if you're interested in that area, I'd be pleased to have you stay with me."

"I would like that very much. Are you sure you wouldn't mind?" I hated the awkward, stiff feeling that suddenly came down between us, the feeling that arose between two people when one was not sure of the nature of the other's intent. I didn't want to push myself on him if he was just being polite, but I was more than happy to meet him halfway if he truly wanted to continue our relationship, even if it was fated to be only for a short time.

"I wouldn't have asked if I didn't want you, Kathie."

I leaned down to kiss him and told him I would hold him to his words. He gave me an unfathomable look, and said simply, "I'm counting on that, love."

We missed the first round of panels that morning, but sat together for the remainder. I had to admit my mind wasn't wholly focused on them what with having Iain so close to me, distracting me whenever our legs or arms would occasionally brush against each other in that casual, but highly erotic, *new lover* way that made me catch my breath each time it happened. At one panel we sat at the rear of the room, Iain with his arm draped over the back of my chair, his fingers tangled in my hair, gently stroking the nape of my neck. I used the opportunity to lean into him and let my imagination wander. Things were looking very rosy indeed: I would be with Iain for at least the next few days; I would be in Scotland, a place that had long made my heart beat fast with desire; and that evening Iain was taking me to dinner to meet his eldest son, Archie, who lived just outside of Manchester. Yes, things were looking very good indeed, which just goes to show how blinding love at first sight could be.

"This is very important to me, Iain," I had said that morning as I tugged a russet colored sweater down over my head. "Meeting your children is the middle-age version of being taken home to meet your parents." I didn't finish the thought by telling him that although I wanted to meet his two sons, I also wanted to be sure we didn't hit them over the head with our fledgling relationship, especially since I had no idea where it was going. It was more important that Iain's sons slowly be clued in to the fact that their father had a new someone in his life, someone who did not intend on letting him go without a fight.

I had to sit down on the edge of my bed as the full consequences of that thought hit me. Iain was in the bathroom shaving with the razor I used to shave my legs (and swearing profanely all the while he did so). I sat and stared across the room at a Monet print and examined the thought that glowed like neon in my mind.

I didn't want to go home. I wanted to stay with Iain. *Permanently*. After knowing him for only four days.

"Well, now I know I've lost my mind," I grumbled, and felt around in my bag for my shoes.

"What's that?"

"Hmm? Oh, nothing, I just said that it's important to do these things right. Slow and easy, that's the key, without ruffling anyone's feathers. I don't want Archie to see me as a threat to his relationship to you."

Iain looked at me curiously. "And why should he be doing that, then?"

"He's an adult child. Adult children can find it difficult to accept that their parents have . . . well, you know."

"A girlfriend?"

I snorted. I hated that term. "Hardly that."

He gave me a lazy, lazy grin. "A lover?"

"Yes, well, I don't think we ought to be using *that* word in front of your son."

"Do you think he won't guess?"

"Certainly not. We shall be most circumspect and dignified. He will see that we are friends, merely friends. Surely you have women friends?"

"Aye, I do."

And suddenly, I hated each and every one of them.

"There you are," I said in a light and completely false tone. "There's no reason for Archie to suspect we have anything other than a mild regard for each other."

Iain gave me a disbelieving look, but didn't say anything more. I was determined to hold on to my self-control, no matter how much I wanted to run my tongue around the various nooks and crannies that made up the glorious land of Iain . . . but no, self-control didn't allow for tongues mapping out terrain, no matter how enticing said terrain was.

As I checked out of my hotel later that day and stored my luggage, I mused on the best way to appear friendly but not threatening to Archie. As I made my way an hour later to our rendezvous point at a nearby square, I wrote amusing little snippets of dialogue in my head in which I charmed the pants off Archie, and had him begging me to stay and keep his father from the solitary, lonely life he led. As I strolled across the square to where Iain stood, I mentally rehearsed the dignified greeting I would make upon meeting his son.

Iain was alone, standing by a bench watching the squirrels panhandle a young couple nearby. I gave the couple a swift look. They were talking intently with each other, oblivious to anyone else. There were no other people in the immediate vicinity, so I speeded up my approach, and with a leap that would do a long jumper proud, flung myself into Iain's arms.

I kissed his cheeks, his ears, and his neck. I nibbled on his nose, I sucked on his lower lip, and I bit his chin. I ran my hands over every part of him that I could reach. "I'm so glad to see you," I whispered. "It's been so long. I've missed you terribly."

Two hours is a long time when you're over your ears in love.

Iain didn't answer. He was too busy kissing, nibbling, and biting me back. He also tactilely checked my person to make sure everything was where he had left it.

"Thank god Archie's not here yet," I murmured into his ear, and sighed happily when he turned his attention to kissing me properly.

Two minutes later, just as I was about to pass out from lack of oxygen, Iain broke off the kiss. "He is here, love."

Lips. Iain had such lovely, lovely lips. More than anything, I wanted those lips to . . . "He's *what*?"

He lifted his head and looked over toward the young couple.

Oh, my god, not . . .

"Archie, come and meet Kathie."

There are few words to describe my feelings at the moment Iain invited his eldest son to meet the woman who had, mere moments before, been hanging off his lips, but *mortified* and *please let the earth open up and swallow me, I couldn't possibly be more embarrassed than I am now* were pretty darn close. Poise and dignity went right down the toilet.

For one wild moment I cherished the hope that Archie hadn't seen me playing a round of Tongue Spelunker with his father, but one look at his tight jaw and furious eyes told me he had. Damn.

"Archie, Susan, this is Kathie. She writes books. Love, this is Archie and Susan."

Archie looked for a moment like he was going to refuse to shake my hand, but struggling manfully, he managed to do so without actually shuddering or wiping his hand off afterward. He even went so far as to wave Susan forward to greet me. I gathered they were an item, although it was difficult to tell since Susan uttered only three words to us the entire evening. The rest of her time was spent in nodding to whatever Archie said. Think of a British, blond, female version of Al Gore nodding away behind Clinton, and you get a good picture of Susan.

"It's nice to meet you both," I lied through my teeth, trying to avoid the daggers Archie's hazel eyes were shooting at me. "Very nice."

I looked at Iain. He beamed at me, then at Archie.

"Well then, let's be on our way," he said, taking my hand in his. I loved holding his hand, it was so big and warm and he had fascinating, expressive fingers. I squeezed them in a silent SOS call. He squeezed back and turned toward the parking lot. "I hope the restaurant isn't too far, lad. We have to be off early in the morning. Kathie's coming with me up to the farm," he tossed over his shoulder. I glanced back at Archie. I was lucky looks couldn't actually kill.

We managed to make it to a nearby Chinese restaurant without anyone openly declaring war, but I knew Archie was stockpiling missiles and aiming them directly at me. I reminded myself that although I wasn't old enough to be his mother (he was ten years younger than me), I *was* old enough to act mature and not lower myself to his level of surly snarls and peevish pouts.

"He doesn't like me," I told Iain as we were following Archie's car to the restaurant.

"He's not the expressive type, love," Iain tried to reassure me. "He likes you, he just doesn't say much."

I wasn't having any of it. "Oh, he's expressive enough. I'm just thankful his expressions have been confined to nasty looks and nothing else."

"It's just that you took him by surprise," Iain explained as we turned into a crowded parking lot. "I should have thought to mention I'd have you with me. Don't worry, love, he'll warm up to you."

I didn't say anything to that—what could I say? *Iain, I've known you four days now and I'd like you to disown your son because he hates me*? Hardly likely. I crossed my fingers that Iain was right and Archie was merely slow to take to people, and followed him into the restaurant.

This was one time my fingers let me down. Iain was initially bewildered, but quickly became angered by his son's continued rude behavior. Only Susan of the Nods kept him from saying anything about it to Archie. It was obvious that Archie resented my presence; he spent a good deal of the evening pointedly telling Susan what wonderful times he had growing up with his family.

"When I was younger, Dad and David and I would go up to Loch Ness every summer and go fishing," he stated with an accusatory glare at me. I shrugged to show I wasn't going to contest his childhood memories. "Just the three of us. We had a great time fishing and sleeping in a tent and going for rambles, with no one around to disturb us."

"Oh, surely you must have seen Nessie just once over all of those years spent rambling the loch?" I asked archly, instantly regretting my words when Archie bristled at my interruption.

"Only the daft and witless believe that load of rubbish," he sneered. "But what can you expect from an American, someone who wouldn't know her own arse from her elbow."

"That's enough, lad," Iain rumbled next to me, sending Archie a warning glance that had him biting off whatever else it was he had planned to say to me. I put my hand on Iain's and gave it another squeeze, this time apologetic. He smiled in response. Archie's glare grew blacker.

When Susan and I made the obligatory "Who'd dream of going by herself?" paired trip to the ladies' room, I tried to ask her about Archie, but she replied in monosyllabic answers and spent most of the time staring at me. I checked for anything unsightly hanging out of the available orifices, looked to make sure the back of my dress wasn't tucked up into my underwear, and finally conducted a quick examination for any sudden growths that might have popped up since I last looked in the mirror. In the end, I settled for staring back at her. At least it made her stop looking at me as if I had a nipple sprouting out of my forehead.

"Subtlety is not Archie's strong suit, is it?" I asked her on the way back to the table.

She was behind me, but I could feel her stare anyway. I sighed, smiled at Iain when he held out my chair for me, and, digging deep, managed to find the intestinal fortitude needed to sit through several hundred mind-numbingly sweet stories of how blissful Archie's childhood was and how close his family was, but when he started in on how much his mother suffered after she and Iain divorced, I was furious. Although Archie was aiming his blows at me, his father was taking the beating. And *that* I wasn't going to stand for.

"It's difficult to blame the breakup of something so complex as a marriage on any one individual," I commented sagely when Iain, with a clear look of warning at his son, excused himself to spend a penny. "I assume you were only a child when your parents broke up. I doubt if you were able to understand all of the stresses that drove Iain and your mother apart."

"Oh, I know what drove them apart," Archie sneered at me. Susan fidgeted with her napkin and looked worried. "It was another person, wasn't it? A love triangle, they call it. You'd probably know, you've got the look about you of just the sort of woman who enjoys breaking up a happy marriage."

"Your father is not married now," I pointed out through gritted teeth, ignoring his insult. "What he does is of no concern to anyone but himself."

"It's *my* business to see my dad happy," Archie snarled.

I opened my mouth to protest, but a deep voice from behind beat me to it.

"If that's the case, lad, you'd best be keeping a civil tongue in your head." Iain returned to his chair and gave me a questioning look. I smiled and pinched his thigh.

We made it through the meal, but Iain was clearly angry and edgy. I was annoyed and frustrated, but too new and uncertain with the relationship to say anything more to Archie. A good part of the problem lay in the fact that I was riddled with doubts and questions about our future, questions like Where was the relationship going? Did Iain really like me/love me/worship the ground I walked on, or was he just using me? Was I being mocked and didn't know it? Was he serious? Was *I* serious? Where could I find a big two by four to wallop his smart-ass son?

The doubts were pummeling me left and right. I wanted to face down Archie, but I didn't feel I had that right. Iain, I was sure, wanted to say something to his son, but he was too much of a gentleman to start an argument in front of two women. So we all sat and seethed, with the exception of Susan, who kept her eyes glued on my forehead and nodded whenever Archie paused for breath, which wasn't very often.

After the dinner, Susan and I stood with Archie the Terrible in front of the restaurant while Iain went to fetch his car. We had planned to stroll around Manchester's Chinatown, but things were just too uptight, what with Archie making snide remarks under his breath, and me working in a dig whenever I thought Iain wasn't listening, so we decided to go our separate ways instead, Iain and I returning to his hotel, and Archie and Susan going off to their flat.

While Iain was gone Archie sidled over close to me, smirked, and let me have it with both barrels. "I'm not blind like my dad, Kathie. I know the look of a slut when I see one, but you needn't worry I'll say anything to Dad about you. I'm sure you'll be out of his life and flat on your back for the next bloke in a few days."

I was so stunned by the venom in his voice that I didn't

even rally my wits enough to smack him. I just blinked and
felt my stomach contract into a ball the size of a walnut,
wanting more than nothing else to cry at his meanness. I
couldn't believe he was cruel enough to say something so
vicious to me; couldn't believe that someone related to a
man with whom I was now madly in love could be so cold
and callous. I suspected Archie was lashing out at me because of problems in his relationship with his father, but it
didn't make it hurt any less. Truthfully, it hurt worse because
I felt incredibly guilty about the speed with which I'd
jumped Iain's bones, not to mention the strength of my emotions for him, and now I had proof that my actions had ad-
versely affected someone else.

I had never jumped into a relationship so fast before;
maybe I *was* acting like a slut. Nice women just simply
don't throw themselves into bed with a man they just met,
right? Perhaps Archie wasn't so far off the mark as first
imagined. Maybe I wasn't as blameless as I had thought.
Not only had I jumped into bed with Iain after only a few
days' acquaintance, now I was planning to visit him for at
least a week—possibly longer. I *hoped* longer. And all that
after only one night together? Perhaps what I was doing *was*
wrong. That horrible thought struck me just as Iain arrived,
only just keeping me from bursting into tears right there in
front of Kwokman's.

Instead I turned on the waterworks in his car. Iain, poor
man, was at a loss. He didn't know why I was bawling my
eyes out, but he was driving in the middle of Chinatown, a
very popular and populated area of Manchester, and
couldn't find a spot to stop and figure out what the problem
was.

"Are you all right, Kathie?" he asked, one eye on the
road, the other on me. I nodded and groped through my
purse for some tissue. "Has something happened to upset
you?"

I nodded again and blew my nose.

"Was it Archie?" he asked grimly, his jaw tight.

I looked at him, sniffled, and felt the hot tears well over
my eyelashes. I nodded a third time.

He didn't say anything to that, but eventually found a parking lot and parked, then wrapped one strong arm around me and heaved me onto his lap.

"All right, love, now you can tell me what he's said to you."

I cried even harder. The steering wheel was digging into my hip.

There are many ways of determining how serious a man is about you, but one of the best I know is to weep all over his neck and see what he does. If he provides unconditional comfort, love, and support, hold on to him, he's a keeper. If he tells you to buck up, makes excuses for whatever upset you, or hands you a handkerchief and tells you your nose is running onto his expensive jacket, you may want to rethink your relationship.

Iain was in the keeper category, a fact I found out when I sat in a dark parking lot and blubbered all over his nice tweed jacket. I didn't stop to rationalize my need to seek comfort from him, I didn't care that I was being overly sensitive and acting like an idiot, and I refused to recognize that my own insecurity in our relationship might have some bearing on the matter; all I wanted was reassurance that what we were doing wasn't wrong. I clung to Iain and proceeded to tattle on his son between sobbing gulps of air.

"He said . . . I was a slut . . . and I'd be . . . flat on my back . . . for the next bloke soon. He doesn't like me, Iain . . . I think we have to . . . face that fact."

Iain truly was a prince among men. He didn't tell me to stop my sniveling, he didn't tell me that Archie didn't mean what he said, and he didn't tell me I must have imagined it. He didn't even say one word about the fact that I was watering his favorite jacket, or that I left him with a wet neck and soggy collar. No, he just sat there murmuring lovely little things in my ear and stroking my back until I calmed down enough to converse without great heaving sobs.

It was that evening that I found out there was more to Iain than just a marvelous man with a drop-dead sexy voice, a wicked smile, and lovely eyes. Oh, yes, there was more to him; there was two hundred and forty pounds of incredibly angry Scotsman. He was so very angry that I had felt a brief twinge of guilt at telling him what that rotten Archie had said to me. I honestly didn't want to be the cause of an estrangement between the two.

"It's all right, love," he told me later as he dumped my two bags in his hotel room. "I'll take care of it. It's not as if I've never had a row with the lad before. We've gone round about other things—this gives me the opportunity to clear the air."

Now I did feel guilty. Here I was adding fuel to an already roaring fire and over something that wasn't Archie's doing. "Don't bother clearing the air on my part," I said, worrying that he would do something rash. "It really wasn't that important—it just shocked me at the time. They're just words."

Iain hoisted one of my bags onto the luggage rack and smiled at me. "Take your bath, love, and I'll have a word with the wee man."

Uh oh. *Wee man.* It wasn't *what* he said, it was the *way* he said it—with a carnivore smile that didn't quite reach his eyes. I toyed for a nanosecond with the idea of hanging around the room while he telephoned his son, but chickened out and scurried off to have a much-needed soak in the tub.

I fretted as I added triple the amount of bubble bath liquid to the water (there's just something comforting about a huge mound of bubbles taking over the tub). What a fine start this romance was off to! One day of bliss, and wham! A meeting with his son and instantly thousands of tiny stress fractures crept across the landscape of our fragile new relationship. I hadn't the slightest idea where our future was going—I had a good idea of where I wanted it to go—but I did know one thing: stresses from family conflicts can kill even the best of romances. I stepped into the steaming water, beat back enough bubbles to leave an air passage, and sank down to chin level. I felt like crying again.

"You have'na drowned in there, have you?" Iain asked a short time later as he stood looking down at me. "Kathie? You *are* in there, lass?"

Lass. He called me lass. The very last Scottish word I was waiting to hear from him, not that I had objections to being called his love, mind you. *Lass*. Oh, lord, I *was* going to cry!

I poked a hand through the dense cloud of lavender-scented bubbles and waggled it at him. He squatted down next to the tub, whapped at a few bubble tendrils that reached out to snare him, and took my hand. "Are you planning on hiding in there all night, love, or will you be joining me?"

"I'll be out in a few minutes. Did you . . . ah . . . have your chat with Archie?"

"Aye, I did."

That didn't tell me a whole lot. I didn't want to pry (well, OK, I did, but didn't think I should), but I felt like I had the Wrath of Archie hanging over me, and wanted to do a little air-clearing of my own. My problem was that I didn't know Iain well enough to judge just how angry he was with me for being the cause of dissension in his family.

"Are you angry?"

"Verra."

My heart sank. It was over, it was all over. I would do what I could to try to patch things up, but I knew then that the whole delightful little romance was fractured beyond repair. "I'm very sorry, Iain. I should never have said anything—"

Iain *tch*ed and gave my hand a yank forward. I was propelled up and over the edge of the tub, my stomach resting on the cold edge as the rest of my upper works pressed up against him. I gave a squawk of outrage over my cold belly that was silenced when he put his hands on either side of my face, stared at me for a good long minute with those wonderfully expressive eyes, then kissed me very, very gently.

"You're haverin', love. I'm not angry with you, I'm angry with that pillock son I spawned."

If my heart hadn't already melted into a big puddle of love-struck goo, it would have at that point. I had a hard time getting the words out, so overcome was I. "Havering? Pillock?"

"Aye, he's a right pillock."

I hadn't a clue what a right pillock was, but I hoped it was something quite rude.

"So you're not angry at me?"

Now he looked a bit peeved. "I just told you I wasn't, you daft hen. You ought to know me better than that."

Ah, but that was part of the problem. We hadn't had enough time together to overcome those standard new-relationship doubts, and they kept getting in the way of my common sense.

"Oh. Would you . . . would you like to tell me about what you and he said to each other?"

"No. Will you be much longer?"

"That depends."

"On what?"

"Whether or not you're going to spill the details about your talk with Archie. I can sit here and get very pruney if need be. I'm a patient person."

He shook his head, kissed me again, reassured me that he put the blame squarely on Archie's head, where it was right and proper, and left me to the bubbly contemplation of what an incredibly nice man he was—but more important, I thought about what Cait had e-mailed me earlier, before I had checked out of my hotel.

Hold your horses, sister, am I reading between the lines right? Did you sleep with this dishy Scot? After you just met him? I know I told you to go ahead and break out the rain-coats, but I never thought you would! You're not that kind of a girl! You never *sleep around! What's going on, Kathie? I want the truth!*

I added a bit more hot water to my cooling tub. The truth was that I didn't quite understand what was going on. Iain did something to me—had some miraculous, amazing effect on me that transformed me into someone else, someone un-inhibited and free and completely comfortable with who I was, and who he was. I felt like I'd known him my entire life, and at the same time, tingles of excitement pricked my spine whenever I saw him. It wasn't his voice, or his beau-tiful eyes, or even that lovely chest . . . it was all of him together, the whole package, the whole Iain. He made me feel complete.

I am not a conference slut, if that's what you're about to imply, I had e-mailed back to Cait, although I knew she wouldn't think that of me. She knew how few romantic relationships I'd had, but I couldn't blame her for being surprised by my unexpected level of comfort with Iain. I was as surprised as she was, but I wasn't about to look a gift horse in the mouth. As long as Iain didn't have a problem with our sudden state of togetherness, I was happy.

I spent a little more time cataloging his many fine qualities, but finally had to get out of the tub or turn into one giant gelatinous blob. I dried off, brushed my teeth, donned my most exotic nightwear (an oversized T-shirt), and poked my head out of the bathroom door.

Iain was stretched out on the bed, his hands clasped behind his head, gazing up at the ceiling. He looked contemplative. He looked a bit tense. He looked stark naked.

This last did quite a bit for raising my spirits. How very thoughtful of him to think of me!

"Common courtesy requires I return the favor." I smiled, moving to stand at the foot of the bed. He looked down the long length of his body at me, a puzzled frown gracing his manly brow.

"What's that you've got on, then?"

"Minnie Mouse."

"Tch." He made that noise in the back of his throat again. "If it's planning to sleep in this bed you are, you'd best be removing it."

A fascinating bit of Iain Trivia hit me: When he's under the influence of a strong emotion, his brogue gets thicker. He was still annoyed about Archie, I knew, but I couldn't help but wonder if this reaction was limited to just anger, or if *any* strong emotion would trigger it. I felt I owed it to the linguistic community to check out this phenomenon. For purely scientific reasons I peeled off Minnie and plopped myself down next to him, nudging him and instructing him to roll over. He gave me a curious look, but complied.

"Now," I said, enjoying the vast spread of Iain before me.

There was so much to touch, I didn't know where to start. "We're going to conduct a little experiment."

He stacked his hands together and rested his chin on them. "What sort of experiment?"

I smiled at his behind. "You know, you have a really nice patootie."

"Patootie?" He tipped his head and looked over his shoulder at me. "What's that, then?"

I scooted forward until I was kneeling between his knees, flexed my fingers once or twice, then took two handfuls of firm, muscled flesh, and squeezed.

"Ah. Patootie." He chuckled while I bent down and kissed the sleek line of muscle that indented on either side of his hips.

"So many men either don't have much of a behind at all," I mused as I gave either cheek a little love bite. His muscles flexed beneath my hands. My smile broadened. "Or they have an unattractive one, one that would be hard put to inspire joy in the eye of the beholder, but you, sir, have an almost perfect specimen of patootiness."

"Do I, now? I appreciate the kind words, love, but I'd much rather look at yours." He tried to roll over, but I threw myself down the length of his back and clutched the bedspread beneath us.

"Stay put. I haven't started the experiment yet." I nibbled his ear just for a few seconds, just because it was there and asking for nibbling, but mostly because I liked the way his breath quickened when I did it. Beneath me, his back and shoulders tensed even tighter, then slowly relaxed down into the mattress.

"You're not conducting experiments on my . . ."

"Patootie?" I offered.

"Aye."

I gave it a fond glance, and just one little squeeze as I slid off him, adjusting his legs so I could sit between them.

"No, although that is an interesting suggestion, and one I'll file away for a rainy day. No, this experiment is quite simple. I want you to say 'She sells sea shells by the seashore.' "

I put my hands on either calf, sliding them slowly up toward his thighs.

"What? Why would you be having me say that?"

"Just say it."

Iain looked skeptical, but started to repeat it. "She sells sea shells by the . . . *ah bluidy hell*!"

"She sells sea shells by the seashore," I repeated, raising my head up from where I was licking the back of his knee. His thigh muscles tightened as a little tremor rippled through him, but he sucked in a big breath and relaxed again.

"If I say it, will you do that again?"

I smiled and rasped my tongue up higher on his leg, licking my way in to the sensitive skin of his inner thighs. Advancing the knowledge of science had its own rewards.

"She sells sea . . . *lord, Kathie, do you have any idea what you're doin' to me*?"

I traced the path of the interesting little vein that runs from the back side of a man to the front. His lovely behind tensed as I admired the scenery.

"She sells sea shells . . ." I reminded him, scooting up farther until my lips were nuzzling the small of his back, following the lovely sweep of muscles as they curved from his behind into the swells and valleys of his back. I let my fingers go wild.

That big chest expanded beneath him as he took a deep breath. "By t'sea *ah, god, love, dinna stop*!"

"Fascinating," I commented, enjoying the feeling of his muscles trembling beneath me. I nibbled and licked the small of his back, enjoying the taste and scent of his warm skin before starting up his spine, kissing each vertebra, watching with increasing satisfaction as his smooth, bronzed flesh rippled beneath my lips. "Absolutely fascinating. I wonder what would happen if I were to . . ." I nuzzled his hair aside and licked the spot at the back of his neck at the same time I reached lower.

He said something, but I don't know what it was. He was speaking in Gaelic by that point. My experiments that night were lengthy, but I'm happy to say, conclusive—it *was* any strong emotion that made his brogue, amongst other things, thicker.

Life started out looking very hopeful the following morning, but that was before the other shoe dropped.

"It'll be good to be home," Iain sighed as he whipped through a roundabout with a skill that didn't fail to impress me. We were in his car in the north of England, heading for the Highlands of Scotland. I gazed out the window, my heart singing a happy little song about following dreams and being with the dishiest Scot alive. I had survived Archie. I was with Iain. I was about to step off into a great adventure. And I had discovered that when Iain put his mind to it, he could make me, too, speak in a brogue.

Things, I thought to myself as Iain squeezed my knee and gave me a roguish grin, were looking up after all.

"You'll like the farm, love, although God only knows what sort of a state I'll be finding it in. David's been minding it while I've been gone, but he's not much of a hand alone with the sheep."

David. Oh, lord, I'd forgotten about David, Iain's youngest son, the son who lived in the next town over from his. David was younger than Archie by five years, and very, *very* close to his father.

I closed my eyes in horror, my heart's happy little song withering upon its lips and dying a cruel, lonely death. David. I could only imagine the sort of reception I would receive from *him*.

Chapter Four

I had always thought I had been to Scotland before, but Iain informed me I was wrong. I'd been to Edinburgh. It wasn't the same thing at all.

"Scotland," he lectured as we drove northward, "would be lost without the Highlands."

"I'm sure the people in the lowlands and the borders and the islands and all of the other areas appreciate that sentiment."

He grinned. "Aye, well, that's doubtful, but it's the truth I'm telling you. The Highlands are the heart of Scotland."

He didn't need to sell me on the Highlands. I hadn't read all those Scottish romances for nothing!

"This area now," he waved a hand at passing moorland, "this area is pretty enough to look at, but there's no real heart to it."

I looked out of the window as we sped northward. There were sheep and cattle grazing in pastures, while farther off were the famed windswept moors, resplendent with white heather and Scotch Broom. In the distance, dark, smoky green-purple hills marked the beginnings of the forest. Every now and again I'd see a glint of silver flashing through the green, indicating a loch.

It was all a bit gothic and Jane Eyre-ish. I sighed happily, loving every mile that took me deeper into the heart of Scotland . . . and Iain.

"Tell me about your farm," I prodded him after we had made a quick stop for lunch. The trip from Manchester to the Spey Valley was about six hours, and Iain reckoned we'd be at his home right about teatime. I wanted to be prepared for meeting David. Forewarned is forearmed and all that.

"What is it you want to know?"

Men. Always so keen with descriptions. "Well, for starters, how big is it?"

"Close on eight hundred acres."

"Ah." I waited. Nothing. You'd think he'd be bursting to tell me about his farm. If our situations were reversed, I'd be telling him everything I possibly could.

I reflected on that for a moment. We had been driving for two hours and it seemed to me that I had done just that—told him everything there was to know about my life in Seattle, my books, my reason for coming to England, even about my little problem with regards to Scotsmen (something I suspected I would regret to my dying days, since he knew he only had to thicken that brogue to bring me to my knees). But he hadn't responded with a similar glimpse into his life. It wasn't that he didn't want to talk, it was simply that he wasn't particularly forthcoming with all of the details I desperately wanted to hear.

It was still early days, yet, I reminded myself as we drove northward. Just because we had spent two nights together didn't automatically open up the door to his heart and soul. I was sure that as we grew closer, his reticence to share his thoughts would disappear.

"Eight hundred acres, huh? OK. Sounds big. So, how many sheep do you have?"

He told me how many ewes, how many rams, how many gimmers and wethers, and other types of sheep that I hadn't a clue about. I assumed they all had four legs and woolly coats, but I wasn't absolutely sure.

"I bet they keep you busy. It's just you and your shepherd, you said?"

"Aye, just me and Mark, although David helps at lambing, and we hire a few extra hands for shearing."

"Still, two men for eight hundred acres seems like it's spreading you a bit scarce."

"The hill ewes take care of themselves for the most part."

He went on to explain how the low ground ewes were the more valuable sheep, and they needed more care and direct interaction, while the ewes that lived on the hills that surrounded his farm mostly fended for themselves, being a hardy lot and used to being on their own.

"Do you have those cute black and white dogs that do the . . . um . . . sheepy-type things?"

Iain flashed me a grin. "You'll not be writing a mystery set on a sheep farm without doing a wee bit of research first, will you?"

I grinned back. "No, I promise you I won't kill off anyone on a sheep farm without checking my facts with you beforehand." I made no promise about writing myself into a romance with a sheep farmer, however.

"I've three Border collies: Biorsadh, Rob, and Roy."

"I bet it's hard for you to get away with all that work."

"Aye, it is, although just now there is a brief lull before tupping season starts. We've spent a fair bit of time the last month separating out the lambs for market, and tagging the ones kept for breeding."

I avoided the thought of sending sweet little baby lambs to market. There was no use working myself into a swivet over something that wasn't any of my business.

"What's that sign say?" I asked, pointing to one we were passing that proclaimed *Ceud Mìle Fàilte*.

"Ah, it's a welcome to the Highlands. It means *a hundred thousand welcomes*. It's the traditional welcome here."

"Isn't that nice? Not just one welcome, but a hundred thousand of them."

We both mulled that over for a bit, then, desperate to learn more about his life, I goaded him into talking about it. As the car climbed up into the Highlands, he told me about how he sorted the sheep, how they were dosed for worms, how they were dipped, how he and his dogs moved the sheep where he wanted them to go, and how he and Mark kept track of which hirsel (flock) lived on which hill.

It was all very fascinating, but it didn't tell me what I really wanted to know—how he lived, what he did during the long, lonely evenings, how he spent his free time, who his friends were, whether or not David would be likely to kick up a fuss over me, and oh, yes, there was that one niggling question that I couldn't seem to ask—whether he had been seeing anyone, someone female who would mind if I suddenly showed up and staked my claim on him. As a rule I love alpha males, but Iain was obviously one of a rare subgroup—a quiet alpha—and that quiet aspect drove me mad with the desire to pry information out of him.

As for the possibility that he had someone tucked away back home, I wasn't casting aspersions on his morals. I knew that if he was inviting me to come and stay with him, he wouldn't be trotting out a girlfriend and introducing us. The man had class, after all. But I also realized that we both fell into this relationship much faster than was wise, and he might very well have left behind a loose end back home.

"So, um . . ." I stumbled over the words in my attempt to find out his romantic status. "So, you were married."

He slid me a curious look. "Aye, love, you know that."

"Yes, of course I do, silly me, but . . . um . . . for how long did you say you were married?"

He grimaced, God love him. "Almost ten years."

"That's a long time. I imagine you were divorced a while ago, yes?"

He swore and swerved around a dead thing in the road. "What did you say, Kathie?"

"Oh. I . . . er . . . how long ago did you get divorced?"

He frowned. "Must be near to sixteen years now."

I was getting nowhere fast. I decided to take the less circuitous route. "That's quite a long time. I'm sure there were moments when you must have regretted the . . . er . . . lack of companionship?"

"Aye," he nodded, flipping on the windshield wipers and muttering to himself about the rain.

"I can imagine that living by yourself, there were times you were . . . uh . . . lonely."

He slipped me a quick questioning glance. "What is it you're wanting to know, love?"

I opened my mouth to say the few words that would put my worries to rest. *Iain, are you dating anyone in particular?*

I tried, but my lips wouldn't form the words. *Iain, were you in love with someone else before we started playing squishy-squishy?* Nope. No good. Much too crass. Maybe the straightforward way was the best: *Iain, this weekend aside, when's the last time you had sex? Ack!* I couldn't possibly ask that!

"Nothing," I said at last, and looked out at the scenery, only to find it suddenly drenched in an ugly gray drizzle. Somehow it seemed apropos.

I spent the rest of the trip being alternately very, very happy, or plagued with doubts and questions and concerns that I couldn't seem to put into words. No surprise there—I was, after all, in a car on my way home with a man whom I had met only six days before. It's not, perhaps, the smartest thing in the world to blindly follow your heart without giving your brain equal time, but I had a feeling that Iain and I were meant for each other. Scotland felt right for me. *Iain* felt right. I pushed the doubts to the back of my mind and watched, as we climbed into the Highlands and the rain cleared, the scenery unfold one breathtaking vista after another. As we drew closer to Iain's farm, he started pointing out landmarks.

"Loch an Eilein," he said, pointing to a picturesque castle ruin on an island in a loch. I love castles. I made a mental note to visit it before I left. "Over there sits the Highland Wildlife Park."

"Really? A wildlife park? Here?"

A smile curled the corners of his lips. "Aye, we do have wildlife here. The park has badgers, wolves, lynx—all sorts of animals. I'll take you there one day when we have some free time."

Hmmm. Interesting. That sounded as if he expected me to be around for a while. Which was, of course, another issue that was making me gnaw on my lower lip with worry. The invitation he had offered me to stay with him had been rather vague, without either a time limit or the offer of carte blanche. Now I worried over the intent behind his invitation to stay with him. Was I a houseguest who would be given her own room and sent on my way after a week? Was Iain expecting me to stay with him for the entire three weeks of my vacation? What if I wanted to stay longer—would he want me to? Did he even want me to be there now, or was he already regretting his hasty and lust-induced invitation as he drew ever closer to his beloved farm? What would I do when he turned me out and broke my heart?

I had visions of myself staggering down a long winding dirt road while bagpipes wailed a lament in the distance, dragging my luggage and sobbing as each reluctant footstep took me farther away from Iain, breaking my heart and shattering my soul into a million fragments.

There are times when it doesn't pay to have a vivid imagination.

"Just a few minutes more, now, love," Iain said, interrupting my pity party. I sat up and looked around, pleased with the rural area, noting several large farms as we drove down a winding road that snaked its way through the mountains. Everything was wet and green and absolutely breathtaking.

"This is lovely country," I exclaimed, my nose pressed against the rain-splattered side window as Iain slowed down to give me a better look. Before us spread a valley dressed in rusty reds, rich browns, and succulent greens, the ground sloping gently up to dusky purple- and green-clad undulating hills. The valley sat snug and protected by its surroundings, giving it a timeless, peaceful quality.

"Aye, it's a good land," he replied, his voice belying bone-deep satisfaction. "That bit there is Kin Aird. I share it with a neighbor."

"It's lovely," I repeated as he drove on. "You share it? Is that common here?"

"'Twas a disputed border. We settled the boundary issue last year by agreeing to own it jointly, sharing the expenses and the profits."

"That makes sense. I don't see any sheep on it, though."

"We haven't settled on how to best use the land yet."

He turned off at a small wooden sign that said Dulnain Farm, and started up a long gravel drive. My stomach tightened into a little ball of worry as we meandered up the drive, almost a mile long, past several pastures, barns, and assorted outbuildings. There were a few sheep visible, but not the great big herds of them that I expected.

"Most are out in the parks," Iain answered my question as to their whereabouts. "This is arable soil, here. I plant those fields with turnips, and over there with silage. Across the way, there, is the lambing park. And around this bend is the house."

I thought I was going to throw up at the sight of it. I didn't believe it was possible to work myself up into such a state over the thought of meeting a person, but I was literally worried sick. David would be at the house. How was he going to take his father's showing up with a strange woman in tow?

Added to that concern was my distress over not knowing what Iain felt about our future. Somehow, despite several tries, I hadn't screwed up my courage enough to ask him point-blank whether or not he wanted me in his life. Hell, I couldn't even ask him how long he expected me to stay!

"It's good to be home," Iain said, his voice thick with satisfaction as he pulled to a stop in front of a whitewash and redbrick, two-story, squat little farmhouse. "I've been away too long."

I stood next to Iain's car and looked at the neat grounds and cute little house, and mentally castigated myself for a fool. All I had to do was open my mouth and ask him what I wanted to know: How serious were his feelings for me? Did he catch his breath in wonder when he looked at me as I did when I looked at him? Was he overwhelmed with the same sense of rightness that I was when we were together? Did he want me to stay with him forever and never leave? And most important, who was that dark-haired beauty who ran out of his house and threw herself into his arms, kissing him with a possessiveness that made the hairs on the back of my neck stand on end?

"David, this is Kathie. She's going to be staying with me," Iain introduced me to his son. I dragged my attention off the woman who clung to Iain's arm, and smiled tentatively at David. He looked a bit surprised for a moment, shot his father a quick assessing look, then turned back and enveloped me in a bear hug that brought tears of joy to my eyes.

David looked like a slightly blurred copy of his father. He was big, burly, had nice brown eyes, and a smile that could bring warmth to the coldest of days. I liked him immediately. He turned and waved toward a slight woman with lovely cornflower blue eyes and a shy smile. She'd been hovering in the background, but came forward with a warm handshake to be introduced as David's wife Joanna.

I liked her immediately as well. She was very sweet, English (At last! Someone I could understand without having to be very still and concentrate intently), and had been married to David for almost four months. They still wore that blissful look that all newlyweds have.

"Iain, darling, don't tell me you're reduced to taking in boarders?" the dark-haired Iain-kissing woman drawled in a BBC voice, pulling on his arm.

Iain darling? Iain *darling?*

"Kathie's not a boarder, Bridget. Love, this is Bridget Stewart. She owns the farm to the south of mine." Iain disengaged his arm and turned back to his son. "Kathie writes books."

Darling.

David smiled. "Now, why is it I'm not surprised to hear that? Welcome to the Spey Valley, Kathie."

Darling?

"Oooh, an author. How thrilling," Bridget cooed. "What is it you write?"

Darling!

Iain took my hand and pulled me toward him. "She writes mysteries."

Daaaaaaaarling.

"Does she speak?" Bridget asked in a snotty tone that made me grind my teeth.

"Only when there's someone worth talking to," I snapped, and turned back to David and Joanna.

Darling, indeed! I knew I was overreacting a bit. Just because the raven-haired hussy had wantonly thrown herself at

Iain and tried to suck the tongue right out of his head didn't mean she was a bad person. Just because she clung to him, and cooed at him, and made disgustingly brazen sheep's eyes at him didn't mean she was worthy of my scorn. Just because she called him *darling* right there in front of God and everyone as if she had a right to, didn't mean she was a strumpet and therefore worthy of my contempt. Or jealousy. Yeah, right.

It was all fine and well to realize that later, but at the time I was positively seething, even after I turned my back on her and chatted for a minute with David and his wife. Soon, however, I realized my mistake when the little besom latched on to Iain.

"It's cold out here, darling. Let's you and I go in and we'll let your little writer friend get to know David better."

I noticed she only included Iain in her invitation to go into the house and thaw out. She evidently didn't give a tinker's damn if the rest of us stood outside and caught pneumonia.

"Darling," I ground out to myself, narrowing my eyes and watching her tug on Iain's resisting hand. I think David heard me because he gave me an odd look and seemed to be having some sort of a problem with his lips. They twitched.

Joanna, bless her heart, took pity on us. Agreeing with the she-devil that it was too cold to stand about outside, she ordered David and Iain to bring in the luggage while we womenfolk went in and set out tea.

I felt like a dog with its hackles up as I stalked behind the two women, decidedly out of place, homesick, miserable, furious, jealous, and sorely put-upon. And those were the good emotions.

David and Iain came in with the luggage while Joanna was bustling around in the kitchen, bringing out hot scones, ordering Bridget to cut up the sandwiches, and handing me a stack of cups and saucers to lay out on the kitchen table.

"Dad, David's been sleeping in the guest room," Joanna called out to Iain as he passed the kitchen on the way to the stairs. "I'll change the linens in there for Kathie directly after tea."

Iain paused, raised his eyebrows, looked at me, and winked. "That won't be necessary, love." Then he turned and marched up the stairs with a grinning David following behind.

Now, I clearly had two choices: I could either die right there of embarrassment, which would mean I wouldn't have the satisfaction of spiting Bridget, or I could pretend nothing had happened out of the ordinary. I was, after all, thirty-seven years old. I was a world traveler. I was no shy virgin to be blushing at every hint of intimate relationships. I could do this, and I could do it with poise and dignity.

"Oh, god," I moaned, and sitting down in the nearest chair, covered my face with my hands. "Tell me he didn't just do that."

Joanna had been trying to hold back her laughter, but she gave up the struggle at my moans. "It's all right," she said in between whoops. "It's just family. But oh, if you could have seen the look on your face when he winked!"

Just the thought of it set her off again. She wiped her eyes with the edge of the tea towel and put a hand on my shoulder. "I'm sorry, Kathie, that wasn't kind of me. Or of Dad. He should have a little more respect for . . . for the situation."

"Oh, god," I moaned again into my hands, rocking in the chair. Everyone knew! This was *not* how I had envisioned this meeting going. Why was I forever doomed to have Iain's family members, the minute they met me, know I was more than just a friend? Did I have *Has Engaged in Sex with Iain* stamped across my forehead? Was there some sign marking me that I didn't know about? Were they all psychic? Why couldn't I *just once* meet someone in his family without them instantly knowing we were playing Poor Man's Polo?

I glanced over at Bridget and was immediately chilled by the glint in her eye. I knew what was coming even before she opened her mouth.

"Yes, it's just family. Nothing to be ashamed about. I'm sure you'll be very happy with Iain's room—his bed is so deliciously comfortable. Not that I've actually ever *slept* in it, you understand."

Oh, I understood. She gave me a slow, evil, knowing smile and turned back to the sandwiches.

"Darling," I growled, and amused myself for some minutes by plotting her detailed, protracted demise.

It's interesting how in times of great emotion or stress, our brain sometimes creates a mental release valve by bringing odd little facts or ideas to the forefront of our mind. For example, at the very moment when I was sure I was about to give in to Bridget's goading and strangle her as she deserved, I remembered something I'd read about medieval punishment. It seems that in the medieval times, disputes were sometimes settled by an act of God. The hand of God was deemed to be shown by the outcome of ordeal by water or ordeal by fire. In the former, the accused was lowered into a body of water. If the person sank, he or she was declared innocent. True, the person was drowned at that point, but all in all, everyone went home happy that justice had prevailed. If the person floated, the verdict of guilty was passed. In ordeal by fire, the accused had to grab a red-hot piece of metal. If, three days after the ordeal, the wound had not festered, it was considered to be a sign from God that the person was innocent. An infected wound proved guilt.

As a rule, those medieval folk concerned with meting out justice really knew their potatoes as far as torture went, but they missed one ordeal so hideous, so cruel and inhuman that I almost hate to mention it.

Ordeal by tea.

If only they had had Bridget around in the Dark Ages! I was willing to bet one tea with her and even the most hardened criminals would have sung like canaries. I know that by the end of that first tea at Iain's house, I was ready to commit a little mayhem myself, and I had a pretty good idea of who would be my victim.

"What is it that brings you here, Bridget?" Iain asked as we sat down to tea.

"Darling!" She opened her eyes wide and gave him a smut-laden smile. "As if I need a reason to spend time with you."

My jaw tightened at that horrible, perfect voice. Iain's eyes met mine. We were all sitting around the table, enjoying the tea Joanna had prepared, or trying to enjoy it. It was a little difficult with Madame Tact insisting on being as obtrusive as possible.

Iain looked a little worried about Bridget, which didn't make me feel any better. In fact, I was utterly miserable. What on earth was I doing there? It was obvious I should have inquired as to the status of his romantic life before I agreed to come home with him. It was equally obvious from the distress in Iain's eyes that this was not just a case of Bridget trying to stake out a false claim. They had quite clearly *known* each other, and known each other very well.

Although each second I spent with Iain merged him deeper and deeper into my soul, I would be damned if I was going to be the third corner of a triangle. If that was the case I'd just borrow the dustpan and gather up the fragments of my shattered heart and be on my way, thank you.

"As it is," Bridget continued, arching her eyebrows, "I did want to remind you that you promised a decision on Kin Aird. Tannahill won't wait forever for our offer, and you know we won't find a better opportunity than this to turn a profit."

Kin Aird? That was the delicious little piece of valley that Iain owned with a neighbor . . . Bridget? He owned a piece of land with Bridget? That explained some of her possessive manner, but not all.

Iain's lips tightened imperceptibly. I wondered what it was she was trying to get him to agree to. Whatever it was, he didn't seem any too keen on the idea. Or maybe it was just Bridget. I know her presence brought a grimace to *my* lips.

"I haven't forgotten," he told her. "We'll talk about it later."

"Very well, but we won't find a better chance than what Tannahill offers. . . ."

"Later," he growled, and shoved a plate of sandwiches at her. She smiled a catty little smile at me that made me wonder just what she was up to.

"Darling, I'm sure Kitten is much too uncomfortable being a stranger here to tell us about the conference, so you tell us instead."

I tipped the mug of instant coffee up to my mouth, but couldn't get any fluid in because my teeth were too busy grinding away a few layers of enamel. *Kitten,* oh ha ha.

"Her name is Kathie, Bridget, and she's quite capable of telling you anything you'd be wanting to know." Iain frowned at her. "And I'll thank you to stop acting like your knickers are on fire. You're upsetting her."

Who, me? Upset? I looked up from the gloomy contemplation of the salmon sandwich before me and blinked at Iain while Joanna helpfully thumped her husband on his back. He had been taking a sip of tea when Iain spoke.

Bridget gave me a long look, then turned back to Iain with a purr. "But darling, I have no intention of upsetting your new lover. You of all people should know how much I value your . . . *friendship.*"

I thought longingly of getting her in a soundproofed room with a rubber hose. Just ten minutes, that's all I asked for. I'd settle for five if I had to. Three would do in a pinch.

"Bridget," Iain growled warningly.

Bridget pulled back and raised her hands in a gesture of defeat, then smiled a piranha smile at me. "I concede. He's all yours, Kaye. I just hope you know what to do with him."

Iain sighed noisily and rolled his eyes. Joanna giggled and continued to whump her husband on his back. David tried for a breath and ended up in another paroxysm of coughing.

"Could we possibly talk about something other than my physical relationship with Iain?" I asked in a strained voice.

Bridget looked interested. "Why? Are you embarrassed, dear? Are you ashamed of the fact that you and Iain are lovers?" She gasped a horrified little gasp. "Is it because you are . . . *unfulfilled?*"

"*Gark.*" Now it was my turn to choke.

"Bridget, stop it. Now." Iain's frown was turning quite black.

She looked him over much as you would a bull you were

putting to stud. "But darling, if you're not doing it properly, if she hasn't yet had an—"

"Bridget!" Iain roared, flicking a nervous glance at me. I couldn't meet his eye. I couldn't meet anyone's eyes. I just sat there, in the house of a man I had known for six whole days, three intimately, and listened to his former lover discuss my sex life and what might possibly be lacking in it.

I have never in my life *tried* to faint, but I did so now. Frantically. Desperately. Anything would be better than the hell I was in.

"Well, really! I don't know what you're all so upset about." Bridget took a small sip of her tea and gazed around with her sultry gray eyes wide in disbelief. "If what Karen says is true, there must be something wrong with her. I know Iain, darlings, and I can assure you all it would be physically impossible for him *not* to bring any woman to—"

"Will you bluidy stop?" Iain bellowed, his hair standing on end.

I tried again. I screwed up my eyes and held my breath and willed myself to faint. Or die. At that point, I didn't care which. Either was a viable alternative to being at tea with Bridget.

Bridget looked at Iain with an innocent air. "But darling, if she can't . . ." Her voice trailed off under the effect of his furious scowl. She gave a delicate little shrug. "Fine. We'll let it go, then."

Everyone heaved a not-so-secret sigh of relief. Iain watched me closely, muttering to himself under his breath.

I forced myself to unclench my fingers, then picked up my mug of undrinkably nasty coffee and drank it. I was a strong woman. I would survive this if it killed me. There wasn't anything worse she could say to me than what she'd already said.

Bridget leaned forward and whispered conspiratorially down the length of the table, "If you need pointers on what drives him wild in bed, dear, do let me know. I'll be happy to tell you about those things that make him roar like a lion."

Chapter Five

"Eh . . . love, I'm sorry."

How sweet. Iain, sensing I was one big ole bundle of nerves, was apologizing for Bridget's horrible comments even though it really wasn't his fault. He had, after all, done everything he could to shut Bridget up, finally being driven to hustling her out of the house by her untoward offer of advice on how to sexually satisfy him. He had even known how uncomfortable I was after that scene, and thanked David, kissed Joanna, and sent them on their way as well.

What a dear, sweet, *thoughtful* man. He understood how strange and alone and desperately homesick I felt, and he was doing his best to put me at ease. Now we would have that discussion in which all my fears and worries would come tumbling out and finally be set to rest. Now he would tell me exactly what he thought and felt about us. Now he would finally open up to me. Tears of gratitude pricked the corners of my eyes as I gazed at him. No wonder I loved him. He was nigh on perfect. My knight in shining plaid.

"I've got to leave you for a wee bit. Just a wee bit," he held up his hands when I shot up off the couch. "I've got to see Mark about what's been happening while I was gone, and tend to a few things in the barn."

"Oh. Of course. You have chores to do. You are, after all, a sheep farmer. This is a sheep farm. These things come first. I know that."

I might have known it, but it didn't make me feel any bet-

ter. Of its own volition, my lower lip started to pout. I
sucked it back in and gave him a watery smile.

"Not a problem. I'll just sit here and . . ." I looked around
the room. It had a couch, a horribly worn down old leather
chair, an armchair that held a stack of books, a couple of
wooden chairs, and two end tables loaded down with magazines and more books. The small octagon table next to a
faded green-and-taupe couch held stacks of *The Sheep
Farmer* and *Farmer's Weekly*. In the bookcase on the near
wall were books on animal husbandry and sheep reproduction. I reached out and plucked a book from the case.

"I'll just sit here and read"—I looked at the title—"*You
and Your Ewe*. Sounds fascinating. Been meaning to read
this for ever so long. I heard it was on the *New York Times*
extended list."

Iain grinned and nodded over my head at something.
"You might find that bookcase of more interest to you,
love." Then he pulled me to him and engaged in a few minutes of snogging before leaving.

Snogging, for those of you who aren't hip to British
lingo, is a delightful word that carries the distinction of
being just as much fun to say as it is to do. Snogging means
kissing—while checking the other person's teeth. When Iain
pulled me to his broad and manly chest for a kiss, I knew it
was going to be more than just a little peck on the cheek, I
knew it was going to be a kiss that fair stole my wits away.
When Iain kissed, his whole body kissed with him, everything from the seductive press of his thighs against mine, to
a lovely grind against his hips and the two hands that had a
tendency to roam. I didn't complain, I just kissed him back,
trying to emulate his actions but usually failing dismally because I couldn't hold on to a thought for more than a second
at a time.

"All right," I said once I had pushed back on his chest
and gasped for air. I retrieved my tongue and put it back in
its accustomed holding area. "That kiss will buy you an
hour, but I expect another if you're gone longer than that."

The look he gave me made my uterus stutter. I watched
him leave, then collapsed into a small dining room chair

next to the big bookcase and fanned myself for a bit before looking over to see what the bookcase held. Floor to ceiling it was filled with books—mysteries, fiction, nonfiction, and biographies—a bibliophile's delight.

I put down the sheep book I had absentmindedly been holding and perused the good bookcase, running my fingers over the titles of books I'd read, occasionally pulling down books by authors I hadn't heard of. Up on the top shelf I noticed a familiar title. I smiled.

"I haven't seen this in years," I muttered to myself as I pulled it down. "Imagine that. Iain has a copy of *The Joy of Sex*. My, my, my." I opened the book. Elegant handwriting in the front caught my eye.

> *To the best lover in all of Scotland. Not that you need this, but do let's try page 57. Love, Bridget.*

Damn!

I tossed the book away from me like it was made of spiders, and poked around for another. Eventually I curled up with an old volume of G. K. Chesterton stories, over which I fell asleep. Iain woke me up two hours later when he came in, full of apologies for the time he had been out doing chores, which I accepted after he spent a good long time in front of the fire on a lovely soft wool blanket making up for his absence. His manner of apology—involving the application of bare flesh upon bare flesh—did much to relieve my worries regarding his present state of mind, but there were other concerns that had me troubled, concerns that I knew we'd have to face pretty darn soon.

That thought was first on my mind when I woke up the following morning. Waking up in a new place is always momentarily confusing, but that morning I knew exactly where I was the instant my eyes opened. I lay still and listened to the heart beneath my ear beating strong and true. It was a reassuring sound, relaxing, and comforting. The sound of life, Iain's life. The sound of his life whooshing through his veins, giving him warmth and strength and everything wonderful that made him Iain. I opened one eye. There was a light burning in the hall, spilling through the not-quite-closed door. Because of the dim light, I could make out the shapes of the furniture in Iain's bedroom. A big, dark wardrobe, a heavy wooden chair, and behind me, beneath a window, I knew there was a small desk. A small, very sturdy desk. We had tested it earlier and it had proven to be quite an accommodating piece of furniture.

"Iain?"

His heart continued to beat steadily beneath me. I had to give Bridget credit, she was absolutely right. Iain's bed was comfortable, but not nearly as comfortable as the man himself. I shifted a little, not wanting to get that whole skin-bonding thing started again. "Iain, I know you're awake."

His breath ruffled my hair. I smiled, turned my head to the other side, and snaked my tongue out to where his nipple was hiding in a swirl of hair. His breath hissed above me.

"Iain, I know you're awake because hands don't do what yours are now doing when their owners are asleep."

My personal mattress rumbled beneath me. Iain was chuckling. I let myself melt into a puddle against him.

"Iain, I know that you're awake, and I know that you know what I want to talk to you about."

Long, sensitive fingers began to stroke my back, making little circles around my shoulder blades, long sweeps down the curve of my spine, more little circles on my behind.

"I also know you don't want to talk about it. But I need to, Iain."

My personal mattress heaved a deep sigh that parted my hair.

"All right then, love, we'll talk about it."

I squirmed. "Well, I'm not going to be able to if you're going to do *that*!"

His fingers paused for a minute while he considered, weighing the advantages and disadvantages of continuing. Then he sighed again and removed his fingers to a safe zone. I smiled into his chest. He was such a gentleman. He refused to take the easy way out even when it was handed to him on a silver platter.

Not that my way was easy, oh no! There I was lying on

top of the man with whom I fully intended on spending the rest of my days, the sun not even streaking the sky on our first morning together in his home, and I was about to grill him about his relationship with the Tart of the Spey Valley.

"I have to ask, Iain, you understand that don't you?"

He ran a finger down my spine, feeling each vertebra before he answered. "I suppose I do, love. Bridget was at her worst last night. I could see you were a wee bit upset."

A wee bit upset didn't begin to describe the depth of my feelings, but I let it pass. "She made it quite clear you and she have been an item."

I waited for confirmation of this. I had no need to hear it, really, since Bridget had all but trotted out dates and times, but I wanted to make sure this was thoroughly hashed out between us. I couldn't stay here with him unless I was easy in my mind about it.

Iain didn't say anything, just sent his fingers down to count my ribs. I tipped my head back and bit him on the chin. His eyes opened, looked down at me for a minute, saw that I was not going to let it go, and closed again. He sighed. For the third time.

"Aye, love, we were."

"For a long time?"

"A bit. On and off."

A bit. That could mean six months or it could mean ten years. I decided that particular piece of information wasn't relevant to the situation, and moved on.

"And I take it the relationship is now over?"

My personal mattress stilled for a moment, and then heaved upward. I was sent sprawling, and suddenly found myself on my back with Iain looming overhead. An *angry* Iain looming overhead.

"Do you think I would be here with you now if it weren't?" he demanded.

Oh dear, I had insulted him.

"Well, do you? Because if that's what you think of me—"

I put a hand on his cheek and interrupted him. "No, Iain,

I don't think that of you. I know you would never have a fling if you were committed to someone. I apologize."

His frown deepened. "Is that what you're thinking this is? A fling?"

I looked up at him, speechless. We were smack dab at an issue that I knew needed to be discussed, but I wasn't ready to be there yet. At least, not until a few more questions were answered. But it seemed I didn't have a choice.

"Is this just a fling to you, love?" He wasn't asking, he was demanding.

I didn't know what to say. I didn't know what he *wanted* me to say. If I said yes, it was just a fling, I'd be lying. I couldn't lie to him, not to those lovely warm brown eyes with the little gold flecks. On the other hand, I couldn't tell him no, that he was everything to me, that I'd be permanently shattered if we ever parted. I couldn't put that sort of pressure on him, not yet. Not before we had time to explore just what it was between us. Not before we had time to understand the entity made up of Iain and Kathie.

"No," I whispered, my eyes puddling up at the injustice of the world. Why did it always seem like things went wrong at the very worst moment? Why was life never the way it should be?

He stared at me, his gaze somber and hurt. He started to pull back.

"No!" I yelled, and clutching him, started to sob in earnest. It seems like I was forever weeping on the man. "No, Iain, oh, no."

"No, what, love?" he whispered to the top of my head. "Are you saying you don't want to be here with me?"

"No," I answered, still sobbing, unable to explain but knowing I had to say something or I'd lose him. "No, it's not just a fling to me. And oh, yes, I'd like us to have a chance. I want to be here. I want to stay with you. I don't know what's going to happen to us, where it'll end, but I want to be with you, Iain."

He held me for a long time after that. He held me until I stopped sobbing. He held me until the sky started turning pink above the hilltops. He held me until I stopped being selfish and thinking only of myself, and started thinking about him. He held me until I started holding him in return.

It took a bit of time, but once I stopped thinking about myself, I realized how rude I had been, and apologized for my selfishness. "Iain, I'm terribly sorry for casting aspersions against your good character by insinuating that you would be playing slap and tickle with me while having a relationship with Bridget. I know you wouldn't do that, and as for the other . . . well, *fling* isn't exactly what I meant."

"What is it you were meaning, then?" he asked, still watching me intently, a serious Iain with a frown above those two handsome eyes. I reached out to smooth the frown away.

"I know it's probably none of my business, but yet, in a way, it is. Iain, I can't stay here with you if I don't ask— were you and Bridget still seeing each other when you went to Manchester?"

He caught my hand and stared at my fingers for a minute, then gently, oh so gently, nibbled on the pad of my thumb.

"Is that what's been worrying you, love? That you're taking Bridget's place?"

His voice sounded so hurt, I was thoroughly ashamed of myself. What sort of a person was I that I could doubt he would act in an honorable manner? Hadn't I had a discussion with myself on this very thing on the way up here? Why all of a sudden was I assuming the worst about Iain?

I'll tell you why. Bridget and her damn *darlings*. I was too ashamed to look him in the eye, so I nodded and watched his lips.

"Kathie, look at me."

"I am."

"No, you're looking at my mouth. Look me in the eyes, love."

I looked. His laugh lines stood out white against the tan of his skin. I wanted to smooth those out, too, but Iain still had a hold on my hand. "I haven't been with Bridget in close to four years, so set your mind at ease."

Four years? Four years! Four lovely, long, deliciously Bridget-free years? Let fly the doves, it's been four years!

"Oh," I said happily, and proceeded to smother his face in kisses. Suddenly, something occurred to me. I stopped abruptly. "If it's been four years, then why did she insinuate—"

He made a disgusted sound. "She's playing her game. She's been after me to marry her so I'll join my farm with hers, and hasn't forgiven me for turning her down."

I stared at him. Iain turned her down? That meant . . . "She asked you to marry her?"

"Oh, aye," he laughed, and reinitiated an activity he had stopped earlier to answer my questions. "Several times. Must be five or six at the last count."

Life suddenly looked very, very good. Exceptionally good. My heart swelled and sang and flew around the room without the slightest effort. I pushed Iain back into the pillows and leaned over him, filled with joy, happiness, and achingly sweet love. The tears of an hour before were forgotten, never happened, never *could* happen with such a wonderful, marvelous, fabulous man.

My mind knew what I was going to do before I did. Warning bells and sirens went off loudly in my head. *Don't do it,* my brain shrieked at me. *Don't say it. It's only Day Seven. You know the rules, it has to be Day Fourteen at the very least! It's much, much too soon. Don't say it! Not now—wait! Wait, you fool, wait!*

"Oh, Iain," I said, leaning over him and kissing his nose and his eyes and his cheeks, then trailing kisses all around his adorable lips. Common sense? What was that? "I love you so very much."

The words were out before I realized it. I gasped. I didn't . . . just . . . .say . . . the *L* word! Oh, my god, what had I done?

Iain looked thoughtful.

Immediately, my mind whipped into damage control status.

"Three things could result from the folly of our declaration," my brain informed me. *"One: he could tell us he loves us. Two: he could make a joke of it. Three: he could*

say nothing. Defenses in place, please, people! We have a frail ego to protect!"

I left my brain to handle the defensive actions while I considered the three possibilities; of the three, the second was sure to be the worst, but the third option wasn't far behind it. And yet that's just what Iain did. He said nothing. He just looked thoughtful and continued to hold me.

I'm sure that most, if not all, of you have been in a relationship where one of you had to be the first to mention love. In some relationships, like my first marriage, it is incredibly easy to toss out because it means nothing.

"Do you want to go ice skating tonight?"

"Oooh, that sounds like fun. Gosh, you're so sweet to me—I just love you to death, Kevin."

"Yeah, I love you too, Kathie."

That is, as close as I can recall, a verbatim conversation I had with my first husband. We were both eighteen at the time, were married a month later when we eloped to Vegas, and divorced a few months after that.

That was not love. It was a big crush, and nothing more. But with Iain, it wasn't only my body involved in worshiping him, it was my heart and soul, too. So when my brain shut down and allowed me to tell him just how I felt, I was putting more on the line than just the opportunity to play mump the cuddie with him for a few weeks. I wanted Iain for the rest of my life.

And there he was, flaked out like a great lummox, not saying a damn thing, just humming softly to himself and stroking my back. It was at such a moment that one is allowed a peek at what one's true inner self is like, and let me tell you, mine was not a pretty sight. I wanted to grab him and make him tell me he loved me in return. I wanted to scream and yell and throw things at him, everything but that lovely desk with the excellent action. I wanted to wail over the injustice of the situation and spend the next three years crying. I wanted to run away and never face him again.

Instead I reminded myself that Iain deserved to be given the time to figure out what it was he felt for me without me pressuring him to give me the right answer. So I bit back everything I wanted to say, fought down the urge to throttle the hum right out of him, and instead determined to show Bridget there was more than one way to make a lion roar.

"You're moaning," I gasped some time later, wanting him to admit he was the moaner, but was too distracted by his hands locked onto my hips to do anything but allow him to increase the rhythm of our dance until his moans and my cries of pleasure wove into one bright, beautiful song of euphoria.

Iain didn't answer with words but moaned louder as I moved along his hard length, rising up until my body sobbed with the sorrow of losing him, then sinking back down upon him, sliding so far down that he bumped up against my womb, stretching me, filling me, completing me. His hands slid along my behind, sweeping up the curves of my hips as I rose and fell upon him, my breath coming hard and fast, matching his rasping gasps for air. His thumbs circled my breasts as I arched back on him, angling myself to take even more of him within me. He pulled his legs up behind me, supporting me, his groans of pleasure increasing as my hair swept across the sensitive bare skin of his thighs.

His hips thrust up as I sank down on him, tightening all of my inner muscles around him, squeezing and gripping until his moans took on a desperate quality, his fingers hard on my hips as he urged me faster, thrusting into me hard and deep, joining with me, merging with me until I thought I would scream from the joy of it. His muscles tightened beneath me, his body gathering as it rocked against me, his heartbeat strong and wild deep within me. I leaned down and scraped one adorable nipple with my teeth, tugging gently on it before lathing it with my tongue, sucking hard as he bucked beneath me and gave a wordless shout of completion.

As he shook within me, he pushed me over the edge, into a deep, blindingly bright abyss where I fell, saved from the fathomless depths only by the strong arms around me and the pounding heart beneath my ear. He was joy, he was rapture, he was everything that had been missing from my life, and I wasn't going to let him go.

"I love you," I whispered, gasping for air, my eyes wet with tears of happiness.

He kissed my tears away.

I had started out to prove something to myself, to prove I could drive him to distraction, to prove I could go one better than Bridget, but in the end all I proved was that whatever was between us was of such a great magnitude, I had lost myself to him. It frightened me, this power he had over me, this ability to make me forget myself, to lose myself in him, but at the same time it overwhelmed, it also comforted me, bonding me to him in a manner I had never guessed possible.

I cracked an eye open to look at the clock as I collapsed onto his still heaving chest.

"I did it," I said, kissing the wildly beating pulse in his neck. He tasted salty and aroused and very, very satisfied. "It took me an hour but I did it. You didn't roar like a lion."

Iain turned his head just enough to shoot me an exhausted and unbelieving glare. I let my lips curl into a smug grin and snuggled my head back down into his neck. "You didn't roar like a lion . . . you howled like a banshee."

That was all to the good, of course, but where there's good there's bound to be bad, and my bad was what followed: yet another Morning Ordeal.

Iain sighed as I burrowed deeper beneath his duvet. "Is it going to take you long to overcome this shyness? It can't be easy on you to be blushing every morning."

I pulled my hair off my face just enough to peer out at him. He was lying next to me, arrogantly male, completely oblivious to the fact that he was stark naked. "You're never shy any other time," he grinned, and twitched at the duvet cover. "Just in the mornings."

I grabbed the cover and pulled it up to my chin, glaring at him. How could he be so casual about this? Didn't the man have any modesty?

"It's all well and fine to be uninhibited when one is getting a leg over, but there *is* such a thing as dignity, Iain."

"Oh, love," he laughed. "You're a bit of a prude, that's what it is."

A prude? Me? Never! Of all the nerve! "I'm not a prude, I'm just . . . discreet."

He snorted. He actually snorted, he was laughing so hard. "Were you discreet last night downstairs on the carpet before the fire, then?"

He would have to bring that up. I slapped his hand away from where he was trying to pull down the cover. "That has nothing to do—"

"And later, on the desk there, when you wrapped your legs around my hips and told me you had a better way to polish furniture. I reckon you're thinking that was discreet as well?"

I was hoping he had forgotten that as well. I had no idea what possessed me, but I would forever be fond of that desk.

"And half an hour ago, love, when you—"

I shot up out of bed and slapped a hand over his mouth. "I think we're both aware of what we did half an hour ago. You've made your point, thank you, Iain."

He waggled his eyebrows and looked down. I followed his gaze. He was happy again.

"Modesty be damned," I sighed and gave up, pushing the duvet away as I grabbed his shoulders and pulled him toward me.

It's a distinct disadvantage to find yourself introduced to someone when you aren't sure of your relationship to the person presenting you. For one thing, there's that whole label situation. Friend, girlfriend, bird (or in parts of Scotland, hen), lover, significant other, domestic partner, buddy, mate—the list of possible labels is endless. Fortunately, the first person Iain introduced me to, outside of his family, caused no problem for any of us.

"This is Mark, my shepherd. Mark, this is Kathie. She writes books."

That was it. No other explanation of who I was, what I was doing there, or why my hands were, at that moment, stuffed into Iain's pants pockets (they were cold and my smart suit blazer didn't have any pockets).

Mark simply looked at me, nodded twice, and spat neatly next to my loafers. I had more interaction with his dog, Foster (named for the Aussie lager), than I had with him. Foster at least shook hands with me. Mark just sucked his teeth and turned his stunningly brilliant green eyes on Iain and started telling him in great detail about a problem with one of the rams' personal equipment. Men tend to feel a great affinity for any male animal that has problems with their plumbing, but the issue takes on red alert status as tupping season approaches. It doesn't do for a ram to be running on only three thrusters then, if you get my drift.

I stood next to Iain, my hands jammed into his pockets to keep warm, listening with great pleasure as they discussed whether or not to bring in the vet or try treating the ram themselves. I almost hugged myself with glee. Here I was, a week after meeting the man of my dreams, standing shoulder to armpit with him, his trusty helpmeet, part of this wonderful new world. It was a Disney sort of moment.

Visions of a grand life rolled out before me as I shifted from one frozen-block-of-ice foot to another. Iain and me, side by side, watching the adorable little lambs on a lovely spring morn. Iain and me taking long romantic walks, holding hands and exchanging kisses. Iain and me sitting with his dogs in front of a roaring fire, snuggling and sending each other glances fraught with meaning. Iain baring his soul to me, sharing his thoughts and deepest, innermost feelings. Iain and me giving that desk in his bedroom another whirl. Oh, yes, life was looking very, very good. If only I hadn't lost the feeling in my lower extremities it would be perfect.

"Go back to the house and get David's anorak, love." Iain finally got tired of me trying to crawl into his jacket.

"No, I'm fine," I said around the chattering of my teeth. "It's just a bit brisk out here. I'll warm up once we get moving." I didn't want to admit that it was my vanity that kept me from donning the hideous navy-and-red parka that David had outgrown some ten years back.

"Brisk? It's bluidy freezin', lass." Mark looked at me like I had gone mad. Maybe I had, I couldn't tell. I was too cold.

"Screw fashion," I muttered to myself two minutes later, and started for the house and the anorak Iain had dragged out for me earlier, along with a pair of David's old wellies, a ratty white-and-blue scarf, and fingerless gloves.

"Don't forget the trousers!" Iain bellowed after me. He turned back to Mark. "Would you believe the daft woman didn't bring any trousers with her to England?" They shook their heads over the folly of women and continued to discuss the ram's dangly bits.

"Ha!" I said aloud to myself as I dragged my frozen carcass to the house. "I draw the line at wearing the pants. I will wear the parka, I will wear the gloves and wellies, but I'd be damned if I wear a pair of ugly, old, smelly, *itchy* unlined wool pants. No siree. Not me. I might not be a fashion maven, but I do have certain standards."

I straightened my lovely, expensive, russet tweed wool suit jacket (bought especially for this trip), made sure the matching pleated skirt wasn't bunched up in the back, patted the complementary cream-colored raw silk blouse, and with a sigh, donned the parka. The wellies took a bit more ingenuity. I ended up peeling off the parka while I fought with the boots. They were about four inches too big for my feet, and flapped around my legs in a nasty, flesh-slapping sort of way. Crumpled newspaper took care of the feet part, but there wasn't anything I could do about the leg slapping, so I gathered up the gloves, put on the parka, and dashed back outside to Iain.

I took perhaps five steps out to them and suddenly lost my footing. Right onto my behind. In the mud.

"Bloody effing hell," I muttered as Iain ran over to help me. "No, I'm not hurt, it's these stupid boots. They're too big and my feet are sliding around in them. How bad is my bu— er . . . behind?"

I hiked up the parka and turned around to present Iain with an unobstructed view of my derriere. No response was forthcoming. I peered over my shoulder at him. "Well?"

"Well, what, love? Do you want a compliment on it?"

I sighed. Men. They simply had no sense where important things like fashionable and expensive wool suits were concerned. "No, of course not! How muddy am I? It feels wet." I tried to look over my shoulder at my butt, but couldn't see anything but wadded up parka.

"Oh, aye, you're muddy. It'll dry." He turned back to Mark, who had been examining my muddy behind with a disapproving eye.

"Iain!"

He looked back at me, his eyebrows raised in question.

"Aren't you going to wipe it off for me?"

He grinned. "I would, love, but there's no use in dabbing at wet mud. Wait till it dries before you clean it."

Lovely. I would get to walk around all day with a big old mud print on my butt. I mused sourly on this for a bit, then gave myself a little lecture about enjoying the day (which was not raining) and company (Iain, Iain, Iain!).

I ignored the faint wet feeling around the calf of my right leg, determined to enjoy the experience of seeing real live sheep up close and personal. We started off for one of the hills, both Iain and Mark whistling up their dogs. I slid around in the wellies, falling twice on the rain-slicked grass until Iain told me to hold on to the back of his mac as we climbed the hill.

Going up wasn't too difficult, but crossing the hill demanded all of my attention. And breath.

"All right, love?" Iain yelled over to me as he paused next to an outcropping of rock to wait for me.

"Oh . . . mercy . . . yes . . . just . . . fine . . . lovely . . . outing," I gasped, trying to smile. No wonder the man was so fit, climbing mountains every day. I tried to focus on how good the day's trek would be for my heart and not on the wet wool skirt clinging to my equally sopping legs. Just then it started to rain.

"Just . . . what . . . I . . . needed," I grumbled to myself as I plopped down on the rock next to Iain.

"What's that?" he asked.

"Nothing," I panted. He looked at me for a minute, then hauled me up next to him, planted a kiss on my forehead, and told me to sit where I was while he and Mark climbed higher to check for strays.

"You're fagged out," he pointed out when I protested— between gasps for air—that I could follow. "You just sit here and enjoy the view. We'll catch you up on the way back."

Oh yes. The view. The one I would have enjoyed if I could have seen it, but the misty rain that had chosen that moment to commence effectively blotted out most of it. I sat shivering in David's parka and made rude faces at the sheep.

Iain has two breeds of sheep, he told me on the journey up. The Hill Cheviots are the pretty ones of the bunch, being lovely white beasties with black noses, which look very scenic and pastoral spread out on the hills. Their wool goes for the sweater trade. The rowdier sheep were the Scottish Blackfaces, a shaggy gang that were always jostling about with one another. As I looked around me at the sheep grazing nearby, I came to the conclusion that up close, sheep lost a lot of their attraction.

For one thing, there's something that people who haven't been around sheep don't know. They look scenic and pretty on the hills, yes. They can be charming and cute as a bug frolicking around at a fair where they have been bathed and coiffed. Some people like them in a stew. But when they are in their natural state, in the rain and mud, they smell.

A lot.

We're not talking spring flowers and roses here, either. We're talking wet, dirty wool with an animal attached. Fortunately, Iain's sheep didn't seem to be any happier to see me up close than I was to see them, so they gave me wide berth. Until the stampede started, that is. And then I was convinced they were in cahoots with Bridget.

I was stamping around the rocks trying to get the feeling back in my toes, waiting for Iain and Mark to fetch me when I heard them yelling and whistling sheepy sorts of commands, like *away to me* and *easy*. Suddenly sheep came over the top of the hill at a fast walk. I stood and watched them with an open mouth.

Herding dogs in action are a wondrous sight to behold. The dogs don't just act on the commands of their handlers,

although that is a major part of their training. They have
been taught to think about what they're doing, and so they
must anticipate the sheep's movements. They have to know
how to find the balance point (the spot that forces the sheep,
avoiding the dog, to move to the dog's handler), and how to
encourage less than willing sheep to move.

As the sheep poured over the hill toward me, I watched
with fascination as Iain and Mark and the dogs worked the
sheep down the hill. It wasn't until the leaders swerved past
that it struck me.

I was directly in their path.

I looked up the hill. Suddenly they didn't seem so benign.
Suddenly the Cheviots seemed like a huge wave of white
four-legged minions of Bridget, intent on sending me tumbling down the hill to my demise. It was a veritable stampede of sheep, and I was dead-on in their path!

Iain told me later me falling off the hill was my own
fault. He pointed out, as he was helping me soak my
sprained ankle in a bucket of hot water and Epsom salts, that
sheep don't stampede.

"They would have avoided you completely if you hadn't
run like a madwoman into the middle of the flock."

"I was trying to alert them to my presence," I replied with
great dignity. "So they wouldn't run over me by mistake."

"Ah, but love, waving your arms and screaming at the top
of your lungs didn't help, did it?"

"Your sheep are not exceptionally bright, are they, Iain?"
I parried his question sourly.

"Which is why I've my doubts as to your opinion that
Bridget was behind a plot to have the sheep murder you."

"At the time it seemed perfectly reasonable," I grumbled.

And it did, it all made perfect sense to me at the time. In
my attempt to avoid being trampled to death by the herd of
wild, man-killer marauding sheep—despite what Iain says, I
swear their eyes were bright red, and their mouths were
frothing and slavering at the sight of me—I slipped in
David's too-big wellies and twisted my ankle as I tumbled
down a slope.

I wasn't really hurt, more annoyed than anything else because despite the protection of David's anorak, by now my entire lovely—and did I mention *expensive?*—russet tweed suit with complementary cream-colored silk blouse was covered in mud. Iain wouldn't let me up until he had seen that I could wiggle my toes, which meant I had to sit even longer in whatever it was that was cold and wet and seeping through my lovely, expensive, russet tweed skirt.

As it turned out, it was sheep poop. I found this out when I put my hand down in it to lever myself up on one leg. And bless him, Iain didn't once say "I told you to wear the trousers." No, he didn't. He just helped me to my feet, slung an arm around my shoulders and hauled me up next to him, then carefully walked me down the side of that damn mountain.

"I feel terribly guilty about this, Iain, leaving Mark to manage scooping the herd by himself."

"It's called lifting, love, and he's done it before, it'll not be a problem for him."

"Oh. Well, would you do a me a favor, then?"

Iain stopped. We were about halfway to his house, on the flat part of the land. "You want me to carry you?"

"No. I want you to tell your dogs to stop looking at me like I just killed their best friend."

Iain chuckled and reassured me again that it was nothing to worry about, but I avoided meeting his dogs' eyes after that. I just couldn't take the accusation I saw in them.

It took us twice as long to make it back to the house as it took us going out, but Iain was patient and even offered again to carry me. What a sweet man. I couldn't let him do it, of course, since not only would he have given himself a hernia hauling me around, but by then I was completely covered in mud and sheep manure, while he remained more or less spotless. So he slowed his pace down to my hobble, and amused me with anecdotes of the first summer he spent on the farm.

I might have noticed the strange car in the drive when we got back to the house, but at that point all I remember thinking was how much I wanted a hot bath and a handful of aspirin. I mentioned this to Iain.

"Aye, love, you've told me that seven times now. A hot bath and some paracetamol."

"Maybe the aspirin should come first," I mused as he paused in front of the door, his hand on the doorknob. "What? Why are you staring at me like that?"

"I was wondering if I shouldn't hose you off outside first. You look like a pig that's been at the wallow."

I raised my chin. I was mucky, but not that mucky. "Oh ha ha, very funny. Open the door, buster."

He grinned, opened the door and swept a low bow for me to enter before him. I limped in with as much dignity as I could muster and ran smack dab into Bridget.

I should have known that life wasn't bad enough at that moment. It wasn't enough that I should be walking like I had two bulldogs stuffed down my pants, looking like one of the dung balls those little African beetles take such pleasure in. It wasn't enough I should be covered in mud and manure when I had gone to such pains to appear before the love of my life in a stunning ensemble guaranteed to drive home what a bargain he would be getting in me. No, it just needed Bridget to add that surreal touch to the day. Now you know why I was convinced she was behind The Great Sheep Murder Plot. It was simply too much of a coincidence that she should be here now, after her sheep henchmen had done their best to remove me from the scene.

"Iain, darling, you look scrumptious as usual. I could just eat you up. Kimmy—is that the new look from America, dear?"

I ground my teeth and stood on one foot, holding the other off the ground in hopes that the throbbing would lessen.

"Bridget, what the hell are you doing here?" Iain looked annoyed to see her. The day suddenly looked a little brighter. He managed to hold her off when she rushed over to lay her lips on him, but I could see the battle had only begun. She was not a woman to surrender without a fight. "Give me your foot, love."

I put my hand on Iain's shoulder for balance as he bent

over to remove the boot, and shot Bridget a victorious smile. She bared her teeth in return.

"Can you make it up the stairs by yourself, then? Or do you want me to carry you?"

It was tempting, I have to say that. What an exit, to leave Bridget in the dust while Iain carried me off to his bedroom. I could almost hear the *sheik and the harem girl* music playing in the background. But I had my pride to think of, and I didn't want her being able to throw shots at me about being feeble, so I declined and hobbled up the stairs by myself. I will admit, however, that the thought of the succubus downstairs made me a wee bit speedier than I might normally have been changing my clothes. I peeled off the no longer lovely but still expensive tweed suit, threw it to the floor while grabbing a clean dress, snagged a pair of flats on my way out of the room, and hobbled barefoot down the stairs, donning the dress and shoes at the same time. It wasn't easy, but needs must when the devil drives and all that.

I was just in time, too. She had him pinned in the kitchen. I pushed the door open and hovered. Eavesdropping? Damn right I was!

"If we don't make the offer to Tannahill in the next few days, he'll start looking at other locations. We'll never have another chance like this, Iain. We *have* to act now."

Iain stood next to the huge black stove, frowning down at Bridget as she stood pleading before him. "There's no guarantee that even if Tannahill agrees to put the abattoir at Kin Aird the council will grant us the zoning exception."

Abattoir? Wasn't that a fancy name for a slaughterhouse? Iain was thinking of allowing a slaughterhouse to be built on his land? My heart turned to lead as I thought of all those sweet little lambs being led off to their deaths.

Bridget made a derisive noise and put her claw on his arm. "Darling, I've *told* you not to worry over the council. Graeham has guaranteed there will be no trouble getting the necessary permissions."

I stood silent and unseen in the doorway, heartsick at the thought of Bridget's plans for the lovely and peaceful valley they shared, but aware that I had no right to voice my opinion.

Unless Iain asked for it, of course. I began to plot a way to make him seek out my advice.

"I'm not happy with the thought of throwing money after something we're not sure of. We could raise a steady profit grazing the land."

"If you would look at the report Tannahill left—"

Iain glanced over her shoulder to where I was standing. He smiled. "Aye, I will. Later."

Bridget made a nasty face as he turned to rinse out a brown teapot.

"I would appreciate it if you could tear yourself away from your new playmate long enough to see farther than the end of your cock."

My eyes bugged out at the vicious undertone in her voice. Iain didn't seem to take exception to it, though, because his was steady enough, although it had a granite, no-nonsense edge to it that brooked no further discussion.

"I'll look at it later, Bridget," he repeated.

Evidently she took the hint, because she immediately changed the subject. "I don't know why you're being so stubborn about the NFU."

I found out later that NFU stood for National Farmers' Union, the big organization that all farmers belong to.

"You're the only one who can help me, darling."

Oh, *puh-leeze*! Pull the other one, it has bells on it!

"Bridget, you've been dealing with the Union by yourself for eight years; why do you need my help now?"

Because she's desperate to get you into her evil clutches, my sweet innocent Iain.

"You know how they are, Iain. They frown so on women. If you would just act as my representative—"

Iain *tch*ed and pushed past her. I limped into the kitchen proper. Iain was heating water—I hoped some of it was for my foot.

"It's not women they frown at, Bridget, it's fools who don't know how to manage their farms."

Oh, good shot, Iain! That made two for us and only one for her.

"If you were to hire yourself a competent manager, you wouldn't need to be running to me each time something went wrong. I've told you before—I've got my own work to do, and no inclination to do yours as well."

Plain speaking. You have to love it.

Bridget, evidently, didn't. She turned on a brittle, brittle smile and aimed it at me. "Kristin! So quick, dear. And what a . . . *charming* little frock. Something from the Oxfam shop?"

More teeth grinding. I wouldn't have any teeth left at this rate if she stopped by often.

"I'm afraid I'm not familiar with the Oxfam shops," I lied, eyeballing her well-cut wool pants and obviously pricey mohair sweater. "But they *appear* to have some nice togs."

She laughed a gay little laugh that was sharp enough to scratch glass and turned back to Iain, who was rummaging around under the sink for something. He pulled out a bucket and a box of Epsom salts.

"Come and sit, love, and we'll soak your foot."

"Oh, what a shame. Your little"—Iain shot her a steely look—"friend hurt herself. I hope it's not too serious, dear. You know they shoot lame animals out here," she laughed.

"What's all this, then?" A sturdy, red-faced, brassy-haired woman stomped into the kitchen and stopped to glare at me. "Who's that? And who tracked in mud all over my floor?"

Iain was squatting on the floor next to where I sat, pouring hot water from the kettle into the cold in the bucket. Bridget stood next to the table, tapping her fingers and watching him with a calculating look on that too-perfect face.

Iain glanced up at the newcomer. "This is Kathie. She's staying with me."

The redhead eyed me with obvious disfavor. I sighed. Another person who wasn't happy to see me. "For how long?"

Ah, that was the question, wasn't it? Iain shot an unreadable at me, then turned back to the bucket as he swirled in a handful of salts. "For as long as she likes. Kathie, this is Mrs. Harris. Put your foot in now, love."

Ah, Iain's charlady. He had spoken of her briefly the evening before when we made dinner together. He hadn't mentioned that she was built like a bull and had a scowl that could peel a potato from thirty paces. I eased my foot into the hot water. Mrs. Harris glared pointedly at the muddy footprints leading from the door to the bench where I had taken off my wellies and dumped the dirty anorak.

"Oh, don't worry about that, I'll clean it up," I assured her.

"Like hell you will. You stay where you are and keep your foot in that water," Iain said as he noticed me trying to ease it out (his idea of warm and mine were not the same). "I'll clean up the mud later."

Mrs. Harris made the feminine version of Iain's *tch*. "You've work to be doing. I'll clean the floor as soon as you've all left me in peace." She glared at all of us as if we were collectively the one blot on her existence that kept her from being truly happy.

"No, really, I don't mind," I protested, worried that I was off to a bad start with Iain's help. I started to pull my foot out of the water. "I'll just clean it up now before it dries."

"Stay where you are," Iain growled, and added more hot water. I yelped and socked him on the arm. "Put your foot back in there, Kathie. I said I'd clean it up."

"Those who make the mess should clean it up," Mrs. Harris sanctimoniously intoned to the wall. "But if your *guest* has lamed herself, I'd best do it. Likely the job won't get done right unless I do."

"Really, I don't mind—"

"I said I'd clean the bleedin' mess up! Now, will you put your foot back in the water?"

"It's not your mess to be cleaning—" Mrs. Harris started to say.

"No, truly, it's not a problem. I can clean it up quickly—"

"Fer Christ's bluidy sake!" Iain bellowed. He took a deep breath.

Bridget eased her hip against the table, pushing it just enough to make a slight noise as the table leg shifted on the floor. We all looked at her.

"Well don't look at me, *I'm* not cleaning it up!"

"If there's nothing else you're wanting, Bridget, you can leave." Iain kept his hand on my knee, forcing my foot underwater. I grimaced at the pain and smacked at his hand. Mrs. Harris harrumphed at such familiarity between a mere guest and the master, and pulled a pink houndstooth wraparound apron from her carrier bag.

"Darling, I just stopped by to be neighborly to your *friend.*" She eyed Mrs. Harris for a moment, and then addressed me. "And of course, I wanted to see how things went last night with poor Katrina."

Oh, god, tell me she wasn't going to do this. Not here. Not now. Not while Mrs. Harris was eating up every word. Then again, why was I surprised? Everyone else who met me was privy to our most intimate details, why not the char, too?

"Last night?" Iain narrowed his eyes suspiciously at her. I made a mental note to have a talk with him about giving her such an opening.

"Yes, darling. In bed. You and Karrie. Whether or not . . ." She glanced over at a fascinated Mrs. Harris and dropped her voice to a stage whisper. "Whether or not she managed an orgasm. I thought I would see if she needed any advice, or suggestions, or had questions, or wanted the name of a good sex therapist."

Bridget brought me a new understanding of the word *mortification.* I was too horrified to do anything but sit there with my foot in a bucket of hot water and gaze at her with blossoming abhorrence. Questions? Advice? *The name of a good sex therapist*?

I was formulating a zinger about how she would know if a therapist was any good or not when Iain slowly straightened up from where he had been squatting. I couldn't help but smile. She'd done it now—she'd pushed him too far. "Out, Bridget."

"But darling, I'm only trying to help."

"Out!" The man had a powerful voice when he unleashed it. My ears would be ringing for days.

"You're living in the Dark Ages, Iain. Everyone talks about this."

"Not in my house! I'm warnin' you for the last time, Bridget. I'll not have you upsettin' Kathie with your talk. Now, get yourself home!"

She slid off the table with sinuous grace and reached for a down-filled jacket. "As you like, of course. But I do think you could both be a little more open-minded about this. How is Karmel ever going to overcome her frigidity if you can't talk about it in a reasonable and mature fashion?"

Iain looked like he wanted to punch something. I hoped it would be Bridget.

She leaned past Iain and patted me on my shoulder. "If you need anything, dear, ring me up. I have only your best interests at heart."

"I'm surprised to hear you have one," I muttered *sotto voce* but loud enough for Iain to hear. He grinned at me.

"If I could have just a moment more of your time, darling," Bridget put a hand on Iain's arm. My teeth started grinding again at the way she caressed his biceps with her thumb. "My car is making the most obnoxious noise, all ticking and rattling. Would you look at it for me?"

Oh, *sure* it was. What a flimsy excuse to get Iain into her wicked little grasp for a few minutes! I gave her a look that let her know I was on to her game. She arched her brows in return.

Iain grimaced and swore under his breath, but being the gentleman he is, agreed, and followed out the door after her. I gazed at the window that ran parallel to the drive and wondered if I scooted over to the wall next to the window whether I could see Bridget's car.

"That was an earful," Mrs. Harris said, looking at me sourly. I didn't say anything but nudged my bucket over toward the wall.

"No doubt you're expecting to eat here with MacLaren?"

I had really taken about as much as I could in one day. I could see by her expression that I was in for more of the same from her, so I thought I'd put an end to it before she could rip a strip off me.

"Why, yes, Iain did offer to feed me now and again, just so I don't keel over and leave him explaining to the police how he came about having the body of a dead American on the premises." I eased my foot out of the water and hauled the bucket over to a chair closer to the window. I could see the back end of Bridget's car, but not the front.

"*Tch.* Much he cares if he makes more work for me. Well, I don't suppose there's anything I can do about it if he wants to flaunt his sinful conduct in the face of the Lord."

"Not a bloody thing," I answered cheerfully, and scooted over to another chair. If I leaned way back and turned my head just so, I could see Bridget's arm.

"Ought to know better at his age," she muttered, and rattled around in a broom closet until she emerged with a battered tin bucket and a mop. "A man of his standing bringing a woman into his bed . . . it's shameful, that's what it is."

I moved over to the last chair and pressed my back against the window. If I craned my head I could see Iain bent over the engine of Bridget's car, tinkering with something. She stood close by him, her hand resting on his back. "Look at it this way, Mrs. Harris. It could be worse. Much worse. It could be a sheep he's living in sin with."

I thought she'd drop her teeth right there. She gaped at me in horror for a moment, then snapped her mouth closed and didn't say another word to me the rest of the afternoon.

We take our victories where we can.

Chapter Six

The following day I was bored. I had spent the entire day on the couch, resting the ankle I had wrenched, my laptop before me as I caught up on my e-mail. Mrs. Harris, who was cleaning and cooking that day, gave me several nasty looks, but didn't say anything.

I can't believe I'm bored, I e-mailed my friend Cait. *This is ridiculous, I'm in Scotland, romantic Scotland, and I'm bored. Iain's been out all day, only coming in for a half hour to scarf down his lunch, and then he had to go out again. Evidently there's something wrong with a fence or dyke or whatever they call it here. All I know is I'm stuck here on the couch with a slightly swollen ankle and I'm bored.*

Cait promptly e-mailed me back. *Petulant, eh? Sounds like the honeymoon is over. That went quick. But then, you didn't really expect that this little romantic episode would last, did you? I mean, get real, Kathie! You jumped this guy's bones a few days ago and you're talking like someone who's lived with him for months! I don't understand what's going on in your head. This isn't like you at all.*

Welcome to my confusion, I replied, then turned the laptop off and spent the rest of the afternoon reading, waiting for Iain. He came in shortly before dark, kissed me, then sat on the couch and massaged my ankle.

"How are the sheep? They're all OK, aren't they?"

He gave me a worried look, absently rubbing farther up my leg than my ankle. Was I about to point out the mistake?

No sir, I was not! "They're fine, love. Stop feeling guilty about your fall."

"Yes, well, I made a right *bourach* of the whole day."

Iain's lovely lips curled in amusement. "Where would you be hearing that, now?"

"*Bourach?* From Mark, when he was trying to bring back the sheep that were scared off when I fell down the hill. He said quite a few other things as well, and I'd like you to explain them if you would."

"What was it he said?"

I told him. He started coughing and immediately changed the subject, but he didn't fool me. I knew his cough originated as a laugh. I mentally filed away the words in my "of a dubious origin" folder, and returned my attention to Iain as he continued to rub my leg.

"Ah, well, it's good of you to bring up what happened yesterday. I don't want you coming out with me tomorrow, love. Now, hear me out!"

My lower lip threatened to commence immediate pouting. Didn't want me out on the fields with him, did he? One little unavoidable accident and I was unfairly banned for life, eh? Thought he would leave me in the house alone with Mrs. Harris, huh? Well, I wasn't about to let him get away with that. "Ha! You can just think again, buster!"

"You can't be walking about in the muck with naught but your skirts and baffies. Until you're kitted out properly, I want you to stay here where you won't be running into trouble."

By process of elimination I narrowed the word baffies down to mean some sort of footwear. "And if I had wellies that fit? You'd let me accompany you on your rounds?"

"Aye, if you've a mind to."

"Oh. Well." That was a different situation altogether. I would, after all, have to get pants and boots if I intended on remaining for a while, and since that is exactly what I intended, it made sense that I should outfit myself appropriately as soon as possible.

It was time to do some shopping! Unfortunately, convincing Iain my ankle was well enough to hit the shops was something else. He made me stay put for another day while my ankle recovered to his satisfaction, but I managed to pass muster the following day. Even then I almost didn't make it out shopping, because Iain had work to do on the farm and couldn't take me.

"What?" I asked him the following morning, appalled that I would have to spend another day sitting in the house by myself. "You can't go with me?"

"No, love, I have to shore up the dyke on the south park. The ground underneath softened, and part of the wall has fallen."

"Well, hell," I pouted, and was working myself up to a nice hissy fit when Iain stopped me.

"If it's just an outing you need, you can take my car and go into town yourself. I'll give you directions."

"By myself?" I asked, simultaneously intrigued and horrified by such a thought.

He nodded. "You know how to drive, don't you?"

"Oh, sure, just . . . not *your* car, your new car, the car you just bought at *great cost,* after years and years of saving and scrimping."

"It's not hard to drive, love. You'll be fine."

"And not on the wrong side of the road."

"You'll be fine," he repeated. "It just takes a bit of practice. By the time you reach the town, you'll be used to driving on the left."

"Mmm." I had my doubts, and almost backed out of the plan in order to wait for him, but the thought of staying indoors (it was raining again, *quelle surprise*) with no one to talk to but Mrs. Harris was enough to give me backbone.

Iain handed me his keys, and made sure I had the directions on how to get to town and where I would find a car park convenient to the shops. He didn't look worried in the least over the idea of me driving off in his car, whereas I felt like I was going to ralph big-time. After a few false starts—such as me sideswiping a gate (no damage to the car, thank god)—I got the feel for driving the "wrong" side of the car on the "wrong" side of the road, and soon I was zooming

along, singing aloud to Moray Firth Radio, planning my
shopping list.

I needed pants, several pairs. As far as I could see, pants
were *de rigueur* for life on the farm. I would save my styl-
ish suits and dresses for wear in the house, when they would
be sure to dazzle Iain and/or any uninvited females who
happened to drop by in order to bait me and seduce him.

Boots were another must-have item. Both wellies, and
something with a bit more style. Sweaters were also high on
my list. My blouses weren't going to cut it in this weather,
and it was only going to get worse. Although Iain's house
had central heating, it had chilly spots, and a sweater or two
would be a definite plus. Especially if I wanted to stay the
winter. And I very much wanted *that*.

I wracked my brain on the drive to town trying to think
of something I could buy Iain as a thank-you gift for having
me stay with him, but I was at a loss as to what he'd like.
Books were always a good choice, but I hadn't made a detailed list of who his favorite authors were, or books in particular that he wanted. I noted the location of the local
bookstore as I passed it, however, and made a mental note to
drop in and browse for an hour or four.

Katherine's Kloset was my first planned stop, and armed
with Iain's excellent directions, I made it there with only
three false turnings and one major "I'm lost, where the hell
am I?" panic attack. Katherine wasn't present when I visited, but her two sales assistants, Penny and Pamela, were.

"You can call us P and P," one of them, the shorter one,
said with a giggle that seemed to infect her cohort.

"Ah," I said brightly, and set off to look around the shop.
P&P followed—together—which led me to the conclusion
that they were sympathetic Siamese Twins. Never once during the entire two hours I was in the shop did I see them separate. They didn't look like each other in the least—Pamela
was a slight girl with mousy brown hair and glasses, while
Penny stood taller than me and had coal black hair and beautiful sapphire eyes—but they seemed to share some sort of
symbiotic relationship. One of them didn't nod; the pair

nodded. If one giggled, the other was sure to be giggling with her. They even finished each other's sentences.

"We have all sorts of clothes here," Penny answered my question of what they stocked. "Separates, dresses—"

"—outerwear, casual and formal—" Pamela broke in.

"—and fashionable country wear," Penny finished triumphantly.

"Ah, good. Sounds like I'll find everything I need here." I smiled. They nodded with perfect synchronization. "Yes, well, the first thing on my list are pants. I desperately need pants."

They looked a little startled, but both nodded again. I told them my size, and asked what styles were popular in the area.

"Of *pants*?" they asked together.

"Yes," I replied, wondering why a simple request was meeting with such puzzlement. I could see a couple of racks of pants along a side wall, but I wanted to find out if there were any locally made ones that were better over continental imports. Buy British, and all that.

Pamela looked at Penny. Penny looked back at Pamela. They both looked at me. "Well, I guess the most common are Y-fronts," Penny said. Pamela nodded. "That's what my dad wears."

"No, you don't understand. I'm not looking for pants for a man, I'm looking for them for myself."

They smiled at each other in relief. "Oh, you want knickers. They're on the table in the far corner. Was there something in particular you wanted? We have some lovely red lace—"

Knickers I knew. "No, I'm not interested in knickers," I interrupted Pamela. "It's pants I want. Just pants. And sweaters . . . er . . . oh, what do you call them . . . jumpers. If you could show me some jumpers that would go well with the pants, I'd be grateful. Local wool jumpers would be marvelous if you have them."

They looked at each other out of the corners of their eyes and both edged slightly nearer the corner of the counter that held the cash register and the telephone.

"You want to wear the jumpers—"

"—with the pants?"

Now they had me concerned. Maybe I was breaching some little known Highland pants–sweater protocol. "Er . . . shouldn't I?"

"Noooo," Penny said thoughtfully. "I suppose there's no real reason you couldn't wear them together. But you might find the knickers more comfortable."

"Yes, ever so much more comfortable. Our red lace silk—" Pamela started to join in, but I interrupted her before she could finish singing the praises of the red lace undies.

"I don't need any knickers. I have knickers aplenty. I've got more knickers than I know what to do with," I argued. "I just want a couple of pairs of pants. Look, those right there. They look like they're made out of natural fibers. Why don't I try on a pair of them?"

Their heads followed my finger to where I was pointing to a rack of pants.

"The . . . trousers?" Pamela asked carefully. "You want to try on the—"

"—trousers?" Penny finished in an equally wary tone.

"That's what I've been saying. I want to try on some pants. Trousers. Those ones there, the brown ones. And maybe those navy ones, too. I'll need several pairs. Do you have any in black?"

Comprehension dawned in Penny's beautiful eyes as she started giggling again. Pamela joined in immediately. "You wanted to wear . . . pants . . ."

"—with a jumper."

"Pants," guffawed Penny.

"Tightie-whities," whooped Pamela.

I couldn't help but wonder if Katherine knew her Kloset was inhabited by a pair of loonies. It took another five minutes before they could speak without setting each other off, but once the explanation was made that *pants,* to the British, means men's underwear, aka Y-fronts, we got along swimmingly.

I just hoped Iain would never hear the tale of how I wanted to wear men's underpants with my sweater.

*   *   *

Right about the time I was modeling my new trousers and wellies for Iain, my mother received the letter I had mailed a week before, telling her about this marvelous Scot I had met at Murder in Manchester. My mother was not online, but she occasionally used my sister's account to send e-mails to friends who were traveling. As soon as she received my letter, her Mother Radar went off big-time and she whipped over to my sister's house to leave me a worried e-mail.

Dear Kathie,

How is England? Are you having a good time? Everyone here is fine, including Rob and Laura Petrie, although I think Laura has laid another clutch of eggs. Do zebra finches ever quiet down? These two always seem to be talking and it's a bit distracting. I'm thinking of moving them to the front room until you come home.

What sort of man is this Iain that you met? How much older is "older than you"? Did you have a nice dinner with him? I suppose you know enough to tell if a man is really divorced, or if he's just saying he's divorced. . . .

It was standard mom stuff until I got to the end. I almost missed the zinger because it was the last line of the e-mail, and by that point she'd gone off into typical "Don't walk around by yourself at night" and "Be sure to keep your money and passport in your money belt" type of statements.

I don't suppose I need to tell you this, but be sure you use protection. Love, Mom.

Protection? *Protection?* Even my mother, half a world away and out of contact with me for almost two weeks, knew Iain and I were having a bit of how's-yer-father? Did *everyone* in the world know? Was it on the BBC? Had the United Nations made a statement about it? How on earth could my mother read between the lines like that?

Maybe it was the drool marks on the stationery that gave me away.

I don't care how old I'll live to be, there was just something embarrassing about talking to my mother about my sex life. Or hers, for that matter. A case of too much information, if you will. I mentioned my dilemma to Iain about how I should answer her e-mail, how I should deal with the Big S issue.

Iain looked confused, and put down the book he was reading. "What issue?"

"The issue of us being together." I was lying on the couch with my head in his lap, my own book at hand. It was a position I found particularly comfortable and pleasing, especially since I had talked him into letting the dogs lie on the floor next to the fire. Iain had quite a few things to say about me bringing his dogs in, but after a few initial grumbles and pointed remarks about how they were used to sleeping in the barn, he let it go and we curled up for a cozy evening of reading before the fire.

"There's an issue with us being together?" he asked, sneaking sidelong glances at his book. I figured I had his attention for two, maybe three more minutes before I lost him to the lure of Peter Guttridge.

"The issue of us being together. You know. Us. *Together.*" Criminy, I sounded like a teenager who couldn't bring herself to mention the word. Unbidden, a blush started heating up my cheeks.

"Ah, *that* 'together.' Is it a problem with your mother, then, or are you just afraid to tell her you've been lusting after my manly parts?"

I slipped a hand under his jumper and prepared to tickle. "Really, Iain, it's no laughing matter. You could show a little more sympathy for me. It's not like you have a parent telling you to be sure to *use protection*. Of all the indignities!"

He smiled and picked his book back up. "Mothers are like that, love. It's just as well you've the matter in hand and can set her mind to rest; I'd hate to have your entire family after my blood."

I agreed and snuggled down, preparing to read my own book. Suddenly, what he had said made two synapses sit up and spark.

I put my book down. "What did you say?"

"Mmmm?" He didn't look up.

I pulled his book down and frowned up at him. "What did you say about putting my mother's mind to rest?"

He frowned in return. "Just that—you can set your mum's mind to rest regarding us having it off."

I let the euphemism go without comment because a nasty suspicion was forming in my mind. "You mean birth control?"

"Aye." He tried to pull his book out from under my hand but I clamped down even harder. The ugly suspicion was fast turning into a full-fledged nightmare.

"Iain, are you trying to tell me you think I'm using some form of birth control?"

He stopped trying to peel my hand off his book and went very still. "You aren't?"

Oh, god. Oh god oh god oh god. Oh. God.

"No, I'm not. I don't need to because you had a vasectomy, didn't you?"

He looked horrified at the thought of such a thing. "No, I haven't."

"But you said so!"

"I never did!"

"Oh my god! Iain, that night after dinner . . . the wild-flower night . . . didn't we have a talk about this? About the need for condoms and such? And didn't you say something about not having any more children after your operation?"

Iain's face was a picture of shock, but it was nothing to what I was feeling. "I was talking about my gall bladder, lass! You asked about my scar!"

"But you mentioned not having any more children after that—"

"Aye, because my wife ran off with the bleedin' MP!"

"An MP!" I stared at him in unabashed horror. "What on earth were you doing telling me about your wife and an MP when we were supposed to be talking about birth control?"

He looked just as horrified as I felt. "If you'll remember, love, neither of us was particularly coherent. I thought you were asking about my wife and why she left me."

I jumped off his lap. The dogs jumped up with me, confused by the sudden shouting. He was right, but that was nei-

ther here nor there. Oh, god. "So you *haven't* had a vasectomy?"

"No. You're not taking those pills? Or using one of those
contraptions?"

I felt like crying. "No, I can't take birth control pills, they
play merry hell with my hormones. And I didn't bring anything else because I didn't think I'd be jumping into bed
with the first man I clapped eyes on. Oh my god, Iain, what
are we going to do? I'm too old to have children—I'm
thirty-seven! You're forty-seven! And I've only known you
a week!"

I'm afraid I was wailing by the last bit. Iain was taking
things in a much calmer manner than I was, but then, it
wouldn't be him in the maternity ward trying to push seven
pounds of baby through an opening that fit snugly around
the cause of the whole problem. "Calm down, love, we'll
sort through this. When's your next time due?"

I stopped pacing around the dogs and did a quick bit of
mental calculation, then burst into tears. Luckily for our
peace of mind there was an all-night pharmacy only an
hour's drive away. We had that do-it-yourself pregnancy test
home and in use before you could say *Jock McRobinson*.

After the big baby scare turned out to be nothing but a
scare, things settled down for a few days. Iain and I quickly
established a comfortable routine. We'd go off together in
the mornings, me trailing around after him as he did his
morning chores (ostensibly I was helping him, but we both
knew I was more of a hindrance than a help), then out to the
fields with Mark, or off to do work on an outbuilding, or taking care of the animals, or a million other things that life on
the farm required. I particularly enjoyed the lambs. Unlike
their elders, the lambs were a joy to be around, frolicking,
romping, butting each other, and never once stampeding me.
I started naming my favorites, something that made Iain roll
his eyes, but I ignored him. He was just a grump over the
lambs.

The balance of the working day was less pleasurably
spent. We'd make lunch together, sometimes under the disapproving eye of Mrs. Harris, sometimes blissfully free of

her presence, and then I'd go to work on my laptop while Iain went back out for the afternoon's chores in the fields. Dinner was always an adventure for the first few weeks. I'd had limited exposure to home-cooked English fare, and none to Scottish food. So dining à la Harris was an experience, and not necessarily one I looked forward to.

Iain was a sheep farmer. He raised sheep. He sold some off for slaughter, some for breeding stock. Naturally lamb and mutton would be a large part of his diet. But I didn't understand why, after the first dinner that featured lamb, dead sheep were present at every meal for the next three nights.

"Surely you buy or barter for some *other* type of meat?" I asked him.

"Aye, love, I do. Why do you ask?"

"I was just wondering if you normally have lamb four nights in a row."

Iain looked thoughtful for a minute. "Now that I think on it, we have been having lamb a fair bit. You might want to mention it to Mrs. Harris."

Me? Speak to Iain's disapproving char? If I couldn't even bring myself to speak to *him* of important subjects—the love of my life, the man who made me whole—how on earth was I supposed to chastise the woman who viewed me as a wanton temptress bent on dragging Iain's good name through the mud? Speak to her? I didn't think so!

"Iain, I can't. She's *your* help."

"But you're here now." He pushed back from the table and grabbed his mac in preparation for bedding down the animals. "Just tell her what you'd like her to cook, love. She probably isn't aware you don't care for lamb."

A little light bulb went off over my head. How could I be so dense? Of course she knew I didn't eat lamb, she was there that first night when I confided my guilty secret to Iain.

I mulled over the issue while I did the dishes. Surely Iain's comment proved he expected me to be around for a while. Surely it indicated he had faith in me and trusted me beyond that of a mere friend. So why was I having such a hard time picturing myself ordering Mrs. Harris around with confidence?

"Because you're a boob, that's why," I told myself as I drained the last of the wash water out and dried my hands off on a soft, worn linen dishcloth. "If you had a brain in your head you'd realize that the very act of him asking you to take care of things demonstrates his confidence in you."

Slowly I convinced myself that was what he had meant. The light of battle dawned within me that cold evening. Iain had placed his trust in me, and if he wanted me to speak to Mrs. Harris, then by god, I'd speak to her!

I had to wait two days before she returned for her four-day shift. During those two days I raided Iain's freezer and cupboards, and spent long hours studying and assembling glorious, lamb-free dinners, with leftovers consumed for lunches the following days. It was a very happy time. We were frequently silly, alarming the dogs once or twice with our hijinks on the carpet before the fire, glorying in being alone together.

But the entire time I waited with growing trepidation for Mrs. Harris to return to her duties. I was out with Iain the day she arrived, but once we returned I had the opportunity to speak with her. Girding my loins with the remembrance that Iain counted on me to de-lamb the weekly menu, I bearded the lion in her den—the kitchen.

"Mrs. Harris," I began pleasantly, a list of Iain's favorite nonsheep dinners held behind my back. "Iain has asked me to speak to you about supper for the upcoming four days."

Her jaw dropped. "He's done what?"

"Iain asked me to plan the suppers with you. It seems he doesn't care for lamb four nights in a row."

"He's said naught of it to me!" Mrs. Harris was a big woman. Not big as in fat, just big. All over. She reminded me of a football player—all beefy arms and no discernable neck. So when she huffed her chest out and adopted an offended look, I took notice. I backed up a step or two and waved the list in front of me.

"He's mentioned one or two dishes that he particularly likes. I thought we could start with a steak and kidney pie for tonight. I took the liberty of pulling out a round steak and a beef kidney from the freezer for you."

"And you'll be eating them yourself, then, won't you?" She harrumphed and turned her back on me, and commenced scrubbing down the kitchen table that I had just cleaned. I'm sure she took up a layer or two of wood with the vigor by which she tackled it.

I knew full well I had no power with Iain's char; I couldn't make her do anything she didn't want to do, and she knew I knew it. I couldn't fire her, I couldn't punish her, I couldn't even reprimand her. But I could take a leaf from Iain's book.

When a man and his dogs herd sheep, they do so by narrowing the sheep's options until the sheep "choose" to go the way the shepherd wants them to go. I'd simply have to do the same with Mrs. Harris.

I made a show of taking down the battered cookbook that resided next to a bag of oatmeal. I could feel her steely gaze on my back as I hummed my way through the cookbook.

"Mushy peas," I murmured to myself. "He'll want mushy peas as well. Let's see, Guinness Stew, Lancashire Hotpot, ah, here it is."

It was too much for her. I could see her fighting the urge to ask, but it didn't take long before she caved. "And just what do you think you're doing with that book?"

I manufactured a look of surprise on my face. "Why, finding the recipe for Steak and Kidney Pie, of course. Iain expressed a particular desire for it." I hoped she wouldn't notice my fingers crossed behind my back. "So he shall have it. Since you don't feel you're up to the challenge, I'll make it for him." I smiled pleasantly and returned unconcernedly to the cookbook, waiting for her response.

It took her three minutes—three long, agonizing minutes—to speak up again. "Have you ever made Steak and Kidney Pie?"

"Hmmm?" I feigned confusion. "Why no, I haven't. But I'm sure I won't muck it up too badly. It can't be *that* difficult."

She *tch*ed. "You'll make a right hash of it, that's what

you'll do. I suppose I'll have to change my plans, then, if it's what MacLaren wants." She snatched the book out of my hands and stuffed it away in the cupboard, muttering to herself about the inconvenience of some people, never thinking of others, only making work for those who toil to make an honest wage.

I couldn't help myself. I had to push her just a wee bit more. "I'd be happy to help, if you need assistance. I'm told I have a light hand with pastry—"

The words had barely slipped out of my mouth when she spun around and glared the hair right off my head. "Ye'll be making no pastry in *my* kitchen! MacLaren's done with my pastry for more than ten years now, and that's what he'll be getting tonight."

She nodded to push home her point and stalked out of the kitchen bristling with indignation. I smiled nonetheless. It was my first lesson in food warfare, and one from which I learned well.

There were many other lessons I learned in those first few weeks while I was adapting to life in Scotland, not the least of which was how *not* to stare at a man wearing a kilt. Now, next to the sound of a burly Scottish sheep farmer speaking, the only other thing guaranteed to turn my knees to pudding was the sight of a man in a kilt. I knew I wasn't alone in this keen appreciation of kilted men, because I'd seen the glazed look in other women's eyes around kilted men. I knew that glazed look; I'd worn it often enough.

Some claim it's the sight of men's knees exposed where they are traditionally covered that makes kilt-wearers titillating, but that theory doesn't hold water, not really. Anyone who's been to the beach has seen men wandering nearly naked. I can take or leave your average Joe in a Speedo, but toss a kilt on him, and he's instantly captivating.

A few days after my triumph over Mrs. Harris, Iain and I were out picking up a few groceries when I spotted a man in a kilt leaving the store. Iain thought my immediate fascination was amusing.

"I don't understand it," he said, shaking his head as he

loaded grocery bags into the trunk of his car. "It's just a kilt, love."

"Yes, that's it, it's a kilt! It's so . . . *mmrrowrr*!"

He rolled his eyes and made a rude comment.

"Oh, you're just jealous. I bet you don't even have a kilt!"

"Aye, love, I do."

My jaw hit the ground. "You do? You have a kilt? A real one? One for your clan?"

He nodded and held the car door open for me.

"So why don't you wear it?"

He frowned. "It's for special occasions, and even then I don't wear it. I always feel as if someone is going to peek underneath."

I snorted. "How do you think women have felt wearing skirts over the centuries?"

He gave me a jaded look. "It's not the same, love."

"How's that?"

"Your arse isn't hanging out there bare as the day you were born."

"There's a nifty little invention called underwear that you might want to investigate."

He looked horrified at the thought. "You don't wear pants under a kilt, love!"

"You don't?"

"No. It's not done, not by a proper Scot."

"Ah." It turned out that although some men do don undergarments, in Iain's set—the manly set—it wasn't the thing to wear undies with your kilt. I imagine it was something along the hair shirt line of reasoning: Wool on bare flesh is *good* for you! Made me itchy just thinking about it, but think about it I did. I wanted badly to see Iain in a kilt.

I began to plot accordingly.

Chapter Seven

Two weeks after I arrived at Iain's house, I lay in bed very early one morning and listened to Iain breathing. It was a relaxing thing, listening to someone breathe. Very calming and peaceful, and given a drowsy just-woke-up state, almost meditative. For some reason, from the very beginning of our relationship, I woke several mornings to find myself lying on top of him. I was embarrassed about this at first, assuming he would see it as some sort of a not-very-subtle hint that I wanted to play, but he reassured me that he was aware I was asleep when I rolled over and plopped myself on top of him.

I'm sure a psychologist would have a lot to say about my nocturnal behavior, but since it didn't bother Iain—and he could still breathe when I was flaked out on top of him—I wasn't too worried about it.

So there I was in the middle of November, lying on top of him very early one morning, listening to him breathe and wondering just how my life was going to play out. I had settled quite comfortably into Iain's life, and that worried me. I was worried because it seemed just too perfect, too easy. I went to England, met a man, and whammo! I was living it up in rural Scotland with the love of my life and no cares in the world. Even to me, it was almost too unreal to be true.

But I was real, and Iain was real, and we were really there, together, and happy. At least I assumed Iain was happy, he certainly seemed so. He just never said anything about how long he expected me to stay on. Blast those quiet alpha males and their lamentable lack of communication skills!

By the time the dark outside had lightened to a rare clear sunrise, the issue had taken on monumental status in my mind. Drat the man, he was making me insane! I had given him as much time as I could to allow him to explore his feelings for me, but damn it, it had been two whole weeks, and if that wasn't long enough for him to know how he felt, then he could just sit right down and figure it out!

I took a deep breath and released my death grip on his chest hair, reminding myself again that I had promised to give him time, and time I would give him, as long as I was still there to have any time to give. However, there was one issue about which I could and would pin him down.

"Iain," I said a few hours later as I tried to avert my eyes from the sight of him laying grilled tomato on his plate. It was Sunday, and Sunday to Iain meant a traditional fried breakfast. Anyone who has never seen an English fried breakfast should count themselves lucky. Just being in the same room with one can raise your cholesterol to a dangerous level. "I'd like to talk to you."

He stuck his head in the refrigerator. "Do you fancy mushrooms this morning?"

Ugh. Not for breakfast, thank you. "No, but if you'd like them, bring them out and I'll fry them up once I'm done with this sausage."

I was manning the sausage and fried egg section of the Aga. Iain had control over the fried bread and tomato grilling operations. He emerged from the refrigerator with a handful of mushrooms while I flipped out a couple of eggs for him and started scrambling two for myself. I will admit to one very great advantage to being on a farm—for the most part, the food was exceptionally fresh. Iain and the nearby farmers all had an exchange program wherein they would trade food products amongst themselves. Pork came from a neighbor's farm, beef from a friend in the next town, and fish came from periodic fishing trips, or swaps with other friends.

Iain had a few chickens of his own for eggs and the occasional stewing chicken, and a goat that provided the best goat's milk I'd ever had. The only thing I was surprised to find was a lack of a vegetable garden, but he told me later he didn't have time to maintain it, so he just bought his veggies at the local farmer's market, or was given them by friends.

"I want to talk to you about my passport."

He looked up from slicing mushrooms. "What about your passport?"

"I'm going to be kicked out of the country in a little over two months."

He didn't look very concerned about the thought of me being sent off, blast his eyebrows. "Why is that, love?"

"Because I'm only allowed to be here three months without a visa. Then it's bye-bye Kathie."

"Ah." He looked thoughtful for a moment. I waited, holding my breath. Would he? Was this the time he'd declare his undying love for me? My heart sang a happy little song as he slowly turned to look at me, his brow furrowed in thought. Life as I knew it ceased until he opened his rugged and manly but extremely adorable lips.

"Do you think bacon or ham?"

Bacon? Ham? *Breakfast?* I stared at him, my jaw hanging down around my knees. Bacon? Ham? That's all he could think about? His stomach? When I was on the verge of being torn from his arms and escorted out of the country, never to be seen again?

Bacon? Ham?

I reached over for the fried egg I had just placed on his plate and threw it at him. *Bacon* me, would he? *Ham* me when I was trying to discuss an issue of the gravest import!

The man had good reflexes. I don't know how he saw the egg coming since he was in profile to me, relieving the refrigerator of its burden of bacon, but he did. He ducked, the egg flying past him to splat against the wall.

He watched it slide down the beige-and-white striped wallpaper trailing yolk and eggy debris, pursing his lips when it finally flopped with a nasty wet noise onto the floor.

"I take it you don't want either bacon or ham, then?"

"I don't give a damn about the bacon or ham, Iain. I'm about to be deported and all you can think about is what part of a pig you want to ingest? Is that it, Iain? I've got one foot out the door and all that's worrying you is whether to go with bacon or ham? There isn't anything else giving you a moment of thought?"

He considered me seriously for a moment, then said, "I think there's a black pudding, if you'd prefer that."

I threw the other egg at him.

Eventually, once the mess from the eggs was cleaned up, I managed to have a serious talk about the subject foremost in my mind. "I'm not kidding, Iain. I looked it up, I'll have to leave. I can only stay for three months, then I have to leave the country, at least for a day."

"Ah. I'm sure we'll work something out. Were the eggs that you threw at me the last?"

"Yes. What do you mean we'll work something out? What sort of something?"

He shrugged. "I suppose I could go see if there are any eggs laid this morning."

I frowned at him, attempting to hide my hurt feelings behind a snarl. "I collected them already this morning. Those were the last of them. I'm sorry if the lack of eggs weighs more on your mind than the thought of me being torn from your arms in a couple of months, but life's a bitch, eh?"

I sat across the kitchen table from him and stared moodily at my breakfast. It looked about as appealing as a plate of manure. Self-pity swept me up in its salty, tearstained grip, singing a masochistic siren song about a dishy Scot who cared more for his stomach than the woman who loved him heart and soul.

Of course the eggs mattered more to him, I sniveled to myself. He needed eggs to eat. He didn't *need* me. I was just a pleasant interlude, a change from the usual women who chased after him. I was just a quick tumble on the desk, and not a damn thing more. For all I mattered to him, I could probably walk out of the room that very minute and he'd never even notice.

I stood up and walked out of the room.

I waited in the sitting room. I waited some more. I kicked Iain's chair. I frowned at his bookcases. I looked at the clock. *Five minutes?* Bloody hell! I marched back into the kitchen.

"Excuse me, did you *happen* to notice that I'd left the room?"

He looked up from his Sunday *Post.* "Aye, I did. Are you feeling poorly?"

"No, but *you're* about to," I muttered, then straightened my shoulders and glared at him. "Iain, as it's evident that you don't give a damn whether I'm here or not, I think perhaps I had better leave."

That got his attention. He put his fork down slowly and frowned. "What are you bletherin' on about?"

"Cute words like blether aren't going to cut any ice with me, mister," I said firmly. One had to be firm with Iain, otherwise one's knees would buckle at the sound of his voice rumbling around one. "I'm talking about the fact that you don't care if I stay or go. I have told you how I feel"—well, OK, just the twice, and it shocked me as much as it did him—"but as you don't . . . don't seem to . . . aw, hell, where's the tissue?"

Iain stood up and handed me his napkin. I bawled into it. It was just too unfair, him meaning everything to me, and me not mattering to him as much as the weighty subject of whether to have bacon or ham for breakfast.

"You're upset about something, love, but I'm not sure what it is. Are you going through PMS now?" He put his hands on my shoulders and gave a gentle "I sympathize with your PMS" sort of squeeze.

"Oh, yes, let's bring intimate body functions into the conversation! This is not about PMS," I wailed.

"Then what is it about?"

"Me leaving. You don't want me here!" I had completely lost it at this point. It wouldn't have surprised me to find myself in a big puddle on the floor.

"*Tch,* love, whatever gave you that daft idea?" He pulled me into a hug and rested his chin on top of my head while I sniffled into his shirt. I was somewhat mollified. He thought my leaving was a daft idea? It wasn't the declaration of his undying love that I needed to hear, but it was better than indifference.

I pushed back far enough that I could look up at him. "Iain, I don't have a choice. I'm going to have to leave come the middle of January."

"Why?"

I would have hit him, except his lovely, warm, peaty brown eyes were full of concern. I started to puddle up again, but I was too upset over the issue of leaving to be annoyed with myself for crying once again.

"I've told you and told you! I'm only allowed to be here for three months. And"—Oh, I really didn't want to say this. But I had to. It was time to have this issue out in the open— "and because I have a home and a life elsewhere."

He just looked at me for a minute, and then pulled me back tight to his lovely warm chest. "No, love, you don't. Now you've a life here, with me."

My tears soaked into his shirt as I smiled into his neck. That was it, that was what I had been waiting for.

"I love you, Iain," I said, wrapping my arms tight around him. "I don't ever want to leave you."

His kisses said *almost* everything I wanted to hear.

A few days after that morning, Bridget decided we had had enough peace, and paid us a call.

"Katriona!" She looked surprised to find me at the house. I was more surprised to see her. I had hoped that after the last incident, she had taken Iain's message to heart and had decided to leave us alone. "Still here, dear? Oh, no, don't tell me darling Iain's fired dear Mrs. Harris and you've taken to drudging for him? Such a come down for you, falling from lover to char."

I shook out the tea towel and hung it up to dry. A good half dozen smart-ass responses were at the tip of my tongue, but I bit them back. It almost killed me, but now that I felt more secure with Iain, I supposed I wouldn't actually die if I were polite to the woman.

"Drudging? No, I'm just making some scones for tea."

She looked at me, expectant. I looked back at her, obstinate. I may be polite, but I'd be damned if I invited her to tea. One tea with Bridget in a single lifetime was enough.

"David and Joanna are stopping by, so you might want to make whatever snarky comments you have to get off your chest and be on your way."

So much for my policy of politeness.

Her eyebrows rose as she seated herself, one elegant suede-clad leg crossed negligently over another. Not one to take hints, was our Bridget.

"How are things going in bed, dear?" She examined me head to toe as if the answer would be obvious. "Finally getting the hang of it, are you?"

"Bridget, I am not going to discuss anything with you so personal as my relationship with Iain. Either say whatever it is you came all this way to say, or please leave. I'm busy."

"Dear, I'm afraid all this domesticity has gone to your head. I've called to see Iain, not you."

My teeth started grinding of their own accord. She finished her examination of me, and turned her attention to her fingernails. I plopped the scone dough onto a floured board and did my best to ignore her.

"He'll leave you, you know, in the end. He always does. Iain is not a man to be faithful to one woman for any length of time. Surely even you must be aware that a man of his *desires* is hard put to practice monogamy."

I ground my teeth harder and punched my fist into the dough. I took great pleasure in imagining it was Bridget's neck my hands were squeezing. "In honor of Joanna and David's visit, I think I'll spruce up the scones a wee bit."

"Has he told you about his other women? The ones he's had recently? I can give you their names, if you'd like. Iain and I are extremely close. We have no secrets from each other."

I added a handful of sultanas and worked them in. "Should I add some dates too or are the sultanas enough?"

"You can't compete with me, you know, not as long as I am tied to his one abiding love. He loves his land more than he loves anyone, including his children."

"No, I think the sultanas are enough."

"So you see, it's hopeless, your plan for Iain. You'll never turn him away from me. You'll never matter as much to him as this farm."

I shaped three mounds and cut them into fours.

"I know you listened to our private conversation about the land we own together, but if you expect to convince Iain against our plans, you are in for a disappointment. He won't listen to you."

I started guiltily. I had hoped to broach the subject of a slaughterhouse on Iain's land despite the fact that it wasn't any of my business, let alone that he hadn't, as yet, sought my advice on the topic. Still, it wouldn't do to let Bridget be privy to my thoughts.

"Avoiding the truth is going to do nothing but hurt you worse, Kelly. You should face up to reality, not try to ignore it."

I dusted off my hands, put my finger to my lips and pretended to think aloud. "Let's see, the egg salad and chicken salad are made, scones are ready to be popped into the oven, and the kettle's steaming. Yes, I think everything's ready."

Bridget *tsk*ed, and stood with a languid grace. "Such juvenile behavior is beneath you, dear, but as you insist on continuing it, I'll wait outside for Iain."

Something sadistic and morbid within me had to know just what she was up to. Was it professional, business concerns that drove her to be so nasty to me, or was it a private, personal vendetta? At that moment I could make a case either way, but I had to know which it was.

"One thing, Bridget, before you go."

She stopped at the door and looked back, eyebrows arched in a supercilious expression.

"Yes?"

"Do you really think you stand a chance with Iain?"

She blinked at me, surprised by the question.

Sometimes I don't know when to quit. "If he didn't want to marry you any of the times you've asked him, what makes you think he'll want you now that I'm here?"

She leaned forward and patted me on the cheek, and with

that gesture I came as close as I've ever come to striking someone. "Ah, but sweet, how long will *you* be here? He'll come back to me in the end. He always does. We have more in common than just sex, you see. We both have a love for this," she turned and waved a hand toward the hills surrounding the farm. "And with Iain, land always comes first."

Well, I asked for it, didn't I?

I was still fuming when Joanna and David arrived. I had no idea if Bridget was outside or if she had left. After her parting blow, she had sauntered outside and leaned on the hood of her car. I did my best to ignore her and whipped up a fruit salad to go with the tea. It wasn't your standard British tea item, but I was not in the mood to debate traditional vs. nontraditional teas. Once that was done I sat down with a book and told myself I didn't care one iota whether Bridget went and found Iain, or whether she was glued naked to the front of her car like a huge car ornament.

I didn't read a single word.

"Kathie, it's nice to see you again." Joanna smiled warmly as she came in a short while later, giving me a little hug. She smelled like cinnamon and apples, and brightened my day considerably. "Oooh, that looks lovely. Let me help you."

She handed me a pot of jam with the explanation that it was her own homemade berry blend, and then we rattled around the kitchen, laying out the plates and cups and saucers. We chatted about nothing in particular until she paused, and with a speculative glance at me, said, "I noticed Bridget's car when we arrived. I assume she's somewhere about?"

I reached for the coffee and my over-the-cup filter. I needed caffeine. Badly. "I have no idea where she is. She came in for a little bear-baiting earlier, but left shortly thereafter."

Joanna's lips twitched. "I assume you were the bear?"

I tapped the tip of my nose and smiled ruefully. "Bridget doesn't seem to like me very much."

I expected her to agree and dish a little dirt with me, but

she didn't. She looked out the window for a few minutes, obviously gathering her thoughts. Then she glanced at the door. "David went to fetch Dad."

She nibbled on her lower lip while I made myself a cup of coffee. "Would you like a cup of tea now, or would you rather wait?"

"Oh, now, please. I'm a little parched. It was the children's story-hour day today, and the librarian who normally reads to them was gone, so I filled in for her."

I handed her the tea, and we sat quiet for a minute, watching through the window as the bare trees moved restlessly in the wind. It looked to me like a storm was coming in.

"Er . . . Kathie . . . this isn't any of my business, and you should tell me to mind my own if I'm offending you, but has Iain talked to you about Bridget?"

Ah, now the dirt was coming. I settled back for a good gossip. "He's told me a little. I know she asked him to marry her."

Joanna nodded. "David mentioned that. Did Iain say anything else?"

I thought for a moment. "Nooo, just that their involvement was finished several years ago."

She nodded again and blew on her tea. "Bridget's a widow, you know."

I didn't know.

"She's been widowed twice, as a matter of fact. Her first husband abused her terribly, or so she says. I don't know for sure, but I can't imagine she'd want to make something like that up."

I withheld judgment on that point.

"Her second husband was much younger than her first. The farm she has now was part of his family's land, and she took it over when he died. His family was very wealthy, one of old families in Edinburgh, you know? They were very high in their clan, very prominent. Well, anyway, when her husband died—I think he died in a bombing somewhere in Greece or Turkey—when he died, his family cut her off. She had nothing from her first husband, nothing from her family, and now nothing from her second husband."

I didn't like this. I didn't like Joanna telling me this—it made Bridget human. I struggled to push down a little bubble of sympathy that threatened to rise.

Joanna took a swallow of tea and with another quick glance out the window, continued in a fast, almost breathless voice.

"Iain could tell you what the husband's family was like—they had a manager overseeing the land, but not running it properly. Iain and the others in the area offered to buy the farm and split it up, but the family wasn't interested in money. Then suddenly Bridget appeared with a lawyer demanding that her husband's property be turned over to her. He had a will, but it disappeared. No one, including the family's solicitor, could find it. So his estate went into holding . . . what's that called . . ."

"Probate?" The word popped out without my thinking. Joanna's tale was making me very uncomfortable. I didn't want to think of Bridget as a victim, or of Bridget as an innocent party. I preferred her snugly in the role she was in now, that of heartless predator after my man, the blood of the slaughterhouse victims dripping from her elegant hands.

"Yes, that's it, how clever you are. Probate. Well, to make a long story short," she laughed and made an apologetic moue, "the family cheated her out of what she had coming as her husband's widow, and she ended up with only the farm. I guess the family thought it was worth the least of all his property."

Snippets of conversations started to merge together in my head. Bridget asking Iain for help with the Farmers' Union. Iain telling me she wanted him to help her with her farm, telling her to get a better manager. Bridget warning me that she and Iain had something in common that went deeper than a physical relationship—their love of the land.

Oh, God.

I really didn't like this. I didn't like this feeling of pity I had for her. I tried to tell myself that it didn't matter that a three hundred acre chunk of rock and valley was all she had. I tried to remind myself that she had hinted she would play as dirty as necessary to get what she wanted, and what she wanted was my Iain. I tried to summon up the picture of her hand on Iain's arm, flexing her fingers familiarly against his biceps. I tried to rally a smidgen of contempt, but I just couldn't. There was too much pity getting in the way.

I don't wonder that I felt sympathy for Bridget; she wasn't the man-eating monster I had first assumed, she was just a lonely, scared woman, holding on to what she had, fighting to keep her independence and that which mattered most to her—her farm.

No, I don't wonder that I sympathized with her situation. I just wonder that I underestimated her passion so greatly.

Chapter Eight

Fate wasn't through with tossing Bridget my way, not by a long shot, but it took a strange twist when a few days later I met Bridget's closest friend, a small, round woman in her mid-forties with soft, curly brown hair, dancing eyes, and a pleasant smile. Her name was Annie Walker, and she and her husband Niall owned the farm that ran alongside Iain's farm's north border. I didn't know that she was Bridget's friend, though. Iain, who surely must have known that fact, didn't tell me.

"Annie," he said as we were on our way to the Walkers' farm, "never has a bad word to say about anyone. You'll like her, love, both her and Niall."

"I'm sure I will," I agreed, a bit nervous, regardless. This was the first time we'd gone somewhere together in a social couple status, the first time I was to meet Iain's friends, and I was on tenterhooks. I wanted everything to go right this time, not turn into the debacle that comprised my meetings with his family. Accordingly, I reiterated with Iain how much I disliked the word *girlfriend*.

"You will please refrain from referring to me as either your girlfriend or lover," I instructed him. "Or bird, or hen. Or, for that matter, not that I hope it would occur to you, as your old lady, or the ole ball and chain."

He swerved to avoid hitting something small and black. A stoat? Cat? Fox? "You're worrying about nothing, love. Niall and Annie will like you well enough."

It was a cat, a black cat. I saw it when it shot across the road behind the car. Oh great, just the omen I needed.

"Just remember what I ask, Iain. To date, everyone you've introduced me to has known instantly that you and I are . . . have been . . ."

"At it?"

"Exactly. I'd like to meet your friends without introducing the topic of our intimate relations."

He grinned.

I didn't trust that grin. That was the very same grin he wore the first morning I woke up in his house, when he informed me that it was an old country Scottish tradition for hosts to see to the bathing of their guests. Mind you I didn't turn the offer down, but I didn't believe for one minute that it was a real tradition. Especially after I had Joanna look it up in a book about country lore.

The Walkers had a bigger farm than Iain's, with more of it consisting of arable soil. In addition to crops and sheep, they had a herd of those adorable Scottish Highland cows— or coo, if you want to go native—with the shaggy heads, pigs, and a variety of other livestock.

Iain walked over to shake hands with Niall Walker and his son Calum. Calum looked to be about fourteen, had one brown eye and one green eye, and a shy, sweet smile.

"This is Kathie. She writes books," Iain introduced me as soon as he and Niall were done exchanging friendly insults and pounding each other on the back. I reached out to shake hands with Niall. "Kathie's my bit of all right."

I stopped with my hand in midshake and stared at Iain, my mouth hanging open.

He cocked an eyebrow at me. "Something the matter, love?"

"What did you just call me?"

"*Bit of all right?* That wasn't on your list, was it? Would you have preferred crumpet? Mare?"

If looks could kill, Iain would have been six feet under. "How about *friend*?"

"Oh, aye, she's very friendly," he teased, winking at Niall, who grinned back at him. I gnashed my teeth for a moment, then gave up. It was quite clear to me that I would never meet anyone in the entire blasted country who was not to be instantly apprised as to the exact nature of my relationship with Iain.

I smiled politely and slipped my hand around the back of Iain's arm and pinched. Hard. The beastly man didn't even flinch, just took my hand in his and held it as we headed for the Walkers' house. Calum jumped to my other side and gazed at me with an intensity I found a bit unsettling. I wondered if it was because I was American or Iain's trollop?

"Am I right in thinking you'll be staying with Iain for a wee spell, Kathie?" Niall asked as he waved us through the door.

"That's debatable at this moment," I muttered, glaring at Iain, but told Niall that I was very much enjoying the Highlands and would be staying for a while. Calum stuck to my side like a burr. Niall introduced me to his wife, Annie, who was in the kitchen with their two teenaged girls, Diana and Rose.

Annie gave a little gasp when she saw Iain and me, and immediately shooed the girls out of the room. She nodded politely at the introduction, but avoided shaking my hand. I assumed it was because she was in the middle of making sausages, and didn't want to take the time to scrub the goo off her hands. Calum parked himself on a tall stool and stared at me with an open mouth.

"Come and see my new baler, Iain," Niall said shortly after the pleasantries had been exchanged. "Close your mouth, Calum, you'll be letting the midges in leaving it open like that. Are you coming with us?"

Calum snapped his mouth closed and shook his head, never once taking his eyes off me. Niall shrugged, and the two men went off discussing the various merits of one baler doohickey over another. Annie turned her back on me and continued shoving a mass of raw meat into an old-fashioned sausage grinder.

I waited for Annie to invite me to sit down and have a cup of tea. I waited in vain. The clock above the kitchen table ticked loudly over the smooshing sound of meat being ground together. I mentally reviewed the two or three sentences I had spoken for evidence of something offensive. Nope. Nothing. They checked out clean.

I glanced at Calum. He was still staring at me with an avidity that made me want to throttle Iain. His larking about had just the effect I had expected it would—now everyone at the Walkers' farm thought I was a tart, a floozy, a woman of loose morals. A *bit of all right*.

I debated my choices: I could either slink off as if I was ashamed of being madly in love with Iain, or act like a mature adult and hope they would respond likewise. I cleared my throat. "Well, Calum, how old are you?"

"Thirteen."

"Ah." Thirteen. What were thirteen-year-old boys interested in? Girls? Cars? Pokemon? I was about to ask him, when he shot a quick look at his mother and suddenly fired off a rapid-fire stream of questions at me.

"Where in America are you from? Is it anywhere near Houston, Texas?"

"I . . . uh . . . no, I'm from Seattle—"

"Have you ever met Hakeem Olajuwon? Is he nice? He seems nice, not like some of his teammates."

His odd eyes were earnestly pleading. I looked nervously at his mother. She had her back to us, still stuffing sausage meat into the grinder. "Oh, well, as to that, I'm afraid I don't follow . . . er . . . basketball?"

"Do you know how I can get his autograph?"

"Um . . ."

"Calum, go and do your schoolwork," Annie said in a tight voice, never turning around.

"I've done it, Mum," he replied, his mismatched eyes locking me in their fervent gaze, waiting impatiently for me to answer his questions.

"I'm afraid I don't know any basketball players, or how they give out autographs, but I suppose if you were to write to the team they might be able to tell you. Or this Wakim person might have a fan club if he's well known."

Calum nodded his head quickly and watched me closely for any other stray tidbits of information I might have about my person. I wracked my brain to think of something. Judging by the stiffness of his mother's back, that was all the conversation I was likely to have there.

"There's . . . um . . . well, you could always try looking to see if this guy has a website. Do you have Internet at your school?"

He thought about that for a moment, then shook his head.

"Well, perhaps your library does." I looked longingly at a cushion-bedecked chair, but I didn't want to offend Mrs. Walker any more than I apparently already had by plumping down uninvited. I leaned against the wall, and crossed one leg over the other. "Other than basketball, what are your—"

"Calum, go and do your chores now and stop pestering Miss Williams." Annie turned around long enough to send her son a steely look. "Now, lad."

There was no mistaking that tone of voice, it was a mother's best weapon. Calum closed his mouth over the protest he was about to make, and with one final reluctant stare at me, he dragged himself off.

I let the second hand sweep around a few times before I tried again. I still had no idea what I had done to annoy Annie—perhaps she had something against Americans, or was very religious and objected to Iain and me living together, or maybe she just took an instant dislike to me right off the bat. Whatever it was, the *smoosh-tick smoosh-tick* silence was getting on my nerves. I just wished she'd tell me what I'd done, so I could apologize and we could go on from there.

I looked around the kitchen, seeking inspiration for conversational gambits. "What a lovely kitchen," I said cheerfully, wincing at the inanity. "That's charming wallpaper you have there. It's a lovely shade of blue, and I like the apples. Apples are always so kitchenish." Kitchenish? No wonder the woman wouldn't speak to me, I was gibbering like an idiot.

Annie mumbled something and continued to grind meat. Strike one.

I wandered over to stand nearer her. "Making sausages?"

Brilliant observation, that. "I imagine that's quite a bit of work, but fairly satisfying, yes?"

"Aye." If she'd snapped her lips closed any faster, the word would have been severed in half.

Strike two.

I searched the kitchen again for inspiration. There was none. "So, how many children do you have? I met Calum and your two girls—do you have any others?"

"Two daughters at university."

Steeeeerike three, you're out! *Smoosh, smoosh, smoosh* went the meat grinder. *Ticka-ticka-ticka* went the clock. *Tap, tap, tap* went my finger on the table.

I stood for a minute, watching her hands feed the chunks of meat into the grinder, which then spiralled out into a bowl on the other side. I was at a loss—she clearly didn't want to talk to me, but I couldn't imagine what I'd done to offend her. I wished she'd just tell me what was on her mind.

I'd give it one last shot, then go out and admire Niall's baler, whatever that was. "Have you lived here—"

Annie spun around, her hands clenched and covered in raw pork. "I'll not ask you to leave since you are here with Iain, but I'll be telling you right now that you're not welcome in my home."

Well, *that* was getting it out in the open.

I have to admit that I was acquiring a bit of an inferiority complex by that point. With the exception of David and Joanna, no one Iain introduced me to seemed to like me. I didn't understand this instant animosity. I knew a lot of people had strong feelings about Americans, I just didn't know it extended to *all* Americans.

I swallowed back the *Yeah? And so's your mother!* retort and tried to be reasonable. Maybe I appeared threatening in some way?

"I apologize if I've offended you somehow, but I assure you it was unintentional, and I—"

"Unintentional, was it? Is it unintentional to steal a woman's intended?"

Huh? She couldn't be talking about . . . no, that was too

far-fetched. "I beg your pardon? You think I've stolen Iain from someone?"

She compressed her lips into a thin line for a moment, and then nodded. "I do. It's well known in these parts that Iain has an understanding with a local woman, and that you've sidled your way into his house with some scheme to marry him. I'll be telling you now that we don't approve of that sort of behavior here. If you had any morals, you'd be on your way and leave him to the woman who's waited for him all these years."

Well, I guess it wasn't as far-fetched as I first thought. I heaved a depressed little sigh. "You wouldn't happen to be talking about Bridget Stewart, would you?"

"Aye, I am. She told me you two had met and that she'd explained her situation to you. I'm sorry to see you haven't had the decency to leave Iain be."

"No, I haven't," I agreed pleasantly. "But that's primarily because Iain doesn't want me to leave."

She started to puff up, but I wouldn't let her speak. "As far as Bridget goes, you'd do best to ask Iain about his relationship with her. I did, and it was very enlightening. Since you're so busy, I'll let myself out."

I gathered what dignity I had and walked out of the house. The men were nowhere to be seen. I stood for a minute in the yard, alone, isolated, friendless, a stranger in a country filled with people who didn't like me. My lower lip quivered as I debated going down to one of the barns to look at the animals, or over to Iain's car for a long cry.

The car won. I started off toward it when Annie appeared in the doorway, wiping her hands on a cloth. "Wait! Kathie, I'd . . . please come back into the house. I'd like a moment to talk with you, if you would."

To yell at me on Bridget's behalf? I didn't think so. "Will you give me a cup of tea?"

"Aye, if you like."

"Well, as a matter of fact, I don't care for tea, but I'd be happy to talk with you."

We returned to the kitchen, and she waved me over to a chair, then went back to her bowl of ground meat and started

adding seasonings. I was the injured party, so I just sat quietly and waited for her to muster her thoughts.

"Would you be caring for a glass of cider?" She brushed
off the last of the sausage and washed her hands.

"Thank you, I'd like that." I loved cider, both hard and
soft. Annie fetched two glasses, poured out the cider, then
came and sat across the table from me.

"Slàinte," I toasted her.

"Slàinte mhath," she responded, and watched me closely
as I took a sip. Ah, it was hard cider. Just what I needed to
survive the killing frost of Annie's kitchen.

"What you said a few minutes ago . . ." she looked down
at her glass briefly, then back up at me with a wary gaze.
"I'll ask Iain, you know."

"I hope you do. It's not for me to tell you Iain's history
with Bridget, but I can assure you that I wouldn't be here
now if he was involved in a relationship with another
woman."

"That's not what Bridget says."

"Bridget is—" A liar. A scheming woman who would do
anything to get Iain. *Desperate.* "Mistaken. I asked Iain
point-blank, and he assured me his involvement with Bridget was over quite some time ago."

Annie stared hard at me for a few moments, then made a
disgusted sound and slammed her glass onto the table. She
muttered in what I assumed was Gaelic. I braced myself for
more slurs on my character.

"I'll throttle the little . . . playing me like a fool. Of
course you've moved in with Iain, and why shouldn't you?
Hasn't he been sniffing around Fiona MacLeod this past
year? And Bridget's telling the tale . . . well, I shan't be so
foolish the next time."

Fiona MacLeod? Iain's been sniffing around a Fiona
MacLeod? Why hadn't her name come up in the little discussion of a few weeks past, the discussion we had before
jumping into bed? I did a little mental rearranging on my list
of things I wanted to discuss with Iain, and topped it with
Just who the devil is Fiona MacLeod?

Annie took a deep breath followed by a healthy slug of

the cider, then placed both hands on the table and leaned forward, her curls bobbing emphatically as she spoke. "I'd like to apologize for the things I said earlier, Kathie. I ought to know by now how Bridget exaggerates when she's upset. I'm heartily ashamed of myself for being so rude to you."

Oh, lord, I was going to cry if she kept that up.

"It's not your fault, really, you were just standing up for a friend. Bridget and I have a little difference of opinion—she thinks she'd entitled to Iain, and I think she's off her rocker. I'm just sorry she's dragged you into this."

"I'm thinking she's a greater fool than me."

"I'm thinking you're correct," I laughed, and downed my cider.

We settled down quite well after that. Annie told me a bit about her life, how she enjoyed her crafts and cooking, and asked several questions about my life in the States. We didn't mention Bridget again—neither one of us wanted to reopen that topic. We had a lovely hour together, sipping cider and swapping life stories, and I was truly sad our time ended when the men came back from baler-watching.

I debated to myself whether or not to mention the episode to Iain. He'd be annoyed at Bridget, which was always a good thing, but I hated to have him think poorly of Annie. I decided not to mention anything.

On our way home he asked if I had a pleasant visit. "Marvelous," I gushed. "Annie is a lovely, lovely, lovely woman, Iain, and I'll not have you thinking unkindly of her. It's not *her* fault if she's so protective of her friends. That's a good trait in a friend, really, don't you think? I think so. I like her. She's lovely, just a lovely, lovely woman."

Iain shot me a glance out of the corner of his eye. "It sounds as if you got along well, then. Enough to take a nip or two together?"

Was he implying I was snockered? I bristled at the implication. "We had a little cider, if that's what you are inshinuating. Not enough to get ripped on, though."

"Ripped?"

"To the tits," I answered, and nodded for good measure. "Takes more than a little cider to get me squiggled."

I was pleased that he was in such a good mood, actually laughing so hard he had to wipe back tears, and would have asked him what he and Niall had done to put him in such a lovely, lovely mood, but I was too sleepy. The rest of the ride home was a bit of a blur, but I do remember waking up drooling on the car door at one point.

It occurred to me that maybe Scottish cider had a bit more of a kick to it than the stuff back home.

A few days after my meeting with Annie, I got a phone call from my mother. She'd received the letter I'd sent saying that I had no plans to return home for at least a month or two. I didn't tell her I was going to become a permanent fixture in Iain's life, but she must have sensed something, because she ignored the cost of an international call and rang up one evening.

Iain climbed out from where I was lying across his lap reading a book and toddled off to answer the phone. I dipped back into my book and paid no mind until he came back into the room.

"Your mum's on the phone, love."

My mother? "Huh?"

"She's waiting to talk to you. She sounds like a nice woman. I can see where you get your sense of humor." He picked his book up and commenced reading.

Iain talked to my mother? My mother called here and Iain talked to her? They joked? My *mother* joked with Iain? I sat on the couch for a minute trying to digest this strange news until Iain gave me a little shove. "She's waiting, love."

I ran for the phone in the hallway. My mother made the stereotyped frugal Scots look like immoderate spendthrifts. If she had invested in an overseas call, it must be something serious.

"Mom? Are you all right? Do you hurt anywhere? Who's dead? Are Rob and Laura Petrie OK?"

"I'm fine, Kathie, and your birds are fine, although I think Laura laid more eggs."

"You called to tell me my bird is laying eggs? She always lays eggs. No one is hurt?"

"No one is hurt, and if you'd stop interrupting me, I'll tell you why I called."

Why is it that even at thirty-seven your mother can still make you feel like you are eight years old and been caught saying a dirty word? I hooked a chair with my foot and dragged it over to the telephone table. "Fine, it's your money. Why are you calling?"

"I just wanted to talk to you. I'm concerned over this plan you have to stay in Scotland with a man you've just met and hardly know when you have a good life and good friends and family here."

Well, I knew it was coming. I took a deep breath and remembered Iain and the way he maneuvered the sheep. "You talked to Iain, didn't you?"

"Yes. He seems like a very nice man, but really Kathie, aren't you a little old for this *love at first sight* sort of thing?"

"Iain is a nice man, Mom, a really nice man. I'm very happy with him. I'm sorry if it seems like I'm abandoning you, but I want to stay with him, and he wants me to stay, so . . . I'm staying."

"That's just being foolish, Kathie. I'm sure Iain is nice and all, but you hardly know each other!"

"I know him well enough to know I'm in love with him, Mom."

"And what about him? Is he in love with you, too, or is he just keeping the cow to get the milk for free?"

I sidestepped the question of Iain's feelings and focused on the slur. "Well, thank you very much, Mother. Oh, how I love being likened to a cow. Thanks oodles."

"That's not the issue, Kathie, and you know it."

"No, the issue is you butting in to my life."

"The issue is you acting irrational and irresponsible. What are you doing about your apartment? Do you expect me to keep these birds of yours forever? What about your books? Kathie, you can't just give in to heedless whims like this. You have your future to think of."

I thought of the wonderful man I just left. "I am thinking of my future, Mom. It's here with Iain."

The rest of the call went downhill from there. My mother is not a sheep and she resisted being herded in the direction I wanted. By the time I hung up, we were both angry and hurt. I glared at the phone for a minute, then ran back to the one person who would make me feel better.

"Have a nice chat with your mum, then, did you?" Iain grunted as I threw myself on him.

"No. Hold me." I snuggled as tightly as I could against him, and thought about what my mother had said.

Iain wrapped his arms around me, rested his chin on my head, and stroked my back with one hand. After a few minutes, he picked up his book and continued to read. I nuzzled his neck and pondered my life.

I'd known all along what staying with Iain would mean—I would give up my apartment, most of my belongings (shipping them abroad would be just too expensive), and only rarely see my friends and family. The first two didn't cause me even a moment of hesitation, assuming I would be bringing my entire book collection over, but the last point weighed heavily on me.

It was a simple matter of Iain vs. my old life. Which did I want more, and did I have the balls to go after it? I looked ahead as far as I could see and decided the road might be a bit rough in spots, but it was the only one I wanted to take. What I didn't see were the potholes in the way, one of the deepest of which was directly in my path.

You're what? Cait had e-mailed me earlier that day when I told her I had decided to stay with Iain. *You're staying forever? FOREVER? What about everything here? What about us? You're my best friend, you can't move to Scotland!*

I had replied with a list of reasons I would stay. *Cait, use your head. I'm single, self-employed, have no ties other than a pair of promiscuous zebra finches, and I am madly in love with a man who welcomes me into his life. There is no choice to be made. Even with the specters of Archie and Bridget looming before me, I know that Iain is the person I am supposed to spend the rest of my life with. Friends and family are taken care of with phone calls and e-mail, and my work is something I can do anywhere.*

So I sat snuggled up against Iain and felt his chest rise
and fall beside me, his breath ruffling my hair, and listened
to occasional *hmmms* of interest as he read his book. There
was no question in my mind that this was where I should be.

That's when those thoughts started hitting me. You know
which thoughts, *those* thoughts. Those thoughts that included not only the *L* word, but the big one: the *M* word. The
one my mother had mentioned in the phone call. The one I
had thought of only in a vague sort of "I don't want to jinx
this" way.

I looked up at the underside of Iain's jaw. That's an incredibly sexy spot, the underside of a man's jaw. Ticklish,
too, much of the time. I pressed my lips at the spot where his
jaw met his neck.

He loved me, of course he loved me. Even if he hadn't
ever mentioned the fact, he must love me. He wasn't the
type of man to toy with a woman, stringing her along and
then dumping her after he tired of her. No, he was a serious,
one-woman kind of guy. Of course he loved me. I loved
him. We loved each other. Therefore—I took a big mental
breath—we ought to be married.

I waited, prepared to flinch away from the pain that the
thought brought with it. Nothing. Hmmm. I gently probed at
the idea. Hmmm again. No pain there, no shrieks of horror,
no feeling of *this is not a good thing,* just a pleasant warm
glow about it. I leaned into Iain and nibbled my way along
his jaw line and over to his ear, where I sucked his earlobe
into my mouth and gently chewed while I thought it over.

He loved me, therefore, we should be married. It would
solve all of the problems of my having to leave the country
every three months or obtaining a visa to stay longer. I could
just imagine what sort of a scene that would be, my asking
the British government for a visa so I could stay in my illicit
Scottish love nest. No, we loved each other, we were going
to spend the rest of our lives together, and thus we should be
married.

"Erm . . . love . . . I take it you're finished with your
book?" Iain's lazy voice rolling around the room, reverber-
ating deep out of his chest, couldn't fool me. He wasn't as

unaffected as he'd have liked me to believe. I had my hand inside his shirt. I could feel his heart beating, and the cutest little nub of a nipple.

I released his well-tenderized earlobe. "Why, no, I'm only halfway through it. Why do you ask?" I scooted a little lower and slipped my other hand into his shirt, feeling around for his ticklish spot. What a surprise! A second adorable nipple! Isn't there a saying along the lines of *A nipple in hand is worth two in*—no, I guess not.

"If it's not readin' you're interested in," Iain mumbled a few minutes later, his mouth being occupied at that moment with making sure my tonsils were where they should be, "maybe there's somethin' else you'd be wantin' to do?"

"Oh, I don't know," I said when I could string enough words together to make sense. "Cards, perhaps?"

I arched my back when his wandering hands found *my* ticklish spot.

"Cards, aye, sounds marvelous. I love a guid card game."

I let the fingers of one hand wander over to the scar on his rib cage where an angry ram had broken his ribs. "Gin Rummy?" I asked breathlessly as he unbuttoned my blouse. With his tongue.

"Nay, not Rummy," he murmured against the mole on my stomach. I sucked in my breath when his fingers splayed over my bare breasts, making them tighten beneath his hands as he stroked his palms over my sensitized nipples.

"Surely you must be uncomfortable what with all of those clothes weighing you down so." I did my best to relieve him of such a terrible burden. It was the least I could do. "If you don't like Rummy, what about Crazy Eights?"

I was having a hard time getting air into my lungs. I wondered briefly if that was a bad thing, then decided his mouth and hands on my breasts were more important, and returned my attention to uncovering a tiny birthmark I had noted on him a few weeks before. I wrestled briefly with his belt buckle, pushing down his zipper as I tugged his pants off. He kicked his way out of them and his underwear, returning his attention to my upper half. I squealed when his lips closed around one taut breast, heat spreading from his mouth to all points across my torso, pooling low, deep within me.

Iain surfaced briefly for air. "I dinna ken how to play Crazy *Eeeeeeeeeiiiiii!*"

I had found the birthmark.

"Well then . . . oh, my! . . . perhaps you might be interested in a round of . . . of . . . oh, Iain!"

He sucked a hot path to my neck as warm, strong hands slid up my thighs. I parted my legs and let him peel off my underwear, a sob of delight catching in my throat as his hands returned and he let his fingers do a little walking.

"Round of what, love?" he murmured.

I chased his tongue out of my mouth so I could answer. "Go Fish?"

"Ahhh, I thought you'd never ask!"

The three dogs lying before the fire heaved heavy, imposed-upon sighs, and moved out of the way just before Iain and I hit the floor. He bent me forward over the coffee table, his long, muscled thigh parting mine as he nipped at my shoulder, pinning me down with the weight of his chest behind me. The cold of the coffee table against my raw, aching breasts made me shiver, just as the heat of him at my back made me melt. Those feelings were lost in joy as he nudged my legs open wider and suddenly thrust into me. A low moan of pleasure escaped me as I arched my back beneath him, allowing him in deeper, reveling in our closeness, wild with the rapture he gave me, thrilled with the hot blast of his breath rasping against me as he held me tight and slammed into me with short, hard thrusts.

He loved me. I just had to get him to admit it.

The night after we played *cards* Iain asked if I minded if he went down to the local pub.

"The lads are asking about me since I've not been in for the last few weeks," he said.

I looked up from where I was working on my laptop, in the throes of revisions.

"Huh?"

"I know you're busy writing now, love, and thought you

wouldn't miss me for a bit if I went and saw the lads at the Twa Brithers."

Wouldn't mind? I was furious. "Do you mean to tell me you've been ignoring your friends to stay home with me?"

"It's not been a great sacrifice, love," he leered at me. "I'd rather spend the evening with you than a group of men."

"And I'm thankful for that small mercy, but really, Iain! You make me feel like a great big ogre keeping you from your fun! Is there anything else you used to do that you've stopped since I came?"

"Oh, aye, love, but I won't miss that." He winked, and whistling a jaunty little *got the last word in* tune, went off to the pub.

When two people move in together, there are a lot of adjustments to be made by both parties. When one person moves in with another, there are even more adjustments, since the movee is often in a territorial position, while the mover is in a lesser, interloper position. The adjustments become greater still when you have two people who have been living alone for a long time, and thus are set in their ways. Toss in a puckle of cultural differences, and you're looking at my situation.

For the most part, the transition went smoothly. The issue of whose furniture to use was moot—there was no way I was going to ship my furniture to Scotland. We agreed that Mrs. Harris should remain on the job, allowing me to work the hours of the day when Iain was out tending the farm. Money, however, *was* a bit of an issue. Part of the problem was that neither of us had any, but the biggest trouble stemmed from the fact that Iain had a head of household mentality, which meant in his eyes any money that came my way was mine and wasn't to be added into the household fund.

Bollocks, said I, and after a few no-win arguments on the matter, shrugged my shoulders and proceeded to slip money into the kitty whenever I could. I had a suspicion Iain knew full well what I was doing, but as it allowed him to save

face, and me to contribute to our survival, we both pretended it didn't happen. Once those little differences were
hashed out, I came a cropper on one that would rear its head
time and time again, ultimately ending with Bathsheepa.

It was no secret to anyone that I had some issues with
Iain's farm. They were my issues, not his, and although Iain
respected them, he couldn't do anything about resolving
them without destroying his entire way of life.

I knew this, and I understood it. I knew what line of work
he was in when I met him. I may not have understood everything a sheep farmer did when I moved in with him, but I
wasn't stupid. The number of lamb dishes that regularly appeared by Mrs. Harris's hand was a big hint that Iain was not
raising sheep just so they could frolic on the hills and look
scenic.

I didn't like it, but there was little I could do about it, just
as there was little I could do to sway Iain away from allowing a slaughterhouse to be built on his land. I tried bringing
the subject up, but never felt comfortable expressing my
hopes and wishes that he'd forgo Bridget's plan for something less murderous.

"Kin Aird is really a lovely piece of property," I said
brightly one morning at breakfast. "Have you thought of
buying Bridget's share?"

Iain looked up from his bowl of cereal and the paper.
"Aye, we both have thought about it, but neither of us has
the money needed to buy the other out."

"Oh." I poked at a cold piece of toast with my knife and
wondered if I dared suggest a loan. It couldn't hurt. "Well,
you could take out a loan—"

"No."

The abrupt manner the word was ejected from his lips
spoke volumes. A loan was clearly out. I didn't know a lot
about his financial situation other than the realization that
cash was a bit tight, which was no doubt why Bridget's proposal looked so good to him.

"This . . . um . . . abattoir," I said, hesitant to continue on
a subject which was so clearly not any of my business. I

gnawed my lower lip as I watched him closely. "This abattoir would bring in a lot of money if you had it built?"

"Aye, it would." He munched cereal. I gnawed lip.

"It seems a shame to ruin such a lovely piece of land with a horrible, bloody building. That spot is so tranquil, so peaceful."

He raised both brows at me in a quizzical look.

"It just seems a shame," I told his eyebrows.

He chewed slowly. "That it does."

Damn the man! Why did he have to be so reticent to discuss everything? Did I have to drag every opinion out of him? We'd been together a month, shouldn't he have started to open up to me by now? I gritted my teeth at him. "Given that it's a crime to waste that lovely land, why are you going to allow Bridget to have that horrorhouse built on it?"

"Horrorhouse?" A faint frown teased his brows.

"Slaughterhouse. Abattoir." I waved my fork around. "The place where you take innocent little animals to be murdered. Whatever you want to call it."

His frown increased. "They're livestock, love. Their purpose is to be used for food. You eat beef, you know where it comes from."

"Yes, but I'm not personally acquainted with the cows that gave up their lives so we could have a roast! And besides, cows aren't as cute as lambs. I can't believe people eat cute, adorable, fluffy little white lambs."

He was going to roll his eyes, I just knew he was, but he stopped himself in time. "We've had this discussion before. I'll not make you eat lamb if you don't like it."

"But that won't stop you from sending them off to slaughter," I muttered as I pushed my toast around on my plate.

Iain reached out and took my hand in his, rubbing his thumb across my knuckles in a manner that sent little tendrils of fire snaking up my arm. His lovely peaty eyes were dark with distress. "Love, you knew I was a sheep farmer when you agreed to come up here. I told you that first day out in the parks that they weren't pets, they're livestock, even the lambs."

I was the most selfish being in the whole wide world. How could I make him feel bad about doing his job? The need to comfort him warred with the desire to beg him to not sell sweet little lambs for slaughter, but my love for him won out.

"I know. It's just that the lambs are so cute and . . ." I stopped speaking at the look of sorrow in his eyes. I knew he hated the fact that I hated the reality of life on the farm, but there was nothing either of us could do.

He released my hand and sat back to finish his breakfast. "'Twill make you feel better to know that I've decided not to go ahead with the abattoir."

I stopped slouching dejectedly over my toast and beamed at him. "You have? Oh, Iain, that's so wonderful! I knew you wouldn't go through with it!"

He started shaking his head the minute I spoke. "I'll not have you believe it's because of how you feel, love. I decided it was too much of a risk counting on the council to approve plans for a commercial business to be built in an agricultural area."

I jumped up and flung myself into his lap, kissing along his jaw until I could capture his lips. "I don't care," I whispered against them, delighted with life. "I don't care why you're not going along with Bridget's plan, I'm just pleased you've scotched the idea."

A smile flirted with the corners of his mouth as he hugged me closer. "Aye, well, I *am* a Scot. . . ."

There might not have been anything I could do about Iain's livelihood, but there was something fully within my ability to change, and change it I did. Within days of Iain's and my coming to terms over my staying, I had arranged for his three dogs to spend their nights in the house. I had already supplemented their diets with table scraps (which they approved of), given them baths when they came in up to the oxters in mud (which they heartily disapproved of), and fought for their right to laze around the fire on the cold winter evenings (approval rating was very high on this as well). Iain thought I was mad.

"They're working dogs, love," he pointed out the first night I bedded them down in the kitchen. I had found some old blankets in the back of Iain's linen cupboard, and after making sure they weren't old family heirlooms, I arranged them near the Aga, and invited the dogs to lie down on them. "They're used to sleeping in the barn. They're not pets."

"They're dogs," I reasoned, and grabbing Rob by his collar, put him into position on his blanket. I gave him the command to lie down. He just smiled at me, his head cocked to one side, his tail wagging slightly at the game I was playing with him. "Dogs can be both pets and working animals. Lie down, Rob, lie down."

Rob continued to look at me, expectant, waiting to see what this game entailed. I tried forcing him into a down, but he stiffened his legs and resisted my efforts.

"Why won't he lie down? I'm giving him the command you use."

Iain folded his arms across his chest. He wasn't going to help me.

"Well, don't tell me I'm going to have to use your blasted whistle! I'll never learn the whistle for down."

Iain smiled.

"Rob, you darling dog, wouldn't you rather lie here nice and toasty in the kitchen than out in the cold, damp barn?"

Rob offered me his paw. Iain smirked and leaned against the wall. Biorsadh leaned against Iain.

"Roy, you handsome thing, you! Come over here and let's get you settled by your brother. He'll be soooo jealous once he sees how comfy you are!"

Roy backed off, growling. Iain snapped a command at him that stopped him in his tracks.

"Fine, Roy, be that way. Biorsadh, my friend! Come and see what a lovely blankie I have for you!"

Biorsadh wouldn't even look me in the eye. I glared at Iain.

"I told you, love, they'll be happier in the barn."

When I staggered out of bed to check on them the following morning, all three were curled up on the blankets. I smiled smugly at Iain, and went about putting the kettle on and getting the dogs' breakfast ready. I thought my point had been made, but alas, there were still lessons to be learned.

Lest anyone think that I had pushed back my plan to wring an admission of love—not to mention a marriage proposal—out of Iain, I hasten to correct that false impression. It was still uppermost in my mind. I had dramatically changed my tactics at that point, however, and I had high hopes that my new plan would do the trick. Rather than shying away from mention of the *L* word, I took every opportunity to tell him how madly in love with him I was. My reasoning was that he might not have been told he was loved in the past, and therefore, he was hesitant about saying it himself. I made sure he knew just how I felt about him.

"I love you," I told him in the morning when we woke up.

"I love you even more than I did a half hour ago," I told him when he was brushing his teeth.

"You're so adorable when you eat a sandwich! I love you!" I told him at lunch.

"Tea's ready. Oh, and I love you," I told him in the afternoon.

"Mmm, this is great stew," I told him one night. "I love it, but not as much as I love you!"

I shouted it to him across the parks, I whispered it in his ears, I mumbled it against his lips, and I gasped it at moments when our bodies and souls merged into one. I admit I might have gone a little too far the day I marched into the bathroom and went into a three-minute soliloquy about my love for him while he was engaged in business of a personal nature, but still I felt it necessary to drive home the point that I didn't just love him when he was seen at his best.

I slathered the man in love, and waited for him to tell me he loved me in return.

Chapter Nine

As November rolled into December my new policy of making Iain feel he was the most loved man on the face of the earth was firmly in place. I carried out my plan accordingly, much, he told me later, to his pleasure. He never once complained that I was going a bit too far with my campaign to force him to declare his love for me. No, truthfully, he always looked pleased when I told him I loved him. He'd hug me and kiss me in response, then go back to whatever it was he was doing when I interrupted him.

The days passed, and I worried more and more that my tactics were having no effect other than some exceptionally pleasant interludes. I fretted over whether I should ask him point-blank whether or not he loved me. I was sure he did, but I reasoned to myself that it was more important that he say the words on his own rather than having me drag them from him.

I became obsessed with hearing him say the words.

"Just three little words," I muttered to myself one morning when I was folding laundry. "Just three simple words that I know he feels, so why can't he say them?"

I did everything I could to get Iain to say them, too.

How's the romance scheme going? Cait asked one morning in e-mail.

Lousy, I responded. *I have arranged for romantic dinners and even more romantic après-dinner activities. I make sure to give him time to himself, so he will cherish our time together all that much more. I make silly, romantic gestures*

*like tucking little notes into his mac pocket in the morning,
where he would be sure to see them later in the day. I even
started knitting him a sweater!*

Cait was impressed by my diligence. *A sweater? Does he
not realize how inept you are at needlecrafts? Does he not
realize this is a declaration more meaningful than mere in-
substantial words?*

"I guess not," I answered her question aloud, sighing. I
had done everything I could; I let him know I loved him for
more than just his lovely eyes, knee-melting voice, and exceptionally fine body. I told him I loved each of the parts
that made him up individually as well as the sum total, and
still he just kissed me and held me and made mad, passionate, wild bunny love to me. It was wonderful, but I still
waited to be told that he loved me in return.

Christmas was beginning to loom ahead, and we talked
about having it at the farm, rather than going to Joanna and
David's flat, as Iain usually did. I was nervous enough about
having Archie and Ewen (Iain's brother, whom I had yet to
meet) come for the holidays, but I was almost panicky at the
thought of facing Archie without Iain's acknowledgment
that he loved me. Without that, I was just another tart in
Archie's eyes, not the woman his father loved. If only he
would just . . . say . . . the . . . words!

Sometimes you find that what you've been seeking isn't
really what you need.

Two weeks before Christmas I pulled up the long drive
that led to Iain's house, and tried to figure out what I was
going to say to him. I had been crying, and just the thought
of facing him made me sick to my stomach.

I had killed one of his cats, and I was surely going to rot
in whatever hell was set aside for those people who were responsible for the deaths of innocent animals.

I looked behind me at the two boxes on the backseat. One
of them held Mouser, one of the barn cats, but the other was
empty. It was Clara's box, and she was dead. She died under
anesthetic while on the operating table at the vet's office
where I had taken her to be spayed.

Without Iain's knowledge. Or permission. Or approval.

When I first arrived at the farm, Clara had four seven-week-old kittens, and Mouser's litter had just been given away. Both were barn cats, living in the barn, keeping the rodent population under control. Mouser was a lovely marmalade-colored cat with part of one ear missing, while Clara was a neat gray-and-white with four white paws. They were both friendly cats, coming up for treats or pets, winding themselves around your legs in that lovely way cats have.

I asked Iain what he did with their kittens.

"Give them away," he said in a garbled voice, trying to speak around the hindrance of a cat's tail in his mouth. Clara loved Iain. She'd come running whenever she heard him in the barn, following him around like one of the dogs. She'd talk to him and pat at his legs until he would sling her up onto his shoulders, where she'd ride around on him as he mixed grain, fed the goat, gathered eggs, and so on.

"Give them away to whom? Are they good homes? Did you check the people out? I hope you made them pay something so you don't get any of those research people who just want free lab animals."

"Most of them went to Brannock. Foxes took his barn cats, and he was looking for a few good mousers." Iain batted Clara's tail out of his face, but she just flicked it back across his upper lip. It was a game they played.

"Oh, yes, *that's* a good home," I said sourly. "And when the foxes take this batch, you'll just fire Mouser up again and have her kick out a new lot of kittens, is that it?"

By that point in time, Iain knew how I felt about animals, so he didn't try to argue with me. We had two different viewpoints, and he was wise enough to know it would take time to find common ground on the subject.

I had been raised to be responsible for my animals, always having them spayed or neutered unless there was a particular reason for breeding them. Rob and Laura Petrie, my zebra finches, were the exception to this, but that's only because my vet turned down the chance to practice her sterilization arts on the birds. So I was naturally outraged by Iain's cavalier attitude about the reproductive habits of his barn cats. I decided that they both should be spayed, and after finding out how long I needed to wait before it was safe for Clara to undergo the procedure, I arranged for their surgery.

I am the first person to admit that I should have consulted Iain about this, but I was still suffering the trauma of having to find good homes for Clara's remaining three kittens (one died shortly after I arrived). I didn't want to go through that nightmare again, so I packed up the cats one Monday morning, and drove them off to the vet.

They called six hours later with the news that Clara had died during the surgery and that Mouser would be ready to go home that afternoon.

I would have confessed my sins right then and there if Iain had been within hailing distance, but he was out in the Land Rover with Mark, checking the fences on the farthest part of the farm. So I cried and chewed on my nails and made a nuisance of myself to Mrs. Harris. She gave me an *I told you so* lecture about people who meddle in the affairs of others, and left me to my misery.

I brought Mouser home and shut her into the downstairs bathroom with a bowl of water, a litter pan, and a hot water bottle covered with a blanket. She was still a little groggy and seemed happy to lie there and sleep. I avoided meeting her eyes (She knew! She knew I had killed her best friend Clara!), and went off to wait for Iain to return to the barn.

It was raining a nasty, cold, sleety type of rain, the sort of rain that makes a sound just like the Gaelic word for wet—*fliuch*. I stood around in the barn, huddled in my anorak, telling Mabel the goat my sins. When I heard the Land Rover outside, I girded my loins and tightened my belt, and went out to confess.

I noticed two things right off the bat: it was a raining even harder, and Iain was in a foul mood. He had the body of a dead ewe in the back of his Rover.

"What happened?" I asked, huddled under the dripping eave of the barn.

"I don't know," he answered, grim-faced and scowling. I knew the ever-present worry of disease was uppermost in his mind. He pulled a tarp over to the Rover, rain running in a steady stream off his hat. "There's a section of fence down near the stream."

"Oh. That's not good, is it? Can you fix it?"

He grunted a no and opened up the back of the Rover. "'Twill need more fencing than I've available, but I'll have to do what I can with that lot until I can pick up more."

Mark came around the side of the car, his hand swathed in a bloody piece of cloth.

"What happened to you?"

Mark grimaced. "Cut my hand while we were shoring up the fence so the ewes wouldn't go through it."

"Oh, geez, I'm sorry, Mark."

He ducked his head in acknowledgment.

"Then the bluidy Rover mired three times coming home," Iain grunted as he and Mark heaved the dead ewe onto the tarp. "I'm thinking I punctured the oil pan on the way here, but that'll have to wait as well."

I watched them with dismay as they covered up the ewe and dragged her over to the barn. This was obviously not the most opportune time to tell him that his favorite cat was dead.

Mark and Foster went off to their cottage at the south end of Iain's property. I stood in the rain wringing my hands and watching Iain toss fencing supplies into the back of the Rover as he swore to himself. The third time he turned around to find me lurking directly behind him, he snarled at me in an exasperated tone, "What is it you want, woman?"

"I need to talk to you," I wailed.

"Then talk, but do it out over there, out of my way." He grabbed another chunk of fencing and hauled it over to the Rover.

I wiped the rain out of my eyes. My hands were shaking with cold and nerves, but I figured I'd best get it over with. "Iain, I know we didn't talk about this, but I took your cats in to the vet today."

He pulled his hat off, wiped his face, and replacing the hat, asked, "Why would you be doing that? Were they hurt?"

"No, I took them in to be spayed."

He didn't say anything, just gave me a long look and walked back over to the fencing and got another armload.

Oh, god, I'd done it now. If he was pissed about me having them spayed, he'd be livid about Clara's death. He'd never forgive me. I might as well just rip my heart out now and stomp it into the mud, because my life with him was over. I took a deep breath and tried to explain my reasoning.

"Iain, it's not right that they should have litter after litter of kittens. It's not good for them, and it's not responsible ownership."

He fetched two more loads of fencing before nodding at me. "Aye, you're right."

I was? Oh, no, I wasn't. The tears welled up again. I was surprised I had any left.

"There's more, Iain." I waited until he was on a return trip empty-handed, and took a deep breath. "Clara died under the anesthetic. Dr. Bruner says it doesn't happen often, and there's no way of knowing beforehand, but she still felt very sorry that it happened and apologized. She's going to do an autopsy to see if there was something else wrong with Clara."

He didn't say anything, just looked at me with those lovely brown eyes that had gone almost black in the rain, then turned back to the fencing.

"Iain," I grabbed his arm and stopped him. "I'm so sorry. I can't begin to tell you how guilty I feel—if I hadn't taken her in to be spayed, she'd be alive now. I know how much she meant to you, and I'm really, really sorry. I feel terrible about it, and I know nothing I can say will make you feel any better, but I want you to know how I feel. . . ."

He nodded, shrugged off my hand, and reached for another load of wire.

"Iain, I know you're angry with me. Please don't feel like you can't yell at me. I have it coming, God knows I do, and I think it would make you feel better if you did. I know it would make me feel a lot better."

He finished loading his supplies, slammed closed the Rover's door, and started toward the barn. "It's just a cat, Kathie, not the end of the world."

Just a cat? His Clara? I stared after him for a minute, stunned by what he said, then started yelling at his back. "Iain, dammit, I know you loved that cat. I know how much she loved you! Why can't you just admit it? Why can't you yell at me and be angry? Why can't you, just once, say that you love something? I know you don't want to admit your feelings about me, but you can bloody well admit that you loved that cat without a loss to your precious male dignity!"

I was screaming the words at him, tears streaming down my face, rain soaking us both, but I honestly didn't care. If he could be so cold and uncaring about the needless death of an animal I knew he adored, what did that bode for us?

He turned around slowly. "What is it you are bletherin' on about now?"

If I could just get him to admit he cared for Clara, I'd know it would be all right between us. "Clara—"

Two long steps and he was directly in front of me, scowling something fierce beneath the brim of his brown hat. "This isn't about Clara, love. What's this about me not wanting to admit my feelings for you?"

I goggled at him. He looked so indignant. How could he look so indignant when he was the one who suppressed his emotions? I sniffled. "You don't. You know you don't. I tell you I love you every day, and you've never . . . once . . . said . . . it."

"I bleedin' well have!" Iain wasn't indignant anymore, he was furious.

I goggled at him even more. "You have not! When have you ever told me you love me?"

"I tell you every damn day!"

I continued to stare at him, the rain running down my forehead into my eyes, my mind turned to treacle. He told me he loved me every day? Had I missed something? Did he whisper it when I was asleep?

"When do you tell me? Iain, you've never once said—"

He grabbed my arms and gave me a little shake. "Are you daft, woman? I tell you every morning when we wake up. I tell you at night when we cuddle up reading together. I tell you every time I love you. *I tell you every time I kiss you, you daft hen!*"

The world stopped spinning. It slowly ground to a halt, and sat waiting, breathlessly, for something profound to sink into my thick head. Standing there in the mud, rain pouring down over us, it suddenly, unexpectedly, finally became clear.

Iain *had* told me he loved me. He had been telling me he loved me in everything he did, every look, every touch, every action, only I was too caught up in my own image of the perfect man to see it. Why was I waiting for mere words to be uttered when everything he did proclaimed a thousand times over that he loved me?

I didn't think it was possible, but I cried even harder. I had killed his cat and completely misread the depth of his character, but still he had the patience, *and love,* to stand there and explain it all to me and not strangle me as I deserved.

I threw myself in his wet arms and kissed his adorable rain-soaked face. "I'm sorry, I'm so sorry, I'm the stupidest woman alive, but oh, Iain, I do love you more than anything in the world."

He waited until I took his handkerchief and blew my nose before giving me a swift kiss, then headed out to fix the fence. I watched him drive off, sending fervent thanks that I'd found him.

By the middle of December, I had been with Iain for almost two months, and I was feeling pretty secure in our relationship. I knew I was there to stay, I knew he loved me, life definitely had a rosy tint to it. There was only that one tiny issue remaining to be taken care of, and I was determined to resolve it before Christmas.

I spent long hours making lists of arguments guaranteed to be so persuasive, Iain would be helpless against my logic and overcome to the point where he married me on the spot. Late at night, I'd lie awake and mentally write the perfect proposal scene.

Me [at breakfast]: Iain, would you pass the marmalade?

Iain [clutching the marmalade to his breast as he falls to his knees before me]: Marry me, Kathie! Make an honest man out of me! I'm beggin' you! You are the light of my life, the apple of my eye, the heart in my haggis.

Me [fluttering my eyelashes shyly]: Oh, my! How unexpected! I shall have to think upon this honor you do me. Do you need an answer right away?

I wallowed in the warm glow such a scene presented until the other side of my imagination, the dark side, the bane of my existence, kicked in.

Me [shoeless, in rags, holding out a newborn babe]: Mr. MacLaren, sir, I beg of you, this is our fifth child! Please, oh please, if you would just marry me and legitimize them . . .

Iain [not looking up from his newspaper]: I've told you before, woman, I'm not the marrying sort of man. Women are here for only one purpose. Now get upstairs to that desk, and I'll demonstrate that purpose.

Me [falling to the floor in a swoon]: Oh, if only I had listened to my mother!

While I knew full well Iain wasn't the dastardly villain my unchecked imagination painted him (and for some reason he always had a mustache and a black cape in those scenes), I still felt that it was a logical progression of our relationship to move into the *discussing marriage* stage.

I began to plan.

The first step in storming Iain's castle was to take a long look at his past history. As I saw it, there was one major problem. I had gotten the impression from the few times Iain discussed his marriage to his ex-wife Mary, and his disgust with how Bridget had repeatedly tried to pressure him into marrying her, that he entertained no little loathing for the married state. I certainly felt that we should be married sometime in the near future, but I wanted him to feel likewise. I knew if I mentioned it, he would agree to marry me just because it was the honorable thing to do, and because he knew I wanted it.

And then there was that subject of Bridget and her many proposals. My pride—oh, surely the most foolish of all human traits—got all up in arms whenever I thought of beg-

ging Iain to marry me. I didn't want him classing me with
Bridget, just another female who wanted him only for what
his protection would bring. I wanted *him* to want to marry
me. Getting him to that point . . . well, that was the tricky
part.

"Exactly how long have Joanna and David been married?" I asked one morning at breakfast, canny as could be.
I had spent some time perfecting my battle plan, and all that
remained was to put it into action. I marshaled my troops.

Iain *tch*ed at something in a farm journal he was reading.
"Since the summer."

"Ah. And how long had they known each other before
they were married?" Clever as a cat, I was. I gave my troops
the signal to move forward. With luck, Iain would never
know what hit him until he was my prisoner.

He looked up. "Oh, it must be three years, now. Why is it
you're wanting to know?"

I widened my eyes in innocence. There's no sense letting
the enemy get an accurate count of your men. "No reason in
particular. Just idle curiosity."

"Ah." He went back to his article on sheep dip.

I buttered another piece of toast, smirking to myself. This
was going to be like taking candy from a baby. I gave the
order to charge. "Three years is an awfully long time to have
known each other before you're wed, don't you think?"

He looked up again and frowned slightly. "No, it doesn't
seem overly long to me. David was only nineteen when they
met."

It was a telling blow, but I didn't think I had lost too
many of my troops. I ordered the archers to return fire. "Oh,
well, if they were *young*, that's different."

Iain nodded and turned his eyes back to the journal.

I sipped my coffee, and prepared to order the troops up
the ladders. "It's not as if they were older. Say, for instance,
in their thirties or forties." I offered him my profile as I
gazed out of the window in apparent contemplation of
everyone I knew who might possibly be in their thirties or
forties and in a position to consider marriage.

No comment was forthcoming. I peeked back at Iain. He

hadn't noted my contemplative profile. Perhaps, being a man, he needed it spelled out a little more. I ordered the troops to load up the catapults. "Young people of that age, after all, often make foolish mistakes. Unlike their mature counterparts."

"Mmm," he agreed, turning the page. Blast him, his defenses were stronger than I had allowed for!

I tapped my spoon on the table. He looked up. I looked down at the spoon in mock astonishment. A spoon! Whatever was it doing there in my hand? "Nineteen is definitely too young to be married."

"Aye, it is."

I commanded some of the troops to search for a bolt hole. We would storm Iain's castle from the inside! "Er . . . how old were you when you married Mary?"

"Nineteen," he answered without looking up. Great. I stuck the spoon on the end of my nose (one of my many talents) and ordered the troops back to me. Swiftly I brought up the left flank for a direct attack.

"My point exactly. You were both far too young for the responsibilities of marriage."

He looked up just as I whisked the spoon off my nose. "Aye, it was the biggest mistake I've ever made. Except for the boys, of course."

"Of course." Drat. Marriage as a horrendous nightmare was not what I wanted him to focus on. I waved up the right flank. "Children can make up for a lot. But I wouldn't think they are *vital* to a successful marriage. If, for instance, you had married Mary later in life—say at your age now—"

He scowled as he helped himself to the last bit of ham. "It would still be the worst mistake of my life, and there's naught you could say to convince me otherwise. The boys were the only good bit to come out of it."

My troops lay dying on the field of battle, their lifeblood seeping into the ground. I wandered amongst their corpses and tried to rally the remainder of my army for one last siege. "But you're older now, and thus much better suited to marriage—"

He slaughtered the rest of my troops with one disgusted

snort. "There's some things that will never change, love," he
said as he turned the page in his journal.

I looked about me. My troops were dead. My siege machinery was destroyed. All that remained was one shiny,
stainless steel catapult.

I fingered my spoon and toyed with the thought of loading it up with jam and firing it at Iain's forehead.

"The trouble with Iain," I later told Biorsadh, the elderly
Border Collie whom Iain had forcibly retired shortly after I
settled in, "is that I can never quite tell if he is pulling my
leg or not. He's a master at deadpan. This morning, for instance, when I was discussing marriage with him . . . was he
simply being obtuse, or was he having me on?"

Biorsadh yawned and decided a little personal maintenance was in order for the day. I tapped my pencil on my
laptop as I considered the question, decided to give him the
benefit of the doubt, and proceeded to initiate my next plan:
to scatter big hints hither and yon.

Wednesday afternoon, hint number one:

"Oh, my, look at this fascinating article about traditional
Island weddings," I said nonchalantly as I dropped the
newspaper in his lap. "Fascinating customs you fascinating
Scots have."

"Mmmm." Iain glanced at it briefly, and then returned to
sharpening a knife. "Fascinating."

Thursday morning, hint number two:

I poured water into my coffee filter, humming a song.
"Blast! I can't get that song out of my head. Mrs. Harris was
singing it the other day. I can't remember the name of it—
do you know what it is?"

Iain swallowed a mouth of tea. "What song?"

I hummed it for him.

His brow wrinkled in thought. "Sorry, love, it's not familiar."

I struck a pose, my finger tapping my lips. "It's Highland

something." I hummed a little more. He shrugged and poured himself a bowl of cereal.

"Ah! Highland Wedding, that's it! I knew it would come to me."

I smiled and batted my eyelashes at him. He smiled back at me. "Would you fetch me the milk, love?"

Friday evening, hint number three:

While Iain was out of the room using the bathroom, I whipped out a book Joanna had given me earlier and pretended to be reading it when he returned. We settled back into our reading positions. I waited five minutes.

"Um, Iain, what is *uirsgeul*?"

"Hmm? *Uirsgeul?* It means a fable."

I kissed his chin and thanked him, then went back to my book. He gave me a strange look, then returned to his own book. Two minutes passed.

"I hate to interrupt you again, sweetie, but could you tell me what *luaidh* means?"

His brows rose. "What is it you're reading?"

I showed him the book. "It's a poem. *Duan na Bainnse. The Wedding Poem.*" At least I hoped that's what it meant; the notes I had taken of Joanna's Gaelic-speaking co-worker were a bit muddled.

"*The Wedding Rhyme*, love." He pinned me back with his gaze. "I wasn't aware you read Gaelic."

I trotted out my innocent smile. "I don't, not really, but it looks so very fascinating. I thought I would give this a whirl. *The Wedding Rhyme*, you say. How very interesting. And it's about a wedding. Yes. So enthralling."

"Mmmm." He watched me for a minute while I pretended to read words I couldn't for the life of me understand, then went back to his book.

Monday midday, hint number four:

As Iain walked into the house, I hung up the phone while shaking my head and laughing softly to myself.

He peeled off his wellies and mac. "You're in a good mood."

I agreed and waited for him to ask why. He tossed the mail on the table and sat down to sort through it. I decided to take pity on his dormant curiosity.

"Is it true what Joanna was telling me—that she made David carry rocks around the town?"

He cocked a brow at me. "What?"

"She said it was a tradition in the Highlands for a bride-groom's friends to make him carry a basket on his back filled with stones until his fiancée kissed him. *Creeling,* I think it's called."

"Oh, aye, she did." He smiled as he went back to sorting the mail into stacks. "She made him carry that creel all the way down Main Street before she took pity on him."

"Such a very quaint *wedding* custom," I said without the least shred of subtlety.

"It is," Iain agreed, then swore when he opened a bill. His tirade against the phone company had all the earmarks of going on for some time, so I took the letter he had slid my way and sat down to see what my mother had to say.

Dear Kathie, Thank you, dear, for the lovely box of sta-tionery. I think your idea of a pleated skirt would be perfect for your sister Mo for Christmas. Are you planning on mar-rying that Scot, or are you going to take years off my life by continuing this cohabitation?

Some days you just can't win.

Chapter Ten

Iain had three crofters who rented land from him. Mark was one of them, although technically he had his cottage and land rent-free; Ben and Joan, a nice older English couple, had the second croft where they raised a small herd of red deer for market; the third croft was rented by some new arrivals from Canada: Phillippa, Miracle, and Bob. Miracle was ten going on thirty, Phillippa and Bob were in their early to mid-thirties, and a few minutes after meeting them, I felt like I was a hundred years old. With a headache.

Shortly after the death of Clara I went with Iain to meet his new crofters. I spent the morning talking with them, or rather, *trying* to talk with them, but really I was being talked to, hence the headache. All three of them talked at once, which made for a confusing time, especially since they didn't all discuss the same thing. The headache lightened a bit once Bob took Iain out to see his new ram. At least then the conversational stream was limited to Phil discussing home schooling and weaving, while Miracle yammered on about how babies were born. It seems she'd just come into possession of the pertinent facts, and was eager to share them with me.

"You're married to Mr. MacLaren, aren't you?" she asked shortly after the men had gone off to do manly things with the ram.

"Uh, no, as a matter of fact, I'm not married to him," I smiled my best *aren't you precocious, don't you have something else to do?* smile and tried to follow her mother's stream of consciousness conversation which threatened to crank my headache up to an intolerable level.

"I can't tell you how wonderful we think Scotland is, Miss Williams, although you should be the very last person I have to tell, having moved here yourself for just that reason, and look where it got you! Now let me put the kettle on to boil—don't you just love saying that? It's so English! *Put the kettle on to boil. Have a booger and mash. Help me boob.* I just love it here! It's so foreign! Do you know what *help me boob* means, by the way? It's not an obscenity, is it? Anyway, as I was saying, Bob is quite convinced that we will be able to stay for at least three years, which works into my plans just perfectly because I plan on starting my own shop, you see, and I will count on you to spread the word to all of your Scottish friends here about the shop. If I can make it pay, we can stay longer than just three years, and that would be grand, wouldn't it?"

She tipped her pert little pageboy to the side and gave me a rather intense, almost scary, smile. She was clearly waiting for me to answer her. I had a hard time deciding where to start, then decided that her rapid-fire method of conversation was probably the best. I doubted if I'd have many chances of responding to any conversational gambits she tossed out. I took a deep breath.

"Thank you, I don't drink tea. Please call me Kathie. Yes, I adore Scotland, although I moved here only after I met Iain, just a little bit over a month ago. It's actually *banger and mash,* and *help m'boab,* although you can say the *me* part of *help m'boab* if you like, and no, it's not an obscenity, it's kind of a gentle form of bloody hell which, I guess is an obscenity if you don't like saying the word hell, or even bloody, but since I don't mind either, I just usually say bloody hell and leave the *help m'boabs* to those who can say it properly, and yes, it would be so very lovely if you could get your shop off the ground and stay here forever and ever and ever."

I was rather proud of my little speech. Phil, unfortunately, appeared to be one of those people who lacked a sense of humor. Which, in hindsight, was good, since my sarcasm tended to be the wallop you upside the head kind, rather than the subtle kind.

"Yes, I'd like that. It's so much nicer here than Windsor [the city in Canada they emigrated from]. Now don't fuss over the tea, I'm going to make you some of my special tea. You'll like this, it's herbal. I make it myself from rose hips and blackberry leaves and all sorts of other good things."

Phil began an explanation about how she made her herbal tea, cutting right across my polite refusal for any of this delicacy, her voice trailing after her as she went off to the kitchen to put the kettle on. I seriously doubt if she stopped talking the whole time she was out there.

Miracle, who reminded me nothing so much as a small Hillary Clinton, complete with Phil-matching pageboy and headband, watched me silently for a moment, then set down her Pokemon toys and marched over to me.

"I know where babies come from."

I stared at her, worried by the determined set of her little jaw. Clearly I was not going to be allowed to escape without allowing her to unburden herself. "How very nice for you. And what do you intend to do with this fabulous knowledge?"

She shrugged. "My mom says I can watch the baby lambs being born. She says it's a wonder of nature and will be very educational for me. I know how babies are made, too. They're made with sex. My mom told me. She says I can watch that, too, although my daddy says I'll have to wait until next year. Do you have sex with Mr. MacLaren?"

My jaw hit the floor. What sort of horrible demon child was this? And worse yet, what were her parents doing promising she could watch them make babies next year? And what the hell was I going to say that wouldn't come out a babbled shriek of indignation?

I looked at the blond Satan's imp standing so innocently in front of me, my mind still reeling from the blows it had taken, and stammered out, "I . . . uh . . . they're going to let you *watch*?"

The imp nodded solemnly. "Daddy says I can't watch this

year because the sheep are already going to have babies, but I can watch next year."

I fervently hoped she was talking about the rams and the ewes, and not something else.

"Uh . . ."

"Mom showed me a book with pictures on how babies are made. She said it's the same with the sheep except they don't lay on their backs. They stand up."

"Uh . . ."

She leaned up against side of the armchair I was sitting in and tipped her head to the side in an eerie imitation of her mother. "Men have *penishes*. Girls don't have *penishes,* they have *uteruses* where the baby grows. You're a girl, so you have a *uterus.* Have you ever seen your *uterus*? Mom says you can't see it unless you go to a special doctor, cause it's way up inside you. *Penishes* are on the outside. My daddy has one," she added proudly.

I stared at her. I couldn't help it, the conversation was so horribly gruesome, it was fascinating. "I'm so very pleased for your father," I said, trying to be polite. "You don't happen to know someone named Bridget, do you?"

She shook her head. "No, but I know a Brian. He was in my class. He had a *penish* too. I saw it. He showed it to me before we left home." A thoughtful look stole over her little devil's spawn face. "I thought it looked gross. Do you think *penishes* look gross?"

"I believe," I said with as much dignity as I could summon, all the while wracking my brain for a subject of discussion that didn't include references to genitalia of any form, "that it is an acquired taste. Er . . . like. I mean, that is it say, it's something that grows on yo— uh . . . it's something that you learn to appreciate."

"What is something you learn to appreciate?" the imp's mother asked, coming into the room with a tray loaded with tea items.

"*Penishes,*" her demon daughter answered, and jumped up to relieve the tray of a particularly nice looking jam tart.

"Oh, yes, certainly," hellspawn mom replied without batting an eye, and handed me a mug. She must have seen the shocked look on my face, because she added, "We believe in answering any of the questions Miracle has with honesty and forthrightness. It's been proven that children cope with the difficulties of life today so much better if they are in possession of facts, not silly mistruths or ignorance."

I smiled weakly.

"Recently we've been having a discussion about reproduction, haven't we, pumpkin?"

Pumpkin nodded, unable to speak because her mouth was full of jam tart. "Miracle has asked a number of insightful and intelligent questions, proving the point once again that children are open to complex subjects such as reproduction when it is explained to them in a supportive, loving environment."

She beamed at her hellspawn pumpkin, then turned back to me. "Now, you'll enjoy this. It's not regular tea, you understand. It's herbal. Much better for you, and of course, it's all natural with no chemicals whatsoever in it, so it's perfectly safe. I do hope you're staying away from foods with preservatives in them, they just strip your body of all the nutrients you need. I had a college friend who almost died of malnutrition because she ate nothing but foods with preservatives, and it ended up destroying her immune system, and she couldn't absorb any of the nutrients she was getting, even after she stopped eating foods loaded with chemicals, not even when they tube-fed her. She almost died from preservatives."

"Ah."

"Now you drink this up, and I'll send some home with you. Did I tell you about Bob's plans for our manure? He's had a wonderful plan for fertilizing the vegetable patch."

I crossed my fingers that she meant the sheep manure.

"I know where manure comes from," a reedy little voice piped up. "My mom told me. It's poop, but it's called manure when it comes from animals."

"Yes, that's right, Miracle." Phil gave me a *aren't children wonderful* look, and patted the demon child on her head.

"I've seen the sheep poop, but I haven't seen them make babies. Have you seen them make babies?"

"Well . . . uh . . . as a matter of fact, I have."

"Mom, Mr. MacLaren has a *penish*. Kathie doesn't think it looks gross. She says it's an acquired taste."

The small headache residing quietly in the back of my head suddenly blossomed into a full-fledged dilly of a throbber. Phil shot a startled glance over at me and put a supportive and loving arm around the minion of hell who was standing at her knee, munching on her third jam tart. I smiled weakly at them both and tried to rally my wits into protesting my innocence, but the Evil One got in the last word.

"I don't think anything so gross would taste good, but Kathie says you learn to appreciate it."

I don't believe we'll be seeing Phil and Bob too much. I have a feeling they'll be keeping Miracle away from us now that we've been formally crowned as the Oral Sex Fiends of the Highlands.

If I thought Bridget was going to take Iain's refusal to her plan for the slaughterhouse quietly, I would have been surprised by the vehemence of her objections, but even my brief acquaintance with her was enough let me understand that she wasn't going to take the news well.

"Iain, you don't comprehend how important this is," she snapped at him, her face tight with anger.

It was a few days after Iain had told me he wasn't going to agree to the abattoir plan that Bridget had stopped by to pressure him into signing the commitment papers. I was at the kitchen table pretending to write a letter to my mother while Iain sat on the floor and tried to fix a portable heater he used in the barn for ailing lambs and ewes. Bridget stormed around him, her hands making sharp, expressive little movements as she alternated pleading and threatening him.

"This is stupid, this is so unnecessary! I've told you the council would be no problem, so there's no reason that we can't make the offer to Tannahill."

"It's not just the council, Bridget, as you well know. The abattoir was just one idea for the land, and as it would require more capital than I can free up and you have available, it's not feasible. We'd be better put to agree on some other plan that won't require buying favors or a large outlay of cash."

I rested my brow on my palm as I bent over my letter, peeking through my hair at Iain and giving him a smile he didn't see. Bridget wasn't a force to take lightly, but Iain didn't seem to be having any problem standing up to her, even when he was sitting on the floor. He let her rant and wail and addressed her barbed questions calmly and with a patience I would never have achieved.

"Darling," she imparted a venom to the endearment I hadn't thought possible, "I never thought I would be forced to say this to you, but you're just not thinking. You're allowing that little bint of yours to sway you, and you'll be sorry, Iain, you'll be very sorry when Tannahill takes his abattoir to Kinrushtie and we're left with nothing but an unproductive piece of ground that no one wants!"

Iain set his tools down and got to his feet, brushing off his pants as he frowned at Bridget pacing before the Aga. He said only one word, but that word hit Bridget like a two by four.

"Out."

Her head snapped around and stared at him. Even I stopped pretending I wasn't listening and looked up. I'd seen Iain annoyed and angry, but I've never heard the chilling note of true fury in his voice as I did then.

"What? What are you talking about? What do you mean, out? We're not finished talking about this. I'm not going to let you throw away—"

Iain walked over to the back door and held out Bridget's coat. "You're leaving now, Bridget. If you want to discuss the issue of Kin Aird later, I'll expect you to have an apology for Kathie."

Bridget's smooth face turned red with poorly concealed anger. "*What?* Apologize to her? To that—" Iain took one step toward Bridget, but the menace in his eyes was enough to shut her up. I sat with my mouth hanging open slightly, amazed that Iain would get so angry over an unkind name. It's not like Bridget had never played her nasty little game with me before. I gave Iain a secret little smile, amazed and flattered that he would jump to my defense, my heart swelling with love for him as I slid my gaze over to watch Bridget work through a craw full of anger and frustration, seasoned by a dollop of blazing hatred. I thought for a moment she was going to blow, spewing all sort of slurs and foul accusations, but she was made of sterner stuff.

"Darling!" She laughed a shaky little laugh, swallowing the last of her bile and turning her brittle smile on me. "You mistake me. I have only the best wishes for your sweet friend. I certainly did not intend you should get so unreasonable over an ill chosen word or two. I'm sure Kestie wasn't offended."

Kestie thought it best not to answer that statement.

Bridget waved away any hurt feelings I might have over being called a bint and continued on, ignoring both the coat Iain still held out to her, and his mammoth scowl. "Iain, darling, if you need reassurances that the council will do as I told you they would, I will get them for you, so you can see how silly you're being by denying us the opportunity to make a sizable profit from an otherwise useless piece of land. As for the other issue," her hands fluttered gracefully as she waved them away as well. "I will raise my share of the money needed, and surely now that you have another income available, you'll have no trouble with finding the funds."

I opened my mouth to tell her there was no way on God's green earth I would allow my money to be used to help fund a slaughterhouse, but closed it after seeing the weary look on Iain's face. The last thing he needed was for Bridget and me to be squabbling.

He sighed and gave her a steady look. "No, lass. I won't agree to it, not now, not if you have the entire council in your back pocket, so you might as well start considering the other options."

"Other options?" Bridget spat, stalking over to him and

snatching her coat from his hands. "Other options? There are no other options that come near the profits we'd be guaranteed from Tannahill." She shot me a glittering, razor-sharp glare, then turned back to Iain with a faint sneer on her lips. "I can see I am outnumbered. Very well, I will tell Tannahill you refuse to cooperate, but I warn you, darling. I will settle for nothing less than the profits I would have seen had you been thinking with your head instead of your cock. It's up to you to figure out how we're to make them."

She stomped out in a whirl of nasty looks and muttered imprecations. I set down my pen and watched as Iain ran a hand through his hair.

"Sweetie, you know if there's anything I can do to help you with the farm, I'll do it. I don't have a lot of money, but what I have is—"

He stopped my offer with a swift, hard kiss that did much to warm my heart. He loved me, he'd turned down certain profits by refusing to allow the slaughterhouse, and he made Bridget leave when she called me names.

"I've no need of your money, love, but I thank you for the offer. There's other options available to us with Kin Aird; Bridget just needs a bit of time to see the value in them."

I kissed him on the tip of his nose and smiled to myself as he sat down to finish repairing the heater. Everything was looking up. Things were going to work out just fine.

Chapter Eleven

Deck the halls with boughs of holly, falalalalalalalala.

"Mrs. Harris, please, I've told you three times, I'd like that mistletoe left above the door. It forms an integral part of the decorations for the sitting room. If you move it from here . . . oh, blast, now the sag is swagging."

"What?"

"The swag is sagging. That one, right there, the one you're pushing aside."

"*Tch.* Are you telling me you need this in every room in the house?"

"Mistletoe is very important. People might want to kiss in every room in the house."

"You've got it in the loo!"

"Stranger things have happened."

"*Tch.* All this folderol! All this work putting everything up—it'll just have to come down in a few weeks, and who'll be taking it down I'd like to know? And clean up the mess? If you think I'll be climbing ladders to take down those rubbishy bits of branches you've put up on the walls, you're daft."

"Happy Christmas to you too, Mrs. Harris."

Tis the season to be jolly, falalalalalalalala.

"What the hell is that smell?"

"Oh, there you are. I'm mulling wine—I thought I would try it out before everyone arrives, but I think maybe I got the recipe wrong. It doesn't look right. Here, taste this and see what you think."

"*Gark.* Erm . . . love, you might want to throw this out and start again."

"Blast! Mrs. Harris has done it to me again! That's the last time I ask her for a recipe. Is it really that bad?"

"You try it."

"*Aaaaaaagh!*"

Don we now our gay apparel, falalalalalalala.

"I don't know what it is you're thinking to do with this, love, but I brought you the tree you wanted. I took it off the top of Clachaun." Clachaun was one of the hills surrounding the farm.

"Oh, Iain, my Christmas tree, thank you! It's going to be perfect! I'll put it in the sitting room and decorate it and put presents underneath it. Let me see it! Is it outside? How big is it? Will it fit through the door? I hope I bought enough lights."

"That's it, there, on the table."

"Oh, it's . . . why, it's . . . it's simply . . . Iain, have you ever seen *A Charlie Brown Christmas*?"

Troll the ancient Yuletide carol, falalalalalalala.

"Well, hell. I don't know where we're going to put everyone, Joanna."

"Oh, Kathie, I'm so sorry. I'll just tell Mum and Dad that you can't put them up after all. They won't mind staying at the Stag's Head. It's better than sleeping on our couch. They'll understand that with Ewen and Archie and Susan you will have a houseful. I feel terrible about asking you to put them up to begin with."

"No, no, I didn't really mean that, I want to have them. We'll get everyone tucked in, it's just going to take a little finessing. Um. Didn't Iain say there was an old box room in the attic that had a cot or something?"

"I think so, but I'm sure it's not heated up there, and I doubt if anyone's cleaned there in years and years. If it's in the old part of the house, it's probably damp, too."

"Heh heh heh—we'll put Archie up there. Your mom and Susan can have the boy's old room, and Ewen and your dad can share the spare room."

"I'm not sure that attic room is a good idea, Kathie. Even with airing, it's bound to be musty and uncomfortable, and Archie . . . oh. Hee hee hee."

"I knew I liked you, Joanna."

Yes, Christmas was coming. I had taken a stand and demanded the right to hold Christmas at Iain's house. Joanna's parents were coming up to spend the holiday with the newlyweds to celebrate their first Christmas together, and the joyous news that Joanna was pregnant. Archie was coming for three days, and Ewen, Iain's elder brother, had rung up to find out what his plans for the holiday were. Ewen gladly accepted an invitation to stay with us for a few days. I spoke with him briefly on the phone, and was reassured by his nice voice and lack of obvious hostility.

I had promised everyone that I would prepare a good old-fashioned American-style Christmas dinner, which meant I had to do some frantic e-mailing to my sister in an attempt to find out just what makes up a good old-fashioned American-style Christmas dinner, and how you go about preparing it. My family, not in the least bit Italian, always had spaghetti for Christmas gatherings.

Armed with recipes for various stuffings, green bean dishes, my mother's creamed onion recipe, and a charge card whose company would love me for the next three years, I ran out and bought enough food for the entire Kingussie Shinty Club. They weren't expected, but I wasn't going to take any chances on being caught short.

I had my plate full, and then some. There was a house to be decorated. There was food to be cooked, including some traditional British dishes that Joanna insisted I must include (she paid for that—I dumped those dishes on her. *Never cook a Christmas pudding if you can help it* was my new motto). There was Mrs. Harris to be mollified and persuaded into doing some extra cleaning. There were presents for family and friends in the States and in Scotland to be bought and wrapped, and in some cases, shipped home.

There was a Scot to be persuaded into marriage.

I managed to keep up my hint dropping to Iain despite a continued lack of response. His attitude was beginning to worry me, though. After the first few hints, I was sure he was on to my plan, but as Christmas drew closer he seemed preoccupied and less inclined to play the game.

A few days before Ewen was due to arrive, I decided it was time to tackle something that had been worrying me.

"Iain, I'm going to have to go home."

Iain was flat on his belly trying to force an ancient Christmas tree stand into holding my little tree. The tree was so tiny we had to fill out its trunk area with wood blocks so the tree stand screws had something to bite into.

He worked out a few Gaelic curses, then sat up. "That's as good as it'll get."

"It's tilted."

He cursed again and went back under the tree, muttered, and made adjustments.

"How's that, then?"

"Perfect. Did you hear what I said?"

"Aye, you're going home."

"For a man who professes his love for me with his every action, you certainly are taking that bit of news well."

Iain wrapped his arm around me, and hauling me up to his side, considered the now righted tree. "I haven't had to muck with this foolishness since the boys were young."

I elbowed him.

He grunted and tightened his arm. "I had assumed, love, that you mean to go back to the States to pack up your things, not that you intend on leaving me. Am I wrong, then?"

"You big toad. Of course you're not wrong. I was thinking that you might want to come with me. You know, as sort of a vacation. Together. Just the two of us. As in a trip. Romantic, hmmm?" Did I have to *spell* it out for him?

"I'm thinking that this damn tree is more trouble than it's worth."

I elbowed him again. He sighed. "I'd have to have someone watch the farm, but Mark might be willing to postpone
his holiday to do it. I wouldn't be able to be gone long,
though, love. It would have to be a short holiday."

"How short is short?"

He thought a moment. "A week?"

A week. Seven days. Five if you counted two travel days.
Could I pack up my entire apartment, disburse what I didn't
want or couldn't take, box up the remaining belongings for
shipping to Scotland, and yet still have time to introduce
Iain to my family and friends? Damn straight I could.

"Done," I said, and offered him my hand. He shook it
gravely then proceeded to show me how they seal a bargain
in the Highlands.

"Well," I said breathlessly once I had made sure he didn't
have any cavities, "if that's the way you seal a deal, I bet
your bank manager loves it when you come in for a loan!"

"Aye, she does," he grinned.

"Smart aleck." I pinched him.

"You should see what we do when we close on something
of importance."

"What's that?"

The dogs shot us disgusted looks when our clothes went
flying.

"'Tis the season," I murmured some time later, panting
and looking up at a slightly wonky Christmas tree now be-
decked with a sock and my bra.

"I hope I live to see it through," Iain moaned, lying prone
and naked before the fire, still sucking in great quantities of
air.

Once I could rally my wits enough to entertain coherent
thoughts I ran down my mental list of tasks to be accomplished: one issue down, one big one to go, and a houseful
of people to prepare for, half of whom I'd never met. I was
starting to wonder what I had gotten myself into when I
looked over at Iain, drowsing before the fire. Even flat out
on his back, stark naked except for (how had he managed
that?) one sock, one hand on resting over his heart, the other
under my head, he was a sight to inspire any woman.

I could get through this. It was just family. Not, as yet, officially *my* family, but I'd make bloody well sure they were thinking they were by the time they left.

"So—how do you go about getting a kilt made?" I asked Joanna, now known to one and all as "The Belly" even though she didn't yet have much of one.

She looked startled. "A kilt? For whom?"

"For my brother. His wife thought that as long as I was here, I could buy him one."

"Your family's not Scottish."

"Does that matter?"

It turned out it did, if you wanted to do it properly. People not of Scottish descent could wear the couple of generic (non-clan specific) tartans like Black Watch, but even that is pricey to get custom made into a kilt, and my brother wasn't the sort to wear an off-the-rack kilt.

"Strike one," I muttered, and peered out the car window as Joanna steered us through the holiday shopping crowds. We were out on a joint expedition of Christmas and pregnant clothes shopping. I would have preferred to avoid the latter, but Joanna had become my closest female friend in Scotland. She was a warm-hearted, loving woman who cherished her family—both her own and David's—but she wasn't without a streak of silliness that greatly appealed to me. David and Iain rolled their eyes many times when they caught the two of us giggling together over something inane. Much like my friendship with Cait, it didn't take a whole heckuva lot to set Joanna and me off.

"Oh, look, isn't this cute, Kathie?" she asked at one of our stops. I looked. It was a Paddington bear wearing a kilt (I'd just like to know which clan claimed him).

"Cute, but I already have the gollies for my brother's little kids, and I don't have any other babies to buy for."

She glared at me.

"Oh, I'm sorry, Joanna. How could I possibly forget the next generation you're hauling around there. Was that a subtle hint? A little something for the baby shower?"

"No, I don't want it, I thought you might. It's wearing a kilt."

"I am not," I said with dignity, "so enamored with kilted beings that I get my jollies from seeing them on a stuffed bear. I don't like teddy bears."

She smiled one of those annoying madonna smiles and waggled the bear at me. "It wasn't for you. I thought perhaps you and Dad might like to give David a little brother or sister."

My jaw hit the floor. "You're looped!" Her smile became even more maternal. "Joanna, you're got to be kidding! It must be all those pregnancy hormones in you! In case it's escaped your attention, Iain has two adult children, one of whom is going to make him a grandfather in six months. I'll be forty in a few years! *And we're not married!*"

She snorted and put the Paddington back. "You don't have to be married to have a baby, Kathie!"

I ignored her and let her browse amongst the pregnancy pants while I gathered my wits enough to look at my shopping list.

"Let's see . . . my younger brother Max is easy, he just wants whisky. His wife is also easy, she'll love one of those cute stuffed sheep I saw in Inverness. Their kids I've already taken care of. Now, Mom . . ."

My mother was a problem. She had everything she needed, she got most of her books from the library, and the few interests she had, like gardening, I couldn't cater to because of agricultural import laws.

"Any inspiration?" I asked The Belly.

"You could get her a Grandma Book," she leered at me.

I gave that comment the consideration it deserved. "Hrmph. What about jewelry?"

We were strolling down Main Street by that time, peering in windows for ideas.

"Oh, look, there's a humidor. You could get that instead of a kilt for your other brother. It looks nice."

"It looks expensive. How about Aran jumpers for everyone?" I asked, pointing at a shop with a nice display.

She wrinkled her nose. "Those are Irish."

I waved a hand dismissively. "Ireland, Scotland, close enough. They'll never know the difference."

She laughed and told me my heart wasn't in the expedition. I bought sweaters for the remaining members of my family, and was heading back for her car when suddenly my eye caught a glint in a shop window.

"Oh my god, Joanna, look!"

"What? Where?" She looked all around, but missed . . . *it*.

"There. Oh my god, it's . . . it's . . . glorious! Come on, we have to go in to that shop. I see the most perfect gift for Iain, and you know how hard he is to buy for."

My breath lurched in my throat as I pushed her into the shop, greeted the owner politely, and dashed toward the display in the window. I stood before it, panting slightly, still clutching Joanna's arm.

"Isn't it beautiful?" I asked reverentially.

"You're joking with me, aren't you?"

"No," I breathed, staring at it, trying to take in all of its magnificence at once. I'd never seen anything so marvelously wonderful before. It was perfect for Iain! I had already bought him one present, but it was a practical one, one he wouldn't have any fun with, but this . . . this was utterly bewitching!

"No, it's not perfect for Dad, Kathie. I'm sorry, I can see you've developed some sort of strange, unaccountable desire for that, but you know how Dad is—he won't even wear a kilt. What makes you think he'd want that?"

I reached out a finger to stroke it. "Oh, god, it's perfect. Can't you just see him with it?"

"No, I can't."

"That's because you're not trying hard enough. Close your eyes and just imagine Iain with this."

She shot me a look that indicated I was being extremely trying. "Kathie, we really ought to be looking at practical gifts if we are to have time to go to the Lady Madonna shop and buy me pregnant knickers."

"Let the knickers have their own babies, I want this!"

"It's a fine piece, isn't it?" the shop owner said from behind us. Joanna just rolled her eyes and started for the door, but I nodded my head quickly and fervently. A fine piece, oh yes indeedy, what a very fine piece. And it was mine!

"Oh, very fine. How much does something like this run?"

She told me. I didn't actually pass out, but things did go black for a moment. I was, however, pleased with how quickly my mind snapped back into place and started scurrying around figuring out how I could afford it.

"You'll notice that's ebony just there."

"Ebony," I whispered, reaching out to stroke it. "Iain would love ebony."

"No, he wouldn't," came from the doorway, where Joanna was opening and closing the door to make the little door chimes chime.

"Stop that, Joanna. You have to excuse her," I said, leaning closer to the saleswoman. "She's pregnant and a mite testy about it."

"I heard that! I am not testy! Now let us go and buy me clothes that fit and bigger knickers!"

"Shall I bring it out for you to look at it a little closer?"

I almost danced I was so excited. I pulled Joanna away from the door to the counter while the saleswoman brought it out, and with one hand flipped open a bit of blue velvet, then laid it on the cloth.

"Oooooh," I said, staring. It got better the closer I got to it. "Pretty."

"Oh, lord," Joanna said, snorting as she moved off to look at the jewelry case.

The shop owner and I both ignored her.

"Yes, it is lovely, isn't it? And as I said before, all handmade."

Two ladies who were in the shop came over to look. I resisted the urge to lunge over it protectively, and instead smiled a modest smile at my obvious good taste in Christmas gifts.

"It's for my sweetie," I said, running a finger down the ebony. "See? Ebony."

"Ebony," the two ladies said, admiring it.

"Burnished Macassar ebony," the shop owner corrected me.

"Burnished Macassar," the ladies dutifully repeated.

One of them leaned closer to admire the ebony. "My Joe would like one of those, don't you think, Claire?"

Claire pursed her lips. "He'd kill himself with it."

"Mmm. P'raps you're right. He did break his thumb two years ago hanging up the new curtains."

The ladies laughed. I smiled a superior *my man could quite easily handle this fine gift* smile.

"You'll notice the drooping quillions," the shop owner pointed out. "Those are quite distinctive."

"Oh, mercy, yes, very distinctive quillions," I said, looking it over and wondering what the quillions were. Drooping quillions, yet. The ladies looked impressed at the thought of distinctive quillions.

"And the quatrefoils are picked out in brass," she continued, waving toward what I assumed were the quatrefoils. They looked brassy.

"I just think it's fabulous, and I know my Iain would be thrilled with it."

Claire looked a bit skeptical at that, but I could see her friend would have been on Iain's lovely gift in a flash if I didn't have my claim staked out quite clearly. I rested a possessive hand on a drooping quillion.

"He's Scottish, is he? You wouldn't be taking this out of the country?" the owner asked. I reassured her that Iain was Scottish, and explained that we lived nearby.

"These pieces combine grace and power, and it takes a very special man to handle it," she warned.

"Oh, Iain is very special," I nodded, a bit of a wheedling tone entering my voice. I had a horrible fear that if she didn't think Iain could handle it, she'd refuse to sell it to me. "He's very strong and very graceful. It's just perfect for him, really it is."

Claire's friend looked a bit hopeful.

"Well," the shop owner, playing the three of us like we were prized trout, "I hate to let these pieces go, they are just that special, but you seem to be quite sure that your friend would like it, so I believe it will have a good home with you."

"Oh, an excellent home," I said, fingering the quatrefoil. "The very best. Um . . . you do take credit cards?"

She assured me they did, and under the watchful gaze of Claire and her covetous friend, I purchased the best gift I would ever find. Minutes later I was floating out beside Joanna with it clutched to my chest. I couldn't wait until Christmas. I couldn't wait until Iain saw the perfect gift. I couldn't wait until I saw the look on his handsome face when he opened the package and saw it in all its glory.

A 55-inch-long burnished Macassar ebony-gripped, quatrefoiled, pommeled, and drooping quillioned two-handed claymore. With scabbard!

Chapter Twelve

We decided on the second week of January for our trip back to the States. The day after we decided this, it struck me that Iain might not have a passport. If so, he didn't have much time to apply and receive it before we left. If we delayed the trip, I'd have to leave the country for a day before I could return since I'd almost run through my allotted *three months without a visa* time.

I waited impatiently for Iain to come in for lunch, then pounced on him and asked if he had a passport.

"I had one, but it expired."

"Oh, Iain! What are we going to do?" I wailed, wringing my hands yet again (you'd think I would have permanent wring marks on them I had taken to doing it so often). "Even if you ran out and applied today, you'll never have it by the tenth!"

"Aye, love, I will. I've already applied for it." He went to the sink to wash his hands.

I stopped in mid-wring and stared at him. "You did? When did you apply for it?"

"Oh, must be a fortnight ago."

I did a swift mental calculation. "You what? But that was before Clara died! That was before I was sure you really loved me. Why didn't you tell me you were getting a passport?"

He adopted that injured look men everywhere get when unjustly accused. "You never asked."

I blinked at him for a few moments, the fury building

slowly like a bubble rising in a pot of porridge. "You mean that you knew at the beginning of the month that you were going to the States with me, but you never mentioned it? Do you mean," I took a deep breath, "to say that you let me wallow in my own tormented nightmarish hell while I tried to figure out if you loved me, and all the while you had plans to come home with me? And you *didn't mention it*? Not one little word?"

I'm afraid my voice rose a wee tad bit by the end of question. Iain put down the towel he was drying his hands on and pulled me into an embrace. "You never told me you had these doubts, love. I thought you know me well enough to know I'd not hurt you like that."

I struggled against succumbing to his warmth. "Do you or do you not mean to tell me that you knew all the way back those two long weeks ago that you were coming to the States with me?"

"Aye, I knew."

I felt like my head was going to explode. He knew and he didn't tell me? He let me go through that horrible period of doubt without bothering to mention it to me? After everything we'd been through, after all the time we'd spent together—two whole months!—he still couldn't bring himself to share his thoughts and plans with me? I fisted my hands to keep them from wrapping themselves around his throat. "Why didn't you say anything?"

Iain shrugged and pulled me back to his chest. "It didn't occur to me to, love."

I took a long, deep breath. Luckily Iain had clamped me firmly to his chest, so my breath was Iain-scented, which went a long way to soothing the anger. It's hard to stay mad at someone when half your mind is too busy being girlish and giggly and tingly to work up to a proper hissy fit.

It was also fortunate that I didn't have time to mull over the injustices created by miscommunication between the one open American and one quiet alpha Scot because Ewen was due to arrive the following day. Despite having spoken with him on the phone, I was still a wee bit nervous about meeting him.

I spent the day running around making sure the million and one things that needed to be done before guests came were accomplished, and closed myself up for long hours with cookery books planning meals that would not shame me or Iain. Mrs. Harris, in a spirit of one-upsmanship (the source of which I ignored), offered to prepare a couple of multicourse dinners, only one of which involved lamb. I humbly and gratefully accepted her offer, and breathed a little easier.

I have learned well from my mother's knee. If you kept people fed and warm, she said, you were more than halfway there, but to be honest, I didn't feel halfway to anywhere but the madhouse when I contemplated Ewen's arrival. Although he sounded friendly enough the one time I spoke on the phone with him, I wasn't convinced he wouldn't turn on me in the presence of family. I worried myself into quite a stew by the day he arrived.

Iain was out finishing his chores when a sleek gray-blue Daimler pulled up alongside the house. I peered out the kitchen window with a frown on my face since I was in the middle of making a Buck Rarebit, and wondered aloud if Iain's brother had arrived early.

"Oh my god!" I exclaimed once I got a good look at the man exiting the car. "That can't be Iain's brother! This guy has to be an actor who's lost his way. Will you get a load of that hair! And that suit! Hooo baby!"

The Adonis in the front yard turned to the house, noticed me with my nose plastered up against the window, and smiled and waved. I waved the hunk of cheese in my hand back at him.

"Jeezumcrow! Did you see that? He's got *dimples*! Good Lord, who is he? And what's he doing here? Do you think I should go out and ask if he's lost? That can't possibly be Iain's brother, he doesn't look anything like Iain! That man's gorgeous!"

"'Tis MacLaren's brother all right." Mrs. Harris sniffed, peering over my shoulder. "Always was one for wearing those fancy waistcoats."

I couldn't tell how fancy his vest was, but his suit

screamed custom tailoring. Expensive custom tailoring. And his shoes. And his hair. I stayed glued to the window until he walked around to the seldom-used front door.

"Aaaaargh!" I shrieked and tossed the round of cheese at Mrs. Harris, who caught it nimbly while chopping celery. "I wasn't expecting him for another three hours! I haven't even put on a clean dress!"

Muttering dire curses upon men who were inconsiderate enough to arrive early, I dashed to the front door and let Iain's brother in.

"You must be Kathie," he said, holding both of my cheesy hands in his and blinding me with a smile that could knock the knickers off of a woman at thirty paces. "I'm delighted to meet you at last. Iain's spoken so much of you that I feel as if I know you."

I extracted a hand and clutched at the wall. This was Iain's *brother?* His *elder* brother?

"Um." I was sure I had a silly, vapid smile on my face, but I couldn't for the life of me think of what to say to the vision standing in the hall. "Um. Welcome. How nice to meet you."

He kissed me on both cheeks, continental style, and stood waiting for me to invite him in. I blinked at him a few times, unable to believe the vision before me.

Iain's brother?

I made a frantic effort to get a grip on myself. *Iain's brother?* "I was just making some lunch . . . dinner . . . lunch. Whatever you call it. If you'd like to . . . um . . . join us—"

"Sounds delightful, my dear. Lead the way."

This couldn't be his brother. This man sounded as English as the Prime Minister. Upper class plummy sort of English. And he looked like something off a suntan lotion commercial. Maybe I was confused. Maybe Iain had more than one brother. Maybe he had a younger, English brother, who was the secret shame of the family, and thus wasn't spoken of.

I stopped in the middle of the kitchen doorway and turned back to him.

"You *are* Ewen, aren't you?"

"In the flesh. Ah, Mrs. Harris, how nice to see you again. You're just as lovely as I remembered."

Huh? I looked at Mrs. Harris with a speculative eye. She was as big as Ewen, and probably a bit stronger. Her red hair frizzled out around the kerchief she always wore when cleaning or cooking. She wasn't ugly by any means, but lovely?

"*Tch,* MacLaren," she said coyly, and I swear she blushed. Mrs. Harris! Blushing? She waved a half-peeled potato at him. "Get on with yourself, I don't have time to waste words with a scoundrel the likes of you."

I stared at the two of them bantering—no, *flirting*—and I upped my prior impression of Ewen's prowess. Any man who could make Iain's char blush and giggle girlishly was a man with serious virility wattage. I stepped back a bit, lest it splash over onto me. I could easily imagine that if I weren't heels over ears in love with Iain, I'd probably be drooling like a spaniel over Ewen.

He took an appreciative deep breath. "Something smells delicious. Could it be whatever is bubbling there so enticingly on the Aga?"

"Ack!" I'd forgotten the leftover lentil soup I was warming up for our lunch. "Um, soup. Lentils."

Great. I sounded like a raving idiot. Ewen was probably making a mental note to grill Iain about his choice of women. I dragged my eyes off the personification of manly beauty and picked up the cheese. It wasn't easy to continue grating cheese while Mr. Handsome insisted on being of assistance. He was too distracting, slathering Mrs. Harris and me with compliments, stirring soup, slicing bread, and generally making me worried silly that he'd get something on that gorgeous suit. I could swear it was raw silk.

"Damn," I muttered as my hand slipped for the third time, grating my knuckles instead of the cheese. I just hoped no one minded a bit of skin in the rarebit.

"Problems, my dear? I wish you'd let me do that, I'm an old hand with the cheese grater. Isabella insisted I be properly trained."

Ewen took my hand in his, and flicking off a piece of cheese, examined the scraped knuckle. "There, nothing to work yourself up about, it's just a little scrape. Shall I kiss it and make it feel better?"

There was no mistaking that roguish twinkle in his eye. He was Iain's brother all right, and a right flirty one, too. I tried to remember what Iain had told me about Ewen's marital status as he kissed my hand. He was separated or divorced—which, I couldn't remember. Either way, he was trouble.

"I might have known you'd be in here trying to seduce Kathie," Iain rumbled as he strolled into the house, dumping his wellies in the corner.

What? Seduce? Him? Me? Never! I snatched my hand away from Ewen and hastened over to Iain to fling myself in his arms.

"Iain, darling!" I never call Iain *darling*, not since I heard that word on Bridget's lips. "You're back. I'm so happy! Look who's here, it's your brother! Isn't that lovely? He's early. I'm making you Buck Rarebit for dinner. Are you hungry? Did you bring Mark? How was the sick ewe? Did you get the rams shifted? There's leftover soup, too."

I was babbling like an idiot, and I knew it, but I couldn't seem to shut up. Iain peeled me off his chest, kissed me soundly, whispered in my ear that it was all right, he understood, and greeted his brother with a hug and a couple of thumps on the back that would have brought down a lesser man.

The two chatted nonstop through lunch, ragging and teasing one another as well as exchanging news and gossip. Feeling myself at a decided loss when I heard about what sounded like an extremely glamorous lifestyle, I apologized later to Ewen over the plainness of our lunch. He seemed to be genuinely surprised by apology. "My dear Kathie, don't think of apologizing for that delicious rarebit! I don't remember when I've enjoyed such a nice one."

"Aye, love, don't let Ewen's fancy feathers mislead you. He's put away more neeps and tatties than any man alive."

Ewen tried to look modest, but had little success.

"I find it difficult to believe you're brothers." I couldn't help but mention this. They sat chatting comfortably over the kitchen table, sipping ale and mopping up the last of the rarebit with leftover bread.

"Oh, aye, it's because Ewen speaks like a bleeding toff. It's the public schools he went to that are to blame."

"No, little brother, surely she's thrown by the fact that you've a face like a horse's arse while I . . ." he ribbed Iain good-naturedly, and flicked an imaginary piece of lint off his immaculate suit.

Iain responded with what I assumed were like-minded insults in Gaelic. Ewen just laughed.

I looked from one to the other. They were so dissimilar, and not just in their speech. "You didn't go to the same schools?"

"Good lord, no," Ewen laughed. "I was not cut out for the life of a farmer, my dear, and that's all Iain thought of from the time he could walk. He always had his hands, and usually his bum, in the mud."

The two grinned at each other. Even their smiles were different. The only resemblance I could see was around their eyes.

They finished catching up on each other's lives while I cleared the table and did the dishes, and soon turned to reminiscing.

It was fascinating to watch Iain with his brother. He treated Ewen almost as he did his sons—with a fond tolerance, but definite authoritative air. I wondered how the two could be so different in personality, and why Ewen, the elder brother, put up with being treated as he did.

The last thing I want to do is to give the impression that Iain was not the handsomest man alive. He was, but I recognized the fact that he was probably the handsomest man alive only to my eyes. I was willing to admit that he would not be deemed overly droolworthy by conventional standards, especially not when compared to the perfection of face his brother bore.

Iain had brown eyes, brown hair shot through with a few threads of silver, a nose that was a wee bit too big, and a very stubborn jaw. Ewen had honey blond hair that waved back from his brow in a manner I knew many women would kill for, hazel eyes that changed color depending on the lighting, eyelashes so thick I'm surprised he could see past them, a perfect nose, perfect mouth, perfect jaw . . . he was just perfect. As if that weren't enough, he also had dimples. It was almost enough to make you swoon on the spot, or throw yourself on him, and from what Iain said later, both were fairly common occurrences.

I stood next to Iain—my Iain, the Iain who had swept me off my feet not with a handsome face, but with warmth and character that sent me reeling in love—and stared back and forth between the two of them. The curiosity was driving me nuts.

"Uh . . . which one of you favors your father? Or mother?" I was still half convinced that one of them was a changeling.

Ewen laughed. "I told you, brother. It's that homely bit of muck you call a face that's thrown her."

Iain grinned and pulled me down onto his lap. "If it helps, love, we've different mothers."

"Oh." It did help. At least it explained why they looked so very different from each other.

I had just decided to do a little gentle prying about their relationship when Iain booted me off his lap and they went out to bring in Ewen's baggage. We settled him in the boy's old room and warned him he would be sharing his accommodations with Nate, Joanna's father. I left them joking and insulting one another while I ran back downstairs to greet the just arriving Joanna and David.

"So, how's the campaign going?" Joanna asked when we were alone in the kitchen. I put the kettle on for tea and settled down for a quick gossip. I had told her a short time before that I had hoped that Iain and I would marry sometime within the next year. She fully supported this idea, and went out of her way to assist me in my hint-dropping plan.

"Is Dad still being thick as a plug?" she asked now, ferreting out where I had hidden the cookie jar. Iain discovered a hitherto unknown passion for my Moravian Spice Cookies a few weeks back when I was trying out the recipe, and since then I had to hide any batches from him lest they were consumed in one sitting.

"No, leave them out," I said when she went to stash the cookies back in behind a bag of rice. "Iain wouldn't dare eat them all when other people are here to witness such gluttony. And yes, he's still either stringing me along, or not taking my hints, which, I must admit, have gone beyond the hint stage and are now pretty much outright demands."

She snickered and dipped a cookie in her tea. I suppressed a shudder at that and was about to go into a mini tirade about Iain's refusal to take a hint when it walloped him upside the head, but the men came down just then.

Ewen was stunning in a gray-and-green tweed hacking jacket, gold V-neck sweater, and a pair of jeans that I doubted had ever seen the light of day. They had a crease on them that could slice bread. In his hand he held a pair of spotless wellies. I swear they were polished—even my wellies, when brand new, never had that sort of a shine to them.

It brought to mind all of those Regencies I had read where the poor valet sat for hours polishing a pair of Hessians with nothing but champagne and elbow grease. The image of Ewen polishing his wellies with champagne amused me, so I shared it in an undertone with Joanna, who promptly broke into peals of laughter.

The men eyed us with a collective jaundiced eye. "Well, they're off again," David pronounced, and with a disgusted shake of his head (and lips twitching in a smile—he really was a good guy), he suggested they be on their way before we went completely loony.

All three men snagged a handful of cookies on their way out the door.

"They are to provide sustenance," Ewen said as he flashed his dimples at me, "in case we should be attacked by wolves while out viewing the wilds of Iain's farm."

"Ah, is that so?" I asked with a smile of my own while Joanna snorted, and watched the men march out to do whatever it is men do when they look at livestock.

I suspect a lot of it is exactly what Joanna and I had planned—to have a good gossip. They just did their gossiping in a harsh, manly man sort of environment. Women have more sense. We do it in the kitchen over beverages and sweets.

"So what do you think of Ewen?" Joanna asked, corralling another cookie. I'd have to make another batch at the rate they were disappearing.

I smiled. She grinned.

"I know, isn't he the end?" She giggled and dunked. "I almost dropped my teeth when David introduced me to him at our wedding. Imagine that—me standing there in my wedding gown, staring like a spotty teenager at my new husband's uncle! Melinda—my maid of honor—tried to seduce him, but he wouldn't give her a second glance."

She thought for a moment, munching the cookie. "Even my mother was a bit giddy around him."

Giddy. Good word to describe the effect the MacLaren men had on women. Iain made me giddy, David made Joanna giddy, and Ewen made a good seventy-five percent of the heterosexual female population giddy. "What I can't understand is how they can have the same father and look and sound completely different. Archie and David don't look too much alike, and yet they are clearly brothers."

"Well, you know Ewen and Dad have different mothers." I nodded.

"David told me that Ewen's mother was some sort of heiress. Oh, not an *heiress* heiress," she reassured me as my eyebrows shot up, "just an only child whose father had a bit of the ready. Quite a bit, actually. Anyway, she married Alec and had Ewen, but decided she didn't like living in Scotland, or being married to an engineer, so she took Ewen and went back to Daddy."

"Daddy, I presume, was living in England?"

Joanna nodded and took another cookie. "Somewhere near Cambridge. She got a divorce, Alec married Iain's mother, and that's why they don't look alike."

I popped a cookie into my mouth. "Well that explains a lot," I said around the cookie. "It's nice to see they have such a good relationship despite growing up in separate households."

"David says that Ewen's mother didn't really enjoy having a child, so she sent him to Alec for the summers and such." She contemplated this for a moment. "Still, it takes your breath away when you first meet him. Not that Dad isn't nice-looking!"

I smiled again and patted her hand. "He may not be gorgeous to anyone else, but he is to me." I remembered the question niggling in the back of my mind. "Iain said Ewen was divorced?"

"Mmm . . . separated, I think. He had his latest wife, Isabella, with him at our wedding. Stunning woman, she is— all blond hair and long legs and chat about her villa in Majorca. I don't think they've divorced yet, but since she's not here with him, they've probably called an end to the marriage."

There's just nothing so fascinating as the intimate details of another person's life. "His *latest* wife? He's been married before?"

Joanna's tea went down the wrong passage. She coughed it up and sputtered, "Oh, lord, yes! He's had . . . let me think, I've known David for three years . . . he's had at least four wives, and there may be others. I know David's talked about four, including the glorious Isabella."

"Who'd have guessed?" I murmured, before turning the topic to the upcoming MacLaren family Christmas. "I'm a bit worried about Archie, but I think everything else is well in hand."

"You'll be fine," Joanna said comfortingly, and slid another cookie out with a wink at me. "It's Christmas! Nothing will go wrong, you'll see!"

Chapter Thirteen

On the first day of Christmas, my true love gave to me . . .
. . . news about the arrival of his firstborn.

Iain popped his head into the sitting room. "Eh, love, Archie's here."

"Lovely," I smiled at him, thinking all sorts of foul things about this news bulletin. I held the smile until he went out to greet the prodigal son. Joanna, sitting next to her mother, grinned as if she could hear my inner thoughts.

"If you'll excuse me a moment, Bev, I'll just go out and say hello to Archie. You've met him, right?"

"Oh, yes, at Jo's wedding. Nice boy, very quiet."

"Er . . . yes." I gritted my teeth and marched out to the kitchen, where the men had just come in from a visit to the barn. Archie and his lady friend Susan were removing their coats.

Iain told me he had a little talk with Archie prior to inviting them up for Christmas. While I'm sure he did, I didn't have the slightest confidence that it would do any good, not after witnessing the venom Archie had poured out at me in Manchester. I was instantly wary.

"Susan, how delightful to see you again. I hope you had an easy drive up? Yes? Good. Archie, welcome."

OK, maybe using the word *welcome* was the wrong thing to say to a man arriving at his childhood home, but the stick-up-his-behind manner in which he turned and surveyed me set my teeth on edge.

He opened his mouth to say something, something incredibly nasty, I was sure, but slammed it shut when Iain moved up behind me and put an arm around my waist.

Ha! The little twerp. I kept the smug out of my smile and explained the sleeping arrangements. Archie immediately took umbrage at being assigned the attic lumber-room.

"Sorry," I said with a rueful smile. "We're full up, that's the best we can do. You're welcome to find digs in town if you think you'd be more comfortable."

Iain's hand tightened around my waist. Damn. I guess I wasn't allowed to bait Archie, either. I patted the hand and added, "But I'm sure you'll be just fine. Your father unearthed an electric heater for you, and there are plenty of blankets." And a whole lot of damp, as well as spiders the size of golf balls, but I wasn't about to mention them. Given Archie's character, it was the spiders I was worried about.

On the second day of Christmas, my true love gave to me . . .

. . . .two requests to stop sniping at Archie.

"He started it, Iain! The little bast . . . blighter made a snotty reference to the Yorkshire pudding thinking I had made it. Then when he found Joanna and Bev had, he made a snide comment about Joanna not knowing any better, given her training."

I was sitting on the edge of our bed, my feet tucked under me, watching Iain disrobe (to my mind, always an exciting event, and one worthy of my full and undivided attention). The look on Iain's face was enough to shut me up. Poor man, he was so pleased to have his family here, and I was making things worse by allowing Archie's barbs—never muttered in Iain's presence—to get to me.

I held up my right hand and stopped Iain before he could say anything. "I'm sorry, Iain. I promise, I won't take potshots at Archie anymore."

He kissed the palm of my hand. "It's just tomorrow, love,

then Christmas and Boxing Day, and he'll be on his way. I'll have another talk with him."

"No, don't, it's not necessary. He's just being testy with me, not outright nasty. I want you to enjoy your Christmas."

"Would you be letting me unwrap a present early, then?" He eyed the belt of my bathrobe.

"That depends." I smiled my wicked smile, the one I keep tucked away for special occasions. "Will you be leaving me with visions of sugar plums dancing in my head?"

"Oh, aye, love," he said, reaching for my robe. "If it's sugar plums you've a cravin' for, I've got the very thing you're wantin'."

I stepped forward into his arms and let him kiss me until we were both breathless and heated. He scooped me up and deposited me on the bed, following me down until he was stretched out on top of me, his hands touching me everywhere with teasing little strokes that incited flames of desire within me.

"Ah, love, you taste so sweet," he groaned into the underside of my breast as he kissed a path across my chest. "You taste like cinnamon."

"Cookies!" I gasped, grabbing his head as he slid down and nuzzled the part of me that wept tears of passion for him. "I was baking cookies earlier. Oh, lord, Iain, I don't think I'm going to be able to wait if you do—"

The words dried up on my lips as he put his mouth to the center of my pleasure and sucked hard, swirling his tongue in sweeping circles that had me arching up off the bed while starbursts of rapture flared behind my eyelids.

"Dear God in heaven, that almost killed me," I wheezed when I had enough strength to move my mouth. Iain chuckled and stretched out beside my still trembling body.

"Ah, love, I just wanted to put visions in your head."

I rolled an eye over to look at him, allowing a smile that promised much retribution to play about my lips. "About those sugar plums you promised me," I cooed, closing my hand around the twin globs resting at the top of his thighs. "I believe I'll have a little taste if you don't mind, just to make sure they're fresh."

His eyes closed in ecstasy as I rasped my tongue along a sensitive spot.

"Merry Christmas to all," I whispered just before I began my torment in earnest.

"And to all a good night," he groaned.

It was a *very* good night.

On the third day of Christmas, my true love gave to me . . .
. . . the desire to kick him in the shins. Soundly. In front of everyone.

Bev and Nate, Joanna's parents, were wonderful people. I liked them from the moment I met them, when Bev, an older version of Joanna, hugged me and presented me with a fruitcake. Nate, a small, balding man, was originally from Yorkshire or one of those regions in England where it takes a residency of at least twelve years before you can understand the inhabitants, but he was very fond of jokes, and had an endless store of them. He'd pop into a room where Joanna, Bev, Susan, and I were sitting, and deliver a joke. We'd laugh, he'd chuckle happily and leave with a sense of a job well done. Once he was out of the room I'd look at Joanna and Bev and ask for a translation. I don't believe I understood more than three or four words he'd said the entire visit, but he was a sweet man, and he seemed to enjoy his time with Iain and David. He also developed a special affinity for Catriona, the cat we acquired to replace Clara, probably because he insisted on taking over the twice daily milking of Mabel, and he'd squirt milk at the cats.

The morning following Archie's arrival, Bev and Nate went to have breakfast and spend the day with Joanna and David. Ewen insisted on preparing breakfast for us, claiming, as he kissed the back of my hand, "I will never be able to live with myself if I know that your fair hands were slaving away night and day simply to provide me with daily sustenance."

I blinked bemusedly at his statement. I had discovered that when he combined his dramatic method of speaking with his dimples, it was an almost overwhelming combination. Only the fact that I knew he was the biggest flirt on the face of the earth kept me from worrying about his intentions.

There was, however, a moment when I would have gladly kissed him.

After viewing Ewen's handling of a frying pan and an innocent piece of ham, which he butchered into odd polyhedron-shaped chucks, I relieved him of breakfast duties. "Isabella may have trained you well with the cheese grater, but that's about it. Sit down and look pretty, and let me do the breakfast."

Susan helped me assemble one of those artery-clogging fried breakfasts that were so dear to the British. Susan was one of the nice surprises; she was much more human than the first time I met her, but she seemed a bit uncomfortable at times, frowning at Archie whenever he fired off a zinger at me. She was one of those peacemaking people who tried to calm everyone down, even going so far as apologizing twice to me for Archie's comments.

We had the breakfast ready before Iain and Archie came in from doing the morning chores, but Ewen overruled my suggestion that we wait for them. He positively inhaled the fried ham, however, so I was busy frying up more when Iain and son came in.

"Ah, little brother," Ewen pushed his chair back, patted his jumper, and let out a discreet but sated burp. Iain grimaced at the *little brother* comment, knowing Ewen did it just to get his goat, and accepted the plate of food I handed him.

"You are one lucky man. A life that suits you, sons to carry on the illustrious MacLaren name, and a woman who can make ambrosia from the most mundane of foodstuffs."

Iain agreed and tackled his breakfast. Archie scowled at me briefly, then picked through his food like it was full of ants.

"Yes, you are a lucky man. When are you going to marry this paragon of virtue?"

I dropped the fork I was using to turn the ham, and spun around to look at Ewen. He had his hands locked behind his head and was gazing at Iain with one eyebrow cocked. My head snapped around to Iain.

What would he say? Would he acknowledge that he intended on marrying me? Would he admit to his brother and disapproving son that we loved each other? Would he inform them that I was here to stay and not some passing fancy? I held my breath, my hands clutched before me, my heart racing as I waited for him to speak.

He dabbed at his mouth with a napkin. He reached for a piece of toast. He looked up at Ewen. His mouth opened. The words were coming out . . .

And they were in Gaelic!

On the fourth day of Christmas, my true love gave to me . . .
. . . a great big belly laugh. And then some.

Cait asked me later in an e-mail why I didn't kill Iain right there on the spot. It was true that there were times when Iain drove me abso-bloody-lutely mad, for no matter how close I thought we were, we evidently weren't close enough for him to be forthcoming with his deepest, innermost thoughts.

The rotter.

I began to wonder if he ever would truly open up to me, or if he would continue on as he was now, assuming everyone was privy to what was going on his mind. Iain certainly always acted surprised when I accused him of holding something back.

When Iain answered Ewen's question about when (not if—and you're crazy if you think I didn't notice that) we were going to be married, I couldn't decide if I was furious for his answering in Gaelic, or insane for thinking it was absurdly funny.

For sanity's sake, and because I didn't want to spend the holiday being angry with Iain, I decided to squelch my pissy mood.

"Ha ha," I laughed gaily, turning around and stabbing a knife viciously into the ham. Wouldn't answer in English, eh? The great coward. He just did it because he knew I'd start crying when he told Ewen he had no intention of marrying me. "As if I would marry *that* big lout. Ha ha ha! It is to laugh!"

"Ah, now there I cannot help but fault you," Ewen said, and carried his plate over to the sink, thereby earning a bonus point for Isabella and her training. "My brother may not be much to look at, but beneath that muddy exterior beats a heart of gold. And you, madam," he took my knife-gripping hand and bowed over it, neatly avoiding impaling himself on the blade, "have captured that heart if I am not mistaken."

Oh, lord, why couldn't Iain talk like that? Why did one brother get all of the verbal skills, while the other got the adorable personality? I looked over at Iain. He grinned at me and shoveled in a mouthful of eggs. I would have killed to know what he said to Ewen, and why Susan looked so worried about Archie, but I'd was damned if I asked in front of Iain.

Things went from bad to worse when Mrs. Harris showed up to do a little dusting and start in on the grand supper she had planned (pork stuffed with dates and pineapple). She took one look at the mess in the kitchen—Susan had offered to help clean, but I sent her off to use the bathtub while she could—and hit the ceiling.

"If you're thinking I'll be cleaning up after this great lot, you're mistaken," she stormed as she shook her apron at me. "I work for MacLaren, not for you. I'll not clean up after an entire houseful of people!"

I was worried she'd go haring off and not make the dinner, so I placated her as best I could and tackled the kitchen while she did a little light cleaning elsewhere. The men, of course, disappeared in that time-honored fashion men have whenever it comes time to clean the kitchen. Susan came down from her bath, looked around worriedly for Archie, and went off to find him.

On the fifth day of Christmas, my true love gave to me . . .

> *. . . .a desire to possess a flamethrower. One of the industrial models. But no rings, gold or otherwise.*

"Fine," I snarled to the sink of greasy water, and plunged my hand into it to drain it and refill it with fresh. "Be that way. All of you can just go off to the ends of the frigging earth as far as I care. Oh no, it's not enough that I have to cook the breakfast, I have to clean up after it, too as well as put up with the most annoying man in existence. Sure!" I slammed a greasy frying pan into the water, drenching the front of my blouse. "Let's just all go have a gay old time and leave Kathie here to wallow in self-pity. Bloody hell, now what?"

I dabbed at the water on my blouse only to find it wasn't all water, some of it was sausage dripping from the pan. Great. In addition to my personal life being a mess, now I had destroyed a favorite blouse. What other lovely surprises did life have in store for me?

"Hallo?"

Oh, god, no. Not that. Not today. Please, I can't deal with that.

"Is anyone home . . . oh, Karrie, you're still here?"

Bridget. Bearing a package. Just what I needed to complete the morning.

"Hello Bridget." It took an effort, and I had a hard time unlocking my jaw to get the words out, but I did and I'm damned proud of that fact. "Happy Christmas."

"Yeees," she drawled, and looked around. "Where's my darling Iain?"

"Bridget!" I shrieked. She blinked in surprise. "No! Is it true? You have a darling Iain, too? Tell me, do, is he anything like *my* darling Iain?"

She smiled a tight little smile. "Very amusing, dear, very witty. Did I interrupt you at your feeding time?" She gave my damp blouse a pointed look. "Soda will work wonders on stains, although if you have a problem reaching your mouth, you really ought to consider wrapping yourself with a towel. So much easier than destroying your *lovely* garments."

"Is there something in particular you wanted, Bridget? A cup of tea? A piece of Bev's fruitcake? Cyanide?"

"Dear one, such spite is most unbecoming. It'll sour that too, too sweet personality if you let it. And speaking of that—"

Oh, lord, why did I ever think I could fence with her? She was a grand master at the art. I knew for a fact the stab to my heart was coming next.

"—I hope you haven't become too settled here at the farm. I hate to be the one to pass along gossip, but I *am* thinking of what's best for you."

I finished drying the plates and stacked them carefully. "Go ahead, Bridget, hit me with your best shot. What is it? Iain has been seen with another woman? Another man? You? No, the first two maybe, but I know Iain well enough to strike off the last."

She bared her teeth in a predatory smile. "I can see you're not in the mood to discuss the issue, dear. I do hope that when you are finally forced to confront the reality of Iain's wandering ways, you'll remember that I tried to befriend you."

I placed the dishes in the cabinet, said a mental apology to Mrs. Harris for leaving a few dirty pans behind, and grabbed my coat. "Consider your charitable holiday task accomplished, Bridget. If you'll excuse me, I'm off to find *my* Iain and his family. Is that a present? How thoughtful. You may leave it under the tree. I'll be sure to tell Iain you brought it." I started for the door.

"I would have thought that you'd be more concerned about Iain dating other women while you're still in his bed, but if it doesn't bother you that he's been seen—twice—with Fiona, then I shan't worry about it anymore."

She gave a delicate shrug, set the package down on the kitchen table, and smiled a feral smile at me as she passed by.

God help me, I tried to keep my lips clamped, but I just couldn't. "Fiona MacLeod?"

Bridget paused with one hand on the door. "Why, yes. You know her?" She put a hand to her mouth and widened her eyes as she gasped.

"Don't tell me you go in for those kinky three-ways? Such a shame, really. Iain never had the need for another woman when I was in his bed. Happy Christmas, dear. I hope Father Christmas brings you everything you deserve."

"And I hope you get everything coming to you, too," I said as I watched her saunter to her car, then grabbing my gloves and jamming my wooly hat over my head, I went out in search of Iain and his kin.

> *On the sixth day of Christmas, my true love gave to me. . . .*
> *. . . the burning desire to do someone bodily injury.*

By the time I found the men down by the lambing shed examining a new footbath Iain and Mark were building, I was fuming. This was not the way I had pictured Christmas. Archie took every opportunity to be unpleasant, Iain was being obstinate just to annoy me, and Bridget's evil little ploy had struck a nerve. I knew full well Iain wasn't dallying with this Fiona person, but if he had been seen with her recently, why the hell hadn't he mentioned it to me? And to top it all off, on my way down to find the men, I discovered the chickens were loose.

I spent a half an hour herding them back into their pen, and then stomped off in a fine fury to vent a little spleen on whoever was foolish enough to get in my way.

It was Iain, as luck would have it. I almost rubbed my hands with anticipation over the verbal drubbing I was going to give him.

"Ah, there you are, love. I was just coming up to fetch you. Come and take a wee walk with me."

"I don't wish to take a walk, wee or otherwise, thank you. It's too cold for a walk."

Iain looked around him in surprise. "Today? Nooo, it's not cold, just a bit brisk, isn't that right Ewen?"

"Oh, yes, just brisk, my dear. Pay no attention to the ice forming on my eyebrows."

Iain muttered something rude at him, and took me by my gloved hand. "Come along, love. If you're chilly, a walk will warm you up."

He walked, I fumed. I nursed my grudges carefully, fan-

ning the flames until I had built them up to a red-hot inferno.
Then I'd scorch him like he'd never been scorched!

*On the seventh day of Christmas, my true love gave to
me . . .
. . . a hike in the Highlands.*

We walked through the gate and into one of the parks.
Iain took my hand. I took it back. He took it again and
tucked it into his arm. I took it back.

"A wee bit miffed about something, are you, love?" He
took my hand again and this time held it tight. I tried to re-
trieve it and failed.

"Miffed? No, Iain, I'm bloody furious. Bridget dropped
by while you were down in the shed." I tugged harder on my
hand. Iain held on to it firmly.

"Oh?" His eyebrows rose cautiously. "I take it she had
words with you."

"You could say that," I managed to grind out, giving my
hand one last heave. Iain just squeezed my fingers and
marched on, dragging my resisting self behind him.

My fury was fast turning to self-pity. This was supposed to
be a wonderful holiday, my time bonding with Iain's family,
and yet it was nothing but a big old sham. Iain didn't want to
marry me, and he didn't even have the balls to say so to my
face. In a language I could understand. Bridget picked on me,
Archie hated me, and Ewen was probably mocking me with
that charming dimpled smile even as I stomped alongside his
heartless brother. Life was just so bloody unfair.

"Do you feel like climbing to the top of Durna, love?"

No, certainly not. I did not feel like climbing to the top of
one of his hills. Not me. Not in that cold. Not when he
couldn't bother answering a question in a proper manner, I
didn't. Not in this or any other lifetime.

"Sure, why not. Maybe I'll get lucky and contract hy-
pothermia up there."

Iain just chuckled and started up the side of the Matterhorn. I gritted my teeth (not an easy thing to do considering

they were chattering) and fought back the tears of self-pity
that threatened to swamp me.

Oh, sure, he may say he loved me (now and then, when
it suited him), but when it came time to put his money where
his mouth was, he wimped out.

"Watch that rock, love."

Love. He was always calling me love. But it didn't *mean*
anything. He called Joanna love. He probably used to call
Bridget love. And that Fiona woman. I bet she was a love,
too.

"Isn't it a fine day, though?"

Yes, sure, it was fine if you were a sheep. But if you were
human, and had human needs and desires and wanted to
know you mattered to someone who meant more than life itself to you, then it was a bloody miserable day, thank you.

"Fine."

Iain shot me a quick glance, then continued tugging me
up the side of Mt. McKinley. I wondered if I dropped down
dead on the spot if he would bother to haul my corpse back
to the house, of if he'd just leave me out there to be eaten by
the crows. I had a mental picture of Bridget showing people
around the farm, pointing to my bleached bones and telling
everyone the story of the foolish American who thought Iain
loved her.

"Still in a wee bit of a snit?"

Just one the size of the Grand Canyon. "Yes, as a matter
of fact, I am."

"Ah."

That's all he said. *Ah.* Not, "Oh, dear, I'm sorry my ex-
mistress came round to torment you." There was no, "I'm
sorry I sired such a cruel and vindictive son." Not even an,
"I'm sorry I can't be bothered to tell you what's on my
mind." No, just an *ah,* and that's it. The tears started forming. It might have been the wind, but I doubted it. Iain
hauled me up the last bit of K-2 and turned to look back over
his valley.

He stood for a few minutes, puffing ever so slightly,
damn his fit self, and held me up as I gasped and wheezed
for air. "It's a good land, this."

Oh, yes, good if you were a man and you didn't care what anyone thought as you sat safe and secure on your good land.

"I've lived here since I was twenty-two. I knew I wanted to live here the first summer I spent on the farm."

I had heard all of this before—how Iain's father had purchased the farm as an investment, but Iain had fallen in love with it at the ripe old age of seven when he spent six weeks there during the summer. He had told me how he had begged his father to let him run the farm, how his father insisted he go to college instead, and how he finally talked his dad into letting him attend a prestigious Scottish agricultural college. Oh yes, I had heard all of this, but what did it have to do with me? I was just the leman, the mistress, the woman who warmed his bed at night but was unworthy of acknowledgment or commitment before his family.

Iain started talking about how much he loved being a sheep farmer, but I was too miserable to listen. I wallowed deeper and deeper into my pit of self-pity until something he said penetrated the dense, dark thoughts. "What? What did you say?"

He looked vaguely annoyed. "I asked you if you thought you'd be happy here."

I gaped at him, my mouth hanging open. It couldn't be. I couldn't have missed it. No, not something as important as this! Oh, god, I had! I had missed it! The most important moment in my life and I had missed it! Think, Kathie, think quickly. How was I to salvage this? Oh, god, my brain had stopped! I couldn't think! I had finally done it, I had burned out my brain!

"What . . . Iain, what exactly are you asking me?"

"You ought to know, love, you've been hinting at it for the past fortnight." He was smiling now, a dear, sweet, wonderful smile. An Iain smile. An Iain smile full of goodness and promise and heartwrenchingly fabulous joy.

Oh, god.

"I'm asking you to marry me, Kathie."

It's amazing I didn't just slide off of the side of that hill, great big puddle of goo that I was.

On the eighth day of Christmas, my true love gave to me . . .
. . . who needs gifts when you have a true love?

Iain did actually give me gifts on the top of that wind-blown hill. He gave me himself, which was the biggest and best gift of all. He gave me a life in a country I had always loved, but never known. He gave me the freedom to be exactly what I wanted to be. He gave me countless other things, starting with the sweetest kiss imaginable, and ending with the patience and kindness to put up with my self-centered pity party.

There are always people who want to know about the more tangible gifts, however, about the *hardware*. Well, Iain gave me a gift that fit that description, too. He gave me a luckenbooth brooch. He pinned it on the sweater under my coat, and told me it was a traditional Scottish gift given to women on their engagement.

A luckenbooth brooch has two hearts entwined with a crown on top—a leftover from the time when Queen Mary gave one to the less than admirable Lord Darnley. The one Iain gave me had a lovely garnet in it, and just looking at it pinned on my sweater over my heart made me puddle up. But those of you who expect that I wept at such a tender moment will be surprised to find out I didn't.

Instead, I sobbed.

I flung myself on Iain and cried all over his coat. I bawled, I wailed, I laughed. I jumped up and down and kissed him and did a little jig and got the hiccups. And then I tripped over a rock and fell down the side of the blasted hill again.

This time I did more than just muddy myself and wrench my ankle, however. This time I broke my wrist.

Chapter Fourteen

I'm sure there are other people who've spent their Christmas Eve in the Accidents and Emergency section of a hospital. I doubt, however, that anyone had the lovely time I had. There was just something about pain medicine and a proposal of marriage to make everything seem not quite so bad, even if your wrist had swollen up to the size of a grapefruit.

I didn't know my wrist was broken right away; I just thought I'd bent it backwards and wrenched the muscles. But as Iain helped me back to the house, and the pain blossomed in relation to the swelling, we began to suspect it was a bit more serious than a mild strain.

So I spent the day in the A&E ward, Iain by my side, trying to get through to my insurance company to see if they would authorize the post emergency treatment. A half-dozen X rays, a lovely, lovely purple pill, and one plaster cast later, and I was on my way back to Iain's house.

There was a rueful smile playing around his lips. I mused on it in a muddled, painkiller induced hazy sort of state. "What handsome lips you have. They are especially nice when they are kissing, but when they part to speak, as they are doing now, they are still awfully nice to look at."

"That's what I like about you, love."

"What's that? My charm? My innate sense of grace? My appreciation for your lips? The wonderful way my eyes cross if I don't concentrate on keeping them focused?"

"Your sense of drama. Any other woman would have

simply accepted me and left it at that. You had to break your arm for good measure."

At least that's what I think he said. I was dropping off when he spoke, but he told me later that's what he said. He also told me he carried me into the house and upstairs to bed. I don't remember any of that.

I do remember waking up in the middle of the night with a terrible thirst and a hot, heavy arm. I was also confused because I was sleeping on Iain's side of the bed to keep my arm from being bumped during the night. The first thing that came to mind, after the pain and discomfort and the clumsiness of using the facilities with my left hand, was Christmas dinner.

That is what I got for planning such a feast! A turkey dinner for ten (Mark was joining us) and me with an arm that I had to keep elevated above my heart. Iain helped me back to bed, gave me a glass of water, and reassured me that he put my luckenbooth brooch away in a safe spot.

"Don't be worrying about dinner, love. You've family here now," he said as he brought out another pillow and tucked it under my arm. "We'll take care of everything."

Family. What a nice thought. I snuggled back down clinging to that thought. I had family now, and they would take care of everything. It was Christmas and I had the thing I wanted most—Iain. How could the day be anything *but* perfect?

Those of you who've had to prepare a holiday meal for family are probably ticking off the disasters on your fingers: the time Aunt Amber set fire to the kitchen with her Flaming Volcano drink; the time the dogs got to the turkey before anyone else; the time the power went off halfway through the cooking. The disaster potential of a holiday dinner is limitless, but I have to admit that this particular Christmas dinner turned out nigh on perfect.

And I owe it all to Joanna's mum, Bev. Bev wasn't comfortable unless she was in charge of a kitchen, with lots of people to cook for. She took one look at my menu, my scattered notes that scarcely resembled recipes, and marshaled her forces. Joanna and Susan were immediately pressed into action. Breakfast was the first order of the day, and it was accomplished with a minimum of muss and fuss.

"Mmmmm," I said, wiping strawberry juice off my chin awkwardly with my left hand. I had planned a breakfast that included Belgian waffles, but Bev changed them into the most delicious crepes stuffed with clotted cream and strawberries. I decided right then and there that we'd spend all future Christmases at her house. "Bev, you are a genius."

The others agreed, in various stages of coherence, everyone's mouth being busy at the time scarfing down the delicacies. Once breakfast was over, the men hied out en masse to do the chores quickly so we could open presents.

There is no irony in the fact that one of the presents was opened while the men were off doing chores. I planned it that way. As soon as the door closed behind them, I called Joanna into the sitting room, where I was installed in Iain's favorite chair, and pointed out a package to her.

"That's Bridget's gift to Iain. I'm a bit worried about it."

"Why?" she asked, turning the package over in her hands.

I reached out for it with my good arm. "You know Bridget! It would be just like her to give him a Kama Sutra doll or something embarrassing like that."

"Good point," said she.

"What do you suppose it is?" I carefully shook the package. It thumped mysteriously.

Joanna looked around to make sure we couldn't be overheard. She took the package back and gave it a speculative shake. "Would you like me to find out?"

I blinked at her. "How can you do that?"

She smiled. "I'm very good at wrapping gifts." She gave me a reassuring pat, and making sure no one was watching, slipped out to the bathroom with the package in hand.

Four minutes later she returned, her lips pressed tightly together. "It's one of those . . . you know . . . those *things*," she said in a hushed voice, a faint blush pinkening her cheeks.

I stared at her. "No, I don't know. What things?"

She quickly handed the package back to me. "One of those man things. *You* know."

Her eyes implored me to understand. I did my best, but I wasn't catching her drift. "Man things? You mean it's an athletic supporter?"

She stared at me in confusion. "A what?"

"An athletic supporter. A cup. You know, the things guys wear when they do sports and don't want their dangly bits to get squashed."

"Oh, a box." She blushed a little harder. "No, it's not that. I'm talking about one of those . . . things. The . . ." She peered over her shoulder, then leaned in close to me. "The things women use when they don't have a man. To satisfy themselves."

I blinked at her. "A vibrator? Bridget gave Iain a *vibrator*?"

"Shhhhhh!" she smacked me on my good arm and took another peek toward the open door to the dining room, where her mother was in conversation with Susan. "No, not that. The other kind. You know."

I thought for a moment. My experience with man things was somewhat limited. "A dildo?"

"Shhhhh!" She whapped me again and turned bright red.

I was beginning to feel a bit flushed myself, but the conversation held such a bizarre fascination, I just couldn't help but asking, "Joanna, you must be mistaken. Why on earth would Bridget want to give *Iain* a dil—"

She clapped her hand over my mouth and smiled over my shoulder. Susan walked in and settled herself with a book on the couch across the room. I leaned toward Joanna and whispered, "Whyever do you think Bridget would give Iain *that*? What possible use could he have with it?"

She stared at me, her mouth hanging ajar.

"Oh, don't look at me like I'm a ninny, Joanna, of course I know what he *could* do with it, but he wouldn't, and Bridget surely must know that. So why would she?"

"It's not for him, it's for you," she said in a vehement whisper. "Don't you see, it's the ultimate slap in the face for you. For both of you!"

I pursed my lips and considered the matter. "I suppose anything's possible with Bridget."

"What are you going to do?" she asked.

"I don't know, what do you think we should do?"

"What are you two whispering about?" Joanna's mother asked, leaning between us and whispering herself.

We both jumped. I looked at Joanna. She blushed even deeper and rolled her eyes.

"It's the present Bridget brought Iain," I whispered back. "Do you know about Bridget?"

She made a face. She had heard of Bridget.

"Well, she brought this present over for Iain earlier, and Joanna peeked—" Joanna kicked me on the ankle. "She suggested we look at it, so she did, and Bridget has given Iain a dildo."

Bev's eyes bugged out. "Are you sure that's what it is?"

We both looked at Joanna. She turned even more shades of red under her mother's knowing eye. "I am a married woman, Mum. I'm pregnant. I know what one looks like."

I nodded my agreement. "I wouldn't put it past Bridget. She's out to make trouble for Iain and me."

"What will you do about it?"

"I don't know, we hadn't reached that point yet."

Susan suddenly squatted in front of me and leaned into the conversation. "What is it? Is it Archie? Has he said anything to you—"

Joanna, Bev, and I looked at each other, then back to Susan. "No, it's not Archie," I reassured her, speaking for the group. We were all still whispering. "It's Bridget."

"Who's Bridget?"

I gave her the basics in succinct terms. "And so, you see, Joanna thought it was best—ow! Oh, all right, *we* thought it was best if she looked in the package."

I handed it to Susan. She looked down at it, then up at us. "What's in it?"

I looked at Joanna. She looked at her mother. Bev answered. "A phallus."

Susan looked interested. "Really? Is it one of those glass

sculptures by that American artist that are all the rage? I've heard of them, but never had the opportunity to see one."

"No, Susan," I said gently. "It's not a piece of erotic art-work. It's a dildo. A working model, from what I gather."

She dropped the package as if it contained poison.

We all stared at like it was about to explode.

"What are you going to do?" Joanna asked again.

"Well I'm not going to let Iain open that in front of his brother and son, that's for sure."

"We can throw it away," Susan suggested.

I thought about it for a minute. "No, Bridget's sure to ask Iain what he thought of her present, and then he'll suspect I tossed it into the rubbish out of spite."

"What you want," Bev said slowly, prodding at the package with the toe of her shoe, "is some way to nobble this Bridget."

"Mum!" Joanna said indignantly.

Bev gave her daughter a weary look. "I don't say a thing about you recognizing a sexual aid and you raise a fuss over a bit of nobbling!"

"Your mother's right," I said after a moment of thought. "What I want is a way I can fix Bridget and the horse she rode in on."

"A substitution," Susan said.

We all smiled at her. "Bright girl. Joanna, take that package in the corner wrapped in the gold paper with the blue stars. That's a jumper I bought for Iain. Do you think you can transfer Bridget's tag onto it?"

"Oh, yes, certainly. What a good idea. But what will you do with . . . er . . . *it*?" She motioned toward the package.

"Take it upstairs and put it in under Iain's bed. I'll show it to him later." And settle Bridget's hash at the same time.

Bev nodded, satisfied. We all exchanged conspiratorial smiles. There's just nothing like a marital aid crisis to bring on a bout of female bonding.

Once the men came back in, everyone filed into the sitting room. I was given a seat of honor, propped up on the couch with several pillows, and tucked in with a woolly plaid throw. I had solicited Joanna's help in dressing after

The Dildo Incident—Iain had helped me into a corduroy jumper (that's an American jumper, or British pinafore) before breakfast, but I wasn't about to sit through the festivities in that. I hadn't gone out and specially purchased a lovely rustley taffeta skirt and silk blouse just to sit around in corduroy, no sir!

Once garbed thusly, I sent Joanna off and spent a half hour trying to find where Iain had tucked away my brooch. We hadn't told anyone yet about the engagement—what with me wailing over my arm, there hadn't been time—but Iain mentioned earlier that he would share the news later in the day.

I have to admit that it would take a better person than me to not look forward to telling Bridget the news. Archie was a different matter. He'd be right pissed about it, and I feared he'd ruin Christmas for Iain when he expressed his opinion. So it was with a bit of worry that I pinned, crookedly, the brooch to my blouse, grabbed a cardigan, and walked carefully downstairs.

"Ah, there she is. And what a picture of holiday festiveness in that lovely ensemble. Stop right here, my dear, and let mine eyes behold your glory."

Archie made a rude noise.

"Why, Ewen," I said as I stopped beneath the mistletoe and struck a pose, "how perceptive you are! Flattery will get you anywhere!"

He smiled, paused a minute as he spied the luckenbooth brooch peeking out from beneath the sweater, then leaned forward and kissed me. "I couldn't be happier," he whispered in my ear, then with an arm around my shoulders, marched me past a scowling Archie and helped me get settled on the couch.

The flurry of wrapping paper was almost blinding as presents were opened, admired, and passed around for general approval. I hadn't expected much since I was not a member of the family, but was touched when Joanna and David gave me a lovely soft wool sweater with little pink rosebuds on it. Iain gave me a set of four first edition Dorothy L. Sayers early mysteries. I sniffled over those, since he knows those four books were my favorites, and they couldn't have been easy for him to find.

When Iain unwrapped Bridget's replacement present, the eye of every woman present was upon him.

"Er . . . it's a jumper," he said, holding it up. We women all smiled our approval. Iain didn't know what to do with it.

"Should I wear it, do you think?" he asked me in a worried whisper. "Or would it be making you happier if I were to put it in the kist?"

Like hell he would. I spent a fortune on that jumper, picking out one in lovely shades of red that would set off his dark coloring well. "No, it's quite a nice jumper. I don't think it would be at all polite to just tuck it away. I'm sure she meant you to enjoy it," I lied, knowing full well she meant to embarrass him and humiliate me. Two could play that game, I decided, and set my plans for revenge aside for later. I had more important things to focus on. I had a gift to give Iain!

I saved Iain's present for last, making him and everyone else open all of the other presents first. I had flattened several boxes and used them to disguise the shape of the sword, then wrapped the resulting strapped-together flattened boxes with newspapers, and tied a big red ribbon around it. I brought it out on Christmas Eve and let everyone get a good look at it. I hadn't told anyone what it was, and swore Joanna to secrecy. Once everyone was through opening their presents, I brought Iain his.

He started opening it at the end with the handle, and peeled back the boxes enough to peer into the opening. He looked up, surprise writ all over his handsome face. "It looks like . . ." He peered back into the boxes, then stood up and reached in and pulled out the sword.

Nate and David ooohed appreciably. Archie blinked once or twice, but didn't say anything. Joanna grimaced. Bev passed a hand over her eyes.

I sat across the room, clutching my books to my chest with one hand, chills rolling down my spine at the sight of Iain standing over the carcasses of several freshly killed boxes, the sword held easily in his manly hand, a strong, vibrant warrior with a somewhat perplexed look on his face. It was a hell of a moment, one I wouldn't soon forget.

"There's a leather thingy for it, too," I said, my breath catching in my throat as he ran one hand down the gleaming length of the blade. "Do you like it? Isn't it magnificent? It's a *claidheamh-mór*," I added, as if he wouldn't recognize what it was.

"Aye, that it is," he said, still looking a bit stunned about the eyes.

"It has drooping quillions," I said, pointing them out. "And that's ebony."

"Ebony's a good wood," Nate nodded.

"Sturdy," David agreed.

I didn't take my eyes off of Iain. He made a couple of extremely controlled passes with the sword, then looked up at me, his eyes crinkling as he smiled.

"Ah, love, it's . . . erm . . . a grand gift."

I felt like the floor dropped out from beneath me. He didn't like it! He thought it was stupid! It didn't suit him at all. What had I been thinking? Joanna was right after all. I swallowed the lump that suddenly appeared in my throat, and dug my fingernails into my palm. I'd be damned if I sniveled in front of Archie and everyone.

Iain sheathed the sword and set it against the wall, out of everyone's way. I went out to check on the teakettle, and stood in the kitchen fighting tears.

"It's the second grandest gift I've ever had."

I didn't turn around. He would be upset if he saw I was upset, and I didn't want to ruin his Christmas.

"Well, I'm sorry I couldn't give you the grandest gift."

"You already have, love," he mumbled against my neck, his arm snaking around my waist.

"No, I'm serious, Iain."

"So'm I, love."

I let him turn me around to face him. "'Tis a grand present, Kathie, but not as grand a present as you gave me yesterday."

"I fell down your hill yesterday. I didn't give you anything you didn't already have."

He shook his head and pulled me closer, then held up my left hand and kissed my palm. "Aye, you did. You gave me something I've waited my whole life for. You gave me your heart and your hand and without them, I'd be lost."

His finger traced the hearts of my luckenbooth brooch as his words sank down into my soul.

"I was wrong."

"Wrong about what, love?"

I let him nibble my neck for a moment or two. "I didn't think you were comfortable telling me what you felt, especially about romantic things, but that was the sweetest thing you've ever said to me. Do you really like it?"

He growled softly in my ear and rubbed his hips against mine.

"Not that, I know you like that, I mean the sword. Do you like it?"

"Aye, love, I like it."

"I thought you needed one."

"Verra thoughtful of you."

"Being in the Highlands and all."

"Aye, 'twill come in handy no doubt."

"Marauders," I said, getting into the spirit of his nibbling.

"Feudin' clans," he said, doing things to my nape that made my hair stand on end.

"Sassenachs," I offered, and slid my hands under his jumper.

"Wolves," he suggested, and was just about to investigate my upper hemisphere when there was the noise of a throat clearing politely in the doorway. I peered over his shoulder. Susan was holding back the rest of the family, blocking them from coming into the kitchen.

I really liked her!

Shortly after the present opening the women dispersed to the kitchen to check on the turkey, and begin preparation of the remaining dishes. I tried to offer my one hand as help, but was soundly chastised for interfering, and sent back to the sitting room.

I curled up next to Iain and smirked at Archie, who glared

back at me. I didn't care. I knew I would get my own back later.

Surprising enough, he took the news of our nuptials rather well, with only one little scene. At the time. I didn't know until later that he had what amounted to a temper tantrum privately with Iain.

Dinner was a marvel, and turned out to be perfection. I sat between Iain and Ewen, Iain there to cut things up for me, and looked around the table filled with happiness. I might not have known these people for very long, but we already fit together comfortably. We laughed, we argued, we pulled together. They were family. I started getting a bit maudlin on the thought of family—my family that I was missing, and my new family who was coming to mean so much to me—but thankfully was stopped by Ewen before I turned into a blob of mush before their very eyes.

He rose and looked around the table, then raised an eyebrow at Iain. "No champagne?"

"No."

"Surely this warrants it, little brother?"

"I've whisky."

"Oh, well, then," Ewen nodded, enough having been said. Champagne doesn't stand up to the water of life here in the Highlands. Ewen waited until Iain had passed around the whisky.

"Hey," I nudged him, and frowned at the glass of goat's milk he brought me. "Where's mine?"

"You're drinking milk. You need the calcium."

"A little whisky'll do more for my wrist than milk will."

"It's milk you're drinking, love."

I was about to thin my lips and make a face at him when Ewen rose. "As the eldest, although I hasten to point out it is by no means apparent, member of the family, I take it upon myself to wish each and every one of you a Happy Christmas."

He toasted us. We all lifted our glasses and drank. I sucked off my milk moustache and waited, anticipated, and almost danced in my seat with excitement. Due to the arrangement of the cardigan I had thrown on, no one but Ewen had noticed my luckenbooth brooch.

"And also as head of this family MacLaren, it gives me the greatest pleasure to welcome the newest member. Iain, Kathie, may you both be hale and hearty 'til you're old enough to die, may you both be just as happy as I wish you both to be."

Archie's head swiveled to shoot laser beams of hatred at me. He snapped out an obscenity. Iain, who had leaned over to kiss me, paused for a moment, gave his son a look that I hope to God he never turns on me, and said slowly, "Because this is a happy occasion I'm going to forget you said that, lad." Then he kissed me, and accepted the congratulations of everyone at the table.

Everyone except Archie.

Archie and Susan left on Boxing Day. Their original plans called for them to stay to the twenty-seventh, but Archie was in a foul humor, and Iain was angry with Archie, so all things considered, it was good they left. I thanked Susan for the cloisonné bracelet she had given me in her and Archie's name, and tried my best to apologize for her rush departure.

"It's not your fault," she said softly, watching Archie hurl their luggage into his car. "You have the right to be happy. Best wishes—you and Iain are perfect for each other. Maybe he'll"—she was looking at Archie when she said this—"come around in time."

I doubted it. Iain told me later that Archie had gone off on him, ranting about a midlife crisis and how Iain shouldn't marry me until he, Archie, had a chance to make up what amounted to a prenuptial agreement.

"That's ridiculous," I had snorted.

"Aye, it is." Iain agreed. We were in our bedroom, getting ready for bed. Iain was assisting me in donning Minnie Mouse.

It suddenly dawned on me that Archie viewed me as an impediment to his eventual inheritance.

"Do you think he believes I mean to do him out of his

rightful share of the farm?" I asked once Minnie was pulled down over my head.

Iain was a wee bit distracted, having helped me unhook and remove those garments meant to restrain buoyant parts of my anatomy.

"Iain." I nudged him with my foot. He had a familiar look in his eye. I waved my cast in front of him. "My arm is a bit sore, sweetie."

Instantly he looked contrite for even thinking those thoughts that he had obviously been thinking.

"We were talking about Archie. Do you think he views me as a threat to his future?"

It was Iain's turn to snort. "He'd be a bigger fool than I give him credit for if he does. I'm not a rich man, love, and the boys know that."

"No, not rich in the conventional sense, but you do have a successful sheep farm with almost a thousand sheep. I'm sure Archie feels I'm here to do him out of his share. Either that or he just doesn't like the thought of you remarrying."

Iain plumped up my array of pillows and tucked me in.

"He's always been a moody little bugger. Don't let his comments worry you. He'll come around in time."

"That's what Susan said," I replied without much satisfaction. I continued to gnaw on the problem of Archie for a while, then gave in to the sleepy tug of the painkillers.

Everyone's mood was definitely more jovial without Archie, and it was with a great sense of disappointment that we said farewell on the day after Boxing Day to Ewen, and Joanna's parents.

"Have you set a date?" Bev rolled down her car window to ask. "I hope you'll invite us."

"Of course you're invited." I shivered in my heavy wool coat. "Iain suggested Valentine's Day, so he wouldn't forget it."

She laughed. "That's a wise man you're getting, Kathie."

"Don't I know it!" I smiled and waved as they drove off.

"Alas, parting is never as much pleasure as greeting." Ewen took my one good hand and kissed me, shooting a sly little glance over at his brother. "Just kissing the bride for luck, little man."

Iain, who stands a good four inches taller than Ewen, made shooing motions. "Bugger off, Ewen."

Ewen buggered off, and we were left alone. Mrs. Harris returned to her duties, *tch*ed over my injury, and greeted the news of our engagement with a sour look and a begrudging wish for our happiness in the future. It sounded more like a curse than a congratulation, but I was too elated to care. All I had left to do was tell my mother, then sit back and wait for Bridget to stop by to annoy me to share the news with her. I didn't have long to wait.

My mother took the news well, by now happier that I be married and living halfway across the world than just living with a man she'd never met. By the end of the conversation she had slipped into full mother of the bride mode, and was talking about things like flowers, churches, and whether or not we could drag Great-Aunt Amber to Scotland from sunny Florida, where she was the reigning belle at the Sarasota Retirement Village.

I hadn't the heart to tell her that Iain and I had already decided we were going to be married at a registry office. I figured there was time enough for that later.

Chapter Fifteen

It wasn't until a day or two before Hogmanay that Bridget showed up to torment me and see how Iain liked her gift to him, and in twist of fate that makes me believe whoever watches over us has a tremendous sense of humor, Iain just happened to be wearing the substitute gift that day. I was upstairs having a wee little nap when she arrived. I hadn't been sleeping well since I kept crashing my cast on the nightstand, finally necessitating a return to my side of the bed, but I heard her piercing voice all right once she greeted Iain.

I damn near broke my neck racing down the stairs to see her. Unfortunately, I forgot my apparel, or lack thereof, and burst into the kitchen wearing nothing more than Iain's undershirt and a pair of cotton sleeping shorts. I had on knee socks as well, one of which was up to my knee, the other sagging around my ankle. Couple that with my arm in a cast, sling dangling from my fingers (I didn't want to take the time to put it on), rumpled hair that hadn't been combed since the morning, and, Iain tells me later, sleep lines on my cheek deep enough to moor a trawler, and you have a pretty good idea of what a lovely picture I made.

Bridget looked marvelous in a garnet colored tea-length dress with matching garnet colored boots. It must have cost her a packet, and I will admit to a twinge of jealousy over the outfit. Especially when she burst into peals of biting laughter over my appearance.

Iain helped me on with my sling, then brought a throw in

from the sitting room and tucked it around me as I waved Bridget to a seat at the table.

"I'll take the post out," he offered, gathering up a few bills and letters. "I put the kettle on a minute ago, love. Will you be all right?"

Iain was clearly uneasy at leaving me with Bridget. I wondered if he had told her yet about our engagement, but didn't think he'd had the time.

"I'll be fine. We'll have an early tea when you're back."

Iain shot Bridget a warning look, and began putting on his wellies and mac.

"Oh, Iain darling," Bridget called out, giving me a smug glance. "Before we discuss your latest plan for Kin Aird, do tell me how you liked my little Christmas present."

His brow cleared as he rubbed his red jumper-clad chest. "'Tis lovely, Bridget. I thank you." He smiled happily at me. "Kathie likes it as well."

I closed my eyes and sent up a thank you to whatever deity was responsible for Bridget playing directly into my hands.

Bridget looked shocked for a moment before recovering her composure. "She does?"

"Aye, she says it suits me quite well."

It was Bridget's brow's turn to furrow. "You . . . you think it *suits* him, dear?" she asked me.

"Oh, yes, it's a remarkable fit. Isn't it, Iain? It fits nicely? Like it was made for you? Not too big and not too small, it's just right?"

"Aye, it is." He nodded and pulled his wellies on.

I couldn't resist one last comment. "Yes, we both like your lovely present. I think it does something for Iain. It makes him so . . . so virile looking."

I winked at Iain. He smiled, gave me a quick kiss, and went off to post the mail.

"Virile?" Bridget choked out the word. "You think it makes him look . . . *virile*? Oh, my dear, you are in need of help more than I possibly imagined. Both of you!"

I rose and gathered up two mugs. "Would you mind getting the tea things? I'm afraid I'm a bit handicapped." I waved my cast at her.

Bridget was clearly having trouble coming to grips with our supposed reaction to her present.

"But . . . you *were* there when Iain opened the present, weren't you?"

"Oh yes," I said, thumping down the mugs, and going back to fetch the tea things myself. "We all were. Everyone thought it was a marvelous gift. We made him check the fit right away."

"His . . . *family*?"

I nodded. "All of Iain's family. It was quite a gathering, very enjoyable. I quite felt like one of the family." I set the jug of milk down in front of her. "Which, of course, I will be after Valentine's Day."

Bridget dabbed at the slosh of milk that spilled when I set it down. "Valentine's Day?" she asked in a distracted voice.

I swished hot water around the teapot, dumped it, then added a few careless spoonfuls of tea and filled the rest with hot water. I plopped the teapot down in front of her.

"Yes," I said, savoring the moment. "Valentine's Day. That's the day we've set for our wedding."

She didn't believe me at first. She stared and sputtered, then gulped down a mug of tea and sputtered some more. Finally she got a grip on herself, aided partly, I believe, by my *go ahead and ask Iain* attitude. By the time he returned, she was able to choke out a polished, "So thrilled for you both, darling."

Neither Iain nor I were fooled by her apparent lack of interest in the turn of events, but we both pretended her fingers weren't white with anger as she gripped the table, just as we declined to find anything strange in her immediate change of subject.

"I've been thinking, darling, and I'm just not going to see my way through to falling in with your scheme for Kin Aird. It just won't serve to plant crops on soil that could be better used in another, more profitable, manner."

Iain accepted the cup of tea I handed him. I rounded up some leftover holiday cookies and set them out on a plate

next to Bridget. She ignored them and me both with breathtaking disregard.

"I've told you I'd not have dealings with Tannahill," Iain
replied warily.

She smiled her shark smile and leaned across the table,
allowing the neckline of her garnet dress to gape in a most
slatternly way. Iain, no mere mortal man he, kept his eyes
firmly on her face. I determined to reward such good behavior in a very tangible manner that evening.

"Darling, that is old business. Consider it forgotten." I
poured myself a glass of milk and sat next to Iain, watching
Bridget suspiciously. I was certain she hadn't forgiven and
forgotten as her smooth, silky voice implied. I had seen the
hatred in her eyes, and I knew she wouldn't hesitate to hurt
Iain by any means possible. "Nor do I agree with the plan to
let the land, but if you insist on grazing it, then I suggest we
simply use it ourselves." She picked up a spoon and frowned
at it, polishing it on a napkin.

Iain leaned back in his chair and narrowed his lovely
peaty brown eyes at her. "You said earlier you were against
grazing. You wanted the cash inflow. Why is it you're
changing your mind now?"

She bared her teeth at him in yet another sharp, pointy
smile. "Darling, I'm a woman! I'm allowed to change my
mind!"

"Oh, for the love of—" I bit off the oath and stuffed a
cookie into my mouth. Bridget never missed a beat.

"And as you were so kind as to offer to let me graze the
land for the first three years, then I will do so. I'll have my
flock moved into the parks next week."

Iain pursed his lips in thought for a few moments, then
nodded his head. "Aye, that'll be fine."

Her eyelids dropped to give him a sultry, knowing gaze.
"Ever the gentleman, darling?"

Worry shimmered through me at the emotion hidden behind those grey eyes. Something was wrong here, something
was very wrong, but I didn't know what it was or how to
stop it.

Iain nodded his head and stood up to see her out the door.

I stayed put. Bridget allowed him to help her on with her midnight blue wool cape, then paused dramatically by the door. Her gaze scorched me for a moment before turning back to him. "I have always found chivalry to be grossly overrated."

I let out the breath I hadn't been aware I was holding as she left, reaching for another cookie while Iain walked her out to her car. She was taking unfair advantage of Iain by demanding the first three years of grazing rights on Kin Aird, an offer he had made in a generous—and desperate—attempt to appease her after he nixed the slaughterhouse plan, but that wasn't what bothered me. What worried me, what made the little hairs on the back of my neck stand up in warning, was how lightly we had escaped her wrath.

"She's up to something," I warned Iain when he returned. "It can't be as easy as this. She's not the sort of person to turn the other cheek, and she's certainly not going to settle for the minor dribble of income grazing the land will bring when she could have much more. Iain, I have a bad feeling she's going to try to put something over on you."

"There's naught she can do, love," he shrugged. "She'll have the profits from grazing for three years while I have none—if she's after revenge, the thought of making a profit against me will satisfy her."

"In your dreams! Iain, she's a malicious, vindictive, nasty woman! She's not going to be happy until she has you ground into the mud, with me beneath you."

He smiled a warm, slightly smug male smile. I pointed a finger at it. "Oh, don't you even *think* of telling me I'm just jealous of her!"

He laughed, but didn't deny it. Which was good, because I *was* jealous, but as that had no bearing on this particular situation, I figured it was better left alone. It occurred to me that the time had come to tell Iain just what exactly was lurking under his bed.

"Sweetie, I have a little something to tell you." I patted the chair next to me and waited for him to sit down. "It's about Bridget's gift to you."

He looked down at his jumper. "You're wanting me to not wear it now?"

"No, I think it looks lovely on you. I thought that"—I took a deep breath—"when I bought it."

He looked confused. "What are you saying, love?"

"We—Joanna and Bev and Susan and I—switched presents. This is one I had originally given you, not Bridget."

Iain stood up again. "Why?"

"Because we thought Bridget's present was unacceptable."

He looked a bit peeved. "How would you be knowing what her present was?"

"Joanna opened it and looked ahead of time, on my authority, I should add. And I'm glad she did."

He went still. Iain was no fool. He might not approve of us pulling a bit of jumper over his eyes, but he had a long experience with Bridget. "What was it?"

Another deep breath. "A . . . um . . . marital aid. A really big one."

He digested all of the ramifications of opening such an item on Christmas in front of his family, and his jaw tightened. "Where is it?"

"In a box under our bed. Iain, I should warn you—oh, too late."

I heard him leap up the stairs, thump around in our room, then there was a moment of silence, followed quickly by some of the profanest language I'd ever heard.

He stomped back down the stairs, his eyes furious, the box tucked beneath his arm.

I intercepted him on the way to the door. "Where do you think you're taking that?"

"Stand out of my way, love. I'm going to give Bridget my thanks."

I winced at the way he said *thanks.* "No, Iain, you can't!"

He stopped to look at me. "And why can't I?" he bellowed. "Do ye think I'll be lettin' her insult us in this manner?"

"But we've yanked the rug out from under her already," I reasoned. "See, that's why we substituted the jumper for it.

Now everyone but her believes she's given you a perfectly lovely, and extremely good looking if I do say so myself, jumper, while she believes . . ."

I couldn't help myself, I kept seeing the expression on her face. I started giggling. "While she believes you're happy with the fit of . . . of . . ." I waved my hand at the box. "Of that!"

It was a test, this. Would he see the humor in the situation, or would he go off and be pissed about the entire thing?

I waited. For a whole minute. One of the longest minutes of my life. Things didn't look good there for most of it. I was preparing my apology for interfering when the corner of his mouth twitched. Time for me to move in for the kill. "You see, Iain, it's perfect this way! Everyone admires the gift she gave you, while she thinks we're all depraved, sex-starved maniacs with utterly appalling taste."

He chuckled. Finally!

He started toward the door again.

"Wait, where are you going?"

"You don't think I'll be keeping this?" He looked scandalized.

"No, of course not, although . . ." I nibbled on my lip. "Iain, those things are expensive. Or so I've been told," I added hurriedly. "And this one seems to be a super deluxe model. It has some sort of pump system or hydraulics or something attached. Look, I'll show you."

I started to raise the lid off the box but he slammed it back down.

"I've no need to be seeing that again."

"Fine, we won't gaze upon its rubbery glory, but I think we can squeeze a wee tad bit more revenge out of this whole fiasco."

He liked the thought of more revenge, I could see that. Those Highland warriors didn't hang on to their grudges for centuries without some of it filtering down to their modern-day descendants.

"How?"

"We can sell it. It's probably worth at least forty pounds!"

He looked at me as if he saw bats flying out my ears. "Do

you think I'll be putting an advert in the paper for this monstrosity, then?"

"No, of course not."

"Good." He started back for the door.

"Iain, forty pounds is forty pounds! We could sell it and buy something nice with that money."

Iain may not be the stereotypical thrifty Scot, but he's no fool with money. He stopped and turned around to look at me. "Where would we be selling it, then?"

I smiled. I knew those long hours of online shopping would pay off some day.

"I'll sell it on eBay!"

"No."

"Why not?"

"Someone we know will find out you're selling it."

"I don't see how . . ." The look on his face was unmovable. I quickly decided on an easy solution. "OK, how about this. We'll sell it on the U.S. eBay only. No one will know it's me. It's the perfect plan, eh?"

He hesitated.

"Forty pounds, Iain. We can buy a couple more James Bond tapes or have a really nice dinner out." He looked unconvinced. "Or you could buy that drenching gun attachment you've been mooning over."

That did the trick. Nothing says happiness quite so well as something to worm sheep.

Our trip to my home a week later was not without its moments of Bergman-esque absurdities. Mark had been prevailed upon to keep an eye on things and handle the chores during Iain's absence. Despite my daily nail-biting session, Iain's passport *did* arrive on time, I *did* manage to get us booked on the flight I had wanted, and we *did* make it to Heathrow all in one piece: Iain, his luggage (which was made up mostly of books, the States being, in Iain's mind, sadly lacking in book availability), my luggage (made up of clothes and my laptop), a bag of presents for my family, and one extra box containing *The Gift.* Bridget's gift to Iain.

Why would I bring that along with us? Well, it wasn't

that I had grown attached to the thing, as Cait accused me once she heard I was bringing it with me. The truth was that I had sold it on eBay just as I had promised Iain, and since the person purchasing it wanted to keep the shipping down as low as possible, I figured I would just ship it when we were in Seattle rather than having it go out airmail from Scotland. In addition to which, the thought of what I'd have to write on the customs form was giving me nightmares.

Iain disavowed knowledge of the package and me once he spotted it. I had quite a time keeping him in his seat after I stuffed *The Gift* into the overhead storage. He wanted to sit elsewhere.

"You can't!" I punched him in the arm. "I'm wounded. I need help. I can't even open up my complimentary bag of salted nuts!"

"I'll not be seen entering the country with that thing!"

"You don't have to, I'll carry it with my luggage. I don't care what customs thinks of me, I just want to send it off to its new home."

Iain muttered what he'd like to do with it, but as it involved Bridget, I thought it best to pretend deafness.

There's just nothing quite so fun as traveling with your arm in a cast. For some reason, and Iain claimed it was because *The Gift* was cursed, I managed to set off the alarm at every security checkpoint I went through. That meant the security people had to bring out the wand and go up and down me checking for bombs, nuclear missile heads, and what have you. All of them viewed my cast as a suspicious object, clearly a cleverly contrived false one whose sole purpose was to smuggle contraband substances. By the time I made it through the Inverness, London, and Seattle airports, I was ready to rip my cast off.

Iain was ready to toss out *The Gift*. He made me mail it that afternoon, despite the fact that I was suffering from severe jet lag and arm rot from where an itch had set in beneath the cast.

"And here we are," I announced as we arrived at my

apartment, throwing open the door with a flourish. "Home sweet home. Mind your head, this doorway is a bit low."

Iain ducked as he entered the apartment—it was part of an attic in an old house that had been converted to an up-scale flower shop—and looked around. "Ah. It's a wee bit small."

I looked around my apartment. Although I knew full well it was small, it hadn't seemed quite so claustrophobic before I moved into the Highlands. "Um . . . yes, well, there was just me and the birds. I'll just set *The Gift* here and you can put that bag over there. Can you bring in the others all right? Be sure to watch—oh I'm so sorry, Iain. Let me look. Did you break the skin?"

Eventually he hauled all of our luggage in without further concussing himself on my door. I called my mother to let her know we had arrived, and would have given in to the jet lag and crashed, but Iain drove me out to the nearest post office so I could mail *The Gift.*

We spent the afternoon and evening going through the apartment, making lists of what I wanted to take with me (books), what I'd give away (furniture not worth selling), and what I'd leave with my mother to sell (most of my electronic stuff).

The following day was D-Day, the day we drove out to see my mother and whatever family members she had rounded up for the formal Viewing of the Scot. My mother lived in a rural community within a few hours' drive of Seattle. I hadn't thought anything about that, but immediately upon setting out the drawbacks became apparent.

"Hmmm," Iain would say as we passed a big farm. I could see he was scanning the distant fields for little white blobs. Uh oh. Trouble ahead. Sheep farmer in his native element.

"Um, Iain, we are on a bit of a schedule. I know you're finding this all fascinating—heaven knows I gawked plenty when you drove me up to your farm—but I'm afraid all of that noise of honking behind us is indicative of a line of four . . . no wait, there's two more . . . six cars that want you to continue driving."

Iain *tch*ed and waved my nudge away. "They can wait for a few more minutes. I'd like to take a look at that cradle up close."

I looked to where he was pointing. Standing next to a barn was a drafting race with a sheep cradle parked next to it. A race is a long narrow pen with a variety of gates that is used to sort the sheep, one at a time, into holding pens. The cradle is used to flip sheep onto their backs so you can tickle their tummies.

"Yes, but Iain, you're holding up traffic. Maybe we can stop and see the sheep cradle on the way home." I had to promise him we'd make time to stop and see if the farmer was willing to talk shop with him just to get him moving again.

We made it to my mother's house just in time to be greeted by my sister Mo, a woman who had no inhibitions whatsoever.

"Where's the kilt?" she queried Iain as she opened the door of my mother's house. Her question took him by surprise. He looked at me. I looked back at him and shrugged. I had warned him how women were about a man in a kilt.

"It's at home," he replied. "Along with my sporran and bagpipes. You'd be Maureen, then?"

No wonder I love the man. Anyone who can take Mo down a peg is a right Joe in my book.

Mo knows when she's been bested. "Well, as long as you plan on trotting them out when we come for the wedding, we'll let you off the hook this once. Yes, I'm Mo." She leaned around him to peer at me. "You're right, Kathie. That accent could drop a cow."

Elder sisters. They live to embarrass.

My mother was lying in wait for us in the kitchen, making me wonder once again why so much of life seems to take place in kitchens. "Kathie! Iain! There you are!"

She hustled toward us, got a good look at Iain, and stopped dead. "Oh, but you're not wearing your kilt?"

I sniggered. Iain managed not to roll his eyes and greeted her politely. We chatted for a few minutes while my sister made a hurried call to her husband, instructing him to pack up the kids and come over immediately, as well as warning him that Iain was kiltless. We were having dinner with my family, and my mother had pulled out all of the stops, inviting all three of my siblings and their families, my Aunt Grace, Grandpa Lewis (Mom's stepfather), and assorted cousins. Mo had arrived early to help with the dinner.

"Won't you sit down over here next to me, Iain," my mother yelled from ten feet away.

I made an oh my god, my mother is *so* embarrassing face. "Mom, he's Scottish, not deaf."

She dropped the volume of her voice a smidgen. "I just thought it would be nice if I enunciated very clearly so he can understand my foreign accent."

"Och," Iain said with a wicked smile, sitting on the loveseat next to my mother. "Ye need'na be worryin' yer haid aboot that, Carrrrrrrol. Kathie's been whisperin' those sweet nothin's in mah air so lang, ah've lairned t'understand the lass."

Mother leaned forward, her brow wrinkled with concentration as she tried to follow what he was saying.

"You big oatcake," I poked at his shoulder, and sat on the arm of the loveseat next to him. "Mother, Iain does not talk like Groundskeeper Willie. Don't encourage him, or he'll just continue to gargle those Rs."

"Kathie!" my mother scolded. "I'm sure she meant no ethnic slurs, Iain. You wouldn't know it to listen to her, but I did raise her properly."

Ethnic slurs? Where did she get this stuff?

"Hello? Is Kathie here?" My brother Max and his wife Denise had evidently arrived. Denise's voice was clearly audible all the way across the house. "Max, you take the baby. Hi Mo. Is Kathie's fiancé here? Is he as gorgeous as she described?"

No one in my family, even those members related only by marriage, had ever mastered the skill of speaking in a conversational tone.

"He's more gorgeous, and he can hear every word, so don't be saying bad things about haggis," I yelled back. Iain

shot me a look. I shrugged again. No use in trying to be polite around my family.

Denise burst into the living room, a casserole dish in
hand, eyes wide and excited. Her face fell when she saw
Iain. "No kilt?"

Chapter Sixteen

My family is a little over the top. They're nice people individually, it's just when you get them in a herd that they can be ever so slightly overwhelming, which is why I was concerned about Iain taking one look at them and calling off the wedding. He wouldn't, of course, but I knew in my heart that was only because he realized we would be living half a world away.

I mulled this over while my Aunt Grace was saying grace. No one in my family is particularly religious, but Aunt Grace, feeling it a personal responsibility that she live up to the name her parents gave her, insisted on saying a blessing every time there's a family gathering. Unfortunately, she's an agnostic, and has no real idea of what makes up a grace. Hers are always an embarrassing combination of family scuttlebutt, her hopes, and one or two pointed reprimands. The prayer, such as it was, formed an address to a mysterious collection of *graces* whom my aunt wouldn't define, but insisted had to be better than just one god.

"And we'd like to thank the graces that our niece Kathie has returned to our familial arms once again after living in a matrimonial state with a man who was not lawfully her husband. We are particularly happy that our family is grown by one more in the form of Iain MacLaren, who we think is a fine man despite the fact that he disappointed us by not wearing his kilt. We'd like to ask the graces for kind thoughts and good wishes for Bradley as he takes his driver's license test for the fifth time, especially since he's taken the written test so many times he should have it memorized by now."

We all looked up hopefully. Aunt Grace had been droning on now for a good three or four minutes, and the roast was cooling. Grace, however, wasn't going to miss this marvelous opportunity to let every member of the family have their share in the graced spotlight.

"We'd also like to thank the graces that Karen hasn't gotten blood poisoning from all of those piercings, although the graces only know what her parents were thinking when they agreed to the nose ring."

Iain snickered softly. I pinched him to keep him quiet. If Aunt Grace was interrupted, she was liable to start over again. She ran through the rest of the youngest generation, and then turned her attention to the older members.

"It should be mentioned as well that my own son Gene needs the graces' particular help with that little problem he's been having in the bedroom, and, since I'm not getting any younger and he's not making me grandmother, I'd appreciate it if the graces could see to it that his wallop packs a little more punch."

My cousin Gene moaned and glared at his wife. "Fer chrissake, Darla, if you tell my mother anything again I swear I'll cut off your Nordstrom's card."

Iain snickered again. This time I was snickering with him. Mo cast a worried eye at Aunt Grace and hushed us up.

"And lastly," an audible sigh rippled down the table, "we'd like to thank the graces for keeping Dad off the sauce, which he knows full well is for his own good, but we ask the graces if they'd please lend a little assistance in keeping him from trying to pay street people to buy liquor for him. Amen."

Uh oh. I turned to my right. "Grandpa Lewis isn't supposed to be drinking?" I asked my eldest brother, Brother. His real name was Edward, but everyone, including my mother and his wife, called him Brother.

"No, he's taking some blood pressure medicine that alcohol counteracts."

Damn. I turned to my left. "Iain, did you give Grandpa Lewis that extra bottle of whisky you brought?"

Iain flinched slightly as he complied with my mother's bellowed order for him to pass his plate. "Aye, I did. He seemed right pleased with it."

I just bet he was. I made a mental note to have my mother wrestle the bottle away from him, and frowned at Brother's daughter Karen before tackling my food.

"We got off lightly, you know," I told Iain after dinner, when we were taking advantage of the dark spot behind the stairs. "Aunt Grace has been known to dredge up events dating back to the time we were in diapers."

Iain chuckled, and nibbled on a sensitive spot on the nape of my neck. I was about to return the favor when I spied Karen lurking in the background.

Karen was sixteen, had two-toned hair, a nose ring, and ears bristling with earrings. I hated to think of what else she had pierced; Brother wouldn't answer that question, he just shuddered and said it was best I didn't know.

"Your Lolita is watching," I murmured in Iain's ear as he slipped a hand inside my blouse.

"Oh, bloody . . ." He removed his hand and turned around to face Karen.

"Oh, hi, Uncle Iain . . . that is, Iain . . . I, um, wonder if I could ask you a little more about sheep? Because they're like so totally awesome, you know? And my friend Sukie, she's been to Europe and all and I just think it's like so totally cool that you live in Scotland, and I'm sure that if I asked Brother he'd totally let me come and visit you. And Kathie." I was clearly an afterthought. She paused for a moment and added hopefully, "And that would be, like, *so* totally rufous! Sukie would just go like all Springer about it!"

I suppressed a smile. It seemed Karen was just as susceptible to Iain's wonderful knee-melting voice as I was. I thought her infatuation with him was cute. She followed him around all evening, chatting with him about anything that came to her mind, and when she wasn't chatting, she just sat and stared at him. Iain found the attention embarrassing and avoided meeting her eye.

"Perhaps Brother will let you come over for the wedding," I said, slipping my good arm through Iain's. Karen looked confused for a moment.

"You know, our wedding. The one at which Iain and I will be married. *That* wedding."

"Oh, right. Yeah, that would be like sooooo totally cool." She giggled and gazed at Iain with a fervent look of utter adoration.

"Come along, you great big Scottish heartbreaker, you," I teased him, and we went off to investigate the dessert possibilities.

My brother Brother is thirteen years older than me. I'm the baby in the family, the latecomer, the one my mother claims showed up with the milk one morning. She also claims I was conceived when she fell in love with an Italian demonstrator at the Seattle World's Fair, but since I was born before the Fair, I disputed that fact.

My family was pretty much like anyone else's—full of crackpots, boobs (Lesser and Greater), and eccentric persons you couldn't help but worry over.

"So, what did you think?" I asked Iain after we had returned to my apartment from the family dinner. He was trying to make himself comfortable on my bed, which wasn't easy considering it was a small double bed that was not meant for a man who stood six inches over six feet tall.

"I'm thinking I'm glad we're not going to have to sleep on this bed for more than a few nights."

I brought a chair around to take up the excess in the feet region.

"Comfy?"

"Aye, if I don't move."

"That's no problem," I said, rolling over and plopping myself down on top of him. "I'll keep you anchored."

"You'll be the one being anchored if you squirm like that again, love."

I stopped squirming and rested my chin on my good hand. "A tempting offer, and one to which I will give my utmost attention momentarily, but first let me ask you what you thought of the family."

He shifted us over to the center of the bed. "Ah, they're an interesting lot."

I sighed. He meant strange and was just too polite to say that word.

"I'll be admitting that there are a few customs your family has that are bewildering me."

I tipped my head back and admired his manly chin for a moment. "Such as?"

"There's the matter of the starters."

"Starters? You mean the *hors d'oeuvres*?"

"Aye. Do you know what your niece was offering around to everyone?"

He sounded appalled. I mentally reviewed the appetizers that Karen had grudgingly agreed to serve. There were cheese puff things, some of Mo's Special Weenies (so called by her son, a name that stuck), assorted crackers and dips, Aunt Grace's egg salad on Melba toast, and other typical appetizers. I didn't recall seeing anything that would horrify a man who had been known to eat the organs of a sheep cooked in that same sheep's stomach.

"No, what?"

"Horse's ovaries! I've seen caviar, love, but never horse's ovaries. I'm thinking the Scots have taken a bloodying over haggis for no reason when you Yanks eat horse's ovaries."

I started to giggle.

"And what's so amusing, I'd like to know? That sheep-eyed niece of yours shoved a plate of bits and dabs in my face and said 'Want a horse's ovary? Those ones are the best,' and pointed at something that looked like chipped ovary on toast."

I laughed even harder. "Oh, god, Iain. I'm sorry, I forgot about the horse's ovaries. I should have warned you." I whooped a few more times, then tried to wipe back the tears. Iain had a decidedly disgruntled look on his face.

"They're not horse's ovaries, sweetie. My mother can't speak French, you see, not even remotely, and since she can't pronounce *hors d'oeuvre,* she calls them horse's ovaries."

Iain stared at me for a minute, then closed his eyes. "It's a good thing we came visiting *after* I'd promised to wed you, love."

"Oh, they're not that bad," I giggled, and tucked my head under his chin. "At least none of them have cast aspersions about your morals."

"Aye, there is that."

"And I don't have any old flames hanging around to give us grief."

"Mmmm." Iain's breathing started to deepen.

I listened to it for a few minutes, letting my own breathing slow to match his. "There is, of course, my ex-husband, but that shouldn't be a problem. He swears the divorce is legal."

Iain muttered something unintelligible.

"I'm sure it's legal. Kevin wouldn't have remarried if it wasn't."

Famous last words, those.

The following morning was our day for receiving visitors. The first to show up was Brother. He arrived on the way to work, interrupting Iain's traditional morning greeting to me. I was not best pleased.

Neither was Iain. He stopped in midthrust, glared at the door over the top of my leg that rested on his shoulder, and spat something in Gaelic.

"What? Iain, you can't stop now!" I wailed, wriggling my hips and tightening my inner muscles around him. He groaned and dipped his head down to plunder my mouth as he resumed his impression of a really, really talented piston engine.

Another spate of knocking stopped him. He lowered my legs from his shoulders and started to disengage the piston.

"Ignore it," I pleaded, locking my legs around his hips while tugging him down onto me. "It's just the neighbors. Or someone's TV. Or moths."

"Moths?" His eyes closed as I flexed my legs and reached around to fondle that part of him that he enjoyed having fondled. He shuddered and gave a wordless groan as he lunged back where I wanted him.

"Really big moths," I whispered breathlessly, moving my hips to meet his thrusts, praying whoever it was outside the door would take the hint and go away.

The front door shook as the evil person on the other side pounded a fist on it.

"Bluidy hell," Iain snarled, and pulling away, sprang out of bed and stalked over to the door.

"Um . . . Iain . . ." I started to point out he was sans clothing, but didn't get the words out in time. I have a very small apartment and he has a very long stride.

"This'd better be bleedin' important," he snarled as he threw the door open.

Brother looked stunned at being greeted by the sight of a naked, aroused, *enraged* two-hundred-and-forty-pound Scot. "I hope to God you're on the way to the bathroom with that," he snapped, waving toward Iain's personal equipment. "I'd hate to have to challenge you over my sister's virtue!"

"Eeek!" I squealed and dived back under the blankets as he pushed past Iain into my dining room/living room/bedroom, forgetting for a moment that I was not seventeen years old and caught rounding third base with the neighbor boy. I peeked over the top of the blankets. "Brother, what on earth are you doing here? And what are you yammering about my virtue for?"

"Be quiet, Kathie, I'll handle this. I'm the head of the family, if you recall."

Oh no, he was going to go off on one of his chivalrous bouts.

"We're betrothed," Iain pointed out, his hands on his adorable naked hips. "Beyond that, what we do is none of your affair."

"Right!" I chimed in, feeling around under the blankets for any sort of garment. "So bugger off, Brother."

"Kathie! I'll thank you to stay out of this. This is between me and this . . . this . . ." Brother eyed Iain from his ears to his toes. "This lout who is clearly bent on besmirching the good name of Williams."

"Like hell he is!" Outraged, I sat up, then remembered my own state of dishabille, and yanked the sheet out and over me in toga fashion. "Iain's right, Brother. What we do is none of your business. I'm thirty-seven years old, if you recall—"

"You're still my little sister!" he bellowed and turned back to Iain. "For God's sake, man, cover that up!"

"I happen to like him like that—" I started to object, stepping carefully off the bed.

"Go and put your clothes on, love," Iain ordered. "If your brother's wanting to say something to me, he can. I'm listening."

He was also standing in an aggressive posture, hands fisted, eyes dangerous, dangly bits . . . er . . . not dangling. The very picture of a righteously outraged man who had been interrupted while about to grab the brass ring, so to speak.

"I'm not talking to you while you're waving that around!" Brother retorted, glaring at Iain's nether region.

"Brother, for God's sake, will you just get out!"

"If you've something to say, Edward, say it. Else I'll be asking you to leave."

"You can't order me out of my own sister's apartment! And don't call me Edward," Brother shouted (he hates his name).

"I'll not be calling you Brother, if that's what you're thinking," Iain bellowed in return.

"Why not, everybody else does, even my own children!" roared Brother.

"Oh, for heaven's sake," I said in disgust, and grabbing my bathrobe, stormed off to the bathroom. I could hear the two of them shouting at each other about me, Brother's lack of discipline over his own children, and oddly enough, honor.

Brother was a professor at a local university specializing in medieval history, one who spent long hours engrossed in medieval culture and lore. His greatest love was the chivalric songs and stories of ages thankfully past, and he had long annoyed his two sisters by insisting that we adhere to an outdated code of behavior. Hence his reference to virtue and honor. I donned my bathrobe, had a quick one-handed wash, and went out to get rid of my brother.

Iain was a pretty placid guy. He got annoyed about things, but I hadn't seen him really angry but once or twice. As he stood, starkers, and faced down my idiot brother, I could see that he hadn't really lost his temper yet. He was just a bit annoyed at being rudely interrupted and yelled at, but he was on his way to true anger, and that was something I wanted to avoid.

Luckily, Brother yanked his head into the present long enough admit he didn't have a leg to stand on with regards to arguments about my virtue and honor, and came to the point of his unexpected and ill-timed visit.

"We're all going to the waterfront this afternoon. In honor of Tom Jones, here."

"Tom Jones was English," I pointed out, and went to put some water on for Iain's tea.

"Well, Roy Rogers, then." Roy Rogers? I think he meant Rob Roy. I snickered as I hunted through my cupboards for tea. I thought I had an ancient package leftover from when a tea-drinking friend visited a few years back. "The point being that this strapping bit of Celtic manhood is the guest of honor, and you'd both better be there or Mom'll have your hide. Both of them. Speaking of which, I've seen just about enough of his, so I'll be on my way."

"Wait a minute!" I wasn't going to allow us to be shang-haied into some jaunt about town when we had other and better things to do. "No one asked us if we wanted to go to the waterfront. We don't want to go. We want to stay here and—"

Brother eyed that part of Iain's anatomy that was still happy, and interrupted me. "Oh, I think I get the drift of what you'd rather do, but you're going to have to keep your hands off of each other long enough to make Mom happy. One o'clock. Ivar's. Be there."

With one last frown at Iain's personal equipment he left.

"Well, hell," I said, and slammed down a mug. "I'm sorry, Iain, it looks like we'll have to go play touristas."

He scratched at the scar on his ribs. "It's just for one day, love. Your family wants to see you—I can share you for a wee bit."

"I'd rather not be shared, thank you. Oh well, maybe we'll go to the coast tomorrow."

"Your movers are coming tomorrow."

Blast. He was right. I had arranged for a company to come in and pack up those things I wasn't taking with me. Iain went off to take a shower while I slammed a few things around in my minuscule kitchen.

"Kathie? You decent? It's me."

Eek! Not my landlord! I looked down at my bathrobe and did a mental shrug. He'd seen me in less.

"I'm as decent as I'm getting with one arm in a cast. Come on in."

My apartment, being part of the attic, had a cobbled together sort of layout. There was a teeny tiny hallway opening directly up into the one main room which held my bed, table, bookcases, a few chairs, and so on. Off this room was a postage stamp–sized kitchen. Directly across from the entrance to the kitchen was the bathroom (also postage stamp–sized).

My landlord, a thin guy with receding dishwater blond hair and a friendly *Don't I remind you of an adorable puppy?* smile took the three steps down the hallway to speak with me as I stood in the kitchen. As he did so, Iain opened the bathroom door to tell me he couldn't hear what I had said because the water was running. He was still naked, although parts of him were no longer happy.

Iain frowned at my landlord. My landlord smiled at Iain. I reached for another mug.

"Kevin, this is my fiancé, Iain. Iain, this is Kevin, my landlord."

Iain grabbed a towel and wrapped it around his waist, then stuck out his hand.

Kevin shook it happily. "Iain! It's nice to meet you. I'm also Kathie's ex-husband, but I expect she told you that."

Whoops! Guess I forgot to mention one or two things.

* * *

An ex-husband might appear to be a hard thing to forget, but Kevin had been my landlord for much longer than he had been my husband, so it really wasn't that odd, in my mind at least, that I had neglected to mention the subject to Iain. In *his* mind . . . well, he had other opinions about the situation. Trust came into it, I found out, and trust—I knew from past experience—was not an easy thing to give.

I trusted Iain. I had always trusted him, at least once I knew that he shared the same feelings I did, but I didn't know then just how much I trusted him.

"I should probably explain about Kevin," I said in a hurried whisper. Iain and I were in the kitchen, alone. Kevin was sitting on the edge of my bed, watching TV. "We met in high school, and were married two months after graduation. We separated about three months after that, and our divorce was final before I turned nineteen. The first divorce, that is. It turns out it didn't actually take because Kevin hadn't dotted some *I* or crossed some *T,* and I was too naive to know that one is supposed to receive a *final* divorce decree."

I took a deep breath. Iain continued to frown at me.

I frowned back. "You needn't look at me like that, you knew I was married before."

One glossy brown eyebrow rose.

"Oh, all right, I admit I should have remembered to tell you that he was my landlord, but it just never came to mind."

"Are you really divorced, then?" Iain asked.

"Oh, yes, *now*. It all got straightened out when Kevin's new wife, a charming woman named Gail, was pregnant with their first child. That's when Kevin's lawyer, who was dealing with a trust fund set up by his parents, noticed that the final divorce never went through. Fortunately, Kevin and I had remained friends, so there was no problem in getting the divorce finalized and Kevin married to Gail a few hours before she went into labor. When I moved back to Seattle, Kevin kindly offered me the tiny attic apartment over Gail's flower shop."

Iain didn't say anything to that, just rubbed his jaw.

"I've been e-mailing him from Scotland every couple of weeks, keeping him apprised of my intentions, and asked him to drop by to meet you, and to get all the info from me about vacating the apartment."

Iain turned and looked out over the counter that opened into the living area. He eyed Kevin warily. Kevin, deciding our private little confab must be over if we were looking at him, popped up and chatted merrily about his daughters and wife, how my trip was, and how he had enjoyed seeing *Braveheart*. I knew the *Where's your kilt*? question was next on Kevin's tongue, so I hauled him over to the loveseat and told him to sit while I wrote out instructions regarding the movers, Iain's address, etc.

"Kathie," Iain said quietly as I was digging through my desk trying to find a working pen.

"Just a second, Iain. I know I have a pen here, I have millions of pens. I'm always stumbling over them, but would I have one when I need one? Oh no, not then!"

"Kathie," Iain's voice dropped in pitch. That got my attention.

"What?"

"Ye might be wantin' ta poot on some clothin' noo, aye?"

Ooops. He was a bit more upset than I had first thought. I smiled at Kevin. "One moment, please. Iain, sweetie, might I have another word with you?"

"Aye, I'd be likin' a few more with you, too."

We adjourned to the bathroom. It held us both, just barely, but offered more privacy than the kitchen.

"What's the matter?" I asked Iain as soon as the door was closed. "You're not jealous of Kevin are you? Because if you are," I continued without allowing him to answer, "you're nuts. There's nothing to be jealous of. Kevin is a friend—I told you I was still friends with him."

"You never told me he was liable to walk in on you whenever he pleased. That's more than a wee friendship."

I got all huffy for a minute over what he was implying, then reason raised a finger and pointed out that Iain was not overly possessive, and thus there must be something behind his distress.

I pushed him to the only available seat and stood between his knees. "OK, mister, just what's this about?"

He frowned and crossed his arms over his bare chest. Not a good sign.

It took me a while to pry it out of him. I had to pop my head out of the door twice and tell Kevin that we'd be just a few minutes longer. Kevin didn't care. He'd found my stash of M&Ms and was happily watching Ren and Stimpy.

"Iain, I know you're not the jealous type," I said, exasperated after fifteen minutes of going around in circles with him. "So what is it about Kevin being my landlord that is bothering you so much?"

"I don't care if he owns the whole bleeding town," Iain fumed, his chin obstinate. "I'm thinking a woman wouldn't allow such liberties as letting a man walk in on her whenever he pleases unless she wants to encourage him."

I was still confused. He didn't make any sense.

"Do you think we're still sleeping together, is that it?"

He stared at me for a moment. "No, I don't. You said you haven't since you left him, and I trust you."

Warning bells went off in my head. Trust. That was clearly at the heart of the issue, and that could go back to only one thing—his first wife, Mary.

I put my hand on his cheek and said the words I had no idea I'd be repeating later. "Iain, I'm not Mary. I won't treat you like she did. I won't betray you, ever."

I didn't know why I found it hard to believe Iain still carried around scars from his marriage to Mary. I guess it was because my own ended so amicably that I forgot not everyone was so lucky. Despite his reticence in expressing his emotions, Iain was a man whose feelings ran very deep, and I knew Mary's betrayal of him with a man she had been engaged to before marrying him had cut him to the bone.

Trust was not an easy thing to give to anyone, and it was even more difficult when you've given it and had it abused. Iain said he trusted me, and I think for the most part he did, but I suspected there was a little tiny bit of him that was holding back, watching me, waiting to see what I would do when given the opportunity to deceive him.

It was to that small unsure part that I said simply, "Iain, I love you more than anyone I've ever loved before, more than anyone I ever will love. You're everything to me. I will never hurt you. Oh, my Iain, my sweet Iain, *tha gaol agam ort.*"

He didn't say anything to that, just pulled me up close and leaned his bristly cheek against my breast. I wrapped my arms around him.

Trust was not an easy thing to give, but I knew Iain was trying.

By the fourth day of our trip to Seattle, we were both ready to go home. This came as a bit of a revelation to me— not that I wanted to leave, but that Seattle was no longer home to me.

Home wasn't a comfortable, if tiny, apartment; home was Iain and dogs and sheep and a drafty house with a crotchety charwoman. Home was the place we curled up together at night before the fire to read, home was where we argued in the barn over the cat beds I made, home was where Iain chased me around the house in payback for tickling him. Home was were we argued and laughed and cried and made love. Home was where I woke up lying on Iain, listening to his heart beat, trying to separate it from mine but thankfully not succeeding.

"I don't belong in Seattle anymore," I told him. "I am just another tourist, like you, only I have a few bits of baggage to be rid of."

He just looked smug, and although he didn't come right out and say I told you so, he did agree that he was looking forward to going home as much as I was. But first I had to take care of the one last important task.

I had to break my mother's heart.

We drove out to her house, stopping twice along the way so Iain could talk to farmers. The first place we stopped had an owner who was very suspicious of Iain's motives, and kept asking what it was he wanted to sell. Iain gave up trying to talk sheep and we hit the road again. The second farm he spotted (the man had an uncanny ability to see sheep at great distances) was a small livestock farm that seemed to have just about everything—cows, sheep, pigs, llamas, and even emus.

"Maybe you'd better let me do the talking," I mentioned as we pulled up with a flourish to a small cadre of barking dogs. "I thought that guy at that last place was ready to pull out his shotgun when you insisted you just wanted to find out what sort of castrator he used. I think a woman's light touch is what's needed here."

Iain just grunted and carefully unfolded his legs from the car. He snapped an order to the barking dogs, who surprised me by obeying. I guessed there was something universally recognizable in an authoritative voice, no matter what the command.

A blond-haired woman who was probably in her late twenties opened the door, a chubby baby balanced on one hip, his face covered in what I sincerely hoped was yellow baby food.

I explained that Iain was visiting from Scotland for a short time and was interested in exchanging ideas with fellow farmers. The woman's pale gray eyes grew rounder and rounder with each word until she stood there, oblivious to the baby blowing yellow bubbles all over the side of her T-shirt. She stared at Iain as if he were God himself come down to have a quick jaw.

"You're from Scotland?" she asked finally. "*The* Scotland?"

"I only know of the one," he answered, and chucked the baby under his yellow chin.

Her eyes got even bigger. I thought they might pop right out and tried to recall my first aid training, but when the look took on a familiar glint, I relaxed. Everything would be OK. I recognized that look in her eye. It was the kilt look.

"Scotland like in *Highlander*?"

Iain gave me one of the *here we go again* rolls of the eye. "Aye, we live in the Highlands."

"Oh my gosh!" the woman said, gasping. "Oh my gosh. Wait till I tell Jim! We *love Highlander*! Jim wants to get one of those big swords so he can learn how to use it just like Duncan! Oh my gosh, I can't believe you're really standing here!"

"You'll notice he's not wearing a kilt," I pointed out helpfully. "However, he *does* have a claymore."

Iain grabbed me with one hand and hauled me over next to him. "What my fiancée is trying to say is that we're on a wee bit of a schedule, and we're wondering if your husband might be about to talk with us?"

"Oh!" she squealed and did a little excited dance. "Oh, Jim will be thrilled to meet you! Just thrilled! A real Highlander!"

The baby squealed with her and chuckled to himself as he was jogged up and down. I watched his mother's antics with a worried eye. I hadn't had much experience with babies, but I knew that they sometimes exploded if you shook them up after eating. I didn't want to be around if that happened.

"Um, is Jim around? As in nearby?"

"Oh!" She jumped again. The baby squealed again too. I backed up a couple of steps. He looked to me like he was going to blow. Suddenly she stepped to the side and bellowed, *"Jiiiiiiiiiiiiiim! Jiiiiiiiiiiiiiim!"*

A slight man in a Pearl Jam T-shirt and dirty jeans appeared in the doorway of a barn. She waved him over, and soon Iain was being invited to see the barn, examine the livestock, try Cyndi's cream cheese raspberry coffee cake (for which she won a ribbon at a fair), and to answer hundreds of questions about the Highlands, Highlanders in general, and the historical aspects of Scotland that interested them the most: military history and swords for Jim; clothes and food for Cyndi.

Two hours later we managed to escape, but only after exchanging addresses and promising to visit them if we ever came to the area again. I also had a sizeable chunk of Cyndi's coffee cake and a blob of dried baby goo where Charles the baby had drooled on my blouse.

"It was wonderful meeting you," Cyndi gushed as we got into the car. "I'm so glad you stopped by. Although we were wondering—"

She looked at Jim. He looked back at her. They both looked at Iain.

"Why *aren't* you wearing your kilt?"

When we arrived at my mother's house, we were an hour late. She greeted us with that worried mother look, and read us both the riot act for making her envision all sorts of hideous accidents. Iain, who knew what I was about to do, promptly made himself scarce.

"Mom, I have some bad news for you."

"Oh my god! I knew it! When's the last time you had a pap smear?"

"This isn't about pap, mom, it's about Iain and—"

"Good lord, when's the last time he had a prostate exam?"

"Mother!"

She eyed my bosom critically. "You had a mammogram last year, didn't you?"

"Yes, as a matter of fact—"

She clutched my forearm. "Iain doesn't have mad cow disease, does he? Working with all those sheep?"

I stared at her. "They're sheep, Mom, not cows. How could they get mad cow disease?"

"Sheep aren't stupid, Kathie! If they wanted to get mad cow disease and give it to Iain so you couldn't marry him after months of living together, I'm sure they could do it."

"Yes, Mom, sheep *are* stupid. Very stupid; trust me on this, I know. Sheep are—" I stopped. What the hell was I doing arguing over the intelligence of sheep? I took a deep breath. "Iain doesn't have mad cow disease, and neither do I, if that's what you're about to ask next. It's just that we're expecting—"

My mother leaped up from the table with a shriek. "You're pregnant!" she bellowed. That brought Iain into the room at a run.

"Didn't I *tell* you to use protection? When will you listen to me? I don't just tell you these things to hear myself talk!"

"I'm not pregnant," I reassured her—and Iain. "Mom, if you would just sit down and listen to me for a minute, I'll be happy to tell you what the problem is."

Iain took one assessing glance at the situation, and decided he'd be better off in the living room with my mother's two cats and a book on gardening.

"It's nothing to do with my health. Or Iain's health," I said before she could interrupt again. "It's to do with the wedding."

"Oh, saints preserve us, he's already married! I knew it! Didn't I tell you to check him out before you shacked up with him? Honest to Pete, Kathie, you don't have the common sense God gave a gnat!"

I refrained from grinding my teeth. She was prone to dramatics, a fact with which I was very familiar. "No, Mom, Iain's not married."

She gasped and clutched at her chest. "Dear heaven, don't tell me that second divorce Kevin arranged didn't take either?"

"No, Mother, neither of us is married. I just want to talk to you about the wedding—"

"Don't tell me you're planning on pulling an Aunt Sissy!"

My family was very big on weddings. My mother was one of six daughters, all of whom argued and bickered amongst themselves, but there was one thing that they all agreed on, one thing that bonded them together: weddings. It was my mother's everlasting shame that three of her children eloped, and the fourth, my sister Mo, married in Germany without familial presence. She had never been able to hold up her head about this to her sisters, and for years I was her only hope. I took another deep breath and prepared to shatter that hope.

"No, Mom, I'm not going to convert to Buddhism and be married in Nepal. I just want to tell you that Iain and I have decided that we're not going to have a big wedding."

She looked relieved as she gently smacked my hand. "Katherine Anne, don't you ever scare me like that again! Mercy, if it's just a modest wedding you want, that's fine with me. We'll limit the guest list to just family." She thought for a moment. "And Iain is welcome to invite a few people as well."

"That's awfully generous of you," I replied, wondering if perhaps my mother hadn't been right about me having been left with the milk years ago. It just didn't seem possible that I could share her genes. "Um . . . we were actually thinking of having a small wedding. Quite a small wedding. Just a few close family members . . . at a registry office."

I almost ducked when I said those last words. My mother froze with a coffee cup midway to her mouth. "What?"

I squirmed. She was giving me the same look she had when I was twelve and had stood out in the front yard and yelled out as many swear words as I could think of. "Well, both of us have been married before, and we're both older, and neither of us wants a big wedding, and you know how I am about churches, and Iain doesn't care either way, so we thought we'd just get married quietly at a registry office. With his sons and brother and you and whoever in the *immediate* family wants to come to Scotland."

She digested that bit of rambling discourse, then immediately discarded it for happier thoughts. "Don't be ridiculous! A girl only gets married once; you need to do it right."

"I've been married once already," I pointed out.

She waved my elopement away. "That didn't count, you were an idiot then. No, honey, you'll just have to trust me that about this, a mother does know best. We'll keep the wedding on the small side if you insist, but there are just certain things you must have."

"Such as?" I asked warily.

"A small chapel, an heirloom wedding gown, lots of flowers, a nice catered luncheon, and, since it will be in Scotland, a horse-drawn carriage."

Ah, we were to the bargaining stage. I was pleased we had come this far without a big scene. I had to tread softly here, however, lest I push her too far too fast.

"How about a registry office, a nice dress that I can wear again, corsages, lunch at a restaurant, and a tour through the whisky factory?"

She didn't even hear me. Her eyes were focused dreamily on the curtain at the window, and she was tracing hearts on the table with her spoon. "I wonder where you can hire one of those bagpipe and drum marching bands?"

Chapter Seventeen

Negotiations with my mother over our wedding broke down quickly. I made the stand that we were going to have the wedding the way we wanted, and she pulled the mother guilt trip on me. We ended up, after two days of intermediaries and go-betweens, agreeing that Iain and I would find a location other than the registry office to have the wedding, but I nixed all of her other ideas. Or so I thought.

Our return trip home was much nicer than the one out, despite my cast still setting off all of the alarms, and having three times as much luggage. A week after we left for the States, we were back snug in Iain's house, the dogs happy to see Iain (all but Rob still viewed me as an interloper), Iain happy to see his farm, and me happy that we were back home where we belonged.

Things were in a bit of a turmoil for a while. We had to fill out the marriage notice forms as soon as possible, as it could take up to six weeks for the registrar to arrange for a marriage schedule. In addition, since we wanted to be married on Valentine's Day, a very popular day for weddings, it meant we had to find a registrar who had time left in his schedule. Then we had to agree on a venue. I called a few wedding consultant places and played them up for their glossy brochures. A short while later Iain and I sat down to look them over.

"Abbeys are out, ruined or otherwise," I said, and we discarded the pictures of abbeys in the area.

"How about this? It's a castle." I handed Iain a brochure

showing a couple and a piper standing before the ruins of Dirleton Castle.

"Where is it?"

"Um . . . East Lothian, I think. Too far?"

"Aye, if you want to have people here after, it is."

"Hmmm. How about Urquhart?"

"In February? It's a wee bit cold on the loch then, love. Are you set on a castle? There's Candacraig. It looks a mite warmer."

We swapped brochures.

"Hmmm. Not very romantic, is it? I take it this is drivable?"

"Aye, it's in Strathdon."

"Oh." We'd been there. The place Iain was pointing out was a registry office that was housed in a quaint little summerhouse. I heaved an inner sigh. I didn't want to admit it, but I did rather have my heart set on being married at a castle. I figured if we were going to be wed outside of a registry office, I wanted the most bang for my buck. Being married at a castle just seemed too good a thing to pass up.

I looked closer at the brochure to find some flaws with the place, and then started snickering.

"Oh, yes, this is a lovely spot. And look, Iain, we can take advantage of their full services. We can have the Tying of the Knot Ceremony, the Quaich Ceremony, and *oooooooh!* The Midnight Candlelit Ceremony!"

Iain was not the most romantic of men, but he did try. His romantic gestures tended to be low-keyed ones that most people would miss if they weren't looking for them. He shied away from blatantly romantic actions, though, and I knew full well the thought of gushily romantic ceremonies would ax Candacraig as an option.

"Oh, aye, we could," he replied, then hurriedly thrust another pamphlet under my nose. "But we haven't finished looking through these. What about this place?"

I looked. "It's a hotel!"

"Is there something wrong with that, then?"

"Well, shoot, Iain! We're in Scotland for heaven's sake. Romantic, historical Scotland. My family is coming to watch me marry you, a romantic and extremely snack-worthy Scot. I think we can do better than to be married at a hotel!"

He muttered something about it suiting him just fine and picked up the next brochure, then dropped it like a hot potato. I caught him trying to hide it under the pile of discards, and immediately glommed onto it. My shriek startled Biorsadh into leaping up from a sound sleep.

"Oooooh! Medieval Scottish weddings!"

"No, love."

I pored over the flyer. "Ooooh! Listen to this! 'A moving and dignified service conducted for couples looking for a meaningful occasion to embellish their betrothment whilst being transported back to a Scotland freed after the Wars of Independence.' That's just perfect for us!"

"No, it isn't, love."

"And look at the costumes! We could wear costumes! Look at that lovely gown! This is so *fabulous*!"

"Kathie—"

"Iain, just look! The men get to wear swords! *Swords!* Your claymore would be *perfect* for this!"

"No, it wouldn't."

"Look here, it says I don't even have to be Scottish, although we do have to recite our lineage back three generations. Hmmm. Bet I could get that from Aunt Amber."

"Kathie, we'll not be having a medieval wedding."

"This is so cool! These guys are actors! They put on a show for your wedding! And you could bring your sword!"

"Love—"

I peered closely at a picture. "Oh my god! You get to wear a *breacan an fheilidh*! Iain, this was made for us!"

"No, it's not."

"But . . ." I tapped at the flyer. "The wedding ceremony is 'drawn from tracts in the time of Wallace and the Bruce.'"

Iain just looked at me and shook his head. I commenced pouting. "There's a quaich." He didn't bat an eye. "And the couple is piped in. Doesn't that sound perfectly lovely?"

"No, love, it sounds silly."

"Well, fine. Be that way. Be totally and utterly devoid of

any romance whatsoever. Fine and dandy. Suits me just peachy bloody keen."

I snatched up the next brochure for a local wedding company. "Well, here's a lovely spot, but I'm sure *you'll* find something horrible about it." I waved the picture of a ruined castle at him. "Damp, perhaps? Remnants of the bubonic plague lingering on the walls? Or maybe it's just too bloody scenic for you, hmmm?"

Iain rolled his eyes and took the brochure from me. "Loch an Eilein Castle. It's a ruin. We passed it the day we drove up here from Manchester."

"Yes, and it's absolutely the most gorgeous site to hold a wedding, and therefore you, Mr. Wouldn't Know a Romantic Gesture if It Bit Him on the Butt, won't like it. Fine. You pick a place."

"You're acting like a child, love."

"No, I'm acting like a pissed off woman whose potential husband—and I stress the word potential—doesn't see fit to allow her to celebrate the *most important day of her whole entire life* in a manner befitting the moment."

"Ah, now you're sounding like your mum."

"Low blow, Potential Husband Iain. Very low indeed."

Location settled—Iain gave in rather gracefully over Loch an Eilein—my attention was immediately turned to the next most important item on my list: my wedding dress.

"So what does my butt look like in this?"

"Turn around so I can see. Um . . . well, do you want truthful or kind?"

"Truthful. Kind I can get from Iain."

"It's not good."

I sighed. This was the ninth dress I had tried on in the last few hours, and I was already exhausted. "Well, hell, Joanna. What am I going to do? The wedding is ten days away and I can't find a dress. If I don't have one before my mother comes, I'm doomed. She'll make me buy a wedding dress, just you wait and see. Big and white and frothing with a train and a veil and I'll look like a giant cream puff gone bad."

Joanna looked at the discards. "I liked that rose one."

I peeled off the dress and reached for my skirt and sweater. "It makes me look too hippy. Where haven't we been?"

She thought for a minute. "Well, Miranda told me about a new little place over in Kinrushtie. We could try there, it's only a few miles down the road."

"I'm not feeling very good about this, Joanna."

"I know you're not, Kathie, but don't worry, it's all part of the prewedding jitters. My mum always told me it would get better the closer you get to the wedding."

I poked my head through the sweater. "And did it?"

"Well, no, it didn't." She grinned at me. "At least it didn't until the hen party! That was fun."

"Oh, yes, I want to talk to you about that. Are you sure it's a good idea for us to do this?"

"The hen party? You mean because the men will know we're throwing you a party to say farewell to your days as a single woman, and therefore they're likely to throw a stag party for Iain?"

"Exactly. I've heard about these Scottish stag parties. Iain told me what David's buddies—" Whoops. I had forgotten that I wasn't supposed to mention that to Joanna. "Yes, I think your idea is a good one. Let's go to Kinrushtie."

She let me get outside before she grabbed my arm and stopped me. "What did David's friends do at his stag party?"

"Oh, Joanna, truly I'm sorry. I shouldn't have said anything. It's nothing to worry about, just the usual sort of hijinks guys get up to in the name of poking a bit of fun at a fellow guy who's about to be married."

I tried to push her toward Iain's car. She stood firm. "What did David's friends do at his stag party?"

"Nothing that should trouble you." Unless, of course, she counted having a prostitute being the evening's entertainment troublesome. "Come along, I want to get to Kinrushtie and back before Iain's in for tea."

"What did David's friends do at his stag party?"

I sighed. "You're not going to let me go, are you?"

"Not until you tell me."

I looked around the street. "Well, fine, I'll tell you and then you'll be all pissed at David, who will tell his father, and then Iain will read me the riot act for telling you. So fine, Joanna, I'll tell you if you honestly want to make my life a living hell. If our friendship isn't worth enough for you to trust me on this one, itty-bitty thing, then I'll be happy to tell you. Just say the word, and I'll destroy what happiness and trust Iain and I have together, just so you can know what your husband of less than a year, the man who makes you insanely happy and prone to smiles at the least likely moment, the man about whom just hours ago you were raving over and telling me things I really didn't need to know about and yet you insisted on telling, was doing at his stag party. Oh yes, just say the word, Joanna, and I'll be happy to tell you."

I got into Iain's car. She stood for a moment on the pavement, weighing our friendship and my future happiness with her need to know something so trivial and unnecessary as whether or not her husband was disporting himself with a hooker on the eve of his marriage. She gave a little shrug. Clearly our friendship meant more to her than mere curiosity. I felt a warm glow wash over me as she got into the car. I sent her a grateful little smile and started the car up.

"What did David's friends do at his stag party?"

Well, hell. I was cornered and I knew it. "They hired a . . . um . . . a professional to entertain them."

"A professional? What sort of a professional?"

"Oh, for god's sake, Joanna, they were a bunch of randy men celebrating the last night of David's bachelorhood. What sort of a professional do you think I mean?"

She started to laugh. I would have stared at her, but I had to get us out of town and onto a road where I could pull over.

"Oh, Kathie you had me scared there for a minute. I thought something really had happened."

"You don't mind that they had a prostitute at the party?"

"Cerise? She's not a prostitute. Or she was, but she's not now, she's reformed. And no, I didn't mind she was there. I was the one who hired her."

I did pull over at that point.

"You hired a hooker for your fiancé's bachelor party?"

"I told you, she's not a prostitute anymore. I told David's friend Ben to hire her. I talked to Cerise first, and told her how far she was allowed to go. She could take off her clothes, and dance around, but no touching."

Uh-oh. That's not what Iain had told me had gone on. He hadn't been at the party long, having dropped in only to bring supplies of an alcoholic nature, but his description of the activities and Joanna's didn't tally. Silence, I was sure, was the best policy, so I let her go on talking about how she had outwitted the men.

It took two more days of looking, but finally I had a dress I was happy with. It was a vintage-looking dress, almost 1930s in its long, sleek lines, with a pale cream background and big tea roses scattered over it. Definitely not your standard wedding dress stuff, but I wanted something I could wear out to any formal events I might be called upon to attend, all of those formal Sheepherder's Balls and such. The Sheep Tupping Proms. The Manure Mucker's Annual Gala. And of course, the highlight of any farm wife's season; the Sheep Castrator's Annual Charity Auction. Now I could hold up my head with pride.

A week before our wedding Iain and I attended the funeral of his ex-wife Mary's aunt. Both David and Archie were mentioned in the will, so they came for the funeral as well. Iain had always gotten along well with Mary's Aunt Edna, so he decided it would be a nice thing if we attended and paid our respects.

Archie had a row with his father and turned down an admittedly lackluster invitation to stay with us, staying instead at a little hotel in the town where Edna was being buried.

"What did he say?" I asked Iain after he had spoken privately with Archie.

He took my hand and gave it a squeeze. He only did that when he thought I needed comforting, so I assumed Archie had nothing nice to say. "He says he'll come to the wedding."

I looked at Iain. The laugh lines around his eyes stood out starkly against his tanned skin. Not a good sign.

"Oh, sweetie, I'm sorry. Was he awful?"

"Not so bad," Iain said, but I knew he was trying not to upset me. I cursed Archie as I had done a hundred times before. I could live with his sniping at me, but it made me furious when he took out his spite on his father. Iain deserved better than that.

"Did he say why Susan isn't here?"

"No, but I'm gathering things aren't too well on that front."

"Oh, dear." I was secretly pleased for Susan. After our little Christmas bonding session, I had become quite fond of her. She also deserved better than Archie.

Meeting Iain's ex-wife Mary was an experience unto itself. Why was it that in some families the children clearly resembled one parent over the other? In Iain's family, he and David were like two peas in a pod, while Archie took after Mary. Both had sandy, light brown hair and hazel eyes, whereas Iain and David had dark hair and soft, expressive, peaty brown eyes that made me want to melt.

When I saw Mary with Iain at the funeral, I couldn't for the life of me imagine how they ever married, let alone produced two sons. Two more different people you would be hard pressed to find. Mary was petite, expensively dressed, with lots of makeup and a carefully coiffed head. She spoke a mile a minute, never stopping for trivial things like breathing or to allow another person to edge in a word.

To be honest, I hadn't been looking forward to meeting her, given my history meeting Iain's family and friends, especially after Archie had so vehemently stated how close they were and how much she missed Iain. I suspected this meeting would be one long unpleasant, awkward experience. I just hoped Mary would hold back the barbs and nasty comments until Iain was out of earshot.

She didn't, but not because she couldn't wait, but because she had nothing nasty to say.

"I live in London, you know, London proper, that is, in Kensington, not one of the suburbs—well, you *know* how the suburbs can be, some nice and quite pleasant while others are just simply *squalid,* there's no other word for them but *squalid,* but as I said, I live in London."

"Oh."

"It's just me and my dogs now, Charles and Camilla they are—isn't that too clever? Everyone always asks me why I didn't name them Charles and Diana and I tell them it's because I saw *that* tragedy coming for years before anyone else—their divorce that is, not Diana being killed, that was truly saddening, wasn't it? So young. But it's just me and the dogs in our snug little flat, not that it's little, really, with three bedrooms, but Arthur always did call it our little flat, and I like to honor his memory. And I'm not truly alone, you know! I have Charles and Camilla, and of course, the help, but they don't really count because they just come in and clean when I'm out during the day, so I don't really see them, although Simon—he's my therapist, and oh! Such a good one, I'll let you have his number if you ever want a really *quality* therapist—Simon says I am not to trivialize other people's lives just because they don't meet my standards, but *I* say what's the use in having standards if you don't adhere to them?"

I nodded, then shook my head, then nodded again, totally confused by the barrage of conversation and unsure of which response was the one she wanted. It didn't really matter, I found out later. Mary took it as given that whomever she was speaking to was utterly enthralled with her conversation. So she smiled at me and continued on telling me about her masseuse and how delicious his hands were, how terribly expensive it was to live in London, but thankfully her late husband Arthur had left her a tidy sum, what a lovely little shop she had just discovered that had the most divine fabrics from Africa—I should really try them, the jewel-tone fabrics would look lovely with my dark hair and eyes—and just how shocked she was to hear that old Aunt Edna had finally died. I got the impression she had assumed Edna had died years ago, and was surprised to find she'd only now stuck her spoon in the wall. Mary then proceeded to give me Aunt Edna's life history as it related to her, Mary, in full, glorious Technicolor detail.

I tried to picture this glittery, fragile, materialistic little creature slogging around the mud at Iain's farm, and failed. Iain himself was a little wary of Mary. I thought at first it was because they had a less than amicable divorce, but it turned out he just didn't want to get trapped into conversation with her. Once she had her conversational hooks into you, so to speak, it was all over. Only death offered respite, and as poor Aunt Edna had probably found out, even death was no guarantee of escape.

Mary certainly surprised me on another front, falling immediately into the friendly camp. Despite Archie's grim warnings, she was extremely pleasant to me, going so far as to cut short the details about her recent colonic experiences in order to inquire how long we'd been married.

"Actually, we're getting married next week—" I started to say, but was promptly steamrollered into silence.

"No! Well isn't that simply fabulous, although I thought Archie said something about you and Iain living together for some months now, but he must have been mistaken, young men often exaggerate, you know. But a week, why I can do a week quite easily, I was going to stay four days while I sorted through Auntie's things, so really, three extra days will be nothing to me, nothing at all, and of course, I will put *all* of my expertise at your *full* disposal. Imagine, it works out so perfectly that I am here to see Iain married in style! He was my first husband, you know, and while not the best husband, I'm sure you and he are well suited to one another, you look just like a farm wife should. I've told him for many, many years to remarry, you know. 'Iain,' I've told him, 'Iain you simply must stop grieving over me and find another woman to marry!' And now he's done just that and at last I can breathe easier and know he's gotten over the trauma of our divorce. Oh yes, I can do a week quite easily."

I wondered, numbly, when she had time to breathe at all. I was so exhausted by the conversation with her that I hadn't the strength to point out that we were trying to keep the wedding small, and ended up giving in to the inevitable force that was Mary, although I did manage to decline her repeated offer to serve as my matron of honor. But it was a close thing.

Life shifted into hectic gear immediately following the funeral. Mary made arrangements to stay in a nearby town since Iain's house was due shortly to be filled with my family. Thankfully Archie returned to Manchester with plans to show up on the wedding day. Bev and Nate were going to arrive a few days early to spend time with Joanna and David. My family was due to roll into town three days before the wedding, after which they would separate and either fly home, or work in a little vacation, depending on their schedules. Ewen and his latest significant other were planning a whirlwind visit.

In addition to all of the standard wedding chaos going on, I had one other worry on my mind. Shortly after Iain proposed, I had decided to start learning Gaelic. I knew that I wouldn't have time to become anywhere near proficient in the language what with all of those strange diphthongs and what-have-you, but I had one specific goal in mind: I wanted to recite my wedding vows in Gaelic.

That may seem an odd thing to do, but I had a reason for it. Iain's father, Alec, was a very active man in his clan, and had been taught Gaelic at his mother's knee. He was one of the people who pushed quite hard to bring back Gaelic to schools, and had his hand in a good many schemes to work Gaelic back into the life of Highlanders. Iain and Ewen were both forced to learn Gaelic since Alec refused to speak English when at home. Ewen was less fluent in it than Iain, but he could and did, on rare occasions, speak it. Iain wasn't the reformer his father was, but he did make sure his boys had a grounding in Gaelic as well, and gave them the opportunity to learn more. Only David did.

I thought it would be a nice tribute to Iain's heritage if I could recite my marriage vows in Gaelic, and I wanted to do more than just learn them phonetically. I wanted to understand what it was I was saying.

Since this was to be a surprise for Iain, I consulted Annie Walker for help. There was a Gaelic learner's class for adults held in town, but it was in the evening, and my night vision was terrible. The thought of driving about at night half blind didn't appeal to me, so I asked Annie for suggestions, and she recommended a tutor. He told me about a series of Gaelic books and videotapes, and we made arrangements to meet every week for tutorial sessions. The tutor, Graeham MacAskill, taught Gaelic on the side to a local grammar school in addition to his job as an insurance agent. I explained to Graeham how much time I had to concentrate on my studies, and went on to discuss my reason for learning Gaelic. He was very supportive of my cause, but it was not until later I learned what price I paid for that support.

As the time for the wedding drew closer, I grew more worried. I wasn't making as much progress in Gaelic as I had hoped. I increased the number of my tutoring sessions with Graeham, and spent long hours studying grammar, watching the videotapes, and practicing my Gaelic on the furniture.

"Madainn mhath," I would greet the chair in the morning. *"Ciamar a tha sibh an-diugh? Tha i fuar an-diugh, nach eil?"*

The chair never did tell me how it was feeling, nor whether it agreed with me that it was cold out that day, let alone what its name was, where it lived, or what sort of beverage it preferred. Graeham was quite impressed with my ability to order drinks in Gaelic, but that seemed to be the only thing that came naturally to me.

Six days before our wedding, Mary returned to the home she had, some seventeen years before, abandoned on an appropriately dark and stormy night. She had had enough of life on the farm, of motherhood, and of Iain. She ran off with an old beau, a man she had been engaged to secretly when she was sixteen, but whom she left when she was eighteen to marry Iain. She was pregnant at the time, but lost the baby a few months later. Archie was born about a year after that, and David five years later.

I figured the farm would hold some pretty painful memories for her, so when she called to say she wanted to talk with me, I offered to meet her in town. She declined, and after listening to a twenty-four minute monologue about the price of petrol, the follies of her adult step-daughter, the latest urinary tract problems of one of her pugs, and her disappointment with the length of her late aunt's funeral services, I managed to hang up. I went down to the barn to warn Iain of the impending visit. He thanked me and promptly headed for the farthest hill, leaving me to run back to the house to whip up a batch of Moravian Spice Cookies. Cookies could ease most pains, I'd found. Surely Mary would need lots of them coming back to a place that held few happy memories for her. Anticipating a tearful scene, I made sure the tissue was handy.

"Well, this house certainly hasn't changed!" she said brightly an hour later as I helped her off with her coat. "It always was hopeless, and I see that it still is. Oh, not that you're not a perfectly good housekeeper," she patted my hand. "Even if you had a full staff, it wouldn't make the house any more comfortable. Drafty old thing." She shuddered delicately and pulled her cardigan up closer.

"Now, dear, I wanted to talk to you about this wedding. Joanna tells me you have nothing planned, nothing at all, and that, dear Kathie, I just cannot allow. Iain was my first love, you know, or practically my first love; he would have been my first love if I had met him before Cecil, but I didn't and so technically Cecil was my first love, but Iain was definitely one of my first loves, probably number three or four, but still very high on the list and for that reason I *owe* it to him to make sure he is married in style. So I'm here to help you. Joanna insists that you really do want to be married in a wet, deserted old ruin, but you and I both know she's young, and the young are always so prone to overdramatizing things, really, and as you're not young you're certainly much more levelheaded than Joanna. I'm not criticizing the dear girl, you understand, I couldn't love her one bit more than I do, and you know how happy David is with her, and that's quite a change from a few years back when he was the wildest thing you ever saw, always with a new girlfriend on his arm, and never with one more than a few dates in a row.

I was in an almost constant worry over him what with the AIDS scare and him running around with all of these loose women and never paying attention to what Arthur—that's my late husband, have I told you about him? I married him after Cecil impregnated his secretary. Arthur was Cecil's partner at the time, and was so very understanding and kind, well, I ask you, how was I to refuse when he asked me to make his life complete and marry him?"

She paused for a breath, then said suddenly. "Men, you know, are the most unthinking creatures on this earth."

"Um . . ." I didn't really want to comment on that. She had left Iain with two small sons in order to run off with her old flame, Cecil of the pregnant secretary fame, so I figured we'd best steer the conversation to a topic less likely to combust.

"I appreciate your offer of help, Mary, truly I do, but you see, Joanna is perfectly right. Iain and I have decided to get married at Loch an Eilein Castle. It's very roman—"

She started talking again.

"—tic," I finished while she went off describing the details of every wedding she'd ever seen or attended, including Princess Diana's, and sat back to save my strength. I had a feeling I was going to need it.

Iain poked his head into the kitchen a few hours later. "Her car's gone so I'm thinking it's safe to come in. Can you hear, or are your eardrums still ringing?"

I smiled wanly at him and lifted a bloodless hand to wave him in. "How on earth did you endure almost ten years of marriage to that woman?"

He grinned. "The first few years were the worst. After that I learned to stay out in the parks all of the day."

I let him pull me onto his lap, and snuggled against him. He smelled like the outdoors and wool and Iain. "She wants us to have a marquee in case it rains. And chairs so everyone can sit. And musicians. And flowery garlands. And a big buffet lunch."

Iain looked startled for a moment. "That's not what we've planned, is it, love?"

"No, it isn't, but Iain I'm afraid. I'm very, very afraid. Mary is . . . is . . ."

"A right pain in the arse?"

"No. Well, yes. But she's more than that, she's *immovable*. I'm just afraid that she's going to wear me down and I won't be able to say no anymore and we'll end up with a big huge wedding that neither of us wants, filled with relatives and friends we don't particularly want to see, and we'll be utterly miserable, and oh, god, *I'm already starting to talk like her!*"

Iain laughed, which is the only thing that saved me from bursting into tears at that moment.

"Oh, you think it's funny do you? Well just chew on this, Mr. Ha Ha. Once my mother and your ex-wife meet, there's going to be hell to pay. We'll have both of them joining forces against us, and then we'll be toast."

That thought sobered him up.

Chapter Eighteen

Things to Do

February 11: Avoid Mary. Joanna and I to airport to pick up Mom and Mo on 1:15 p.m. flight. Iain to train station to pick up Brother's family at 2:40 p.m. Dinner at Chez Hadji's for fifteen at 7 p.m.

I disliked driving to Inverness. I was still uncertain enough driving that I wanted to avoid driving in well-populated areas, so I asked Joanna if she would drive. She was curious about my family, so she left her mother and father with David, and we set off to pick up the female members of my family who had come for the wedding.

The first words out of Mo's mouth, bellowed across the airport waiting area, were, "I don't see any kilts!"

Joanna looked at me. "That would be your sister?"

She'd know if I tried to deny it. Mo and I looked quite a bit alike. "Yes, she is, but I'd like to point out right now that I am perfectly able to converse without drawing the attention of everyone in the room, unlike my sister. And there's my moth— Oh my god."

My mouth dropped open. I couldn't believe what I was seeing. She didn't! She wouldn't! She *couldn't*!

"What's wrong? That's your mum, there? The lady in the gray coat? The one with the . . . oh, my."

Oh, my, indeed.

"Yes, that's my mother. And that other person is my Aunt

Amber, reigning belle of the Sarasota Retirement Village and renown hootchicoo dancer."

We stared at the spectacle that was Aunt Amber. She was actually my mother's aunt, my great-aunt, and was, by best guess, approximately 150 years old. We didn't honestly know her age, since she ripped off a few years at each birthday. By now, she was probably younger than me.

"She's quite . . . vibrant, isn't she?"

I tried to avoid looking at her. Aunt Amber was color blind, and always wore ensembles of the most garish color combinations. Usually her companion, a woman by the name of Alice, steered her toward the less eye-straining outfits, but Alice had taken the opportunity to visit her family while Aunt Amber was under my mother's care. Mom evidently didn't see a problem with Aunt Amber wearing a blue and green tasseled shawl covering a pink blazer, orange faux satin blouse with marabou tassels down the front, and blue-and-white polka-dotted pleated skirt with gold metallic tasseled belt. Combined with the knee-high nylons and Nike tennis shoes with little red-and-white tassels tied to the shoelaces, and a black hat that vaguely resembled a tasseled Sydney Opera House, she was indeed a sight to behold.

I somewhat reluctantly claimed my family and introduced Joanna. Joanna and Mo quickly sized each other up, decided they were kindred spirits despite a twenty-year age difference, and went off to get the luggage while I herded Mom and Aunt Amber toward the parking lot.

"Yes, Mom, I do have a dress. And yes, I told you the other day when you called that we have the site booked for two hours."

"And the caterers? I can't believe a daughter of mine is doing just a buffet lunch and not a sit down! How am I going to explain that to your aunts?"

"Just tell them we're broke and we can't afford anything else."

"Oh, pooh, you know I offered to help you children with the costs."

Yes, but at a great price. I'd have been under obligation to do things her way if we accepted any monetary support.

"Um, Mom? Does Aunt Amber know that man?"

"What man?" My mother looked around the seating area next to the doors.

I pointed her in the right direction. "That one over there. That surprised-looking gentleman upon whose lap she is now sitting. I think she's tickling his chin with a tassel."

My mother uttered a few words I very seldom hear her utter, and went off to remove Aunt Amber from her perch.

There was a reason Aunt Amber was the belle of the Sarasota Retirement Village. Her years of dancing fan dances, bubble dances, and snake dances in Atlantic City and other venues up and down the East Coast had given her the idea that she was Gypsy Rose Lee, Marilyn Monroe, and Mae West all rolled into one sharp package.

If she were a hundred or so years younger, I'd have said she "puts out." I wasn't sure if she actually did or not, nor did I really want to find out, but she certainly had made the pursuit of the male of the species her *raison d'etre*.

And lucky, lucky us, she was there to watch Iain and me get married! I made a mental note to put two watchdogs on her at the wedding. The thought of what she'd do with any man brave enough to show up in a kilt was too hideous to think about.

Immediately upon returning home, Mom and I had an argument.

"Now, Iain is picking up Brother and Laura and the kids, isn't that right?"

"Yes, Mom, he's there now."

We were in the bedroom that she and Mo and Aunt Amber were sharing. Mo was flat out on the bed moaning about the time change and trying to get up enough energy to call home and let her husband know they'd arrived safely. Aunt Amber was in the bathroom adjusting what were sure to be tasseled undergarments. It didn't bear thinking about.

"Good, good. And you'll be staying at the same hotel as Brother?"

I stared at her. Hotel? Me? What was she talking about? "Huh?"

My mother stopped unpacking and turned around to look at me. "The hotel. The one you're staying at Sunday night."

"Mom, I live here. I don't have to stay at a hotel."

She put her hands on her hips and gave me that mother look, the one all moms worth their salt save for those special occasions when their children don't come up to snuff.

"Well, you certainly may live here the rest of the time, but you cannot stay here Sunday night."

Mo moaned.

"Why not?"

"Because that will be your wedding eve! You can't sleep with the groom the night before your wedding, it's bad luck!"

"I always thought that was a bunch of hooey, Mom. I mean, what could be steamier than a little illicit *we're not married yet* sex?" Mo asked.

"Maureen, I am speaking to your sister, not you. And besides, you know full well that it's bad luck. You didn't spend the night before your wedding with Ned!"

Mo grinned and winked at me. I rolled my eyes and handed my mother a pair of her shoes.

"You must have a room on Sunday night, and that's all there is to it. Or Iain will have to. One of you has to leave."

"Iain can't leave, he'll have chores to do in the morning."

"On his wedding day?" My mother looked aghast at the very thought.

"Yes, Mom, the goat still needs to be milked, and the animals fed. I can feed the chickens, but I haven't yet mastered Mabel. She doesn't like me. Besides, this whole thing is ridiculous. Iain and I have been living together since November, it's hardly likely that one more night together without being married is going to doom us to eternal hell."

She lowered the shoes and squinted her eyes. "Either you stay at a hotel Sunday night, or Iain does. Take your choice."

"Mom—"

"It's your choice!" She stomped out of the room to find out what Aunt Amber was doing so long in the bathroom.

"You'll have to give in to her, you know," Mo commented without opening her eyes. "You know how she is.

She's given up a lot what with you insisting on a small wedding—not that I think you're wrong—but you're going to have to give on this."

"Of all the stupid traditions—what?" I yelled the last out the door to my mother. She appeared in the doorway of the bathroom, her face flushed and wearing an unfamiliar expression.

"It appears Aunt Amber has found some sort of birth control device and is insisting it's hers. Would you please come and identify it for me, so I can give her her pills and she can take her nap?"

Mo snorted as I swore and went to claim the object in question. I heard her clearly from the bathroom.

"If you've got any more of those little presents from Iain's ex-girlfriend, I'd tuck those away as well. Aunt Amber is likely to be enthralled by them, too."

Brother's hotel was booked, but I managed to find one in town that had a single free. I made the reservation grudgingly, my mother standing next to me at the phone to make sure I'd book it.

"Happy?" I snapped as I hung up the phone.

"Always," she said smugly, and patted my cheek.

February 12: Avoid Mary. Pick up cake from bakery. Call caterers to make sure everything is OK. Try not to let Mom and Mary talk together without supervision.

"Where do you keep the olives, Kathie?" Laura, Brother's wife, asked. I reached over her head for a bowl.

"Green or black?"

She made a face. "Black in tuna fish? Yuk. My kids would scream. Green."

"I think there's some in the larder. And while you're in there, would you bring out the second loaf of bread? We're going to need it in order to feed this lot."

We were making sandwiches for lunch. A kind of late lunch/early tea, actually. The ladies in our party had been out all of the morning shopping, while the gentlemen stayed on the farm; the kids playing in the barn with Mabel and the cats, and the older generation tagging around after Iain as he did his chores. Brother was particularly fascinated by the dogs and how well trained they were.

"The eggs are done, Aunt Kathie. What do you want me to do with them?"

I gave Karen the instructions on cooling the eggs for the egg salad, and resumed my place at the soup kettle. Mo peered over my shoulder and crunched a piece of celery in my ear. "Not enough bacon."

"Yes there is, I know how to make potato soup—" I stopped, a horrible thought striking me. "What are you doing in here, Mo? You're supposed to be out at the grocery store with Mom!"

She waved toward a clutch of grocery bags on the table. "We're back. Mom's outside talking to—"

I was off before she could finish her sentence. I had a horrible feeling I knew who my mother was talking to, and I had to separate them before disaster struck.

". . . and I can tell you are a woman who raised her daughters the right and decent way, Carol, but when I tell you the trouble I've had with Kathie, you'll scream, you'll positively scream. Do you know she intends on having the wedding at a ruin? And not even a nice one, but one that's open to the sky and doesn't have all of its walls! Have you ever heard of such a thing? I've been to many a wedding in my time, as I told your daughter earlier this week when I offered her full use of my expertise in taking the everyday event she has planned and making it into something people will be talking about for months, and I know a thing or two about how to put one on, but she insists that she and Iain want to have this minuscule *nothing* affair and not the wedding that my dear Iain needs and deserves. He was my first love, you know, or close enough to my first love to be considered my first love, and for that reason I owe it to him to make sure that his wedding is not a brief, shoddy sort of affair. I told Kathie this, but you know how this younger generation is, not that she's that much younger than me, only eight or nine years at most and I certainly don't think she looks any younger than me, but still, she is naive and young enough to not know her own mind even though she thinks she does, and Iain—well, you know how men are, they'll go along with whatever is easiest with never a thought to what they really want, and need, and deserve—"

Too late. Mary had snagged my mother, Mom was listening to her with the same sort of look a rat gives a cobra, that hypnotized, blank, vacant sort of stare. It was all over for her. I returned to the house a saddened, wiser person.

"Well, that's it, the wedding's off," I announced to the kitchen at large.

You could have heard a pin drop.

"What's Dad done now?" Joanna asked, waving a butter knife at me.

"Nothing. Not a blessed thing. He is innocent of all things but having the dubious taste in marrying Mary."

Joanna and everyone else in the kitchen looked confused.

"The wedding's off," I repeated for effect. "The wedding as we know it is now officially history. Instead of the lovely and charming intimate affair that Iain and I so painstakingly arranged, we will now have a giant, overblown, hideously expensive, fussy wedding that no one but Mom and Mary will enjoy, and which will probably result in years of acrimonious comments between Iain and myself, ending in a bitter divorce and my eventual downfall to alcoholism, while Iain turns into a dottering old man with no friends but his sheep."

You could have heard a feather drop.

"Oh," Mo said, and went back to slicing cheese for the ham sandwiches.

Laura *tut*ted. Bev dusted off her hands and put an arm around my shoulders. "I'm sure it's not quite as bad as you think it is."

"No? You just go out there and listen to Mary and my mother talk. I'll bet you a fiver they're already talking about how they can fit fifty more guests in."

Bev smiled. "I'll tell them lunch is almost ready."

"A fiver, Bev!"

She nodded and pulled off the cloth she had wrapped

around her waist as an apron, and went out to fetch my mother and Mary.

I returned to the soup with a sinking feeling in my stomach, and tried to figure out a time when Iain and I would be alone long enough to escape the house and elope.

Bev returned five minutes later, her face ashen. You could have heard individual atoms of oxygen striking the floor.

Bev straightened her shoulders, and with an effort, gamely met my eye. "How do you feel about a champagne fountain topped with an ice sculpture of you and Iain in between two bagpipers?"

By the time Sunday rolled around, I was following firmly in the footsteps of every other bride before me, and was a nervous wreck. I didn't want to spend the night alone in a strange bed in a strange hotel—I wanted to spend the night lying on top of Iain, begging him to run away with me and save me from the hideous disaster that the wedding was sure to be.

Instead, what I got was dinner out with the ladies—my hen party.

February 13: Avoid Mary. Move to hotel. Hen party.
Iain's stag party.

Joanna and Bev arranged for my hen party. I was pleased Bev had a hand in it, thus ensuring Joanna's wild streak wouldn't show up in the form of a male stripper or something equally as lamentable. Instead, what they had planned was a nice dinner at a private dining room in Brother's hotel, a few gifts, a couple of bottles of champagne, and of course, chocolate, chocolate, chocolate.

What they had planned and what actually happened were sadly two separate things.

Oh, it started off well enough. We all met in town at a cute little restaurant for an early full tea, the kind with clotted cream, cucumber sandwiches, lots of little pastries, and so on. Laura had commandeered Brother's rental car, Mary had her Honda, and I had Iain's Volvo. We rendezvoused, synchronized watches, kept Aunt Amber from wandering off after a couple of construction workers, and soon were settled in the very lilac interior of The Lilacs, a cute little restaurant that specialized in being extremely twee. Tourists ate it up, along with scones, clouty dumplings, and heather honey.

From there we did a few hours of shopping. What else could I expect? I had a group of women who, with the exception of Annie and Joanna, were not native to Scotland. Shopping was *de rigueur,* and who was I to argue with them? After shopping we retired to the private dining room Joanna had reserved at Brother's hotel. To that point, things were going pretty well. I endured a modest amount of chaffing, nothing unusual, and Aunt Amber only once escaped us—while we were all drooling over a blue topaz pendant and ring set, she was offering to show the jewelry store manager how she did her famous half-dollar dance for Harry Truman.

"Don't ask," I told the stunned store manager as he backed slowly away from Aunt Amber. "You truly don't want to know how she holds the half-dollar when she does it."

Once we got back to the hotel, things just kind of degenerated. I blame the chiropractors, truly I do. They had been at a convention in Inverness, and a group of them had taken advantage of the nearness of Aviemore and had spent the day there skiing. Now, chiropractors in general weren't, in my experience, wild and crazy guys. Most of them wore suits and serious faces, had extremely good posture, and nice, clean hands. But the group at the hotel we were at was evidently made up of the Bad Boys of chiropractic care. The problems started when it turned out both groups—the Bad Boys and my party—had been booked into the same private dining room for the same time.

"What are we going to do?" Joanna asked in a near wail. As hostess of the party, she felt responsible for the hotel's mistake and was close to tears.

"Now, don't worry, Jo, we'll take care of that manager." Bev motioned to Mom and Mary, and the three of them went to corner the weasely little manager who had been bribed into allowing the Bad Boy chiropractors to have the room despite the fact that we had booked first.

In the end, because our combined numbers were so small, and half the Bad Boys were tired from their day on the slope, we ended up sharing the dining room: our nine to their five. The hotel staff separated the tables into two lots, and we contrived to ignore the interlopers as best we could.

All except Aunt Amber, who looked upon this circumstance as a gift from heaven, and therefore not to be ignored.

"Any of you boys from around here?" she asked as she hiked up her orthopedic knee-highs. The group of us, except for Mary who thought Aunt Amber was a hoot, collectively rolled our eyes and moved her to a seat with her back to the Bad Boys.

The waiters served the champagne, and Joanna called the party to order. "As the official organizer of this celebration, and soon to be step-daughter-in-law to the guest of honor—"

Mo hooted at that. The Bad Boys looked up at her noise. "Even Brother's kids aren't old enough to be married!"

"As I was saying, as official organizer, I'd like to start the celebration of this important occasion by giving the bride the obligatory symbols of her upcoming nuptials. First," Joanna whipped out a large carrier bag, "the veil and tiara!"

I tried not to roll my eyes as our group applauded when Mo plunked the tiara and a short bit of tulle on my head. The Bad Boys applauded politely as well, then returned to their stories of the hills they had savaged.

"Next, her magic wand!" Joanna bestowed upon me a glittery wand with a silver star at the end. "And finally, to keep her new husband mindful of his manners"—the chiropractors looked up, interested—"a whip!"

"Just like the one I have!" Aunt Amber piped up over the roars of laughter from the Bad Boys and Mo. "Only mine has a tassel at the end. Smarts something terrible, too."

I took the whip and endured another round of bawdy hints as best I could. Even my mother got into the act, offering a few choice suggestions as to what I could do with the whip. Get a little Bolly under my mother's belt, and she really let her hair down.

"Presents! Time for presents!" Bev declared, and I spent the next half hour opening packages containing pairs of crotchless knickers, see-thru baby doll jammies with plastic hearts in strategic locations, a pair of faux fur-lined handcuffs from Max's wife, Denise, who was present in spirit only, and a his and her set of tasseled thongs (and I'm not talking about the kind worn on your feet). This last one was from Aunt Amber, who told us it had taken her almost a whole week of shopping at her favorite adult stores to find just the right ones for Iain and me. His was leopard print (he Tarzan), while mine was zebra (me Jane). I had to promise her we'd wear them on our honeymoon in order to keep her from modeling the zebra one for the chiropractors.

By this point the Bad Boys had given up all pretense of keeping to their own side of the room, and stood up to view every new gift as it was opened. Aunt Amber was in seventh heaven when, as we cracked open the third bottle of champagne, the Bad Boys invited themselves to our table and joined the fun.

"Want me to show you how to do the Lambada the hard way?" Aunt Amber leered at one of them, twirling her gold tasseled necklace and waving it at him. The Bad Boy, whose name was Joe, was game, but alas and alack, no music could be found.

Dinner helped calm things down a bit, since everyone was too busy eating and chatting with the Bad Boys (who had pushed the tables back into the original configuration), but once dinner was over, the fun and games began.

Most of the games were the standard stuff found at bridal showers of the bawdy bend—a round of Truth or Dare, advice to the bride in the form of the older generation recalling the wedding night talk their mothers gave them, and several really bad jokes by the Bad Boys.

Then Joanna and Mo went out to Laura's car and came back with another carrier bag laden with something bulgy. "This is a little game we played at my hen party," Joanna said, and passed around small paring knives.

"What, you do a little cosmetic surgery?" one of the Bad Boys joked.

Joanna smiled a wicked smile at him, and with a flourish, whipped out a cucumber. "This is the Cucumber Game! Mo will pass among you with the bag of cucumbers. You will notice there are all sorts of sizes and shapes in there—please take one (the gentlemen are excluded from participation) that closest resembles your husband's . . . um . . . willie."

"Joanna!" Bev said with a half a giggle. My mother snorted and immediately started digging through the bag.

"Mom," I objected. "You're not married anymore and you're not seeing anyone!"

She snickered and pulled out a cucumber. "There's a lot you don't know, honey," she chirped, and eyed the cucumber speculatively.

Bev giggled fully this time, and after poring over the remaining selection, emerged from the bag with a small, stunted little cuke.

"Mum!" Joanna protested. "Don't you think that's a little on the small side?"

Bev took another sip of the champagne and waved her cucumber in the air.

"Now, does everyone have one?"

The Bad Boys all responded with rude comments. Joanna ignored them. "Fine. The idea is to use these knives and carve your cucumber to resemble the size and shape of your partner's willie. Best carving job wins this lovely"—she dug around in another bag—"this lovely picture of a famous movie star."

She held up a laminated picture of a movie star—a *porn* movie star wearing nothing but a smile. The Bad Boys took one look and protested that a part of his anatomy had to have been retouched and wasn't physically possible outside of the animal kingdom.

Aunt Amber snagged the photo and propped it up in front of her while she carved.

"For inspiration," she told the Bad Boy next to her. He grinned.

I was awarded the picture by virtue of being the bride, and therefore in need of such a thing. Aunt Amber was awarded First Runner-up for having the most lifelike rendition of a male member in cucumber. Mom won a ribbon for most humorous, Bev won the pity award (she pared half of the cucumber away until she had a lump the size of her thumb left, which gave Joanna a severe case of the giggles), Annie won the least artistic award, and Mo won the braggarts award (she did only a tiny bit of carving around one edge of a really, really big cucumber).

"Well, that's it then," Joanna said, after having awarded the last prize. "I hereby declare this hen party over. The bride looks a bit tipsy, and judging from the angle of her veil, I believe we should escort her to her cold, lonely bed before she passes out."

"Ho, the night is young," Joe the Bad Boy declared, and stood up to get our attention. "I've always heard you have strippers at these Hen Nights! I don't see any strippers here." He peered around him in a semisloshed way. "So I guess my mates and me'll just have to stand in for them. Nick, Tom, you two see if you can't find us some music. Will and Ernie and I will keep the ladies entertained until you return.

"Oooh, Chippendales," Aunt Amber squealed, and jumped up and down in her chair clapping her hands, then suddenly dived into her handbag for dollar bills.

Mo snorted, and held a brief consultation with Joanna. I will admit to having had a tiny bit too much champagne, and was convinced that if I waved my magic wand in just the right manner, I could make the Bad Boys vanish. Or at least turn into frogs.

Joanna and Mo, who had abstained from champagne so they could ferry everyone home, strong-armed the manager into helping us dissuade the Bad Boys from either stripping or following us to the various locations. Mom and I did our best to peel Aunt Amber from her chosen Bad Boy (Joe), but I think she still managed to give him her number in Florida.

I was in the car with Joanna, Bev, Laura, and Annie when the subject came up about what the men were doing for Iain. I knew David was playing host to his father's stag party, but I had had a little talk with him a few days before and had made sure he understood that Cerise and her ilk were not to be included on the guest list.

"Don't worry, Kathie," he said with a cheeky grin. "We won't do anything that you ladies aren't doing."

This worried me. How did he know what we were doing? Might he not have a wrong impression of the level of our lasciviousness, and act falsely upon it? And if we were carving cucumbral replicas of our menfolk's manhoods, just what were *they* carving?

"Hey!" I said, still waving my sparkly wand and occasionally bashing Joanna on the back of her head with it. "What do you guys think the men are up to? Hadn't someone better check on them? I think someone had better check on them. I think *we* had better check on them. I don't trust that David. He's a sly boots."

Joanna giggled. "I've never seen you squiffy. I'm going to have to remember this to tell my children."

I gave her head a wave with the magic wand and got it tangled in her hair. By the time I pulled it (and a clump of her hair) free, the others had taken up the subject.

It was motioned, seconded, and unanimously voted in that we drive out to the farm and check up on what the men were doing. Somehow on the drive there the beans were spilled about what really went on at David's stag party. I honestly don't remember being the one to tell it, but someone did. Joanna was angry with David for a week afterward.

"OK, now here's the thing," I shushed everyone in the car as we approached the farm, and made Joanna stop at the beginning of the drive. The second car, driven by Mo, had followed behind us flashing its lights periodically because they hadn't a clue what we were up to. "We need stealth here, ladies, stealth. We have to be very, very, very quiet so the men don't hear us. Quiet is what we need. And stealth."

"What we need," Annie said with a little burp, "is quiet. Stealth!"

"Yes, excellent point, Annie Walker," I praised her. "We need to be stealthy. Joanna, that giggling is a dead giveaway. It's going to have to cease. I have lived here for three months now, and I can tell you that Iain has no giggling animals."

"It's not stealthy at all," Bev said solemnly, and frowned at her still giggling daughter. "She always was a giggler. Liked to have her bum tickled when her nappies were changed."

"Mum!"

I waved my wand for silence as the occupants of the second car piled out. Laura and Mary had remained behind at their hotel, leaving only Mo, Mom, and Aunt Amber.

"Now, this is very important," I told the group. "Stealth! We need stealth. Do we all understand?"

"No, I don't," Mo said. "I thought we were taking Kathie to her hotel? What are we doing here?"

We all tried to explain at the same time, but Joanna hushed us and did the honors. After the questions were answered (all but what the men were carving), we weaved our way up the drive.

"This is stupid," Mo said five minutes later, her teeth chattering as she blew on her hands. "This drive is at least a mile long. It's freezing out here! We could have driven almost all of the way and no one would have seen the headlights."

"Shhhhhhhh," we hushed her. Whispers of *Stealth!* were periodically uttered by members of the SWAT team. Some of us, those who had watched James Bond movies, adopted the zigzag approach to the house to avoid the spotlights and machine gun fire from the guard towers, but this inevitably caused giggling in the ranks, so the zigzaggers had to cease.

We snuck up to the sitting room window with a minimum of *Shhhh!* comments, and ignoring the fact that we were standing in the remains of Mary's flower bed, we soon had our noses plastered against the glass peering in through the crack in the drapes.

"I see a leg," said Mo.

"Is it bare?" I asked, thinking of Cerise.

"No, it has pants on it."

The English members of the group snickered. A time out was taken to explain the pants/trousers situation, then new peekers were assigned to the window. "I can see David," Joanna said, her head tilted at an odd angle. "He's reading a book."

"Reading?" Bev asked.

"Does it have a picture of a naked lady on it? Is it smut?" asked Aunt Amber.

"No, it's something about sheep, I think. *You and—*"

"*—Your Ewe.* Yes, I've read it," I said, waving the book away with my wand and watching the lovely sparkles shine in the light from the outside lamp. "No smut in it unless you're a ewe. What else do you see?"

"I see Dad," Joanna said, moving to the other side of the window. "My Dad, not Iain. He's asleep."

It started to dawn on us that maybe we had jumped to a conclusion as far as what the men were doing. It didn't sound like they were having a wild stag party at all. Several members began to stamp their feet and shiver in a most un-stealthy way. It was motioned and seconded that we return to the warmth of the cars. We were a bit disappointed by the lack of an orgy, to tell the truth, and threw stealth to the winds as we started back toward the cars.

"Something the matter, ladies?" Iain loomed up out of the darkness, causing several members of the Stealth Brigade to shriek and come close to having heart attacks.

"Well, it's a good thing Aunt Amber has on her June Allyson bladder pants," Mom said, clutching her heart. "I sort of wish I had a pair on as well."

"Ooooh," squealed Bev, and slapped a hand over my eyes. "You're not supposed to see the bride, Iain. It's bad luck. What are you doing out here? We were being ever so stealthy."

"Aye, you were. Very stealthy. I was bedding down the animals. What is it you are doing here?"

We all (all but me) looked at one another. "We—left something behind." Joanna said, and betrayed our cause with a bit of a snicker.

I'm told (I couldn't see at the time, Bev being under the impression that if she hid my eyes, Iain wouldn't see me), that he sized up our condition pretty quickly, and after making sure there were sober members of the group to drive us home, sent us on our way.

After he asked one question.

"Erm . . . why is it Kathie is wearing her knickers on the outside of her frock?"

I pried Bev's hand off enough to look down. Sure enough, I had forgotten that I had tried on the crotchless knickers to the delight of the waiters and Bad Boy chiropractors. I didn't have my legs looped through the leg openings; it was being worn more like a deranged garter belt.

"Tradition," said Mo in a moment of inspiration.

"Yes, tradition," my mother agreed. "All of the women of the Williams family wear our underwear on the outside of our clothes the night before a wedding. Doesn't your family have that tradition, too?" she asked Bev.

"Oh, certainly we do," Bev replied, giggling.

"I was going to wear the zebra thong, but they wouldn't let me," Aunt Amber told him. "It has the loveliest hip tassels you ever did see."

Joanna says Iain just shook his head and went back into the house.

I waved my wand in his general direction, and allowed myself to be guided down the driveway. Bev didn't think it was safe to uncover my eyes until we were to the cars, lest Iain inadvertently see me.

February 14: If still alive, marry Iain.

"So, is Iain going to wear a kilt today?" Mo greeted me when I opened the door to my hotel room the following morning.

I pried one eye open enough to look at her.

"Nurofen," I croaked, and staggered off to the minuscule bathroom. How on earth had a herd of elephants found their way into my room, and why had they all tap-danced on my poor little head?

"So, is he?"

The fiendish Satan's imp who resembled my sister had followed me into the bathroom, screaming at me at the top of her lungs. I did my best to peel open my other eye, but it was too much of a strain so I left it closed. "Water. Nurofen."

The imp took pity on me and handed me a glass. "You'd think by now you'd learn not to mix your liquor. You guys slugged back almost a fifth of scotch, you know."

By an enormous output of concentration, I managed to get some water into the glass, and a couple of pills out of the package. Swallowing was harder than I thought, but I got them down and staggered back to the bed to better confront this demon in my sister's clothes.

She wandered over and examined a dress hanging from the front of my wardrobe. It struck me that I wasn't in my room.

"This'll look nice next to Iain. He *is* wearing his kilt, right? I didn't come all this way not to see him in a kilt, you know."

Kilt. Iain. Wedding.

"Aaaaaaaaargh!" I screamed.

The Mo-demon looked over at me. "Did you just moan something at me? Was that a *yes* moan or a *no* moan?"

"Wedding!"

"That's right, baby sister. Got that other eye opened, have you? Good. Whoa, you need some Visine. Good thing I got here before Mom. She'd never stop reading you the riot act if she saw you looking like something the cat crapped."

It all came back to me. The hen party. The chiropractors. The crotchless underwear. Iain outside of his house.

Mo eyed me with concern. "I think you need a bit of the hair of the dog."

"If you have any mercy in your soul, no," I pleaded, carefully propping myself up on the pillows and reaching for the water. "I never want to see whisky again. Or champagne."

She plopped down on the foot of the bed and set the elephants to tap dancing again.

"You haven't answered my question."

I took a tentative swallow of water and waited a moment to be sure it was staying put.

"No, Iain won't be wearing his kilt. He doesn't like wearing them. He wouldn't even wear one to David and Joanna's wedding, and all of the other men there did."

"That's a shame. I'd like to see him in one."

I murmured an agreement and closed my eyes. "Ewen'll probably wear his. Iain says he loves to wear it. It's a babe magnet."

"Ah, Ewen. I'm looking forward to swooning over him."

"Just remember you promised to keep an eye on Aunt Amber. She'll go gaga over him."

It took a half hour before Mo could talk me into taking a shower (while I was in there I took a couple more Nurofens, feeling that I could live without my kidneys, but I couldn't get married with such a head). When I emerged from the steamy womb of the bathroom, Joanna and my mother had joined Mo.

"We're here to dress you," Mom said. "Mo's going to do your hair. Goodness, you do look terrible. Joanna, maybe you had better do her makeup. I wouldn't want Iain seeing her with those red eyes and that blotchy skin."

My mother. Always the queen of tact.

"What color is Iain's kilt?" Mom asked, examining my dress. "I hope it won't clash with the red and pink of these tea roses."

"He's not wearing a kilt." I explained while Mo whipped out a set of hot rollers. I sat in the one available chair and let her comb my hair. "He bought a really nice suit last week and is going to wear that."

My mother looked like she was going to hit the floor. "He's not wearing his kilt? Well, what's the use in his being a Scot if he's not going to wear his kilt?"

I shrugged.

"I think they ought to take it away from him then," she said with a sharp nod. "It's not right, him having one and refusing to wear it."

"David is wearing his," Joanna offered. "Dad didn't wear a kilt at our wedding, but David and Ewen did. They looked marvelous, so don't worry, you'll have some gorgeous examples of MacLaren men in kilts to admire."

Laura and her two daughters, Karen and Melody, arrived while my head was full of curlers.

"Hi, Aunt Kathie," the girls piped in their sweet, charming, innocent teenaged girlish voices that scraped across my aching brain like barbed wire strung with nettles on bare flesh.

"God, you like, look so sick. Are you going to hurl?" Karen asked.

I glared at her as best I could. "If I do, I'll do my very best to aim it away from you."

"This is starting to resemble that Marx Brothers film," Mo said, scooting over so the girls could sit on the floor next to the basket of flowers. They had been deputized as my bridesmaids, and were thus entitled to the rose and carnation corsages made up for the wedding party. Laura handed Karen a packet of pins, and gave her instructions on pinning a corsage.

"So," she said, that task completed. "We can't wait to see Iain in his—"

"Kilt!" Mo and Mom and Joanna said in perfect unison.

I wearily explained the whole anti-kilt/Iain phenomenon, and designated Laura as the person who would take each and every wedding guest aside and update him or her on this bit of information.

"Who's got Aunt Amber?" I asked, suddenly realizing that she wasn't with us.

"Mary does," Mo replied, mumbling since her mouth was full of hairpins. "We thought she could work off some of her verbal energy on Aunt Amber. They were going out to breakfast."

That didn't sound like a good idea, but I figured Aunt Amber was my mother's problem.

"Anybody home?" asked Brother as Melody opened the door in response to his knock. "Good god, you're all packed in here like sardines."

"How's Iain?" I asked, twisting around to see him. I knew Brother had been out to the farm to check on the last minute catering details for me. "Did Archie show up? Is he giving Iain grief?"

"Sit still or you're going to look like Mary Pickford," Mo threatened, waving a comb around.

"Sober as a judge," Brother replied to my question. I didn't think that sounded particularly good. Bridegrooms weren't supposed to be sober as judges on their wedding days, were they? Weren't they supposed to be happy and thrilled and full of appreciation for the Mystery of Woman? "And yes, Archie is there, in a particularly surly mood, but I had a little man-to-man with him and threatened to break his leg if he said anything out of line to you or Iain."

I smiled at Brother. There were times when he had his moments, and this was one of them.

"Iain's not going to wear his kilt," Laura told him, fulfilling her primary duty.

"Ah. He said something about that," Brother nodded, and accepted his boutonnière. He eyed me in that annoying way elder brothers have. "You look awful. Aren't you going to put on a gallon or two of makeup?"

So much for sibling affection. I made a rude gesture at him, which he ignored by opening the door.

"Here they all are," Mary said, pushing Aunt Amber inside. "I told you—lord, it's a bit of a crush in here, isn't it? I told you they'd be here and here they all are. And here *we* are, safe and sound." Mary leaned toward my mother. "I had a little bit of trouble with her once we were finished with breakfast. She wants to know how to get to Gretna Green. Something about marrying a blacksmith."

Mom looked startled. "A blacksmith? I didn't even think she knew a blacksmith. Why would she want to marry a blacksmith?"

"Anvils, Mom," Mo said, tweaking a curl into place. "You know, people used to go to Gretna Green to get married over the anvil. Haven't you read any Georgette Heyer? Aunt Amber got it mixed up in her mind, that's all."

Mo finished with my hair, and I turned around to face the mass of humanity crammed into my small room.

"Mom, why is Aunt Amber dressed like she's Heidi?"

"Oh, she thought that would be a nice tribute to Iain. Sheep, you know."

"Yes, but we're in Scotland. You don't see too many dirndls hereabouts."

My mother just shrugged, and smiled at Aunt Amber, who shot me a dirty look for picking on her (for once) color coordinated, but unmistakably Bavarian, costume. Where she'd managed to find a tasseled dirndl was beyond my comprehension, but I had other things to worry about.

"Were the caterers setting up for lunch?" I asked Brother.

"Yes. Well, one of them was. It seems there was a little accident with your cake, and the other one had gone off to the bakery."

Words that are every bride's worst nightmare: *The groom has run off with the maid of honor/best man; The check bounced;* and *There was a little accident with your cake.*

"What sort of accident?" I asked, tightening the belt to my bathrobe until it cut off circulation to my lower extremities.

Brother looked unconcerned. "I don't know, something about the top layer being eaten by a dog."

There's something to be said for the power of women. Instantly every woman but Aunt Amber and me leaped into action. Mary shot me a *This is what you get for not letting me handle the arrangements* look, and went off to hunt down the caterer at the bakery to ascertain the extent of the problem. Joanna called the house to talk with David and see how bad it was. Bev, having just arrived, sensed from the pandemonium that Something Was Up, and cleared the room of unnecessary personnel. The girls were sent down to wait in the lobby with their father, and Aunt Amber was dissuaded from joining them in hopes of finding a blacksmith.

Mom wrung her hands and alternately lectured me about hiring inferior caterers, and reassured me that everything would be fine, just fine, she felt that in her bones, and heaven knows her bones hadn't lied to her yet.

But Mo was the best. She dug around in my suitcase and unearthed the remains of the bottle of whisky we had been drinking the prior evening, uncapped it, and handed it over.

That was the scene that Ewen found when he tapped at

the door. He picked me out of the crowd and graced me with a devastatingly handsome smile.

"Well, how's the blushing bride this morn? Not having cold feet, are we? No prewedding jitters? Everything running smooth as silk?"

I looked him straight in the eye and swigged the last of the whisky straight from the bottle.

"Yeees," Ewen said slowly. "Glad to see that all is going well. I'll just dash off to check on the groom, then, shall I? Any thoughts of love and devotion you'd care for me to pass along to him?"

I wiped my mouth on the back of my hand, only *just* refrained from belching, and stood up.

"Tell him he's going to regret not eloping when he had the chance."

Chapter Nineteen

*Mìle fàilte dhuit le d'bhréid, fad do ré gun robh thu
slàn.
Móran làithean dhuit is sìth, le d'mhaitheas is le d'ni
bhi fàs.*

*A thousand welcomes to you with your marriage
kerchief, may you be healthy all your days. May you
be blessed with long life and peace, may you grow
old with goodness and with riches.*

Once I was suitably dressed and coiffed, and my bag had
been repacked and I had been checked out of the hotel, we
gathered together in the car park for last minute instructions.
Brother was driving me to the castle. We were to leave fifteen minutes after everyone else in order to allow them time
to gather and be suitably impressed when I arrived in all of
my wedding finery. Ewen had left earlier, in charge of herding the groom and his party to the site. He had left behind
Angel, his latest, a nice, if scatterbrained, hand model. She
spent a lot of time talking to Aunt Amber about the importance of cuticle care. Maps to the castle were distributed,
and soon Brother and I were the only ones left.

"Car or lobby?" he asked, wanting to know where I
wanted to wait out our allotted time.

"How about a bar?" I suggested.

He steered me back inside the hotel lobby, where we
stood around and entertained all of the guests. I didn't think

I looked particularly bridelike, but I guess the bouquet of carnations were a giveaway. That and the headful of flowers that Mo had woven into a fetching hairdo. And, of course, Brother in his morning coat and boutonnière. He was the only man I knew who owned his own morning coat.

Upon reflection I will admit that we looked pretty weddingish, but there was still no call for a nasty old man to make obscene comments about wedding nights and rice.

Nervously, I went over my card with the Gaelic wedding vows on it. I muttered the phrases over and over to myself, but each time I did, I forgot more and more of the words.

"What am I going to do?" I wailed to Brother. "My brain is leaking Gaelic all over the place! I can't remember any of this."

Brother adjusted his boutonnière infinitesimally to the left. "Then just read it off the card."

I glared at him. "Don't you have a shred of romance in your soul? I can't *read* my wedding vows to Iain! I have to say them! They have to come from the heart!"

Brother shrugged. "Write 'em on your hand, then."

I stared at him with an open mouth for a moment, then smacked him on the shoulder.

"That's an *excellent* idea! I'll write them on my hands, and then if I forget any of the words, I can peek down and no one will be the wiser. I *knew* there had to be a reason I was cursed with you as a brother!"

"Hey, Kathie, I was joking," he called out after me as I went to hunt down a black marking pen.

Ten minutes later we were on our way, the main part of my wedding vows filling both palms. Twelve minutes later we realized we hadn't saved a copy of the map to the site for ourselves.

"Well, this is just typical," I ranted, being careful not to hold my flowers too hard lest I smudge my cheats. "First Nate lets the dogs in to eat my cake—the cake I personally consulted with the baker over—and then Aunt Amber propositions the hotel manager so that we'll never be able to stay there again, and now we're lost in the wilds of Scotland while Iain waits patiently for me to come and marry him. Fine. Just fine."

"You'd think there would be a sign or something," Brother muttered, peering at roadside signs. "This is a major castle, right? Something big that all the tourists go to? Where the hell is the sign for it?"

I didn't say anything. It wasn't a huge castle people could visit, but it was part of a lovely scenic walk around a loch. It took us a while (we had to stop for directions), but we eventually pulled into the visitor center carpark. Suzanne, the wedding coordinator I had worked with to arrange for the site, was near tears. She was new to coordinating, and this was her first time at Loch an Eilein.

"There you are!" she cried, visibly relieved. "Did you bring your wellies?"

"Wellies?" Brother asked.

"I sent you an e-mail reminding you to bring boots," I pointed out as I sat in the car and stuffed my feet into my wellies. "We have a bit of a walk to get to the cottage."

"Cottage? What cottage? I thought you were being married at a castle?"

"Don't you read anything I e-mail you?" Exasperated, I put my hands on my hips and glared. "Honestly, why do I send you things if you're not going to read them? Didn't Laura say anything to you about this? The cottage is near the best viewpoint of the castle. That's where the ceremony is taking place. It's very pretty."

He slammed the car door shut and muttered something about being busy at the time. We started off on the twenty-minute walk that would take us around the loch and to the north viewpoint. On the way there, seated on a bench, we spotted Iain's friend Sandy kitted out in full piper's regalia with his bagpipe at his side.

"I'm here to pipe you in," he said with a charming bow.

I couldn't help it. I started to puddle up. There I was in the middle of the Cairngorm Mountains, walking around a loch on the way to the grounds of a deserted castle, about to marry the man I adored more than anything in the world.

And I was going to be piped in by a red-haired, fully kilted piper. *It just doesn't get better than this,* I thought to myself.

I was wrong.

If you've never heard bagpipes echoing off the hills, across a loch, and bouncing off a ruined castle, you've missed an experience of a lifetime. There was a spot on shore on Loch an Eilein where you could stand and yell and hear a triple echo; hearing Sandy walk through that area with his pipes wailing was truly a mind-expanding moment.

As we approached ground zero, the most scenic spot on the whole loch, the spot where you could look across to the island to where Loch an Eilein Castle sat, I started shaking. I didn't know if it was the cold or nerves, but it was probably both. I kicked off my wellies, let Suzanne fuss over my hair and dress for a moment, clutched my flowers carefully, and took Brother's arm in a grip he later told me left bruises.

I was about to be married, and this time it was forever.

As we rounded the last stand of trees, Sandy wrapped up his tribute, and I blinked back the tears enough to see the group of friends, family, and soon-to-be family waiting for us. Mo, Karen, and Melody popped out in front of me, and led the parade down to where everyone was gathered. I tried to pick out Iain in his handsome new herringbone suit, but he must have been standing behind the group of guys in their kilts.

I couldn't help but smile at them. There's just nothing like a man in a kilt to add a touch of class to a wedding. Ewen looked stunning, as usual. Two of Iain's farmer friends, Niall Walker included, were also in kilts. David and Archie stood together, both wearing the MacLaren colors. And Iain, always so handsome, looked breathtaking in his kilt.

My mind slammed into a full stop. *In his kilt?*

I stopped walking, and blinked. Was that really Iain, or were my eyes too weepy to see clearly? The vision in kilted gloriousness stepped forward.

It *was* Iain! And he was wearing his kilt! For me!

Brother shoved a tissue in my hand. "I knew you were

going to do this. I told Iain you'd blubber all over the place if he wore that thing. Come on, he's waiting."

I looked up at Brother, tears streaming down my face. "He's wearing his kilt! The one he wouldn't even wear to his own son's wedding. He's wearing it for me."

Brother's eyes looked suspiciously damp, but he's made of sterner stuff than me. "Are you going to stand there and bawl all day, or are you going to marry the man? He's got to be freezing his ba—He's got to be freezing in that getup."

It's a good thing Brother had the forbearance to arm himself with a pocketful of tissues. I went through a good quarter of them just walking up to Iain. He looked so impossibly handsome with his kilt jacket, and his little ruffled shirt, and his sporran, and even the sghian duhb tucked into his sock was handsome. And he was flanked by his sons and brother, all wearing the same outfit. A lump the size of Arizona filled my throat.

"Are you all right, love?" Iain whispered to me when he took my hand. "You look a bit pale."

"I'm so happy," I sniffled and dabbed at the tears. "But I'm going to get you for this, Iain MacLaren, just you wait and see. Making me cry like this in front of everyone!"

He smiled, wiped a tear off my cheek, and turned to face the officiating registrar.

Most of the ceremony was a blur. I remembered seeing an osprey flying over the castle on the island, and I remembered feeling Iain's warm hand holding mine, but other than that, not a lot of other wedding memories in my mind.

There were two notable exceptions: the first was hearing Iain's lovely voice rumble around us. *I, Iain William now take you, Katherine Anne, to be my wife. . . . I promise to be a loving, faithful, and loyal husband to you, for as long as we both shall live.*

The second exception was when I said my vows. That I doubted I would ever forget.

"*Tha mise Katriona Anna* [sob, sniffle] *a-nis gad ghab-hail-sa Iain Uilleam* [bawl, bawl] *gu bhith 'nam cheile pòsda.* [My free hand reached out to Brother to exchange soggy for dry tissue] *Ann am fianais Dhe 's na tha seo de . . .*

um . . . [There was a long pause when I suddenly realized I didn't remember the rest of the vows. I dropped my chin to my chest and tipped my free palm back to peek, but it was the wrong hand. I looked up at Iain. He was smiling at me encouragingly. I looked down at where he was holding my hand firmly in his. I wriggled my fingers. He squeezed my hand in return. I tried to pull my hand out of his. He tightened his grip and gave me a quizzical look.] *Um* . . . *Ann am fianais Dhe 's na tha seo de* . . . [I gave my hand a big yank, leaned into Iain's chest so no one could see what I was doing, and read the somewhat smeared words. I leaned back, shoved my hand back into his, and continued.] *Ann am fianais Dhe 's na tha seo de fhianaisean tha mise a' gealltainn a bhith* . . . *bhith* . . . [Momentary lapse in memory]. . . *bhith 'nam bhean phòsda dhìleas* [Big sniff and a wee dicht to the nose] *ghràdhach agus thairis dhuitsa, cho fad 's a bhios an* . . . [Slight panic attack as I forgot the last couple of words. Iain held tight to my hand and whispered them to me] . . . . . . ah . . . *dìthis againn beò.*"

I wiped my eyes throughout so I could enjoy the sight of a stunned Iain. His jaw had dropped when the *Tha mise Katriona* came out, but he quickly got hold of himself and beamed at me while I stumbled through the rest of it. He never said a word about the cribbed notes on my hands.

It made all of those days of hard work worthwhile just to see the look of surprise and pride on his face when I managed to get the words out in Gaelic. It was truly one of my better moments.

Chapter Twenty

After the wedding our life quickly settled into the same easy pattern as it had months before—I went out with Iain in the mornings, then stayed inside for the afternoons, writing and editing. Life was as close to idyllic as it could get, which should in itself have made me suspicious. Instead, I lived for the moment, and enjoyed every second spent with Iain.

One afternoon a few days after we returned from our honeymoon in Cornwall, Iain dragged me out of the house, announcing that my wedding present had arrived.

"A horse!" I shrieked, and threw myself into his arms as a piebald mare was unloaded from a trailer. "You bought me a horse! Oh, Iain, that's the nicest present anyone has ever given me! I've always wanted a horse!"

He kissed me and told me to look again.

"Two horses!" I exclaimed as I stood next to the first horse, stroking her velvety black nose while a second horse was unloaded. "I can't believe you're giving me two horses! Why two horses?"

Iain grabbed at the sorrel's halter as the guy unloading him turned to close up the horse trailer. "This one is Tennyson. The mare is Skittles." He scratched Tenny behind his ear, adding, "It wouldn't be right to just give you one horse, love, when the point is for us to go riding together."

I smiled at him over Skittles's investigative nose as she snuffled my sweater. "You're the sweetest man I know, Iain. No wonder I adore you."

"Aye," he leered back at me. "I always knew you loved me for my riding ability."

I made a shocked face at his double entendre that had him snorting with laughter while I looked over his present to me.

"They're lovely, both of them. Did they travel well?" I asked the delivery man as he closed up the horse trailer.

"Well enough," he nodded, then turned to Iain and started in on farm talk. I admired the horses until a word of the men's conversation caught my ear. I turned back to them slowly, a sour feeling in my stomach.

"I've heard naught of that," Iain was saying, shaking his adorable head. "I doubt it's likely. Not here. My flocks are clean. I've not had infection of any sort in ten or so years."

The horse trailer man frowned, tugged up his pants, and slipped a chain across the latch to the trailer door. "Rumor said you had. I thought you'd be likely to know whether it was true or not. I know you run a clean farm, MacLaren, but not everyone is as careful against disease as they should be."

Disease. Infection. Words that made the blood of any farmer run cold with dread. There were so many nasty infectious diseases beyond the normal everyday illnesses that could decimate a flock. I took a step closer. Iain was frowning now too, looking puzzled but, I was relieved to see, not worried.

"I don't know who's put about the rumor that we've disease here, but it's not so. My ewes are all healthy. I've seen no sign of any infection."

"Most likely I heard wrong, then," the man said as he hoisted himself up into his truck. "Glad to know it's not true."

"Where'd you hear such a thing?" Iain asked, one hand on the truck's door.

The man started up his truck. "One of the new men down at the co-op."

The sour feeling in my stomach turned to fury. Someone was spreading nasty rumors about Iain's sheep?

"Ah. 'Tis of no matter, I've naught of that to worry over."

"Glad to hear it," the man nodded, and put his truck in gear.

"She really takes the cake, doesn't she?" I fumed, watching the truck round a bend in the drive. "Imagine Bridget putting someone up to spread nasty rumors about you having infected sheep! She must really be mad at you if she's resorting to that sort of a sick joke."

Iain tugged on his lower lip for a moment as his eyes scanned the surrounding hills. I watched him, wishing I could punch out Bridget's lights for worrying him. Disease was no joking matter to a sheep farmer; one infected ewe and the whole flock might have to be destroyed. If the outbreak was bad, it could spell disaster. It was very difficult making a profit if your farm is quarantined and all the sheep destroyed for fear of spreading the infection.

"You're thinking it's Bridget behind the rumor, then?"

I snorted and stroked Skittles's silky ears. "Of course it's Bridget. Who else has it in for you and has a track record of infantile, petty behavior?"

"Mmm. Even if it is her, it's naught to worry over, love," Iain finally said, turning a reassuring smile on me. "'Tis likely to be a mistake, or at worst is as you say—Bridget speaking spitefully against us."

I put a hand on his arm and gave it a squeeze. "There's no chance that the guy at the co-op could be right, is there? I mean, you'd know if your sheep were sick, wouldn't you?"

He pulled me into his arms and kissed my nose. "Aye, love, I'd know if they were sick, and they aren't, so I'll have you lose that worried look and show me how grateful you are to have such a thoughtful husband."

"I would, but there's a horse nudging at my back, and I'd hate to shock them by ripping off your clothes in front of them."

Iain laughed and smacked my behind as I turned to lead Skittles off to a pasture. Despite his apparent unconcern, I was a bit worried over Bridget spreading rumors about Iain's farm. Other than maligning him in a general way, I didn't see what she stood to gain by it. Iain refused to discuss the matter, telling me about the horses instead. Skittles, he said, was a nicely mannered mare he found on a neighboring farm, while Tenny was picked up at a horse auction, and had, we soon found out, one odd little quirk to his personality—he believed he was a sheep dog. I promptly gave him to Iain.

I knew there were such things as cutting horses used to manage cattle, but I'd never seen a horse willingly take on the task of herding sheep. Tennyson did, though. When Iain would take the dogs out into the parks, Tenny would trot after Rob and Roy and do his best to help with the lifting. The dogs, however, resented his interference, and Iain lost control of the sheep because he laughed so hard at the sight of a great lumbering horse trying to nose the sheep along, so after a few days of horse vs. sheep, Tenny was banned from the parks when sheep were being moved.

"It's a shame, too, because he enjoys it so," I told Iain one afternoon as we watched over the railing at the two horses wandering around their pasture.

"Aye, he's muckle great fool of a horse," Iain agreed.

"Look at him now, isn't that pitiful?" I pointed to where Tenny was standing at the far end of the pasture, watching the sheep in the next field, blowing periodic great breathy sighs of sadness. Skittles ignored him, cropping happily on the grass.

Iain laughed and told me to change while he saddled up the horses. We rode out shortly after that to check the south fences. Even during the winter months, when you'd think there wasn't a whole lot to do because the sheep were all out grazing for long periods of time, there was still a plethora of tasks needing attention. Maintenance on the fencing was always a prime issue, as was upkeep on the outbuildings and cottages on the farm, day-to-day animal husbandry, and keeping tabs on all of the latest farming regulations, news, and information.

It was a marvelous day for riding—the sun poked out from behind the clouds every so often, glinting off the silvery splash of the river as we rode south. It was cool enough to remind me that it was spring, but not so cold as to ruin the ride. Sheep *maa*ed to one another as we rode past them, through the remainder of the heather and gorse that Iain hadn't yet burned, climbing higher and higher up one of the hills until we reached the boundary of our land.

I watched as two hawks circled each other, spiraling upward and crying their high, sharp cries of fury or passion, which one, I couldn't tell. The air was so crisp it left a tang on my lips. It was such a nice ride, it was just a shame that it had to be the south fences we were checking. Those were the fences that bordered Kin Aird, and I couldn't help the dull feeling of dread that roiled around my stomach whenever I thought of Bridget's fury over the land.

"She's got her sheep grazing already," I astutely noted. "Didn't take her long to get them moved in."

Iain nodded, his eyes narrowed as watched a shepherd unload a truckload of ewes with the help of two dogs. One of the dogs leaped into the truck, onto the wooly gray backs of the sheep, sending the flock galloping down the wooden planks to freedom.

"Those are Mules," Iain said, a frown wrinkling his brow.

"Mules?" I looked. All I saw were sheep. "Where're the mules?"

"They're a breed of sheep, love. A crossbreed."

"Oh. Funny name for sheep. Is there a problem with her having Mules?"

He watched the shepherd close the truck, whistle up his dogs, and drive off bumping his way down a rutted track toward a long metal gate. "No, no problem, it's odd, though. Bridget raises Scottish Greyfaces. It doesn't make sense for her to bring in a small flock of Mules just for Kin Aird. 'Twould be more of an expense than it's worth."

I rolled my eyes and put my heels to Skittles. "Iain, sweetie, has *anything* Bridget's done ever made any sense?"

He didn't rise to my teasing and continued to look puzzled as he nudged Tenny into a walk beside me. "Bridget may be many things, love, but where her farm is concerned, she's not foolish."

His words hung in the air for a moment, sending a shiver down my back as I glanced over at the placid sheep grazing contentedly on the shared property. Iain might not suspect her of hatching a devious plan of revenge, but I certainly did. And now she was acting out of character bringing in a flock of expensive sheep. Just what exactly was she up to?

I had little time to wonder about Bridget's latest scheme as we geared up for spring, which meant lambing season. In March I was called on to act as dog chaperone for Joanna and David's puppy Twiglet. David had given Joanna the yellow Lab as a birthday present, but her girth made it uncomfortable for her to attend the puppy obedience class that Twiglet badly needed. Since David was working long hours to save up for the baby, I offered to do the honors for her.

Iain had little patience for the enthusiastic, if sweet, puppy, but he agreed to chauffeur us to and from the class. The evening of our first class he drove us to a nearby grammar school gymnasium and dropped us off, saying he'd be at the local until we were finished. I snapped Twiglet's leash on her, let her have a few moments of walkies time on the grass, then headed into the gym. A small table had been set up near the door with a variety of dog-related products.

"And who are we?" A small perky woman with a pixie haircut and seriously cute smile tipped her head as she gazed down at Twiglet, who was spinning around on the end of her leash much in the manner of a top, trying to see everything and everyone all at once. "My, we're a bit excited, aren't we?"

"We are indeed," I replied. "We always are when we see new people and dogs. We will, however, settle down as soon as we've seen all there is to see."

"Yeees," she drawled, watching with a disbelieving eye as Twiglet, suddenly possessed with the knowledge that cleanliness is next to godliness, sat down to attend to a bit of personal hygiene in the nether regions.

"Please sign in," Pixie ordered, her expression distasteful as she avoided watching Twiglet.

I signed my name, added the puppy's name, and handed over the fee for the class. Pixie deigned to read my information. "Twiglet. That's quite an unusual name for a dog."

"Yes, isn't it." I wasn't about to tell that Joanna had named the puppy for the sweet she was addicted to.

"We're all waiting over there, on the steps, until Frau Blucher arrives." She nodded across the room.

"Frau Blucher?" Wasn't that the name of a character in *Young Frankenstein*? The one whose very name caused the horses to panic?

"Frau Blucher," Pixie said firmly, and pointed her pen to the wall where a flyer had been taped up. I looked closer. Frau Blucher looked like one of my old sadistic gym teachers, Miss Wentwhistle, the one who cruelly refused to allow cramps as grounds for failing to join in the activities. "Frau Blucher is a well-known dog trainer from Germany. We are very pleased to have her, and count ourselves lucky that she chose Cozy Canine Corner to teach for rather than"—she sniffed—"that other establishment."

The other establishment being the only other dog-oriented business in our small town. Their rivalry for customers had become legend in this area, starting on the small scale with occasional bouts of price one-upmanship on cases of canned dog food, and ending with a yearly battle to see who could put out the lushest and most enticing spread at Christmastime, to entice customers into visiting their shop for the annual "Father Christmas and Pet" photos.

"Ah, Frau Blucher," I repeated, pausing to listen for the sound of horses whinnying outside. Pixie just pointed across the gym toward a few steps leading up to a stage. I took a moment to eye some of the nice leashes and collars available for purchase, decided I'd better wait until the puppy was past her chewing on everything stage, and was about to claim a seat on the steps leading to the stage when a small reedy little voice crawled over me.

"I have a puppy, too. It's a boy puppy. What kind of puppy do you have?"

I stiffened. It couldn't be. Not—not the hellspawn imp!

"My puppy has a *penish*."

It was, it *was* the hellspawn imp!

I turned around slowly, a terrible smile plastered to my face.

"Why, hello Miracle. What a surprise to see you here.

Yes, you do have a puppy, don't you. Is he a cocker spaniel?"

"Yes, his name is Toby and he's a cocker spaniel. He's only six months old. I'm nine. How old are you?"

A shriek from across the room indicated that Phillippa had noticed where her child had gone. Or more particularly, to whom her child was speaking.

"Old enough to know better," I said under my breath, and spruced up the smile for Phil.

"Kathie," she said breathlessly, grabbing Satan's Little Helper and hauling her up against her. "I didn't know you'd be here."

"Yes, well, even Iain and I take time off from snacking on each other to do other things," I said with a feral smile.

Phil stared at me in horror.

"This is my daughter-in-law's puppy. I'm just helping out," I added, about to explain that Joanna was expecting, but stopped when I noticed what Toby was doing.

"Uh . . . he's uh . . . very frisky, isn't he?" I asked, using my foot to try to pry him off Twiglet. She was spinning around again, trying to dislodge the dog that had suddenly attached itself to her rear end.

Phil blanched, jerked on the leash a couple of times, and ended up having to bodily remove her dog from mine.

"Are they going to make babies, Mom? Can I watch? You said I could watch when Toby has babies."

"Toby is a boy, dear, remember? He can't have babies."

Miracle nodded solemnly. "I remember. He has a *penish*. But Mom, Kathie's dog is a girl dog. Can I watch her have babies?"

"She won't be having puppies," I replied, wondering if it were possible to get into another class. I had a vision of what this class was going to be like with the Dr. Ruth of the primary school set, and it wasn't pretty. "She is going to have an operation that will make sure she doesn't have any puppies, so there's no use in your asking if you can watch her make or have puppies. And before you ask, no you cannot watch her have her operation."

Phil tightened her protective arm across the imp. Miracle's eyes opened wide as she squirmed in her mother's grasp. "Mom, I want to watch an operation!"

"I think Twiglet and I will just go over there for a bit. Nice seeing you again, Phil."

Phil just stared at me as if she suddenly expected me to strip naked and dance around the room. I tugged Twiglet away from a small moose disguised as a Great Pyrenees puppy, and sat down next to an elderly couple who had two small hairy things resembling largish rats. The hairy rats yapped incessantly during the class, but the couple never seemed to mind.

Mrs. Hairy Rat eyed Twiglet with a disapproving eye while the puppy stood with her head tipped to one side as she watched the interesting hairy little toys dance and sing for her. I tightened her leash, figuring it wasn't going to look good on her obedience record if Twiglet ate one of the other class members' dogs.

"Labrador retriever?"

"Mostly," I said, resisting the urge to reach down and shake one of the Rats into silence.

The woman sniffed and looked significantly over at her husband. He gave Twiglet and me a haughty stare, and went back to counting the number of tiles in the ceiling. Or stretching his neck. Or draining his sinuses. I never did figure out why he spent the entire class time staring at the ceiling. I scootched down a bit and smiled at a woman and her fox terrier puppy, and managed to get Twiglet relatively settled just as Frau Blucher rolled in. Short, stout, with one of the blocky wedge-type haircuts that so many German ladies seemed to prefer, she was one of those women who had an endless supply of energy. She was constantly moving, constantly talking, and I will say this for her—none of the dogs in the class were a challenge to her. She just rolled right over them, squishing them into compliance.

"Velcome! Velcome everyone!" She snatched the clipboard away from Pixie, waved her back toward her table, then strode over and stood in front of the stage area. A few people were still chatting. She clapped loudly for attention. "You vill be quiet, please. Excellent. Velcome, I am Helga

Blucher, and you are here for zome obedience, yes? Yes. I am here to teach you obedience."

She waited for a moment. No one said anything but the yappy Hairy Rats. "But the obedience is for your dogs, yes, and not you? Although you too will be obedient by the end of the class! Ha ha ha ha!"

We all laughed at her little joke. Obediently. I thought it sounded more like a threat than a joke, to be honest.

"Now, ve have here tvelve of you, yes? Yes. And you all have puppies, yes? Yes?"

Mrs. Hairy Rat stood up. "Lalla and Baby aren't puppies any more, but they're small, so that shouldn't be a problem."

Frau Blucher stared at the rats, frowned at them for a moment, then marched over to them. They responded by increasing the volume of their output. She squatted down and clapped her hands in front of their yapping little mouths. "You vill stop that noise this minute!" she bellowed. They stopped. Mrs. Hairy Rat looked a bit put out, and picked up Baby and Lalla, murmuring comforting noises in their little Hairy Rat ears.

"You zhould not let them be the master of you," Frau said sternly to the Hairy Rat people. Twiglet chose that moment to lunge over to where she was kneeling. Twiglet loved people, and was more than happy to greet anyone, whether or not she knew them. She took the opportunity presented to march over and greet this wonderful new person, her whole rear end waggling with the joy of making a new friend.

"Twiglet!" I hissed, reeling in the leash. I was too late. She had managed to give Frau Blucher a few wet kisses on her cheek.

I figured we were in for it now. Slowly Frau Blucher's head turned toward us. She eyed Twiglet first as she wiggled between my feet, then me. I felt like squirming, too. "Tviglet?"

"Uh . . . yes, she's just five months old. I'm sorry about that, she loves people so and I hate to discourage her friendliness."

"No," she said decisively. "It is good, yes? This friendliness is good." Much to my amazement she reached out and patted the puppy on her head. Twiglet was in seventh heaven. Frau Blucher stood and marched back to the center of the gym. "You vill all be praising good behavior and," she shot a stern look at Mrs. Hairy Rat, "discouraging naughty behavior. Kisses are good. Barking is not good. Yes? You have a question little girl?"

Miracle took a few steps out, Toby in tow. "This is my puppy Toby. He's a boy puppy. That's Twiglet. She isn't going to have a baby because she's going to have an operation. My mom told me how babies are made but I didn't know about the operation."

Phil popped up and grabbed Miracle, smiling and muttering things under her breath as she hauled her back toward the steps.

Frau Blucher tapped her clipboard twice, then nodded sharply at Miracle. "Now we can proceed, yes? Yes."

"Well, at least we got away without her mentioning the *penishes*," I whispered to Mrs. Hairy Rat. She looked scandalized and scooted away from me.

By the time the class was over, Twiglet still had enough energy for five dogs while I was so exhausted I could barely walk. Phil had done her best to keep Miracle out of the range of what she no doubt imagined was my bad influence, but I could see by the hesitant glances she shot my way that there was something she wanted to say to me. I figured it was a lecture about stifling her little darling's desire to see Twiglet spayed, but it turned out to have far more sinister overtones.

"Er . . . Kathie . . . do you have a moment?" she asked as I was using a plastic shopping bag to scoop up the gift Twiglet had felt necessary to deposit on the gym floor. Pixie was already heading my way with a bottle of disinfectant and a roll of paper towels.

"Sure. Why don't we go outside," I offered, waving the bag of poop toward the door. Phil nodded, hustled Miracle off to her car, then hurried back to where I was waiting for Iain to pick us up.

"Bob will kill me if he finds out I bothered you with this, but men are so unreasonable at times! He says Iain knows what he's doing, and I'm sure he does, but we spent every cent we had on those Blackface sheep and we can't afford to lose the herd now."

"Flock," I corrected, a horrible suspicion growing. "You aren't, by any chance, about to ask if Iain's sheep are infected with a disease, are you?"

She nodded, her face relaxing from its tight mask of worry. "You see, I knew you'd be reasonable about this! But Bob said it would be an insult to Iain to question whether or not his sheep were liable to infect ours. And we can't afford to have any of them become sick!"

"I assure you, Iain couldn't afford to lose his sheep either," I said dryly. "There's no infection, but I'm curious about something, Phil. Who told you there was?"

"Bob," she responded promptly, not hesitating to shift the blame. "He said he heard it at one of those farmer places he insists on hanging out at three times a week when he should be home helping Miracle with her math. You wouldn't believe the sort of math problems they make children learn over here! It's enough to squeeze the creativity right out of her."

"One of those farmer places?" I could see Iain's Land Rover turning the corner a block away. I didn't want to worry him with word of more rumors spreading about infection on the farm, so I had to make my interrogation quick. "What sort of a farmer place? The co-op? An NFU meeting?"

She shrugged and grimaced as Miracle started honking the car horn. "I'm not sure. One of those places. I just wanted to be sure our flock wasn't in any danger from Iain's sheep."

"No danger," I reassured her with a lot more confidence than I felt. After dropping off Twiglet, I spent the ride home mulling over what possible gain Bridget could have slandering Iain's sheep, but decided the next morning it was nothing more than a petty attempt to annoy him

Three days later the first ewes went down sick.

"Well?" I asked Iain that night. I had spent the day trying to write but unable to because of the dread that filled me when Iain brought word of a half-dozen ewes showing symptoms of EAE, an infectious disease that caused ewes to abort their lambs prematurely. "Is it what you think it is? Are the ewes aborting?"

He peeled off his coat and sank down heavily onto a kitchen chair. The laugh lines around his eyes stood out white against his skin, his face filled with anguish and exhaustion. "Aye, they are. We're not sure if it's EAE, or another infection, but eight of the ewes have lost their lambs."

Poor ewes. Poor Iain. I knelt down at his feet and put my hands on his where they rested limply on his thighs. "Will you have to destroy them?"

He shook his head. "I don't know. The vet'll be out in the morning to collect some samples. We'll know more then."

I held his hands for a few more minutes, my heart breaking at the bleak weariness in his lovely eyes. We had a silent dinner, a depressing evening with Iain checking periodically on the isolated ewes, and a long, sleepless night in which I held him in an attempt to protect him from the probable disaster. Losing a flock of sheep would not devastate us; being forced to destroy all of the sheep within range of the infection would. Iain had mentioned that there was a vaccine for EAE, but the only sure way to eliminate it was to cull the flocks. I wasn't sure if Iain would recover from such a drastic measure, either emotionally or monetarily.

It was with a very grim face that I stopped by Graeham's office the following morning. I had been shopping for a few necessities, and was heading home to hear what the vet had to say. Since Graeham was on my way, I ran in to his insurance office to let him know I wouldn't be at our weekly Gaelic tutoring session.

He stood up, smiling as he held out his hand when I slipped past the outer office into the small, close room that reminded me of a rabbit warren. "Kathie! Don't tell me— you're finally going to allow me to take you to lunch! After four months, I was beginning to suspect you were holding a grudge against me for that regrettable incident."

I forced a smile to my lips, but I was willing to bet it looked pretty sickly from the other side. The regrettable incident in question was his attempt at a grab during one of our early sessions. I came close to smacking him, but managed to get my feelings across with a few sharp words and glares. He had apologized and never tried anything on me since, but I was still vaguely suspicious that he'd go into octopus mode again if I weren't vigilant.

"Thanks, Graeham, I don't have the time today. I'm on my way home, but I wanted to let you know I won't be in later."

"Oh?" He hadn't let go of my hand. I tried to pull it back without being too rude. "Not trouble at home, I hope?"

I fluttered my free hand toward the window and safety, exerting a little more pull on my hand. His tightened. Damn. I didn't want to have to get miffed with him, either, since he was such a good Gaelic tutor, but I wasn't about to play handsies with him when I had a dishy Scot waiting for me. "Oh, you know how life is. It has its ups and downs." I stepped backward toward his door, taking my hand with me. Luckily he decided not to follow.

"Ah, that is too bad. You're talking about the EAE outbreak, of course. I heard the rumor that Dulnain was infected; I'm sorry to find out it's true."

I smiled another feeble smile and started for the door. As I passed his secretary his words sank in. I paused at the outer door to the office, then spun around. Graeham was standing framed in the doorway to his room. His eyebrows rose as I stepped forward a step.

"Graeham, who told you that Iain's farm was infected?"

His eyebrows rose even higher. "Who told me?" He sucked in breath and furrowed his brow. "I'm not sure I can remember . . . Doris, do you remember who mentioned the MacLaren's farm was infected?"

Doris, the blond fifty-something secretary, made a face. "I haven't any idea."

Graeham tugged at his earlobe as he pursed his lips in thought, a calculated move I suspected he thought was an endearing trait, but which made me want to smack his hands. "I'm sorry, Kathie, I don't remember who it was who told me about your farm. Is it important? I can try to find out if it is important to you."

"No," I said, opening the door and smiling at Doris. "Not important. Thanks. Bye."

Not important my Aunt Fanny! Not only had someone been spreading rumors about an infection that just showed up, but they even named it, pinpointing the disease that Iain thought was affecting his sheep.

I hurried home to find Iain seeing the vet off.

"Well?" I asked as soon as the vet waved a cheery good-bye and headed off down the drive. "Well? Is it EAE? Will you have to cull the flock? Can you save any of them? Did he give you a vaccine? Why are you just standing there? Why don't you answer me? Dammit, Iain, I've been worried sick about this and all you can do is stand there like a great big oatcake and not say a single thing!"

A tiny smile touched his lips as he pulled me into a hug and kissed the top of my hair. "Ah, love, what would I do without you?"

I mumbled into his jacket that he couldn't exist without me and hugged him back.

"It's not EAE," he mumbled against my mouth after he kissed me properly. It took me a minute to recover from the effects of those rugged, manly lips.

"Thank God for that."

"Packer thinks it might be Gutierrezia. He's given them oxytetracycline. It doesn't look as if we'll lose more than half the ewes affected."

I blinked. Douglas Packer was one of our local vets, a nice man, but very young, just out of vet college. Iain liked him, but tended to reserve judgment on the vet's calls. "Gutierrezia? What's that? Is it contagious?"

Iain opened the trunk of the car and gathered up the groceries. I hurried for the kitchen door. "It's a plant, love. It acts as an abortifacient."

I peeled my coat and gloves off and followed him into the warmth of the kitchen. "A what? Oh. It makes the ewes abort?"

He nodded.

"How would your sheep get a hold of Gutierrezia? They've never done this before, have they?"

"No," he grunted as he set down the groceries.

"So then how could they get this Gutierrezia? Does it grow around here?"

"No," he repeated, standing still so I could help him out of his coat. He thought I was just being polite to help him; in truth, my motives had to do more with the opportunity to run my hands over that big chest rather than with courtesy. "It doesn't grow in locally. The only way for the sheep to be getting into it is for someone to have given it to them."

I stopped finding excuses to caress his ribcage and stared at him. Grim eyes dark as night stared back at me. "Someone deliberately fed our sheep a plant that would make them abort their lambs? Someone came onto our land and did that?"

"Aye," he responded, his jaw tight and unyielding.

"But how did they get to the sheep? Oh." I remembered that he had told me earlier all the ewes affected were the ones alongside the dirt track that separated the south border of Iain's land with Kin Aird. "They probably used the track, huh? But that only goes to Kin Aird and Bridget's farm. . . ."

Bridget! It had to be her. No one else would be so perverse, so evil.

"That witch! That *bitch!* By God, I hope you sue the pants off her for this, Iain! How dare she retaliate against you like this, just because you didn't want a murder house on your land? How dare she kill those poor little innocent unborn lambs!"

I expected Iain to jump to Bridget's defense, but he surprised me by simply nodding his head.

"You . . . you're not going to say it wasn't Bridget? You're not going to defend her against my tirade? You're not going to tell me that she wouldn't be so cruel as to viciously attack you in this manner?"

"No, love, I'm not. Her Mules have been moved."

Iain looked worn to a frazzle. I pushed him toward a chair, put the kettle on for tea, and started unpacking groceries.

"She moved her sheep? Why would she do that?"

He rubbed the back of his neck. "She'd move them if she

thought there was a chance they might get into the Gutier-rezia. Those are pedigreed sheep she's bought. She'd not be wanting to expose them to the possibility of losing their lambs."

I ground my teeth against calling Bridget every name I could think of. Instead I slammed cans of soup onto a shelf in the pantry. "So what are you going to do about it?"

He lifted his hands in a gesture of defeat. "Our ewes have been treated. We'll probably lose some, but the rest of the flock should be safe. I'll keep an eye on the other hirsels to be sure they're not being poisoned as well."

I stuffed a loaf of bread into the breadbox and slammed the little door closed. "You're not going after Bridget? You're not going to make her pay for what she's done?"

"How can I make her pay, love? I can't prove she's had a hand in this, anyone could have climbed the fence and had access to the track and the sheep. I don't even know where the Gutierrezia came from. All I have is the suspicion that Bridget's decided to pay me back for losing the abattoir by spreading rumors that there was infection on the farm, fol-lowing that up with enough proof to have everyone believin' it." He accepted an apple that I tossed from one of the gro-cery bags, taking a chunk of it with a quick savage bite. "I suppose we should be grateful she only poisoned a few ewes. It would have been much worse if she'd introduced infected sheep into the hirsel."

My blood ran icy at the thought of that.

"Well, hell!" I stomped around the kitchen, putting gro-ceries away with muttered imprecations. "This is so bloody frustrating!"

He agreed.

"So you're not going to do anything at all?"

He beetled his brows at me. "I didn't say that."

"Oh, good." I set the teapot on the table and plopped down in a chair next to him. "So what's the game plan?"

He poured himself a cup of tea. "It's naught to do with you, love."

I stared at him. He wasn't going to go all quiet alpha on me again, was he? Not after everything we'd been through?

Not after we had been married? "Dammit, Iain, now is the time you're supposed to open up to me. You're supposed to trust me. You're supposed to tell me everything!"

He looked surprised by the fact that I was yelling. "I do trust you, Kathie."

"Good," I ground out, poking him in the chest. "Then you can just tell me what you have planned in retaliation for Bridget's cruelties."

He gave me one of his long, level looks, the kind that made me feel like I was being unreasonable despite the fact that I knew I wasn't. "I'll not retaliate, love. I will investigate the matter, but I won't retaliate."

I pouted over that for a moment, toying with the thought of offering myself as a tool of revenge—oh, how I would like to get Bridget in a quiet little room for a couple of minutes, just me and a few common garden implements—but that look squelched the idea. "OK, so how're you going to investigate?"

He shook his head before blowing on his tea. "I've not decided yet."

"You must have some idea!"

He shook his head.

"Well, OK, how about this—we look for the person starting the rumors, then we prove Bridget was behind him. Or her. But it probably was a him."

"That won't prove she poisoned the sheep."

"No, but it will show she had knowledge of illness before it actually appeared, and thus must be guilty."

He shook his head again.

"Well . . . what if I look for the rumormonger while you go after the source of the poison?"

"I'll not have you involved in this, Kathie."

"But—"

"No."

"Iain—"

"No."

I argued for twenty straight minutes, but in the end he made it clear that he had no intentions of allowing me to help. I certainly wasn't going to let Bridget get away with her evil plan, however.

While Iain was working to prove Bridget's complicacy, I'd focus on finding out who had started the rumor of disease on the farm a good two weeks before the first ewe was poisoned.

It was a job worthy of a mystery writer!

Chapter Twenty-one

April meant lambing in our area of the Highlands. A few months before the ewes were due to start popping lambs out, Iain brought in the local vet and handed him a big wad of money to do ultrasounds on all of the pregnant ewes. The ultrasound allowed him to know how many lambs the ewe was expecting. Each ewe was then marked on her side with a bit of paint indicating how many lambs she was carrying— nothing for singles, blue for twins, green for triplets.

In addition to the ultrasound, the ewes were dipped, vaccinated, and crutched. Crutching the sheep meant Iain and Mark spent a long week rounding them all up, and one at a time, clipped the ewes around their hindquarters and under the belly, clearing the way to the ewe's teats so the lambs wouldn't have to break out a tracking dog to find them. The ewes were also crutched at tupping time, with the idea that clipping away the wool gave the ram better access and thus a better success rate.

I like to think of it as a bikini wax for sheep.

Crutching was also done to keep down parasite problems, a subject so repulsive, I socked Iain on the arm when he explained it to me.

As lambing time drew closer, the ewes were separated into groups by their colors, and herded into specific lambing areas, allowing Iain and Mark an easy way to check on the ewes carrying one lamb, the twin-bearing ewes, and even those who were expected to pop out triplets. Lambing time itself was fraught with worry and concern—most of which was for the ewes having one lamb, since they were often the most trouble. Single lambs were usually quite big, and thus prone to getting in awkward positions during the birth.

This lambing season was worse than normal due to the mystery campaign against Iain and his sheep that culminated in the loss of thirteen breeding ewes. Word had continued to spread about the possibility of our sheep being diseased. A week before lambing was due to start, Iain was paid a call by an agriculture official who ordered an investigation into the illnesses with an eye to quarantining the farm should anything turn up infectious.

"What's the worst that could happen?" I asked Iain that night when we were cuddled up in bed.

He shifted beneath me and was silent for so long I thought he had drifted off to sleep. "The ministry could order the ewes to be destroyed."

His voice rumbled deep in the chest beneath my ear, but it didn't take much to hear the unspoken pain that accompanied the words.

"Even the pregnant ewes? The ones ready to pop? They'd kill them?"

"Aye," he said. Just *aye*. No more, no less, but it was enough to fill me with dread.

We spent a tense, stress-filled eight days before the sheep were cleared of infection, confirming the vet's assessment that the ewes were poisoned with an abortifacient, but we didn't have time to so much as sigh with relief before the lambs started dropping.

Most of Iain's sheep were hardy hill sheep, not spoiled rotten *I sleep only in a barn* sheep, so they generally did well birthing by themselves without assistance. Both Iain and Mark spent long days out in the lambing parks and on the hills, however, checking on the low ground and hill ewes, making sure those who had birthed were OK, that the lambs were alive and kicking, as well as assisting in the difficult births. Roughly two-thirds of the ewes lambed without problem; it was the other third that kept everyone busy.

This was my first time at helping out at lambing, and I was a basket case worrying that I might do something to hurt either the ewe or the lambs. I had no idea what to expect other than the gruesome scenarios presented in Ian's sheep books.

"It'll be all right, love," he reassured me. "You'll not be asked to do something beyond your experience."

"What experience? I have no experience! I have no experience whatsoever in birthing things! I know squat about it!"

He grinned. "You'll know more than squat by the time April's over."

If I survived it, I would. Not a very reassuring thought, that.

I dogged Ian's footsteps the first few days, watching how he helped with a breech birth—one of, if not the worst case birthing scenarios—and one in which one leg or another was folded back. My admiration for him shot sky-high when I saw how gentle he was with the ewes—even though they were livestock, not pets, he still treated them with great compassion and did his best to ease the ewes who were having troubles.

We all carried satchels with lambing supplies in them: iodine, twine, towel, sharp knife, rope, antiseptic wipes, antibiotics, and so on. At one point I looked at the rope and wondered what Iain expected me to do with it. Hang myself if I couldn't get the lamb out? It seemed reasonable to me at the time.

Once a lamb was born and it seemed to be thriving, its ear was tagged, and its number and the ewe's number were recorded in notebooks we all carried. My notebooks tended to have more information than just the normal numbers, sex, and date of birth. Mine had descriptions of the lambs, little head sketches, and notes about any characteristics that I found particularly amusing.

Ian didn't find this amusing at all, but then, he knew what was coming, and he knew me. I didn't understand his attitude at first. He wasn't a cold, callous person, and yet that was the attitude he struck with the cute, adorable, fluffy white lambs.

"They're not pets," he said for what seemed like the hundredth time when I showed him my notebook so he could transfer the information to the master book.

"No, of course they're not, but that doesn't mean I can't find them cute! Just look at the sketch of Cottonball I did—isn't that the cutest little lamb you've ever seen?"

Iain sighed. "Kathie, don't make sketches of them. And don't name them. All that's needed is the basic information."

"I can't help it, they're so adorable! I want to take the camera out with me tomorrow."

"Just don't get attached, love. You know where they're headed."

Yes, I did, and I had a couple of big issues with that, but it didn't seem to be the time to hash that out. Iain was coming in exhausted each night. He barely had enough energy to eat supper, then he'd crash on the couch, a book resting on his chest as he snoozed a few hours away before heading back down to the barn to tend the orphans. Poor man. Lambing season wasn't an easy time.

David and Joanna normally helped out at lambing time, but with Jo preggers, she was excused from duty, so it was that I ended up apprenticed to David as he made his rounds. We were given morning patrol of the twin lambing park so David could get a half day's work in at his regular job.

David and I marched out each chilly April morning, our breaths collecting in clouds on the pure, sharp air as we flung satchels over our backs, climbing the hills to see how many new lambs were born, and who might be having problems. We tagged their ears, trimmed and swabbed iodine on the umbilical cords of the newborns, made sure the ewe was dropping milk, and checked to make sure the placenta had been passed.

The only thing we didn't do right off the bat was dock tails and castrate the ram lambs. I drew the line at docking tails. Even though I knew why it had to be done, it still grossed me out royally, although later I became quite handy with the ring castrator. I think it kind of worried Iain that I was so proficient. Men get a little funny when one of their wife's talents takes the form of castration.

"Mmm," David said our third morning out. "We've got a problem ewe here."

I had been watching a newborn lamb nurse happily, his tail wagging furiously. I looked over to where David stood. Whoops! There was a nose sticking out of the ewe's hindquarters. Not good—lambs in proper presentation were born with their noses between their front feet. This little fellow's feet were nowhere in sight.

"Well, there's nothing for it but to see how he's laying." David stripped off his gloves and cleaned his hand, then smeared a lubricant on it and lying on the ground, slipped his hand in alongside the nose. Just the sight of his wrist disappearing up the ewe made me nervous. We hadn't had any problem births the past two days, and Iain had said he would handle any serious problems. This looked mighty darn serious to me.

"Um, David, I can go yell down your father if you want."

"Ah, I found a foot. No, it's under control, let me see if I can't figure out which foot belongs to which lamb."

That was the problem with multiple births. Sometimes the leg that was coming out was not attached to the "first out of the chute" lamb.

He worked on that ewe for a good twenty minutes, pushing the nose back in and pulling the proper legs forward until the first lamb was born. His brother soon followed, and we were rewarded with the sight of the ewe making those lovely mom noises and *maaa*ing at her babies while they *maaa*ed back at her.

"It'll be your turn next," David grunted as he wiped down his hand and arm.

Me? No way! "Huh-uh! Not me. I don't know nothin' 'bout birthin' no babies, Miz Scarlett."

He gave my shoulder a pat, and watched the lambs. "You're a sheep farmer's wife now, Kathie. I'm afraid you're not going to have a choice."

He was wrong. I knew Iain, and if I absolutely wanted nothing to do with the lambing, he wouldn't say a word about it. But I had wanted Iain, I had wanted a life in Scotland, and I wasn't about to refuse to help him when he needed every pair of hands, so when the next problem ewe came up, I wiped off my hand, greased it up, and with only a few "Yuk! I can't believe I'm going to stick my hand up a sheep!" comments, I set about to learning what the inside of a sheep felt like.

It was warm. And slimy. And absolutely fascinating. The first thing I felt was a smooth little hoof. It was pointing in the right direction, and the flat side was down, as it should be. "There's a hoof," I told David. He nodded. That was good, front hooves should be the first thing to come out. I followed the hoof up as far as I could and found the lamb's face.

"OK, I have a leg and a face. I'm pretty sure the leg belongs to the head, so that's good, right?"

"Right, that means it's the leg for the first twin. Can you feel the second one?"

"Lamb or leg?"

"Leg."

I followed the lamb's jaw to the underside. "No, there's nothing." I tried following the head down to the lamb's shoulders, but the ewe's pelvic bones prevented further exploration. "Crap, I think that leg is folded back."

"Can you ease it forward, or do you want me to try?"

I looked up to him. I was lying on my side in a cold, muddy field, my face inches away from the least attractive part of a sheep, my arm doing things I never imagined it would be doing, and oh joy of joys, it was starting to rain.

Iain's wife. I was his wife now, and that meant I had to do sheep farmish type things, even if I didn't particularly care to. I took a deep, sheep-scented breath. "No, just tell me what to do."

David walked me through it. Luckily, the leg wasn't bent as far back as I thought, and the twin wasn't pushing the first lamb too far forward, so I managed to get the lamb pushed back a little, then his legs forward. A few gentle tugs, and *gooooosh!* One lamb, very gucky, but breathing.

I couldn't have been prouder if I'd given birth to the lamb myself. I looked up at David. "I did it! I birthed a lamb! I can't wait to tell Iain!"

He laughed. "Well, technically the ewe did, but I know what you mean. It's always a good moment when they come out alive and active."

We pushed the baby around to the mom, who promptly cleaned its face clear of membrane, chewed off the cord, and started licking the rest of it. Ten minutes later, she stretched out her neck, her head pointed up to the sky, grunted twice, and popped out a second lamb.

Mom and babies were doing well when we left.

Bathsheepa and her sister were born toward the end of lambing season. Their mother rejected them, evidently the second time she had rejected her lambs. Iain put her in the adopter—a small enclosed area that gave the ewe time to learn her babies' scent, or to be fooled into adopting an orphan lamb—but it did no good.

That was about the time I learned how to tube-feed lambs. I was horrified at the thought of doing it, having heard Iain's many warnings about being careful when sliding the tube down their throats—if you did it wrong, you could send the tube into their lungs, killing them when the fluid was injected.

"Keep it to the back of their throat," he told me time and again, then he'd demonstrate. I hadn't done it without supervision when David came up to the house one rainy afternoon with two newborn lambs tucked under his coat.

"Dad says you need to warm them, and feed them colostrum. You know how to do that, don't you?"

Who, me? I'd seen it done, but never had tried it on my own. I got out the heat lamp we kept in the house for warming the newborns, and made sure they were dry. They felt cold. I would have asked David to do the feeding, but he was just as tired as Iain, and was also trying to put in as much work as possible at his office.

"Sure, I helped Iain just yesterday feeding triplets. Go on home, David, and let Joanna pamper you."

He gave me a tired grin. "It's not quite what you thought it was going to be, is it?"

The lambs started to shiver, a good sign. It meant their bodies were trying to keep them warm. "No, not quite."

He handed me the feeding tube and syringe, then fetched the bottle of colostrum from the fridge and popped it the pan of water kept warming for just that purpose.

"You're sure you'll be all right with them?" David asked as he stood at the door, his eyes—so much like his father's—weary but filled with concern.

"We'll be fine," I reassured him, and watched him leave with a growing sense of panic. A few minutes later I got the bottle of warm colostrum and stared at it, hoping directions would suddenly appear on the bottle.

Colostrum was the first thing a lamb got from its mother—it was full of immunoglobulins and other good things a lamb needed to survive. The ewe stopped producing colostrum a short while after giving birth, which is why it was important to have some on hand for the newborns and orphans who couldn't nurse off their moms.

I knelt on the floor next to the two little lambs lying together in a box under the heat lamp. They weren't struggling to get up, or trying to lift their heads, both bad signs. I looked at their ear tags. Ewes number 6288 and 6289. Both were Hill Cheviots, adorable little white things with black noses. 88's eyes were closed, but 89 watched me warily.

"Come on girls, we need to get a little food into your tummies. Work with me on this, OK? You'll feel better if you do."

I felt around the side of 88's mouth for the gap where there were no teeth, and slipped the tube in. She didn't fight it at all.

"Keep it at the back of the throat," I told myself, and carefully slid the tube in, watching for any coughing or choking that would indicate I had the tube in the lamb's lungs.

Once I had enough of the tube in, I listened at the end of it, but heard no signs of breathing. I sat there for a minute, my stomach balled up, my heart racing, my hands shaking. I'd never done this by myself before, but if I didn't do it, the lambs would die. Two sweet little lambs that Iain had entrusted to me, two little lambs that I could save if I could just get a grip on myself.

I attached the syringe to the tube, and slowly pushed the plunger, emptying an ounce of the colostrum into 88's stomach. She didn't cough.

"Good girl," I told her, and pulled out the tube. I refilled the syringe, and taking a deep breath and sending a prayer to whatever entity watches over lambs, tube-fed 89.

From the start, 89 was the healthier of the twins. Once I had a few ounces of colostrum in her, her temperature rose to normal and she tried to get on her feet.

"You're a frisky little thing," I told her when I was giving 88 another ounce of colostrum. Lamb 89 was standing, wobbly, but standing. "I think you'll be just fine. But your sister here . . ." I looked down to the lamb on my lap. She wasn't frisky. Her neck was stiff, not flexible like other lamb's neck. She didn't open her eyes, and she didn't struggle.

I was alone in the house, Mrs. Harris having gone home for the day, David off doing his own job, and Iain and Mark out in the parks. I couldn't help myself—tears of self-pity started welling up.

"I'm sorry, I don't know what to do for you," I told 88. Her sister had curled up and was resting, her body temperature normal. I would try bottle-feeding her a little later, but first I had to take care of 88.

I gave her another ounce of colostrum. She lay on my lap, her little chest moving as she breathed, but that's all that moved on her. Her eyes were still shut. I carried her with me when I went into the sitting room and grabbed two of Ian's sheep books, then returned 88 to the heat lamp in the kitchen while I read them.

There was so much that could be wrong with her, but I hadn't the experience to judge what she needed. I wanted Iain to come and take over for me, to make the decisions, to figure out what was wrong and make it right. I read and reread the chapters on lambing illnesses, and felt utterly and completely lost.

Iain came in eventually, three hours later, tired and wet and filthy. I had forgotten to turn on the oven to cook the meal Mrs. Harris had prepared, so there wasn't even a hot meal to comfort him.

There was just one sick lamb, one frisky lamb, and me. He knelt on the floor next to me and lifted up 88. I told him what I'd done for her, and how her temperature wasn't rising above 99 degrees, no matter how close I put the heat lamp to her. His face said it all.

"She's dying?"

"Aye, love. You did everything right." Iain knew how terrified I was of doing something wrong and killing a lamb because of my inexperience. "Sometimes they're just too weak or ill to make it."

"But isn't there something we can do? Call the vet?"

He gently laid 88 back in the box. "No, love, there's not. Sometimes you just lose them."

"But—Iain . . ." I looked up at him helplessly. His face was tired and concerned, but I could see the answer there. I sniffled. "If you sit here with them, I'll go put the kettle on and get your supper. I don't want little 88 to be alone. Bathsheepa's just taken a bottle, so she should be ready to go out to the barn after you've eaten."

"Bathsheepa?"

"6289. She's a fighter."

Iain wearily got to his feet. "Love, don't get attached—"

"I know, they're not pets. But she looks like a Bathsheepa, don't you think? Just stay with them for a few minutes. I don't want 88 to be alone. Here's a chair. I'll go put the kettle on for you." I hurried off before he could lecture me anymore.

Lamb number 6288 died less than an hour later. I held her in my arms, wrapped in a towel, sitting on the floor next to the kitchen table where Iain was eating. He tried to take her away before she died, but I wouldn't let him. This was my lamb, a lamb that had been given to me to take care of, and I had failed her. The least I could do was to keep her warm and comfortable until she died. I wanted her to know she wasn't alone.

*   *   *

Where her sister had faded, Bathsheepa thrived. I was in charge of bottle-feeding the lambs in the morning, something I came to love. Bathsheepa was always at the head of the pack to be fed, butting my legs if I didn't get the bottle to her fast enough, or set the bottle feeder—a bucket filled with ewe replacement milk and a bunch of nipples—up in what she considered a timely manner. Although Bathsheepa didn't have any marks to distinguish her from the other bottle-fed lambs, I could always pick her out.

She was my success story, my pride and joy, my sweet little lamb that I had saved from almost certain death. Single-handedly. She was mine.

"No, love, she's not yours, she'll be going off with the rest of the excess lambs come the autumn."

"But Iain, she's my little lamb! My Bathsheepa!"

He threw another bale of wire into the back of the Rover.

"No," he said again. "I'm sorry love, but I did tell you not to become attached. They're not pets, they're livestock."

I bit back the angry words, and kept my voice pleasant. "I know they are, of course they are, they're sheep! All I'm asking for is one little lamb, Iain, the lamb I saved. By myself. When I was alone and frightened."

He just kissed me and told me no again, then went off to mend a fence. I looked out into the park at where the lambs were frolicking and tried it pick out Bathsheepa. I thought of her being herded into a truck and driven to the auction barn or feeder lot, scared, alone, and frightened. I couldn't let that happen to her, not my Bathsheepa. Not the little lamb who followed me around, not the lamb that gamboled and butted and leaped with joy. I'd have to figure out some way to make Iain understand that she was more than just livestock.

You're living a fairy tale, you know that don't you? Cait e-mailed me one day when I had described the lambs to her as they frolicked in the fields. *I can't wait to come out and see it for myself. How come all of the pictures you've sent are of you and Iain? What's the farm like? You never tell me about it.*

Close your eyes, and I'll describe it, I wrote back to her.

Well, OK, open them to read this, then close your eyes. Imagine yourself standing in a valley. If you're lucky, you will have chosen to stand in the valley on one of the early summer days that shows off the Highlands to their breathtaking best. Although it's almost always windy here, the light summer breeze should feel more like a lover's caress as you stand and absorb the warmth of the sun.

I had my laptop with me when I was typing up the e-mail to Cait. I had just finished bottle feeding the lambs, and was sitting out with Biorsadh watching them play. Around me was the glorious beauty of spring turned to summer. Beneath my feet was lush, fertile pastureland that sloped up gently at first, then steeply as it climbed the hills surrounding me on all sides. Green fields were dotted with occasional splashes of yellow, purple, and white—wildflowers. The shades of green were endlessly varying—deep emerald in the valley fields that were empty of sheep for a while, or dirty green with hazy splotches of purple and reddish brown on the lower slopes that have been well grazed. Mossy-colored gray and brown topped two of the peaks to the south, while the northern peaks looked as if they were covered in green velvet so smooth and rich that your fingers ached to feel it. Winding between two of the hills was a shallow river that ran slate gray in winter, but a lovely dark midnight blue in summer. Ferns, small shrubs, and occasional trees followed the path of the river, which never—even in high summer—stopped singing its song.

Take a deep breath, I wrote to Cait, *and hold it—you'll smell fresh-cut hay from one of the west fields, wild sweet peas from the south, and the clear, sharp scent of warm earth and grass from beneath your feet. Closer to the barn comes the earthy tang of manure, or the pungent, tear-starting smell of the compost. Inside the barn are the usual barn smells—sheep, wool, hay, dust, horses—a riot of notes varying from pleasant (horse) to nose wrinklingly acid (mouse droppings).*

I paused another moment, listening to the distant maaing of the sheep as they grazed, noting how nicely the sound was counterpointed by the barking of the dogs as they worked their charges, and couldn't help but smile when deep, masculine rumbles reached my ears as Iain and Mark gave orders to the dogs and each other. I knew just how quickly those orders could change into some inventive Celtic oaths when the sheep were being obstinate. Birds chattered endlessly from the nearby trees and hedges, but they weren't enough to drown out the low drone of farm machinery that was a constant background noise from surrounding farms. I tipped my head, my eyes closed to catch the more distant sounds of cattle as they lowed from a farm next to ours, while closer to home the horses nickered and talked to one another in their pasture.

If you sit quietly in the tall grass, I wrote, *you might hear the silken whisper of one of the barn cats slipping through as she patrols the area. A sharp, high squeak cut off quickly and you know she's on the job.*

I turned my back to the fields and considered what I saw. *With your back to the main barn, you'll see a white and red brick farmhouse sitting square and strong, tucked in next to a crescent of trees. The old part of the house, the part that is 200 years old, is whitewashed, with small windows and a gray slate roof. The newer addition is redbrick, with matching slate roof. It's kind of a strange hodge-podge of a house, but it's comfortable and has a warm, lived-in feel.*

I looked around, still filled with the sense of wonder my surroundings brought me, thinking to myself that the land in and around the farm was much, much more lovely, and infinitely more detailed and rich than I could ever possibly describe with mere words.

I finished my e-mail to Cait and saved it to send later, then turned off the laptop to go find Iain and thank him again for sharing his life with me.

Each day I see something new, Cait, each day the light differs just enough to display some facet of the hills bathed in new colors, or presenting new contours. Each day my breath is taken away as the beauty of the Highlands strikes me anew.

*   *   *

Summer blasted fully into the Highlands, a blissful, but brief, respite from worry. We hadn't seen hide nor hair of Bridget for the last three months, and Iain's attempts to find out who poisoned his sheep had no more success than my covert and unauthorized investigation into who was responsible for starting the disease rumors. We settled down into a peaceful, happy existence, but one that was tainted by an ever-present, faint sense of unease. Although Iain didn't talk about it, I knew he wasn't foolish enough to believe we'd seen the last of Bridget.

As summer wrapped us in her golden embrace, she brought shearing time with her. Iain hired a couple of shearers who worked the circuit of farms, helping out those farmers who needed extra hands to get the flocks sheared. I was absolutely enthralled with the shearing process, spending the day out in the barn watching the men and their spidery-armed clippers that dropped from above as they zoomed up and down a huge woolly mass, slowly peeling off the fleece and revealing very naked-looking sheep beneath.

The fleeces themselves were fascinating, grey and rather ugly on top, but underneath clean and white and soft. I took great enjoyment in watching the sheep's faces as they were being shorn. They lolled around, one minute on their rump, the next on their side, then flipped over to the other side. Surprisingly few of them fought the shearing. Iain and Mark were pretty good shearers, but no one beat Gordon, one of the hired shearers who made cutting the fleece off a sheep an art form. While one hand was running the clippers, the other was moving ahead of it, smoothing and keeping the skin taut so there were no nicks. He rolled the sheep first one way, then another, then voila! A fleece was tossed over to an assistant, who flung it out onto a table and removed the worst daggs, bits of debris, and other ugly parts.

"How's the shearing going?" Joanna asked one morning.

"Fine. Want to go down and watch?"

"Ugh. Give me a few minutes. I have to use the loo again," she said as she hoisted her bulk up from the kitchen chair and waddled off to the bathroom.

We strolled off to the barn, Jo using the time to fill me in on the latest round of bodily discomforts and changes she was experiencing, leaving me to ponder why pregnant women felt it necessary to share information about hemorrhoids and tender nipples with their less fecund sisters.

I felt a bit put-upon until I realized that Joanna, normally a modest and somewhat shy woman, was treating me as she would her sister or mother. Thereafter her tales of backaches, constipation, and other such unsavory symptoms were received with a warm, fuzzy sort of feeling. *We are family,* her confidences said. *We can talk about these things.*

Joanna popped a toffee in her mouth, and surveyed the barn. "Have you never thought of having children, Kathie?"

Just the once, I thought, *a few months ago and it scared the hell out of me.* "No, it never seemed to be a right moment. Either I was in a temporary relationship, or life was too unsettled. And I didn't want to raise a child by myself, which limited me to serious, ongoing relationships, and I haven't had too many of those."

She rubbed her belly and sucked her toffee. "It's not too late, you know. Lots of women have children into their early forties. You and Dad could have a baby if you got started soon."

I almost choked on the toffee she had handed me. "Uh . . . no, I think Iain's happy with the two children he has, and it's rather late for me to be thinking of that."

She did a pretty good impression of Iain's *tch* and wiggled her eyebrows at me, a trick she had also picked up from him. "If it's David you're worried about, you needn't be. He'd love to have a little brother or sister."

I thought desperately of a topic interesting enough to allow me to change the subject. "Well, that's very sweet of David, but honestly, children aren't in our plan. I'm looking forward to just being a grandmother."

She giggled. "Just imagine, you'll be a granny but not a mum."

We laughed over that bit of irony, and after musing on the oddness of life, went in to watch the shearing.

*   *   *

That evening Iain told me that Archie would be making his third visit to us.

"What do you mean he's coming up to help with the shearing? *Archie?* Your least farm-oriented son?"

Iain grinned, and stretched his legs out before him. We were sitting out on a blanket near what had once been a vegetable garden, watching the stars twinkle down at us.

"You wouldn't think it, now would you, but Archie's a better hand at shearing than David is."

"I thought he didn't like sheep."

"He doesn't. But he likes shearing them."

Yes, well, that made a lot of sense. Archie seemed to take particular enjoyment out of being contrary. "Well, I know you'll be glad to have him here, and maybe he's resigned himself to our marriage. It's been four months; he certainly ought to have by now. Is Susan coming as well?"

"He didn't say." Iain pulled me over next to him and started sliding a hand under my skirt and up my calf. It was a very distracting action, but I wanted to take advantage of our time together, so I did my best to ignore the hand creeping up my leg, and the nibbling that was going on around my nape and ear region.

"Um, Iain, about Bathsheepa . . ."

"Not now, love."

"This won't take but a min . . . min . . . um . . . minute. You know, that's very distracting when you do that with your tongue."

"Mmmm."

"As I was saying, about *Baaaaaaaaa* . . . oh, my. Yes. Um. Bathsheepa, Iain. I really want to . . . *hooooo!* Just a hair lower, sweetie. Oh, yes! Ah, as I was telling you, Bathsheepa really means quite . . . a . . . bit . . . it's awfully warm out tonight, isn't it?"

"Warm. Aye. Verra warm."

"No, that's not what I was talking . . . *aaaaaaaa-AAAAAH!*"

Clearly things were getting out of hand. My hands, not Iain's; his were in complete control as they quickly stripped us both of our clothing. I knew that if I wanted to make a pitch for keeping Bathsheepa, steps were going to have to be taken and quickly, before I lost myself to the glory of a dishy Scot in full seduction mode. I decided to turn the tables on said dishy Scot. If he could turn my mind to mush with just a few nibbles on my neck and assorted wanderings of his hands, then I could do the same to him. I'd have him promising me not only Bathsheepa, but also the moon that smiled down on us as well.

"You're in my power now, you lusty Scot, you," I crowed as I pushed him onto his back, straddling his belly and pressing his hands against the blanket next to his ears.

"You're thinking that, are you?" he asked with a smile playing around those manly, adorable lips.

I decided he needed punishing before I pleaded my case for Bathsheepa. Lots of punishing. "I'm certain of it," I replied, and released his hands so I could slide my own over the wonderful muscled planes of his chest.

"Nipples!" I said in mock surprise, and bit his chin as I slid down a little, lowering my head to his chest to get a better look at the unexpected find. "Imagine that, right here where anyone could do wicked, torturous things to them."

"Aye, I keep them there for emergencies," he replied with a definite hitch in his breathing. "I've found it to be very convenient. What sort of wicked, tortuous . . . oh, god, love!"

First Bathsheepa, I told myself, fully engaged in dishing out punishment that would keep a smile on Iain's face for the next week. First Bathsheepa, then the moon. 'Twould be a piece of cake.

That was my thinking *before* his hands got into the action. Once he discovered where I kept my nipples ("Nipples!" he said in the same surprised tone I had used), it was all over for me. I couldn't hold a thought longer than a flea on a rock. I worried about that for all of a nanosecond, then gave it up and focused on my plans for Iain's punishment.

"As you're in my complete and total power," I managed to squeak out, my breath coming in little bursts as Iain's hands and mouth were busy mapping out the exact dimen-

sions of my breasts, "I'm going to have to insist that you follow standard operating procedure."

"Aye? And what's that?" Iain razed his tongue over a nipple that was crying out for just that touch. A moan started
deep in my throat as I pulled away from the hot lure of his
mouth. I located his belt in the pile of our discarded clothing and hooked it around the base of the standing water pipe
a few feet away.

"Hold this," I instructed him, leaning over to place the
ends near his ears.

"What?"

"I want you to hold on to your belt while I'm having my
way with you."

He thought about my demand for all of two seconds, then
reached up and took an end of the belt in either hand.
"You're in one of those moods, aren't you love?"

"One of the moods where I make you take a passive role
and let me frolick upon your feeble man's body? Yes. Yes,
Iain, I am in one of those moods." I wrapped my hand
around the long, hot length of him and leaned forward to
kiss that smug smile off the corners of his lips. "And you are
going to hold onto that belt and not let go of it until I say you
can," I whispered against his mouth. His smug smile got
smugger. Until I gently drew my nails down the soft dangly
parts of him. Then he lost his smile in the groan of pleasure
that rumbled deep in his chest.

"You smell like heather and wind and that lovely spicy
soap you use," I said as I flicked my tongue across his nipple. His stomach contracted as I grazed my teeth along the
adorable little brown nipple nub. "But best of all," I repeated
the action against the nipple's twin, then swirled my tongue
around his belly button. His muscles contracted even more.
"Best of all, you smell like an aroused Iain, *my* aroused Iain.
Your pheromone factory must be working overtime,
sweetie, because the scent of you makes me want you deep
inside me, filling me, making me burn bright with your
fire."

Iain groaned and jerked his arms toward me, the belt prohibiting his movement. "Oh, aye, love, that sounds like heaven to me."

I bit his hip then kissed away the sting. "Hands on the belt, mister! Don't let go of it!"

He groaned again, then lifted his hips as I slid down and ran both hands up his thighs, letting my hair slither down his belly. His whole body jerked again as I nuzzled my way up one thigh, spreading legs and rubbing my breasts against him as I headed for ground zero. A creaking noise made me pause. I glanced up to make sure his hands were on the belt. They were, but the water pipe was listing at a thirty degree angle from the strain of Iain pulling on the belt. I licked and nibbled my way up his thighs until I was flush up against the object of my desire.

"Mmm, yes, I can see you're holding tight to the belt. I believe such good behavior is deserving of reward, don't you?"

A hopeful moan was my answer. I let my fingers go wild on the soft, tender flesh before me as I rubbed my cheek along his velvety hardness. He bucked.

"Did I tell you I'm thinking of learning to play the bagpipes, Iain?"

He didn't say anything, just lifted his head and looked at me with big, pleading eyes. I smiled. "It's true, I am. What other instrument will allow me to squeeze, blow, and finger all at the same time?"

His body went taut as he read the intent in my eyes. I fingered. I squeezed. And I licked a serpentine trail up his claymore o' love, blowing a soft breath along the path. There was a loud cracking noise as his hands jerked down to grab me and pull me up above him. He held me over his hips, positioning himself to impale me, his hips rising to meet me even as I plunged down onto him. Drops of water hit my chest and shoulders as I arched back on him, taking him in deeper, mindless of the fact that he broke the water pipe, mindless of the hard grip of his hands on my hips urging me into a rhythm that drove him deeper and deeper into me with each thrust, mindless of everything but the love that swelled and grew within me until it spilled out into the night. I tight-

ened around him and started a circular motion that I knew
would drive him to the brink of euphoria, reveling in my
power to make him insane with desire, but reveling also in
the power he had to make me feel one with him.

A plume of water arced over us, bathing us both with tiny
little bites of cold as the water splashed onto our skin, but
the cold stood no chance against the fires Iain had started in
both of us. I would have sworn the water evaporated off me
as soon as it touched my heated flesh, but Iain's hands were
slick over my skin as he followed the curve of my hips up to
my ribs, spreading the water along the heaviness of my
breasts, up over my shoulders, sweeping down my back to
curve around my behind. I leaned forward, trailing the wet
ends of my hair along his chest as I licked the water from his
mouth.

"I love you, my sweet Iain."

His mouth opened beneath mine, one hand sliding back
up my spine to cup my head, holding me firmly as I teased
his tongue until he growled into my throat. Grabbing my
hips, he rolled us over until he had me pinned on the soggy
blanket.

"And I'm lovin' you as well," he rumbled just before he
plunged back into the raging inferno he'd started deep
within me. His hips flexed in short, fast thrusts as I opened
my body and soul to him, taking his love, taking his heart,
and giving him back my own. There was moisture on my
cheeks as he spun us into a climax that rocked the world, but
I couldn't tell if it was from tears or the water. I cried out my
love for him as he rose over me, braced on his hands, his
back arched as he roared his love to the night. The image of
his powerful body silhouetted against the silver light of the
moon, caught in that beautiful, brilliant moment of ecstasy,
would stay with me forever.

Oh, he certainly was loving me. He loved me beyond
anything I'd ever known.

Archie arrived the following day. He dropped his bags in
the spare bedroom, greeted me civilly, if coolly, and went off
to the barn to help with the shearing. I took cold drinks

down about an hour later and watched him shear. Iain was right—he was pretty good.

I had the chance to talk with him privately a few nights later. Iain was taking a shower in preparation for a guy's night out at the pub. It was a conversation I was to remember for a long time, not because of Archie being rude to me, but because of what it revealed.

"I understand you're trying to learn Gaelic," he said in a supercilious tone. I was curled up on the couch with two books, trying to decide which I wanted to read. Archie leaned against the frame of the door to the sitting room and watched me.

"Yes, I am. Don't tell me you have objections to that?"

He smirked. "None at all, although Dad might when he learns what's *really* going on."

God, he was a pill.

"Your father knows I'm interested in Gaelic, Archie. He just doesn't have the time to teach me himself."

I could hear Iain starting down the stairs. "Oh really? And what would Dad have to say about what *else* you're interested in?"

He'd lost me. I wasn't sure I wanted to be found. "What are you talking about?"

"I heard you are doing more with your tutor than learning *Gaelic*."

"Are you ready, lad?" Iain called out from the kitchen, then popped in to kiss me before they left.

I was thankful I had only one lamp on, so he didn't see the blush that had swept over me at his son's charge. That little rotter Archie! He was insinuating that I was having a fling with Graeham, and I was willing to bet my next book's royalties that I knew just who had started that bit of nastiness!

Chapter Twenty-two

September rolled in on the back of the brisk, clean air that was a trademark of the Highlands. One bright day late in the month Iain came in shortly before tea time, bringing with him the smell of the wind and hay and the horses.

"How are you feeling, love? Better?"

I blinked, pushed aside the books, magazines, and my laptop, and sat up in bed, yawning. "Oh, Iain. Yes, I feel much better. I had a bit of a nap. I think I've finally got this flu whooped."

Iain sat down on the bed next to me and looked over at a collection of juice glasses, water glasses, mugs with leftover flu medicine, and a soup bowl. My mother always told me to push fluids for both colds and flus.

"Ah, looks like you're keeping something down at least."

"Yup. Like I said, I think I have this bug squashed."

Iain looked slightly worried. "You said that four days ago, love."

"Flus do that sometimes. Come back on you. Just when you think you're getting better, they wallop you again." I heaved myself up, and propped a pillow up behind me, still drowsy and warm in the pool of autumn sun that lay across the bed. "Boy, that was a long nap. I must have really needed the sleep."

"Hmmm." He held something in his hand. Something paper. Something familiar. Something that belonged in the kitchen.

"What are you doing with the calendar?" I asked.

He looked down at it, frowned, and setting it on the bed, leaned back against the carved headboard and pulled me over to his side. He kissed my forehead, checking for signs of a fever.

"I don't have a fever, Iain."

"I know you don't, love."

"But thank you for checking. Did you have your tea? I'm famished. I know we're going out later with David and Jo and the baby, but I don't think I can last that long without a little something to tide me over."

"We'll do tea in a minute." He eyed me with an unusual intensity. "How long have we been married?"

What a stupid question. He knew how long we'd been married! "Almost eight months. Why? Are you going to give me a present?"

"I think I already have."

"Huh? Where is it?"

"Erm . . . well . . . ah . . . Joanna—"

"Joanna has my present? Well, she can just give it back! That's taking step-daughter-in-law-ism too far! I don't care if she is the mother of our granddaughter, you know how I love presents!"

"No, love, she doesn't have your present—"

"Well then, where is it?"

"Eh . . . you're not making this easy, Kathie."

Now he was beginning to tick me off. Here he dangled a present in front of me, and then when I asked politely for it, he got all obtuse on me and refused to give it to me.

"Well if you don't want to give it to me, that's just fine. You can take it back to wherever it is you got it. I just hope you can get your money back for it."

Iain started to chuckle. Really, the man was being quite, quite exasperating. I pinched him to let him know I didn't appreciate being made fun of in my poor, pitiful flu-riddled state.

"Love, I think we're needing to have a little discussion if you're feeling up to it."

"A discussion about men who promise gifts only to

snatch them away before their beloved wives receive them?" I asked darkly.

"No, a little discussion about . . . ah . . . let's start with Joanna and David."

"Why? Is something wrong with Baby Amy?"

Joanna had given birth to a lovely blue-eyed girl two months before, named Amy after her maternal great-grandmother. Iain adored the baby, taking much pleasure in her even when she spat up all over him. The first time I held her, I fixed her with a stern look and informed her she was to forgo ralphing on me. Thus far she had honored my request.

"No, she's fine, love, but as you mention the baby . . ."

I smiled at him and snuggled into his shoulder. Iain was so cute. I had been very careful to keep my granddad teasing to a minimum, but obviously he was feeling his age a bit, what with his first grandchild wrapping everyone around her pudgy little fingers.

"It's all right, Iain, you don't have to pussyfoot around me."

He looked startled. "I don't?"

"No, you're just feeling your age now that you've spawned a dynasty. It's natural! You'll be fifty soon, so you shouldn't fret if you're feeling a bit ancient."

He flinched. Clearly *ancient* wasn't a good word choice. I tried to make amends. "You're really quite young, you know. I'm sure you'll be around to see this grandchild grow up, and any other grandchildren you have. I mean, you'll only be sixty-eight when the baby is twenty."

"Oh, lord."

I patted his hand sympathetically. "I know, it sounds awfully old, doesn't it, but really, you have to face facts. Time is passing, sweetie, and we're not getting any younger, but that's not a bad thing! We're on the threshold of our twilight years—"

"Kathie, stop."

I looked at him. His lovely peaty brown eyes were closed, his mouth was twitching, and his manly chest was shaking.

"What's wrong?"

Iain made an effort to compose himself, and waved a hand at the calendar. "Love, when's the last time you had a look at the calendar?"

I glanced over to where it was sitting on the edge of the bed. Had I forgotten his birthday? No, that was the following month. David's birthday? Joanna's? Some important Scottish holiday?

He reached for it, then handed it to me. "Take a keek. Do you see anything missing from the last few months?"

"I'm not in the mood to play a guessing game with you, Iain. I'm ill."

"No, love, I don't think you are ill. Not really."

I stared at him. Had he missed the many recent sessions when I had dragged my flu-riddled self in to pray to the porcelain god? Fine. He wanted to play games, I'd play his little game. "What exactly am I looking for?"

"Something that's missing."

I looked at the calendar again, flipping back a few months. Appointments, farm notations, MMV, reminders to buy things or pick things up, notes to call people back. Everything was fine.

"What?"

"Now look at the last two months."

I rolled my eyes, but did as he asked. It had the usual collection of appointments, dinners with friends, notations of when I had called my agent. Typical stuff.

"And I'm supposed to see . . . ?"

"Compare the two, love. What's missing in the last two months?"

I flipped back and forth, getting a little annoyed. I have never been good at the "spot the differences" type of puzzles. Suddenly a cold sweat started at my scalp and washed downward, flickering little chills down my spine, making goose bumps stand up on my arms. I flipped back to June and July. There they were—MMV. I looked at August. No MMV. September—no MMV. My palms started to sweat. I wracked my memory. Wasn't it during the last week of July that I had gloated to Iain in the garden that he was in my complete power? The same evening that balmy summer winds (unusual in the Highlands, even in July) made us both more than a bit romantically inclined as we lay on a soft woolen MacLaren plaid blanket, staring up at the stars? Wasn't it on that evening we, acting on the spur of the moment, had thrown caution to the wind and . . .

"Aaaaaaaaaaaghhhhhh!"

There was no notation on the last two months. It wasn't penciled in, it wasn't scribbled on the margin, it wasn't stuck on with a sticky note. Two solid months without the least little mention of *Mister Monthly Visitor.*

Iain wrapped his arm around me and pulled me back to the warmth of his chest. "Ah, love, you're going to make a fine mother despite being on the threshold of your twilight years."

We celebrated that night, celebrated the news that simultaneously scared the dickens out of me, and filled me with a strange anticipation. I hadn't ever thought I'd want children, but seeing how Iain doted upon Baby Amy did a lot to change my mind.

So that evening we celebrated. In a manner of speaking. I was sure Iain was feeling a bit concerned about starting a second family at his age, and I wanted to prove to him that although he might be older than many expectant fathers, he was in perfect shape physically, emotionally, and mentally. I particularly wanted to emphasize his physical perfection and stamina. I figured there was only one way to really prove that.

"Now, let me see . . . have we done this one, I wonder?"

Iain, lying on his belly in front of the fire, moaned an answer. I studied the book. "It says you're supposed to communicate with me in a verbal or nonverbal fashion to indicate whether you want the stimulation increased, decreased, or stopped. Don't forget to do that, now."

I picked up a feather. "So, we were go on the feather, yes?"

He moaned gently into the blanket I had laid in front of the fire.

"Yes. And the faux fur just got sticky on the massage oil, correct?" I slid down from where I was sitting on his behind until I was perched on his calves, and applied the faux fur. Iain moaned again.

"Right. No go on the faux fur." I consulted the book again. "Use gliding, fluid strokes down your partner's back, legs, and feet. Done that."

Iain groaned. I snatched back the feather I was tapping on him.

"Oh, sorry, sweetie. I didn't mean to tickle you just there. Um . . . I think you are supposed to turn over now so I can do your front side."

He groaned louder and heaved himself up and over onto his back. I sat next to him, warming the bottle of massage oil between my hands. "Oh, look, Iain ! It says I get to tease your thighs!"

Iain grabbed handfuls of blanket on either side of him as I loomed over him with my feather at the ready. "I'm thinking it's your turn, love."

"No," I said, abandoning the feather. There were just some things fingers did so much better. "The book says it's very important to complete one massage before you start another. Something to do with not blocking the chakra or something. I skipped that part. Now, let's see if I understand the instructions correctly . . ."

"Aaaaaaaah!"

"Yes, good, I believe you were supposed to do that. At least, the look on the man's face in the book corresponds to the one you're wearing now, so I assume that's correct."

Iain muttered something in Gaelic.

"You'll be happy to know, sweetie, that I'm not supposed to tickle you. The book says that violates the premise of an erotic massage, and that it leads the massagee into distrust of the massager's motives. I wouldn't ever want you to distrust my motives. This is supposed to be highly pleasurable. You aren't forgetting to communicate with me verbally or nonverbally, now are you, Iain? Because the book also says it's very important that you're supposed to give me a signal before blasting off for the moon. Iain? Are you all right?

Sweetie, the book doesn't say you're supposed to be panting at this point. I think it would tell me if you were supposed to. It tells everything else, even down to the look on the guy's face. See?"

"If you have any mercy, love, you'll end this torment!"

I removed the book from where I was showing him the illustration accompanying the particular massage stroke and consulted it once again. Hmmm. I flipped ahead a few pages. "Oh, yes, begging, here it is. That's OK, you can beg. You're just a bit ahead of me. Hang on a mo, and let me just catch up to where you are."

Iain's eyes rolled back in his head while I caught up.

"Did you know, sweetie—oh, you like that one, do you? Do you know that these massage strokes have names? This one is Climbing the Matterhorn."

I paused for a moment at Iain's reaction to Climbing the Matterhorn. "I didn't know you knew how to yodel. That was very good! I particularly like the high notes."

He grinned. Or tried to, it came out kind of a grimace.

"You're not forgetting to breathe, now are you? It says right here," I tapped on the page as I held it in front of his face, but I don't think he saw it. His eyes appeared to be crossed. "It says right here that you are to remember to breathe, and I'm to remind you if you stop. OK, now, the next page has . . . oh, my."

I looked at Iain. He rolled one eye over to look back at me. "Feeling fit tonight, are you, sweetie? Heart nice and strong? No history of strokes in your family?"

"Oh, god, what is it? What horrible thing has that bluidy book wantin' you to do to my poor, helpless body?"

I read the instructions and made a little moue of consideration. "I think it's best if I just show you."

Iain grabbed even bigger handfuls of the blanket.

"It's got a curious name, though. This wouldn't happen to be a Scottish holiday, would it? Like St. Andrew's Day?" I started to reach for the book.

"Love, if you stop, you're going to kill me."

"Oh, sorry, I was just curious about this name. Here, I

think I can do this one handed. Well, maybe if I just hold that with my chin. Look, this one here. Is that a holiday name?"

I propped the book up on his heaving chest. He cracked one eye open to look at where I was pointing. *"Aaaaaaaaaar-rrrrrrrr. Nooo."*

"No it's not the name of a Scottish holiday, or no you're giving me a verbal communication?"

"Uuuuurrrrrrr."

I looked at the book. It didn't say anything about the massagee making an *uuuurrring* noise, although the guy in the picture did have his face screwed up in a way that would indicate he could possibly be saying *uuuuurrrrrr*. I shrugged and went on to the next page.

"Now, this one I think you'll like. I believe from the name it has something to do with perpetual motion. Oh, yes, I can see you do like it. Who knew physics could be so fun, hmmm? Mercy, will you look at that! You've got amazing muscle control, Iain. I don't believe I've ever seen anyone do that before."

I flipped forward through the book. "Oh, wait, my mistake. You're just ahead of me again. The guy here in this picture seems to be doing that as well, although he's lacking your panache."

"Love."

"Yes, Iain?"

"When I die, which is probably going to be in about two minutes if you continue doing that, be sure to tell our ween that I was sorry I couldn't live long enough to see him born."

I frowned and looked back at the book. "I must not be doing this right. I don't think you're supposed to be able to speak coherently. Maybe if I add a little wrist action . . ."

"Gaaaaaaaaaarrrrr!"

"Yes, that's the response you're supposed to have. OK, on to the next one." I flipped to the following page. "Oh, looky! This one is named after a Beatles song! You'll like this!" I started humming.

I was right. He liked it. By the end of our session he was willing to admit that if he could survive my erotic massages and still retain all of his faculties, he would have no problem raising another child.

A cold snap hit our area a few weeks later, but as long as it wasn't raining, I wasn't about to complain. I took full advantage of my new status as mother-in-waiting to loll around late in bed in the mornings, warm and comfy and full of happy thoughts of our future. One morning I tumbled out of bed a couple of hours later than normal, showered, dressed, grabbed a blueberry muffin, and headed off to make sure the chickens had been fed and their eggs collected.

Iain had his battered old pickup truck out, the one he used to haul sheep around. He and Mark were setting up a ramp and some temporary panels to serve as a funnel into the back of the truck.

"What are you guys doing?" I asked them, stuffing the last of the muffin in my mouth as Mark heaved another panel into place. He didn't look at me. Iain's jaw went a bit tight. The hairs on the back of my neck started to stand on end. I looked behind him into the holding paddock and saw it filled with lambs. I searched them, and sure enough, there she was, butting her head against an empty grain bucket. My heart congealed into a dense lump and dropped to my stomach.

"No. Iain, you can't do this. I won't let you."

Iain put down the plank and nodded to Mark, then walked over to me and put his hands on my shoulders. I tried to twitch them off, but he clamped down hard.

"Kathie, I've told you over and over again the lambs aren't pets. I know this will be hard for you, so I think it's best if you were to go up to the house."

"No, Iain, dammit, why not? Why can't I keep Bathsheepa? Just give me *one* good reason why!"

He wiped a tear off my cheek. "Because you won't just have one, love. There'll be more lambs next year, and more the following, and more each year after that. You'll help them be born and you'll warm them and you'll feed them, but you can't keep each one."

"I don't want to keep each one, I just want to keep

Bathsheepa!" I was wailing, but I didn't care. Mark knew how much I loved Bathsheepa as much as Iain did. This was nothing new to him.

"Ah, love, I know you. You've got the softest heart of any woman I've met, and that's something you just can't have if you expect to live on a farm. They're just animals, not children."

"Bathsheepa is like a child to me!"

"That's what I mean, Kathie. You're too attached. You're not reasoning clearly—you're thinking with your heart and not your head."

I couldn't believe he could be so callous. How could he be so cruel and heartless? How could he not see this was breaking my heart? How could he be so damned *logical*?

"Iain, don't do this to me. Please, Iain, I've never asked you for anything before, and I swear I won't ask for anything else, but don't take my little lamb from me!"

He just looked into my teary eyes and shook his head.

"My God, Iain, do I mean so little to you that you can't bend just once? Does our baby mean so little?"

"This isn't about the baby, and it won't be just once, love. You know that."

"Love?" I took a deep breath and said the words I never should have said. "Iain, if you *love* me, don't do this."

His hands dropped to his side. He was quiet for almost a minute. "It's because I love you that I'm doing it. If I didn't, your heart would be broken each time a lamb died, each time a sheep had to be put down. I don't want you to go through that every year. The sooner you learn that they're not pets, the easier it will be for you."

"That's easy for you to say, you don't have a heart!" I was lashing out, and I knew it. I didn't really mean what I said, but I couldn't believe he was going to take Bathsheepa away from me. I couldn't believe he could be so stubborn, so stupid about one little lamb. *My* lamb!

"Aye, I have one, and it's grieving for you just as you're grieving for the lambs." He took my hands in his and rubbed my knuckles with his thumbs. "Kathie, I've tried to make this easy on you by taking the decision away from you and letting you blame me for the consequences, but you're not letting me, love. So I'll leave it up to you. You can have your lambs, the whole bleedin' paddock of them. But we'll have to sell off the flocks and find some other way to make the farm pay for itself. We won't be able to raise sheep anymore."

His eyes were sad, so very sad. It almost hurt me to look into them. Oh, I knew what he was saying. It made sense in my head; either you accepted all that went along with raising sheep—the long hours, the hard work, the joys and sorrows, and inevitably, sending some of the flock off to market each year—or you got out of the business. There was no halfway point for a working sheep farm. Either you did it fully, or you didn't do it at all.

And this was Iain's way of life, the life he loved, the life he had wanted since he was seven and first visited the farm. There was no way I could take that away from him. Oh yes, I knew that with my head, but not my heart.

"Just one lamb would make so much of a difference?" I asked, my lips quivering, tears still snaking down my face.

He pulled me up to his chest and wrapped his arms around me. "Would it be just one lamb, love?"

I rubbed my cheek on his shirt and thought about all of the lambs I had witnessed born. They had all become special favorites of mine, ones I had named and purposely hunted out to see how they were faring. Most were being kept as replacement stock for the lesser-producing ewes Iain would sell a few weeks later. But not Bathsheepa.

I thought of lamb 6288 and how I held her for an hour while she died, and of how I grieved over her for weeks afterward. I thought of all my bottle-fed babies, Blinkin, Toast, Marshmallow, Growler, Turtledove, and all of the others, all of the lambs who would come and nuzzle my hand for the bottles, and who later would run up to me for a handful of oats or corn. They were all so very dear to me. I knew some of them were probably in that paddock with Bathsheepa, and my heart shattered a little bit more.

"They're . . . not . . . pets," Iain whispered into my ear, and tightened his arms around me. I had heard those words hundreds of times over the spring and summer, but never really understood them until that moment. I sobbed into his chest when I finally realized that he was right. I wouldn't be able to stop with just one lamb. Each one that I had to warm, each one that I held in my arms while I slipped a feeding tube down its throat would become more than just a lamb to me.

They'd become my special lambs, my friends, and my woolly little babies. It almost killed me to admit it to myself, but Iain was right. I would adopt every lamb I could if he let me, and would make us both miserable by grieving over the ones he wouldn't let me have. Standing there in the yard, holding onto him, my face buried in his shirt made wet by my tears, I finally admitted the fact that if I wanted to live in happiness, I'd have to learn the first rule of sheep farming.

They are not pets.

Chapter Twenty-three

I have determined that there are times when life, the fates, kismet, whatever you want to call it, sucks. Royally. First it knocks the wind out of you, and when you finally catch your breath again, it drops you to your knees.

Just as I was sobbing on Iain, learning the painful lesson that trusting him when I thought it would break my heart was not easy, but was right, Bridget showed up.

She hadn't been to the farm for a few months, since before shearing when she came with a group of co-op farmers for a meeting. We had both given up trying to prove her guilt with regards to the sheep poisoning, and since she had made no other threatening gestures, we had slipped into the assumption that our worry was for naught, and she had really given up on punishing us.

I clung to Iain for a minute, not wanting to face her, but I told myself that was the coward's way out. And God only knew, if I could admit that I was wrong about keeping Bathsheepa, I was no coward. So I pushed myself back from Iain and wiped my runny nose with his handkerchief.

Mark had disappeared at some point. There was just Bridget, Iain, and me in the yard. She stepped out of her car, cool and elegant as usual. She looked between the two of us and raised a delicately penciled eyebrow. "Trouble? Not more EAE?"

"We've no infection, Bridget, we never did have. What is it you're wanting?" Iain asked wearily, and crossed his arms over his chest. I know he's not in a good mood when he does that, but evidently Bridget had never learned to read his body language.

"Darling, so gruff! I'm simply here to lend my support to you and poor Kendra. I know we've had our little disagreements in the past, but that is all behind us now that we are such good friends. And friends stand by one another in their time of need."

I sniffed and dabbed at my nose. What the hell was she going on about? She certainly wasn't any friend of ours, and she knew it.

"What are you nattering about? Why would Kathie be needing your support?"

I tsked to myself. Iain is an inherently curious person, a fact that Bridget knows and plays upon. If he would only ignore her, I've told him before, he wouldn't play her game and she'd be left without a foot to stand on.

"Why darling, I thought you'd have heard! It's quite the latest on-dit in town. All untrue, of course, I would never question Kyla's loyalty to you."

An ugly, ugly suspicion started to form in my mind.

"Anyone who truly knows the pair of you knows just how malicious the rumors are, but you know how people think. No smoke without fire and such. And after all, comparisons are bound to be made to your first wife having an affair while she was married to you. It simply cannot be helped."

I felt my stomach drop to my feet. My chest grew tight, making it hard to get air into my lungs. She wasn't about to do what I thought she was going to do, was she? And why couldn't I say anything? Why couldn't I leap on her and strangle her before she did? Why couldn't I yell and scream at her that *she* was the one spreading lies about me? About us?

"What are you trying to tell me, Bridget?" Iain's voice had all the warmth of an Arctic winter.

She cast a pitying glance at me. I swear there was triumph in those lovely cold eyes. "Don't tell me you haven't heard—all untrue, of course—that Keiko's having an affair with Graeham MacAskill? Her Gaelic teacher? The one she has been meeting with secretively for weeks behind your back? You do know, of course, that she still meets with him every week? Or has she told you that she's through with the Gaelic lessons until winter?"

She did it. Well, that didn't hurt as much as I thought it would. In fact, it didn't hurt at all. I was too numb to feel any of her barbs thrust home. Numb was not necessarily a bad feeling. Numb was good. I enjoyed my numbness.

Until I saw Iain's face.

It was true I had told Iain in April that I was stopping the Gaelic lessons. It was also true I had continued to meet with Graeham, but not for any amoral purposes. I was planning another Gaelic surprise, this time for Iain's birthday. I wanted to write him a poem, a poem in Gaelic, one that would show him just how very much I loved him.

As I stood there and let Bridget's venomous voice pour over me, I couldn't help but remember how difficult it had been for Iain to trust me completely, to rise above the scars Mary had left him. I had thought our few months of marriage had gone a long way toward erasing those scars, but I truly feared that Bridget would destroy what trust we had built.

"You didn't know?" Bridget asked Iain coyly. "Surely, darling, you've heard the talk in town. No? Well, of course it hurts me to be the one to pass it along, but I thought it best you knew what everyone was saying. Graeham, of course, says there isn't any truth to the matter, but clearly he is trying to keep the knowledge from spreading, and as for your little Kyra here, it's obvious there are some things she's keeping from you, some things she has been *lying* to you about, and who knows what else she is hiding?"

Iain just stared at her, his face a blank mask. I felt sicker than I've ever felt before. Graeham had betrayed me? I wasn't overly fond of him, but I never imagined he'd be a party to something so vicious as spreading nasty rumors about me.

Iain's mask never cracked. "If you're done carrying your tales, you'd best be on your way."

"But Iain, surely you don't intend on turning a blind eye to your wife's infidelities—"

His scowl was truly something fierce to behold. I could see from where I stood that his hands had fisted, his knuckles white with the strain of keeping them from throttling Bridget. At least I hoped that's who he wanted to throttle.

"I'll not be believing Kathie has dishonored me in any manner, and I won't stand for you spreading such lies about her."

Bridget didn't know when to give up. She put a scarlet-tipped claw on his arm. "Darling, if you would listen to Graeham—"

"Good day to ye," he snarled, and turned toward me. "Ye'd best be going up to the house now, lass."

"Iain!" Bridget and I both said at the same time. I started for Iain, to reassure him, to explain to him, but something Bridget said earlier suddenly snapped into place. I stopped in midstride, my mouth hanging open as I stared at her when she followed Iain around the truck. She knew Graeham! She obviously knew him quite well, something he had never mentioned to me. I wouldn't doubt that her knowledge of him extended to the realm of intimate.

Enlightenment flooded me as I stood there shivering in my scrungy chores coat. Anger and fury and pain puffed out of me with each frosty breath. After seven months, she'd finally slipped up and given us what we needed.

"Bridget?"

She turned with a look of vicious triumph on her too-perfect face. "Karmel?"

"How did you know the disease the sheep were supposed to have was EAE?"

She stilled for a moment, then made a fluttering gesture with her elegantly gloved hands. "Someone told me, no doubt. It was no secret. Everyone at the co-op was talking about it at the time."

Iain slowly stalked around the truck, his brow furrowed with suspicion as he held Bridget in his sights. "I heard the rumors as well, Bridget, and none of them ever mentioned EAE. They all said my sheep had a disease, but no one ever said it was EAE. The only people who knew about that were Kathie, Mark, and the vet, and none of them would be likely to be spreading untruths about."

Bridget started to look worried. A tiny kernel of pleasure glowed inside me at that look. She glanced at me, then back to Iain with a triumphant glint to her eye.

"It must be your loving wife, darling. I believe, now that I think upon it, that Graeham MacAskill was the one who mentioned it to me, and surely he could have only learned the truth from her."

The scene in Graeham's office replayed before my eyes. He had known about the EAE, he had mentioned it, but I was so worried about what was happening back home I didn't pick up on what that meant. The bastard! He had been betraying me to Bridget as far back as February. Another piece of the puzzle slid into place. I blew out a long breath and looked up at Iain. His peaty brown eyes were black with anger.

"You're wrong, Bridget," I told her, keeping my gaze fixed on my husband. He was, after all, the only one who mattered. "There was another person who could have told Graeham what the disease was the sheep were rumored to have. You could have told him. You could have told him when you put the Gutierrezia in the pasture for the sheep. You could have told him so he could help you spread rumors of illness even before the sheep were poisoned. You could have told him when you planned and plotted and finally thought of a way to strike back at Iain because he didn't want either the abattoir or you. Oh, yes, you could have told him—Graeham, your contact on the council, the man who you had arranged to get you and Iain special zoning permissions so the abattoir could be built on Kin Aird—you could have told him at any time. Tell me, Bridget, just how much of a kickback did you promise Graeham if he helped you? How much did he take in order to try to ruin Iain?"

She flinched at the last words, but held onto her spiteful smile. "Darling, you're quite mad if you think I would do anything to harm Iain. As for Graeham, it's true he is on the council, but he has nothing to gain from harming Iain."

"She's not mad, Bridget. We've known it was you behind the attempt to harm me, but not had the proof. Until now. I'm thinking an investigation into MacAskill's actions as a councilman would be very interesting."

Bridget stepped back under the influence of the cold look of anger he leveled at her. "Darling, she's lying! She'll go to any length to fool you, don't you see that? She's tried to come between us from the first moment she arrived, and now she has Graeham helping her! Iain, darling, don't let her destroy all that we have together—"

She didn't get any further before Iain completely lost his temper. I'd never seen him so furious, and honestly hope I never will again. Most of what he said to Bridget was profane, but the highlight was when he told her in no uncertain terms to leave, and that she'd be trespassing if she ever stepped foot on his farm again. He also made not-so-vague threats about what actions he'd take if she ever harmed me or his sheep again. I wanted to thank him for putting me first, but after assessing the look on his face, I felt it better to let him work off some of his ire on Bridget. And work it he did.

"Iain, you can't believe—"

"I believe you're a spiteful, vicious bitch!"

"I was only trying to help you!"

"Help me?" His hair stood on end as he bellowed the words at her. "Help me? You poisoned my sheep to help me? You spread foul rumors about my wife to help me?"

"She's all wrong for you, Iain, wrong for you, and wrong for your farm. She doesn't want you to be a success as I want you to—"

He breathed in deeply, visibly struggling to maintain control. "Aye, yer right there. She doesna want me to rape ma land for a few pounds."

Bridget ground her teeth for a moment, then snarled, "I should have known it was a waste of time trying to reason with you. You're so wrapped up with preserving your land you'd rather be poor the rest of your life than realize a profit. I pity you, I truly do, Iain. You don't have nearly the intelligence I thought you had. Instead of being successful, you'd rather grub around on a nothing little sheep farm with a nothing little wife. You aren't even worth the trouble it would take to explain how my actions were for your benefit. You are nothing, Iain, you always have been, and you always will be."

"It's past time you were leavin'," Iain said wearily, rubbing the back of his neck and sending me an unreadable glance.

Bridget's jaw worked once or twice as if she was going to unload a bit more bile, but evidently she realized it would do her no good. She sent me a look that should have dropped me on the spot, and spun on her heel.

Iain stood watching her drive off, saying nothing, his expression dark and brooding. I walked around to where I could face him. There was pain in those lovely brown eyes, pain that should never be there, pain that was put there by that soulless witch. I placed my hands on either side of his face.

"Iain, what Bridget said earlier about me and Graeham . . ." I looked into his eyes and the anguish I saw there as a result of my lie to him made me sob. "Oh, god, Iain, she makes it sound so horrible, but it really wasn't, I was just trying to . . . to surprise . . . you again." I tried to swallow the huge lump in my throat. "I wanted to surprise you for your birthday with a poem, without crib notes, because you liked the wedding vows so much . . ."

It was no use, I couldn't go on, I couldn't face him. The more I said, the more damning it sounded, even to my ears. Bridget had done it, she'd won. She'd destroyed everything, and I had helped her.

I turned away and said the only other thing I could say. "You're my love, my life, my heart and soul. I'm not Mary. I told you that before, and I'll tell you as many times as you need me to say it. I'll never betray you. Never."

His arms went around my waist and pulled me back against his hard chest. "I know you won't, love."

I stopped sobbing at his words. Dear God, could it be that he believed me? I turned around in his arms to face him.

"I didn't have an affair with Graeham, Iain. I was just trying to learn enough to write a poem for you."

His jaw was tight, but his eyes had lost that flat, pained look and were the lovely warm eyes of my Iain again. "I know you didn't, love. I never doubted you."

Oh, he might not realize he did, but I knew the shadow of doubt passed briefly over his mind. I wanted to vanquish that shadow, and there was only one way I knew how to do it. I took a step back from him.

"Iain, a few minutes ago you asked me to trust you." One eyebrow rose ever so slightly. "No, you didn't come right out and ask me, you *asked* me. You asked me to trust that you were right about Bathsheepa. You asked me to trust that even though it'll be the hardest thing I've ever done, you are right in this. You asked me to trust you despite my every instinct which screams to the contrary." I took a deep breath and squeezed his hands. "And now I'm asking you to trust me."

"Ah, love, I do trust you, I always have."

"I know you do, and I know you have, but I also know there's a little part of you that Mary hurt so badly that you've been afraid to let it go. But now you have to, Iain, because if you don't, this'll be the end of us."

He wrapped his arms around me again and kissed my forehead. "No, love, it won't be. You're just a bit emotional at the moment."

"Iain, I know what I'm talking about. You say you trust me, and I think for the most part you do, but if there's the tiniest bit of doubt in you, it'll just grow and grow and eventually consume the trust, and then we'll be left with nothing."

He didn't say anything, just held me for the longest time. I didn't know what Mark was doing, probably hiding out in the barn waiting for the emotional storm front to pass by.

I told Iain that leaving Bathsheepa would be the hardest thing that I would ever do. I lied. Walking away from Iain that morning was the hardest thing I'd ever done. Unlike me, notorious for wearing her heart on her sleeve, Iain had to have time to work through emotional issues. I knew he

couldn't do it with me clinging to him, so I walked back to
the house.

Without looking back at either him or Bathsheepa.

You probably won't be surprised to learn that Iain justi-
fied my faith in him a thousand-fold. When he came back
from taking the lambs to market, he told me he had sold all
but her. Bathsheepa he took to a different dealer and sold as
breeding stock. I'm sure he got next to nothing for her—the
reason he wasn't keeping her was because her mother was
not producing good stock—but the fact that he did that for
me went a long way to easing the sorrow of losing her. I
took back everything I'd ever said about him not being one
for romantic gestures—selling Bathsheepa as breeding stock
was the most romantic expression of his faith and trust, and
of his love, that I could ever imagine.

Despite that, I had a feeling things would take longer to
resolve themselves in his mind.

"You don't really believe I had an affair, do you?" I asked
him later that night. We were snuggled up on the couch, but
neither of us was reading.

"No, love, I don't. I've told you that."

I looked into those lovely peaty brown eyes with the gold
and black flecks, and I saw love shining out at me. But there
was also a shadow still lingering around the edges. I had
done what I could to banish the shadow, but it would take
time to fully eliminate it.

"You know what my mother would say," I said, trying to
broach a subject I knew he'd object to.

Iain groaned. "I've not the slightest idea, although I
haven't a doubt that it would involve horses ovaries."

I tickled his ear.

"Probably. But she'd also say that you're a control freak
and you need to lighten up a little."

He looked astounded. "A control freak? Are you calling
me a control freak? Is that what you're thinking?"

"No, I'm not, but Mom would. She'd see this niggling little worry you have deep inside you as a desire to keep in absolute control of your life."

Iain looked at me like I was nuts. I probably was, but I had a feeling that this trust issue went a bit deeper than the whole Graeham thing. He knew me well enough to know I'd never go browsing elsewhere, so it had to be something even deeper that was disturbing him. I figured I'd use my mother as a scapegoat and do a wee bit of probing.

"Well, love, she'd be wrong. I've no desire to be in absolute control of anything. I never have, and if that's what you're thinking, you're wrong as well."

I tickled his jaw.

"Mom would say that to trust someone with your life, you have to give up a bit of control. After all, that's what the trust is—faith that the other person will take care of you, will not harm you, will do right by you, forever."

He looked disbelieving. This heartened me. I had a feeling I was on the right track.

"Mom would point out that the real issue that's bothering you has its basis in the fact that you've been alone so long, and been self-sufficient so long, so naturally you don't want to let go of any control now."

"I've told you, nothing is bothering me. I'm not worried about losing control over anyone or anything."

"Maybe not, but you haven't seen the shadow, and I have."

"You're seeing shadows now, are you love?"

I let that go. His body language was making it clear I had pushed him about as far as he was going to go.

"What my mother doesn't know, and I do, is just how much Mary hurt you when she left you. I know you had to be even stronger then, especially when she tried to take the boys away from you later."

He reached for his book. I was making him uncomfortable with talk of Mary, but I thought it was time to take a good long look at the scars Mary had left, and see how bad they really were.

"I think it's all tied in together, Iain. I think you're a person who protects his very gentle heart with a seemingly impenetrable wall of self-sufficiency. The foundation of that wall is control, and now I believe deep down inside you, your wall-maker is panicking because you've weakened the foundation by trusting me with your love, and he doesn't want you to weaken it any more. It's self-preservation at its most basic form."

"I think you're a bit daft, love. You're seeing things that don't exist. I'm not worried about control or self-preservation." He opened his book, as clear a signal he was ending the conversation as if he'd stood up and yelled it out.

I stopped talking and leaned into him, tickling his Adam's apple, pleased with him, pleased with life. He was starting to open up to me, slowly, to be true, but at least he had learned he could bare his emotions without reprisal. We would be faced with many challenges in life, not the least of which was resting beneath my heart, but we'd face them together.

I kissed his neck and smiled a secret little smile. Our life together was full of promise. How could it be anything else with the dishiest man to ever don a kilt?

Epilogue

Two days after Bathsheepa Day Iain walked into the house around lunchtime and pushed a box at me.

"What's this?" I asked suspiciously.

"It's a present," he said, and thrust the box into my reluctant hands.

"A present? Does it contain body parts of any sort?"

He rocked back on his heels and waggled his eyebrows at me. That roguish look had me worried. Had Bridget sent him something for me? I gave the box a little shake. "Is it something I will enjoy?"

"Ah, I don't think you're wanting to do that, love. Open it."

"Oooh, it must be something fragile! Fragile things usually mean glass. Wine glasses? A lovely vase?" I looked at the box. It didn't seem to be the sort of box one would put an expensive vase in. It looked to be a box that formerly held cans of baked beans. "Is it bigger than a breadbox?"

"Love, you'll find out faster if you open it."

I looked at the box again. "Is it something for us both, something for the baby, or something for me personally?"

"You won't find out until you open it."

"I'm afraid to, Iain."

His smile faded a little. "And why is that?"

"Think back on what the last box you handed me contained."

He thought. "That wasn't a present, love. I wanted you to throw that in the fire barrel."

"Yes, but you didn't tell me that. You didn't tell me that it contained the remains of a half-eaten hen. You just simply handed me the box and went off to do something else without warning me of the gruesome collection of dead chicken parts inside."

"Ah, but I did pick up the gruesome collection after you shrieked and dropped the box, now didn't I?"

He had me there. He had indeed cleaned up the remnants after I freaked.

"That's neither here nor there. My point is that I am now naturally hesitant to open any box thrust upon me. Might I have your reassurance that this box contains no animal parts?"

"Eh . . . open the box, love."

"It *does* contain animal parts?"

"Open the box, Kathie."

"What sort of animal parts? Edible animal parts?" I was more than a little suspicious now.

Iain rolled his eyes. "Aye, you can eat it if you're really wanting to, but you won't, and if you'll just look in the bleedin' box, you'll be happy."

"Promise?"

"I promise! Now open the bluidy box!"

I looked at the box. It seemed benign. I sniffed it. No odor of rotting bits of chicken. "You didn't answer my breadbox question."

"Oh, for Christ's sake, I'll do it myself."

He snatched the box back from me, but I wasn't about to let him ruin my lovely present. I loved getting presents!

"Hey, that's mine. Give it back," I said as I grabbed the box and pulled.

"Are you going to open this time and not question me about it for a half hour?" he asked, still retaining his grip on the box.

I tugged on it. *Mine!* "Yes, I'll open it, just give it back."

"You're sure? You'll really open it this time?"

"Yes, yes, just let go of it, Iain."

"You'll not be wondering if it contains something nasty,

then?" He tugged the box closer to his chest. Damn it, his hands were stronger than mine.

"No, I won't, just give me back my present, Iain."

He looked down on the box. "I'm thinking maybe you're not serious about opening this fine gift I've given you."

"You haven't given it to me yet, you big goat. Now hand it over."

"Are you sure?"

Iain has a wicked, wicked sense of justice. This was my payback and we both knew it.

"Give . . . me . . . the . . . damn . . . box . . . Iain."

He grinned, and handed it back to me. I took a few deep breaths, vowing to cherish this victory.

"Thank you. And for the gift. I'm sure I'll love it." I smiled at him.

He raised an eyebrow. "You've exactly three seconds to open that, love, or I'm taking it back to where I found it."

One-one-thousand, two-one-thousand . . . "Is it something you found, then, and didn't purchase for me?"

He reached for the package. I danced around the table, just out of his reach.

"No, Iain, I'm opening it, I'm opening it, I just like to build the anticipation a little."

"You'll be doing more than building anticipation if you wait much longer," he muttered. "Open in now."

"Oh very well." I set the box down on the table. "But you take all of the fun out of getting a present." I put my hands on the lid. "Smaller than a breadbox?"

"Kathie—"

"Animal, vegetable, or mineral?"

He started to come around the table. I snatched the box and went running for the sitting room, but despite his size, he's fast on his feet. He caught me at the door.

"One," he started counting, his hand on the box. On *my* present! I tried to squeeze the present by him.

"Two." I wasn't having any luck. He was blocking the door and wasn't budging.

"Three." He started to take my box.

"Nooooo!" I wailed. "It's mine! I'll open it, just let go."

"I'll have your promise that you're going to open it, then."

"I promise. I'll open it." In my own good time.

"Now. You'll open it now."

Well, hell. "You sure are a party-pooper. Yes, fine, I'll open it now."

"Go on, then."

"Right this second?"

He sighed and reached for the box.

"Fine," I said, setting the box back down onto the table. "I'll open it, but I want you to know that you've taken all the fun out of receiving a surprise present. These things are best drawn out, you know, but you've made me rush it and now I won't enjoy it as much as I might."

He looked at his watch. "You've been enjoying it for the last ten minutes. Open it. Yes, now."

I stuck my tongue out at him, and opened the box.

Curled up on a ratty old pink towel, surrounded by bits of crumpled up newspaper, lay a confused looking little black and white puppy.

In this land of livestock and working animals, Iain had given me a pet.

Kathie's Glossary
for the Confused

This glossary is for those of you unfamiliar with BritSpeak and colloquial Scottish phrases, intended so you can enjoy the story without trying to guess the definition of certain words. Or worse, being forced to ask your Scottish minister what exactly *tupping* means. Or *getting a leg over.*

anorak: parka

baffies: slippers

banshee: what you howl like when you play mump the cuddie for an hour

black pudding: a horrible, horrible thing (it's actually a sausage made with blood, but that qualifies as horrible in my point of view)

blethering: talking without really saying anything; babbling

bluidy: bloody

bit of all right: slang for a woman, as in a girlfriend. Not a nice connotation, however, so don't use it unless you want to get your face slapped

bourach: has many meanings, one of which is *a mess*

ceud mìle fàilte: Gaelic for *a hundred thousand welcomes.* Seen a lot on signs in Scotland

contermashious: stubbornly holding to something, even when you are wrong

cropper: to come a cropper means to have a disaster, or something that's gone badly awry

crumpet: technically a food item similar to what Americans know as an English muffin, but used in slang to mean a woman as a sex object

dicht: a quick wipe, or dab

dreich: used in Scotland to mean ugly, gray, endlessly wet weather

fagged out: tired, pooped

fluich: the Gaelic word for *wet,* as in wet weather

frock: dress

get a leg over: oh, come now, must I spell everything out?

grippy: tight-fisted

haggis: Take one dead sheep's organs (heart and liver, usually), mix them with oatmeal, suet, onion, and stock, then place inside the sheep's cleaned stomach, and boil for a few hours. Some people swear by haggis, others swear at it

havering: to blather on like a fool

hen: used in parts of Scotland, it's the Scottish equivalent to the Brit's *bird.* It means a woman

hen party, hen night: a bridal shower

hirsel: a mixed flock of sheep (or the place the sheep eat)

hogmanay: New Year's Day

jumper: sweater

kist: a box, as in a chest in which you would store blankets, jumpers, etc.

knickers: ladies' undies

lifting sheep: moving the sheep from one field to another

mare: yes, it's a female horse, and it's also slang for a bit of all right

mump the cuddie: this is actually a children's game, but adults can play their own variations thereupon. No further explanation should be needed

oxters: armpits

pants: men's underwear

park: field or pasture

pillock: an idiot or boob

poor man's polo: if you can't get the meaning from the context of the sentence, it's best you don't know

puckle: an imprecise measurement, such as a handful of something

serviette: napkin

shinty: a game similar to field hockey, played with curved sticks called camans. Very popular in the Highlands

slàinte, slàinte mhath, slàinte mhor: good health

slaistery: something very messy or mucky about the farm/house

snarky: snide, smart ass

snogging: kissing while checking the number of your partner's teeth, if you get my meaning

stick your spoon in the wall: to die

suspenders: a garter belt

tha gaol agam ort: Gaelic for *I love you*

tupping season: mating season for the sheep. Sometimes a ram is known as a *tup*

twee: too cute for words

wellies: short for Wellingtons, they are rubber boots

wether: neutered male sheep

Well. I'm still here. More than a little groggy and jet-lagged, not to mention bemused, but here.

Pierce was at the airport waiting for me when I came through customs. He looked the same as he always did—tall, good-looking despite the beginnings of a cute little beer belly, confident, with a smile that always made me think he was laughing secretly at something only he found funny.

"Tessa! At last! I've waited forever for you! Mwah!" He planted a sloppy wet kiss on my cheek then held me at arm's length to give me a brisk once-over. "You look like hell, honey, you really do."

My shoulders slumped as I crossed a protective arm over my torso. "Thanks just oodles, Pierce. You sure do know how to make a girl feel good."

He laughed and waved his hands toward the luggage I'd set down to hug him. "Evan, be a lamb and take those, will you? Now, you know what I meant by *look like hell*. Your hair! Tessa, love, I've told you time and time again—a little color is not a bad thing! No one likes that dull shade of brown. A nice magenta cellophane, that's what you need."

"Auburn, definitely auburn," a slim young man with co-pious piercings said as he grabbed my two bags. "Auburn is much warmer. It would go with her skin tone better than magenta."

The two men eyed me for a minute, their heads tipped to the side just like they were symbiotic twins, then Pierce shook his head, tsked, and grabbed my arm to steer me toward the car park. "It's not important, honey. We can fix your hair up later, after the show is over. Now, you've read the rule book, yes?"

"No. Just some of it."

"Excellent," he said, obviously not paying the slightest bit of attention to me as he pushed me through the doors toward a dark tunnel leading to the parking. "Let's see, it's two now, and you have a fitting at four . . . yes, we have time for lunch. Evan?"

"Right behind you, Pee," Evan answered.

"We'll stop at the Cock and Cow for a bit of lunch, then go on to the studio."

"Pee?" I asked Pierce a moment later when Evan scooted around us, heading for a dark blue sedan.

"Isn't he delicious?" Pierce answered, his gaze resting with wicked intent on the younger man as Evan stuffed my luggage into the trunk. "Such a help he is, you have simply no idea how useful I find him."

"Mmm," I said. "I bet you do. He's awfully . . . *pierced*, don't you think? I mean, even if he is trying to live up to your name, don't you think having his eyebrows, nose, ears, and lower lip pierced is going a bit too far?"

Pierce snickered and herded me to the side of the car, his voice low and soft as velvet as he whispered, "His tongue is pierced, too. I can't even begin to tell you how much I enjoy that!"

"Right, I think we're dipping into the realm of *too much information*, so I'll let that pass. About lunch—I couldn't possibly eat. I think I'm going to be sick as is. Could we just skip all the stuff and go straight to the part where I meet this Roger guy and he takes one look at my fleshy form and laughs hysterically, wiping his eyes just long enough to send me home?"

"Stop it, Roger's going to love you," he said as he shoved

me into the back seat. I scooted over so he could sit beside me. "You're perfect for the job, just perfect! You have every quality he's looking for. You're intelligent—"

"Thank you," I murmured, flattered and disbelieving at the same time.

"—and you know just tons about history and all that stuff—"

"It *was* my major in college."

"—and you're American, of course, and related to the Vanderbilts—"

"Distantly," I pointed out. "Very distantly. And so are a lot of other people."

"—and most importantly of all, you're the only one who is free."

He went on for another minute, giving less and less believable reasons why Roger the producer would love me, but I was stuck on the last point.

"What do you mean I was the only one who is free? You said you moved heaven and hell to get me this job, and now you're saying the only reason I'm being considered is because no one else can do it? I wasn't your first choice?"

"Oh, look, we're coming into town. That didn't take long, did it? Traffic around here is normally the pits. How much farther to the Cock and Cow, Evan?"

I sat back and thought about giving in to a pout. The way Pierce evaded my question was answer enough—obviously I was not the first choice as a replacement. Of course I wasn't. What was I thinking?

Lunch looked good. I don't know if it was, because I decided the only way I was going to get through the day was if I had a little liquid courage, so accordingly, I drank my lunch. I poured martini after martini down my throat until a blessed numbness set in. Pierce stopped me after the third one, which may not sound like much, but trust me, for me it was. By the time Pierce caught me sucking the last bit of gin from the olive's toothpick, it was too late.

"I like olives. Don't you like olives? I really like olives. They're so olive-y," I said to him as he hauled me outside to where Evan was waiting with the car. "Olive. Even the name is good. Ooooooooolive. Isn't it nummy? You're nummy too, Pierce. It's just too bad you don't like girls, 'cause I bet a lot of them would olive you. You have a really nice face." I gave his face a pat, just to show him that I really liked it, and wasn't just saying it to be nice.

Pierce shoved me into the car, muttering under his breath something about people who have no tolerance to alcohol knowing better than to drink martinis.

"But I'm better now," I protested, wondering how one of my legs had found its way onto his lap. "I never used to be able to drink, but I can now. I've been practicing. I can have a whole bottle of beer without getting silly now, and I couldn't do that when we shared that apartmen' on Queen Anne Hill. 'Member that apartmen'?"

"Remind me never to volunteer to help Roger again, will you?" Pierce asked Evan. He pushed my leg off his lap. "And as soon as we get to the studio, I want you to find some coffee—black—and bring it to the wardrobe room. Six or seven cups of it."

I tipped my head back and started singing *Werewolves of London*.

Pierce shuddered. "Make that twenty cups."

Thankfully, the buzz from the martinis lasted through the horrors of having to stand in my underwear in front of Pierce and a couple of wardrobe ladies while they measured every conceivable stretch of my skin.

They shoved a couple of dresses on me, but I don't remember much about them except they were scratchy and uncomfortable. Pierce let me have a little nap on a ratty old armchair in one of the wardrobe rooms while various people came up and held bits of material against my cheek to see what looked good.

The buzz, unfortunately, was gone by the time he shook me awake, and frog marched me, dizzy and a bit queasy, down the hall, up a flight of stairs, and into a plush carpeted room dark with heavy mahogany furniture, lightened by a lovely view of the Thames.

Before I could open my mouth to protest Pierce's brutality of dragging me from a sound sleep, a balding man with dark red hair looked up from the massive desk I was pushed before. My stomach seemed to keep moving long after I stopped.

"Oh, there you are! Hello, Tessa, I'm Roger d'Aspry. Pierce has told me so much about you. I'm delighted that you're joining our team—relieved actually, because we start filming tomorrow and what's the story of a duke's life without his duchess at his side?" Roger came around the desk while he was speaking, his voice clipped in a manner reminiscent of expensive schooling. He took my hand in both of his to simultaneously pat and shake it. He was about four inches shorter than me, not terribly unusual as I am almost six feet tall. "I know you'll have a grand time, just a grand time, you're going to love everyone and the house! It's glorious! Pierce tells me you're quite the devotee of history, so you should have no trouble adapting to the lifestyle. You've read the rule book and introductory material?"

I blinked at him and swayed just the tiniest bit while I let his words trickle through the fogged mass that was presently acting as my brain. "Um. Some of it."

"Good, good. We just need you to sign a few releases, merely a legality, I assure you, then I'm sure you'll want to have a bit of rest before the evening's fittings, the audition, and of course, you'll want to read up on the rest of the volunteers for the program."

Fittings? Auditions? He wanted me for the part? He saw me and he still wanted me? Maybe his eyesight was bad. I held up my hand and waved it before his face. "How many fingers am I holding up?"

Behind me, Pierce groaned. Roger frowned at me, then frowned at my fingers. "Three. Is there a reason you are asking me that?"

Oh, God, now I'd painted myself in a corner. If I said no, he'd think I was an idiot, the kind of lunatic who waved her fingers around and asked people to count them. If I said yes and explained that he couldn't possibly want me to be the duchess, I'd have to explain why, and if I had to discuss my overflowing abundance of flesh with one more person, I'd scream. My brain was still fuzzy feeling from the martinis, but I figured the truth was probably the best bet. I'd rather be thought self-conscious than a boob. "Um . . . it's just that . . . well . . ." I waved a hand up and down my torso.

"Honey, I've told you and told you that you're just perfect for this role!" Pierce hurried forward and grabbed my hand. "She has this idiotic idea that she's too fat for the part."

"PIERCE!" I smacked him in the arm. How could he come right out and say the word with no creative euphemisms or polite skating around the issue? "The word *fat* is politically incorrect. I'm skinny-challenged, thank you."

Roger eyed me up and down, from nose to toes, then back up to my head. "I don't see a problem."

I wanted to kiss him.

"Most of the aristocracy were pudgy. All that rich living, you know."

The kiss shriveled up on my lips. "Pudgy?"

He gave me a quick grin. "Sorry. Skinny-challenged. Besides, you have your own hair. I would hate to go through the wig trauma again." He shuddered delicately as he spoke. "And speaking of that, you've met the wardrobe people, yes? Our goal with the *Month in the Life* project is absolute accuracy and authenticity in every facet of life. To that end, we're asking each participant to not only live without items that were created after 1879, but to live by the societal precepts of the mid-Victorian era. Manners, values, etiquette, social interactions—all must conform to the standards the Victorians lived by. Are you willing to do that?"

I blinked a couple of times and carefully cleared my throat. "I'm tolerably familiar with that period, so I don't imagine it will be a problem, although I'm not an expert by any means."

"That's why we included a copy of *The Glory of Womanhood* in the project material. If you have any questions about how you should deal with servants, which fork to use when, how to have a tea for your friends, when you should go visiting, that sort of thing, it's all covered in the book. And just to get you started, we've made up a list of everyone's duties, from the duke right down to the scullery girl.

That's in the packet as well, and I urge you to become familiar with it, because as the mistress of the house, it will be your duty to interact with the housekeeper to make sure the house is run smoothly. You are ultimately responsible for the servants and their well-being."

I kept my eyes fixed on his left cheekbone and nodded slowly. If I looked anywhere else, the room seemed to dip and sway, taking my stomach with it.

"Now, regarding the filming—please, please ignore the presence of the cameramen and the sound people. They will do their best to be invisible, and I'm sure that after a short time you won't even notice they're there. We want you to act just as naturally around them as you would should you be alone, strictly keeping within the guidelines of a Victorian duchess, of course," he laughed. "No turning your hand to a bit of dusting or putting a room to rights."

I gave him a brave smile, brave because I was suddenly struck with how unsuitable I was for this role—not only because of my weight, but because I simply was not raised by duchess standards. How would I eat with servants watching me? Then again, I doubted if Max the architect was brought up in a ducal household. "I'll do my best."

"I have every confidence you will." He tipped his head to the side for a moment, looking at me just as Pierce and Evan had earlier. "You'll quite enjoy yourself, you know. You'll be the mistress of the house, you won't have a care in the world except picking out what frock to wear, and whether to go riding in the morning, or in the afternoon. We have a lady's maid for you, naturally, a wonderful woman who is very experienced in the period. All you have to do is enjoy yourself and live a life most of the world would sell their souls to experience."

My stomach did a half-gainer at that thought.

"Now, on the schedule for this evening is a brief audition—just an interview that we do on film for archival purposes, then I expect the good ladies in wardrobe would like you in for a second fitting, and then we're off in the morning, very early I'm afraid, but we wish to start filming with breakfast. Our film crew will go out to Cheshire later tonight, but they will primarily be filming the servants first thing in the morning, so we'll have time to smuggle you into the house and get you dressed before you make your first appearance." Roger looked up from a stack of papers as someone opened the door. "Oh, Sam, Max, what excellent timing, come in, I want you both to meet our lifesaver. Tessa Riordan, this is Sam Everett, our head cameraman, and Max Edgerton, who'll be taking on the role of His Grace, the Duke of Bridgewater. You'll be working very closely with Sam, Tessa, since he'll shoot all the principle photography, and of course, you'll get to know Max very well during the next month."

Two men entered the room, the first a thin, wiry guy with carroty hair and wire-rimmed glasses. Behind him, a dark shadow flickered in the hallway, then Sam moved aside to allow the dishy man in the photo to enter. My stomach jumped and did a front somersault with a half-twist as I got a good look at him—he was even more handsome in person than he was in a stiff, posed picture. His eyes were what most caught my attention—they weren't just light as the picture showed, they were a clear, crystal blue, a blue topaz blue, a summer sky in early morning blue, framed with sooty black lashes so thick I wondered if he had to comb them each morning to keep them from getting tangled.

Those beautiful eyes, a bit wary as they studied me, suddenly warmed as he stuck out his hand, saying, "It's a pleasure to meet you, Tessa. I can't tell you how thankful I am to know you've agreed to take on the role. I hope you are free for dinner tonight, I'd like to talk about the project with you."

I opened my mouth to say hello, nice to be here, hope you like large women, would you like to have sex after dinner, but all that came out was olives. And three martinis. And the potted meat and black bread and . . . well, basically everything I'd eaten in the last five hours. It all came up, barfed ignominiously onto the plush carpet, a bit of it splashing up onto Max's neat brown loafers.

Pierce closed his eyes in horror and slapped a hand to his forehead as I stood hunched over, one hand clutching the back of the leather chair, the other hand twisted into the front of my thin gauze dress to keep it from dangling into the mess. I released the chair long enough to take the handful of tissues that Roger thrust from behind me, mopping my mouth as I straightened up.

Max looked from his soiled shoes up to my flushed, red, sweaty, tears-of-mortification-shining-in-my-eyes face and withdrew his hand. "I take it that's a no to dinner?"

From *USA Today* bestselling author
Katie MacAlister

The Corset Diaries
0-451-41112-9

No woman in her right mind would consent to wear a corset for a month. Especially a "skinny-challenged" woman like Tessa. But dreams of being debt-free dance in her head at the offer of appearing in a reality TV show. "A Month in the Life of a Victorian Duke" is about real people pretending to live on an English estate, circa 1879. And Tessa's leading man—a real-life Duke—is so handsome she can barely breathe, with or without the corset.

KATIE MACALISTER'S NOVELS ARE:
"FUNNY, QUIRKY, AND ENJOYABLE."
—MILLIE CRISWELL

"WICKEDLY WITTY...DELICIOUSLY SEXY."
—*BOOKLIST*

Available wherever books are sold or at penguin.com

O896